THE SHIMLA LEGACY

From the last decadent days of the British Raj in Shimla to nineteen ninety's England - a story of betrayal, love and tragedy.

Rebecca S Mason

Stylish, moving, mysterious.
Just what is The Shimla Legacy, *how was it created, and who are the beneficiaries? An intriguing family drama*
spanning half-a-century and two continents, set against a backdrop of political, social and cultural change. A great read.
Peter Mason FRGS, award winning Fleet Street journalist and author.

Print ISBN 978-1-7384231-1-8

Published by
Llyfrau Cambria Books, Wales, United Kingdom.
Cambria Books is an imprint of
Cambria Publishing Ltd.

Discover our other books at: www.cambriabooks.co.uk

DEDICATION:

To the late Rev. Canon K and Mrs E Jones whose travels took me on my first trip to India and hence to Shimla, which captured my imagination profoundly and led me to writing this, my debut novel.

ACKNOWLEDGEMENTS:

I would like to thank my husband and family for keeping me going at times of the occasional writer's block and blank-page-staring.

I also wish to thank my Novelists Group for their positive encouragement, and for giving me the dynamism and impetus to write, and for all their freely-given approvals and critiques.

Part 1

1

Shimla 1997:

S trands of light filtered through the curtains signalling the dawn. She woke in a cold sweat, her nostrils filled with an acrid smell. She couldn't breathe. She felt herself choking, gasping for breath. Her body glistened in the half-light as she reached for a towel and mopped the sweat from her face. Fully awake, the terrifying memories faded and she realised she had been dreaming. Again.

She made her way through the unfamiliar hotel room to the small garret window. Smoke-laden air wafted in. Had that prompted the nightmare? She shrugged, and pulled her gown tightly round her body against the early-morning chill.

Faraway sounds of children laughing filled the stillness of the morning. The sky was lightening, and a silhouette of mountains came into view. Faint at first, then, as the sun rose and the air cleared, they sprang into sharp relief. Shanty houses clung to rock faces, appearing to teeter haphazardly on the edge of a cliff. She imagined a labyrinth of pathways worn down by tramping feet.

People coughed in the thin air, and she heard the faint cry of a baby. Pushing aside the pink net curtains she flung the window wide open. Leaning on the sill, she cupped her chin in both hands and drank in the atmosphere.

'I'm here at last.' she whispered. 'Home.'

Jessica had arrived in Shimla the night before on the Toy Train as it strained to reach its destination. Embarking on a long-awaited journey to discover her family history, she'd come to find her parents' graves.

She was born in nineteen forty-two. Just four years later she was shipped off to England from these dramatic highlands, this once-lovely outpost of the British Empire in the foothills of the great Himalaya. Her parents would escape the heat and dust of Delhi during the searing summers, and re-base to Shimla, along with other high-ranking officials of the Crown Rule.

A clock tower somewhere in the heart of town chimed. Jessica closed the window and turned into the room. As she switched on her bedside light, she caught the merest glimpse of a shiny cockroach scurrying under a carved dark wood chest. It startled but didn't surprise her.

Last night, the hotel porter had pointed out the bathroom to the right, along the corridor. Gathering her wash bag and towel, she stepped out of her room, looked both ways, and hurried past doors beside which were an assortment of shoes in neat shining pairs. She breathed deeply and smelled the clean, fresh scent of shoe polish, together with an aroma of coffee drifting up from the kitchen. It filled her with wellbeing and she smiled.

The antiquated bathroom looked the same as it must have looked at the time her parents came to stay at their house in the hills. A deep cast iron bath with claw feet stood solidly behind the door. The square ceramic washbasin had brass taps matching those over the bath, and a large brass plug. The taps were dull, and had, she observed, at one time, been scoured with steel wool, which took away forever the chance of a lick of Brasso to restore them to their original shining glory. Small, wrapped tablets of pink Lux soap adorned the glass shelf above the sink.

Jessica locked the door and turned on the bath taps. Scalding water cascaded into the tub. She mixed it with freezing cold water. The room filled with steam, so she opened the snowflake-frosted window a crack to let it drift out into the morning air.

As she sank into the cosseting luxury of her bath, she closed her eyes, relaxed, and tried to plan her first day. She wasn't sure where or how, yet she knew she needed to find answers to questions and re-discover feelings from her childhood by digging deep into her parent's past. If she was lucky there'd be archives in the church or at the town hall. She'd prepared herself for surprises and inconsistencies to stories gleaned from her aunt and uncle, hence her own need to come here to find the truth.

But she'd have to familiarise first, even do the tourist trail. Go to the museum, the town hall, and Christ Church, the church where her parents married and were interred in the cemetery. She finished bathing, pulled the heavy plug out of the bath and quickly dried herself.

At eight o'clock she was ready to descend to the dining room for breakfast. Dressing modestly, she decided to wear a floral skirt, cream silk blouse, navy blue cardigan and sturdy walking shoes. She hesitated as she was about to fasten her mother's single string pearl necklace around her neck feeling a weird sense of déjà vu, as it occurred to her the beautiful jewels may have been given to her mother here, in Shimla. Perhaps not, she thought, and left it in a drawer. She looked in the mirror and patted her curly auburn hair. She hated her unruly hair—the colour, she thought, was neither red nor brown, and try as she may, she never could make it look sleek and modern. It didn't even go well with her blue-green eyes.

Creaking boards on the polished staircase announced her arrival in the lobby where she was welcomed by the same porter who had taken her luggage to her room. He stood to attention, and, with a quick bow of the head.

'Good morning, madam. We hope you slept very well.'

'Yes, yes thank you,' Jessica lied. 'Where's the dining room, please?'

'Come with me, madam,' and he led the way. 'My name is Akash, please to ask if anything is not right, you know if there is anything we can help you with your problems.'

She thought his offer endearing, and said she would be certain to let him know if she needed anything—in fact, would he be here after breakfast? She needed to get more maps and directions.

'Madam,' replied Akash, 'I travel to home at eight thirty, and will not come here till the night, but my colleague Sanjay he will help. Madam, here is your table, madam.'

'Thank you, Akash.'

Jessica sat at the maroon-clothed table, in a small alcove with an open window. The town was already bustling with activity and buzzing with voices, shouting traders, trucks, and rickshaws, and cars hooting at the wandering Brahmin cows. She had spent her first few days after arriving from London, travelling overland to Shimla, so was already accustomed to the sights, sounds, smells, and the sheer and wonderful chaos that was India.

As she waited for her boiled egg, toast, and coffee, she opened her guidebook, and began to make notes in the margins, when she heard a

5

man's voice.

'So sorry to disturb you…'

The tall, fair-haired man dressed in blue jeans and a black crew-neck sweater nervously adjusted the red neck-scarf. She recognised him as the person who had helped her with her luggage at the station the night before by lifting her suitcase onto the porter's trolley.

'Sorry, I didn't see you there. Ah, you're staying here, too—thank you so much for helping me at the station last night. It was you, wasn't it?'

'Guilty, I'm afraid! I hope you don't mind, but may I sit here? It's about the only seat left.' He gestured to the chair on the opposite side of the table to her.

'No, er…please, do sit down. I was so tired last night and glad to get to the hotel,' she looked up at him and smiled, and his blue eyes smiled back.

'Thanks, yes, it's not a good journey, especially after dark when you can't see the wonderful scenery. Sorry, allow me to introduce myself—Sebastian, Sebastian Shelley. I live and work in Delhi for a British news agency as a freelance feature writer, and I'm here in Shimla for a while to do some research. I come here often, and for long periods sometimes, just to write.' Well spoken, his rugged tanned face put her in mind of an explorer or a mountaineer.

'I'm Jessica, Jessica Delaney-Hartford. Pleased to meet you.'

'Are you staying long?' he asked, glancing sideways at the same time to alert a passing waiter.

'I'm not sure,' she fingered the napkin on her lap. 'This is my first visit here. Well, not *exactly* my first—it's a long story.' Jessica looked at the stranger and grimaced to suggest a hard task. 'You see, I was here over fifty years ago with my parents, just before my father was about to be recalled by the British government after Indian independence. We had a house here, in Shimla.'

The waiter arrived at the table with Jessica's breakfast.

'You don't mind…do you?'

'Of course not, do carry on.' Sebastian caught the waiter's eye and looked briefly at the thin, dog-eared pink paper menu.

'I'll have eggs, bacon and mushrooms, please. Thank you.' He put the menu back on the table and spoke to Jessica. 'You see, when I saw

6

you last night in the bright station lights, I could have sworn, well, you bear a very strong likeness to a woman in a photograph my father has on the desk in his study. In his house in Devon. It's uncanny. This must sound ridiculous, and you'll think I'm totally bonkers, but...' He hesitated and stared down at his clasped hands. Taking a deep breath, he looked Jessica straight in the eye. 'You don't, by any chance, know a man by the name of Meredith Bateman?'

Jessica put down her egg spoon and raised her napkin to cover her mouth. She looked past him with staring eyes, her mind spun with information and images, and with thoughts of the person to whom the name belonged. The name spoken by a complete stranger.

'Meredith Bateman—lawyer?' She looked at him. 'I know Meredith Bateman very well. He is, or was, the executor of my parents' estate, and recently, my aunt's estate. But who is your father? I'm sure it can't be me in the photograph, you must be mistaken.'

'You never heard Meredith talk of Edward Shelley?'

'No, not that I can remember. I was only four when my parents died, tragically, here in Shimla, and I was taken back to England to be brought up by my mother's sister, Aunt Catherine. I can't remember much at all about being here—just vague childhood images.'

'Edward Shelley, he's related to you?'

'He's my father. He was also here in India, an Army officer. He has lots of memories of his postings here in Shimla and sometimes talks about it. I think he did a bit of wheeling and dealing later when the British finally pulled out. He set himself up in a very lucrative export business. That's how I became interested in coming over to explore, and now, to work here.

'My father was, I think, in his thirties when he left. My mother and myself came along later when he'd made a name for himself, and we lived in what is still his country home in Devon, until he and my mother divorced. He did extremely well, importing Indian made goods—rugs, silk, cotton cloth—all the stuff they sold on market stalls in England. Cheap clothing and the like. He was one of the first people to make it big business after the war, in the late forties.'

Jessica listened intently. 'So, your father was stationed here, in Shimla?'

'I don't think he was stationed here, but I know he came here often. He has spoken about it occasionally, especially now, with me living in Delhi. Was your father in the Army?'

'No, my father was a civil servant. He worked in the government offices in Delhi—some sort of advisor to the Viceroy. The government in those days used to move to Shimla in the summer. My Aunt Catherine and uncle weren't here, so it was difficult for them to explain to me what my parents' lives were like in India. My parents died on the same day from a serious strain of dysentery. In fact, I'm here to search records, and hopefully obtain copies of documents such as marriage and death certificates. Apparently, not much found its way back to England.' Jessica paused, looked at Sebastian and continued. 'My aunt came to Shimla for their funeral and to take me home to England, and she took as much as she could back with her, but they said some documents were left behind or lost. I do have my own birth certificate, and a few fuzzy photographs. After they took me to England, my parents' things were crated up and sent on, and some trunks went missing, apparently…but to be honest, everything has become confusing. It was my Aunt Catherine who urged me to come here, just before she died.'

They finished breakfast, refusing the waiter's offer of more toast. Sebastian suggested they retire to the hotel lounge for coffee.

'Well, I can't be too long, I've got to do a lot of legwork today. I've never set eyes on my parents' graves, I'm not even sure if there'll be headstones, or even whether the cemetery is still as it was. Aunt Catherine didn't know much.'

'I understand. Yes, you must do as much as you can first thing, the sun gets hot, and the altitude will take its toll.'

He walked behind her through the hotel lobby over threadbare carpets thrown on polished, pitted timber floors, and across to the stuffy-smelling lounge. Dark red chenille-covered armchairs and sofas were arranged in groups, with small highly-polished carved tables in between. Jessica thought the ones in the bay window the most welcoming, and as they sat down, Sebastian called a waiter and ordered coffee.

'Have you stayed here before?' Jessica was puzzled at what Sebastian had just told her. But she was certain he was mistaken, even though there was the tenuous connection with her family lawyer.

'I usually come to this hotel—it may not be the best place in town, but their rates are good, and the manager is very amenable and pro-active. I've promised myself one day I'll stay at the Imperial instead.'

The coffee arrived.

'Black or white?' Jessica asked as she poured.

Sebastian appeared pensive and distant. 'Oh, yes, black for me, please. But tell me, and forgive me for being so persistent about this photograph, and this will seem to be a totally outlandish question, but have you ever visited Stonehenge?'

'Ha! Well, my goodness, yes.' Jessica pulled herself upright in her chair and looked at Sebastian, bemused and incredulous. 'I was there a couple of years ago with friends, en route to Cornwall for a holiday. We stopped at Stonehenge for a picnic lunch. Meredith Bateman lives in Cornwall now he's semi-retired, near his daughter who has a farm at Trevasey, on Bodmin Moor. In the days when he administered my parents' estate, and just after I turned twenty-one, we had regular meetings to sort out investments and payments. He managed everything while I was at school, and he paid all my school fees out of a trust fund. We've kept in touch ever since. I went to see him whilst we were there.' Jessica remembered. 'Of course! I sent him some photographs a week or so after I got home.' She stared at Sebastian. 'Have you never asked your father about the photo?'

'Yes, that's how I know who sent it to him, but when I asked him who the auburn-haired lady was, he said it was Meredith's niece. My father used to employ Bateman on legal matters for the business. But if the photo isn't of you, Meredith Bateman's niece is your double.'

'I've never even heard of your father, and I'm not Meredith Bateman's niece. But yes, if it is me, the only way your father could have that photograph is if Meredith had sent it to him. But, thousands of people visit Stonehenge every year—I'm sure it must simply be, as your father said, Meredith's niece. You'll see when you go back and have another look, that you're definitely mistaken.' Jessica shrugged, smiled at Sebastian, and drained her coffee cup, relieved and happy at the apparent conclusion of this bizarre conversation.

2

Shimla 1947:

Come on Elizabeth, we'll be late!' James Delaney was standing on the black and white tiled floor at the foot of the sweeping timber staircase. He looked up to the landing, and through the balustrade caught sight of his daughter, Jessica.

'Jessie, go to bed. I can see you. Where's ayah?'

Chandra rushed along the landing, scooped up Jessica and they hurried away towards the nursery, giggling. Elizabeth came into view and followed in their wake.

'Chandra! Chandra—don't forget to make sure Jessica has her cup of cocoa, will you.'

James could hear the muted conversation between his wife and their nanny.

'No, Memsahib.'

'We'll be back around midnight. Make sure you keep the door locked. Let no-one in.'

'No, Memsahib. Goodbye.'

'Thank you, Chandra, you're a treasure.' Elizabeth hurried back along the landing.

'I'm coming, James. Get the car ready.' And with that, she swept down the wide stairs, her sage green silk evening dress billowing behind, her elegant high heels tapping on the bare boards. Her decision to wear the green came only after much deliberation, trying-on, posing, and discarding, in front of her dressing mirror. She wore the stunning emerald and diamond pendant left to her by her mother, and matching emerald tear-drop earrings. Ranjit opened the car door, turned back to the house and went inside. James and Elizabeth heard the clunk and thud of the heavy bolt being thrown on the front door, and they drove off down their long winding driveway.

There had been sporadic skirmishes lately between various political and religious factions, following massive movements of refugees out of the area. It had strained relationships between Indians and the British to breaking point. James Delaney was serving out his last few months in India, and their house, The Laurels, would be boarded up.

The servants were not at all sure what was to become of them. Rumour had it they would be abandoned with little or nothing to show for their loyalty, hard work, and devotion. Some were angry it had turned out this way especially after their unquestioning belief in Gandhi and his promises for the future of a new India.

'James?' Elizabeth adjusted her green silk chiffon stole and straightened her dress to prevent it creasing.

'What?' he was always grumpy driving along the rough road to and from their house. It was so bumpy it made it difficult for him to drive much faster than walking pace.

'Do you know who'll be at dinner tonight?' His wife's nonchalant manner did nothing to disarm James's knowledge of the real reason for the question.

'Not sure, mostly couples from the regiment, some house guests up for the weekend, and Viceroy staff, I suppose.' He didn't need to ask her why the question. He knew full well.

'Oh. Yes. Do you have any idea how many?'

His irritation showed. 'For god's sake, Lizzie, I don't know, and anyway, what the hell does it matter?'

The obvious annoyance indicated he thought there was a distinct possibility Edward Shelley would be present. That smarmy officer, who always seemed to engage his wife in frivolous conversation and exclude him; who was forever in the background, and who often came to their house at Elizabeth's invitation for tiffin, or for sundowners at six. They would be together when he came in from his club, sharing jokes, laughing and smiling. His onetime friend and lifesaver had become, over the years, an unwanted accessory to his household.

The image of him and Elizabeth sitting on the veranda, sharing a softly spoken secret tête-à-tête was forever present when they were in Shimla. He had also noticed Edward taking a very strong liking to Jessica–bringing her gifts of toys each time he arrived at the hill town. He didn't like it and had told Elizabeth not to accept anymore.

For years now, James had suspected Elizabeth and Edward's friendship was more than platonic. But had no real evidence to prove it. His wife's exemplary demeanour was too precious to question, and their marriage too established in society to jeopardise. Yet he wished this well-meaning interloper would one day go away and never come back, and he was prepared to bite his tongue until that day came. It would, he had decided many times, seem churlish to cause a scene. In any case, there may be nothing at all in the friendship, and he would look a fool—after all, Edward *was* much younger than Elizabeth.

Their car crunched to a halt on the dry gravel driveway in front of Hilltop House, a sprawling brick-built residence. A servant rushed down the impressive flight of steps flanked by brick columns with pale blue hydrangeas blooming profusely at their base. With a slight bow, he opened the door for Elizabeth, who stepped out into the night air, holding her skirt, and proceeded up the steps and into the house, whilst James parked the car.

'Dearest Elizabeth!' It was the host, Charles, arms outstretched, who spotted her first, kissing her on both cheeks. 'Welcome—where's James?' Charles, his jolly round face shining to the pate, took Elizabeth by the elbow as they exchanged small talk on the way to a reception room where other dinner guests had already assembled.

'Oh, James is parking the car, he won't be long. Sorry we're a little late, it always takes time to get Jessica settled. And those bumps in the road. I usually have a headache before we even get here.' They both laughed at the thought of Elizabeth's head bobbing painfully over the bumps. They were laughing as they entered the magnificent drawing room. 'Anyway, how are you and Lola?'

'Very well, my dear, so glad you could come tonight. Come and meet everyone.'

Elizabeth walked behind Charles, scanning the room frantically. Where is he? Her heart began to race, her cheeks glowed, and her eyes sparkled at the thought of Edward in that very room. She stood proud and pulled the neckline of her dress a little lower. A mischievous smile played round her lips as their eyes met across the room full of chattering guests, seeing no-one and nothing else, but boring into each other's body and soul.

'...and do you know Fredah and her husband, Philip...and you *must* meet...?' She was shaking hands and saying hellos in a trance, not remembering anyone's names, moving around the room at Charles' behest. 'And, of course,' Charles went on, 'you already know Edward,

Clara and Hermione.'

Their eyes met as she approached him. They pretended small talk. Overcome by a fierce desire for each other, they wanted to embrace. Her shallow breathing excited her senses. Wanting to touch but prohibited by convention and fear, their audacious conversation skirted the very boundaries of wisdom and reason.

Then, in a low aside, 'James has just entered the room,' Edward had been keeping an eye on the doorway. He turned from Elizabeth and engaged Clara in conversation before James reached the quartet.

'Damned car stalled on the driveway, had to get the wallahs to push-park it, hate it—they always bash 'em around. Don't know if we'll be able to restart it tonight in the dark.' His voice was loud, and Edward turned to face him.

'Bad luck old chap, I'll give you a lift later, if you like.'

'No, no, it's all right—it's just over-heated, I'm sure it'll start okay.' The last thing James wanted was charity from Edward, to have Elizabeth, his wife riding in *his* car, whilst he sat, humiliated, being driven home.

'Well, the offer's there if necessary.' Edward turned to leave the group and as he did so, he came close to Elizabeth, brushing his arm on her breast. She could feel his breath on her neck as he squeezed past, and her pulse galloped. She felt flushed and impatient to be with him again. That feeling of elation—was it merely the excitement of concealment, after all this time, or did she really love him? *Please let the car not start*, she thought. James stared at his wife, seeing exactly what was blatantly taking place in front of his eyes.

The dinner gong sounded outside in the hall and people finished their drinks and conversations. Cocktails and small talk over, the assembled guests filed into the dining room. The polished table was lavishly laid with fine English bone china and crystal, gleaming silver cutlery and sparkling candelabra. Charles McAllister sat in a tall-backed mahogany carver at one end of the table, Lola, his wife, at the other end. James noticed Edward sitting between Fredah and Clara, thankfully nowhere near him or Elizabeth. Two or three simultaneous conversations were taking place. Snippets of each were heard in occasional moments of silence as food arrived and plates were cleared. Elizabeth was intent on talking to Lola about Jessica's progress at

Sunday school. Across the table someone was discussing politics in a loud voice, and at some time during the evening, everyone talked about the current unrest, and what their plans might be, after India.

3

Shimla 1997:

Jessica stared uneasily at her empty coffee cup. Still feeling the need to ask questions, she tried to put the conversation she'd had with Sebastian out of her mind. This curious meeting with someone whose family appeared to relate to hers seemed unlikely.

'As you haven't been to Shimla before, would you perhaps allow me to show you round, I do know the place fairly well?' Sebastian drank the last of his coffee and waited for a response from Jessica.

'Well, are you sure you don't have anything else to do?'

'No, nothing that can't wait. It's easy for me to take time off and come up here. This may be your last.'

She warmed to the gesture. He seemed nice, and she thought it would be good to have a chaperone.

'I haven't decided where I want to start. I have a list of must-dos—but I thought you said you had some research to do?'

'It can wait.'

'I'm still in the throes of getting to grips with maps and the terrain. And how *does* one hail a rickshaw?' They both laughed, easing any tension. 'Well, if you think…'

'Of course, I'll meet you in the lobby in five, and don't worry, *I'll* call the rickshaw!' She watched him as he strode confidently out of the room and into the lobby. She picked up her bag and followed. Back in her room, she checked her appearance in the dressing-table mirror, undid the top button of her blouse, and applied just a hint of lipstick. Turning to check her hair, she looked again in the mirror and went to the bedside drawer, took out the string of pearls and clasped them round the bareness of her neck. She put the remainder of her valuables away in the safe. She locked the door to her room, and, walking self-assured and smiling, descended the stairs to the lobby. Sebastian was waiting. He smiled and gestured towards the door.

'Where to first?'

She took out her map and notebook as they stood waiting for a rickshaw.

'I have an urge to try to find The Laurels, my parents' old house where I was born, if it's still standing after all these years. I have a few sepia photographs back home which were taken there, some of the few belongings that made it back to England after they died. I realise I should have brought them with me.'

'I think the first place to start would be the municipal offices. But be warned, there'll be mountains of paperwork, and the archives will need some time to go through. Perhaps we'd better tell the story and let them do all the hard work. There may be a fee to pay, but believe me, in India, it's worth it—bureaucracy learned from the British has grown tenfold since, along with their filing systems.'

They travelled along the main street, The Mall, which was bustling with women in colourful saris and salwar, trailing children, and men in western clothes, topped with warm woollies. A barber sat a client in a chair on the pavement and proceeded to give him a haircut. Four stretcher-bearers with a sheet-wrapped corpse whose stiff grey feet protruded from the cloth, jostled to get past on their way to a funeral, with an untidy group of mourners following behind with bundles of flowers.

As they neared the front of the town hall, Jessica couldn't help but notice people sitting motionless on steps and lawns and around the forecourt, waiting—for what, she wondered. The solid building was showing the ravages of time. The soft stone had not been maintained or cleaned for decades, its walls blackened. Passing down the long dark corridor, rooms to either side were filled with studious-looking clerks behind tiers of dark brown wooden desks bearing typewriters. At each desk sat a white-shirted office worker, shuffling mountains of papers.

Enquiries said the black and white handwritten hanging sign. They went through the open doorway and were greeted by a young man who seemed surprised to see them. Jessica sat down on the chair in front of the young man's desk, and Sebastian stood behind.

'I have come to Shimla to find my parents' graves, and to find the house where I was born,' Jessica's directness and confidence surprised Sebastian.

The young man-made notes on a large feint-lined notepad. 'And what is your name, please?' He stared at Jessica with a look of helplessness on his face, and a tone of pessimism in his voice. 'When did this take place. What year? We keep records only for so long.'

'How long?' Urged Jessica.

Sebastian broke his silence. 'You have archives, don't you?'

'Yes, sir, the archives department is upstairs. Searches must be done by an authorised civil servant, can take some time, and cost money. The municipality keeps records for fifty years, otherwise we run out of space.'

Jessica looked up at Sebastian. 'Fifty years! It's fifty years since I was taken away from here, fifty years since my parents died.'

She spoke to the clerk. 'Do you know where I can find copies of death certificates?'

'All records of births, marriages and deaths are kept in the registry section.'

They were first sent to the surveyor's department and asked about Jessica's early home, The Laurels. They left the office with instructions and moved upstairs to the registry offices.

'This is going to be so difficult.' Jessica was already beginning to lose hope. She looked at Sebastian. 'Everything has to be sifted through. Did you see the piles of papers in those offices? They have no microfiche files or anything. It could take days!' Her voice held a hint of resignation of what she thought was inevitable—that nothing would be found. 'But surely, we can go to the house, at least they will know where that is. It was near the Viceregal residence, I think.'

They sat and explained why she was there, what were her objectives, and gave all the necessary details for clerks in various offices to work on, in the hope of finding relevant records.

She searched Sebastian's face. 'Do you think we should leave them looking for documents and go and find the house. I may even remember something—I faintly remember a bumpy road.' She found herself being captivated by the atmosphere of the place, and childhood memories seemed to flash in and out of her mind.

She held up her map and asked an officer in the surveyor's department if he had heard of a house called The Laurels. She sketched out the story about the sudden and untimely deaths of her parents, and how she was taken back to England afterwards.

'Tell him about your father, Sebastian, perhaps his name might also ring a bell on records and papers.' Her idea was not received well.

'No, my father hardly came here; he doesn't warrant a mention in any formal documents. I won't even bother them to look, they've got enough to do chasing your records. And we're here to get to the bottom of your family, not mine.'

He spoke to the clerk, 'The house had a long driveway, and a large garden.'

Jessica turned sharply and stared at him. She couldn't remember telling him anything about the house. When could she? How did he know such detail—detail she didn't know herself and therefore couldn't possibly have told him.

'How do you know?'

'What!'

'About the house, the driveway, and the gardens?'

He smiled. 'Didn't you say? You must have mentioned it when you were telling me what you remembered about the place. Maybe it was just an impression you gave me.' He quickly turned back to the clerk. 'Near the Viceregal residence, we think.'

Maps were spread out on the counter, and the clerk pointed to the Viceroy's house—now a tourist attraction, and traced his finger along a winding road. 'There it is sir! There, that's where The Laurels used to be.'

'Used to be...but what happened? Isn't it still there?' Jessica's dreams were being shattered before she'd even had a chance to go anywhere.

'Rumour has it the house burned down just before the British left. That was in nineteen forty-seven. A long time ago now.' He put on a sympathetic face, trying to identify with her. 'But it *was* known as one of the finest houses in Shimla. I remember my grandmother telling me about the couple who lived there, apparently...'

Sebastian butted in. 'Yes, Miss Delaney's family. Now, my good man, if you can give us that map, we'll be on our way—thank you very much for helping us.' He took hold of Jessica's elbow, and steered her down the corridor and into the street.

'I thought he knew something more—should I go back and ask?' said Jessica. She was puzzled and shocked by what she'd just heard.

'No, he's just wanting some incentive, it happens all the time. He knows no more than we do.'

'The house burnt down? Why wouldn't Aunt Catherine know this?

If it's true, why didn't she tell me? It was she who wanted me to come back here. She urged me.'

They walked out into the bright sunlight, and Sebastian hailed a taxi.

'Perhaps she did, Jessica, but didn't know how or what to tell you. Perhaps she wanted you to discover all this for yourself.' Sebastian stopped and looked into Jessica's face as the ramshackle vehicle pulled up noisily by the side of the road. He helped Jessica into the lumpy back seat.

4

Shimla 1947:

Elizabeth strolled into the drawing room for coffee along with the lady guests as their men prepared to take after-dinner port and cigars. Her friend, Alice, sidled over to her to make sure they sat next to each other, but Elizabeth decided to make a rush for the powder room. She wanted to look her best when the men came to join them. She was enjoying flirting with Edward and wanted to keep up the charm.

He had recently come back from Delhi. The Indian plains were devoid of eligible unattached females, and with most of the officer's wives at the stations very often left alone and bored whilst their husbands went away, the pickings of elite and sophisticated British women in the hill towns were rich indeed, for an attractive young Major like Edward Shelley.

Their affair had started in July nineteen forty-one when James invited him home for the weekend, along with a small group of visiting officers who gathered at The Laurels before going riding. The Delaney's horses were chosen because they were used to the steep terrain where they were heading. The tracks were very stony and narrow in places, winding as they did round the hillside before reaching lower ground. The return ride was the most dangerous, and a sure-footed horse was essential, especially if the men decided to do the complete trail.

As the riders gathered for the off, Elizabeth, jauntily casual in her usual jodhpurs and cream linen short-sleeved shirt, was bustling around making certain the porters had enough supplies for their picnic lunch. She stood by Kowloon, James's horse, checking to ensure it looked fit enough for the journey. A keen horsewoman, she had never been to the area where they were going, preferring to ride out with the women on her own pony, Rainbow, to safer, flatter areas which were very few and far between in Shimla. That day she was looking forward to a quiet afternoon at home catching up with her correspondence.

'All set, James, do take great care, and come back safely.' She patted the horse's neck and stepped away as, strung out in a neat line, the men walked their mounts slowly through the gates and towards the beginning of the track.

She stood watching, arms folded, and was just about to turn back into the house when the rider bringing up the rear pulled up alongside her. The officer astride smiled broadly, winked, bowed his head dashingly, and, touching his hat, 'Edward Shelley. Mrs Delaney, I presume—I very much look forward to seeing you when we get back. Very much indeed.' And with that, he nudged his horse to trot on and catch up with the rest of the party, looking back at Elizabeth as he departed.

Elizabeth was amused and flattered at this bold advance. The man looked younger than she and James, and she couldn't recollect seeing him around in Shimla before. She watched as he disappeared along the driveway and out of sight. With a spring in her step she went back into the house to tell the dhobi to make sure the guest room beds were made up. Back in the kitchen she gave further instruction for the evening dinner.

Standing at her dressing mirror she straightened her hair, looked at her profile, and complimented herself on being the finest filly in the stable. She'd already had Chandra hang up her dress for the evening and match up the shoes, but as she glanced first into the mirror and at the dress, she decided to change it for a newer one with a lower neckline and a flowing skirt. Fabrics had been very scarce since the domestic political trouble and the escalating war with Germany. The movement of goods around the world had been disrupted, but fortunately for those living in India, homespun silks and cottons were still available from box-wallahs. Elizabeth had them visit regularly, and she had built up a wardrobe full of exquisite and beautiful clothes made from exotic bright-coloured cottons and silks. For a mere few rupees, she was able to get decently fashioned attire run up by the local durzi in no time.

By the afternoon, Elizabeth had still not taken her mind away from the fleeting incident with the dashing cavalry major. Checking the guest list James had left for her to make up the dinner table place names she deduced that his name must be Edward Shelley. The party would be back in time for afternoon tea and a rest before dinner, so she decided to get dining arrangements out of the way beforehand. The dinner guests would be mainly men, but Alice, Lola and Dorothy were to come over to join their husbands in time for dinner, and so with some judicial shuffling of names, Elizabeth managed to seat Edward between herself and Dorothy. She went upstairs to her bedroom feeling pleased with herself, closed the door, took off all her clothes and lay naked on the bed in perfect quiet. Closing her eyes, ripples of excitement coursed through her body at the thought of their new guest.

She was stirred out of a dreamless sleep by shouting voices. There was a commotion in the yard, and assuming the men had returned, Elizabeth leapt to her feet to peer out of the bedroom window. The gardener was calling for help and two house boys ran out towards him. Five horses and one without a rider slowly came into sight. The first horse had two men astride. Elizabeth waited until they rounded the trees before she realised James was slumped up front on Edward's horse. They all dismounted, and straight away went to help Edward and James. Elizabeth quickly pulled on her clothes and ran two at a time down the stairs, through the kitchen and out into the yard.

'What happened, what happened?' She pushed through to get to her husband.

'It's alright Lizzie, I'm okay. Had a bit of a damned fall. This chap pulled me up, saved my life, I'd say.'

She looked back and forth at James and Edward, 'I'd better send for a doctor! Ranjit, RANJIT...' she shouted for the head boy.

'No need Elizabeth, we've checked him over.' Charles nodded his head towards Edward. 'Edward here is a recently qualified St John's man, and there's nothing broken that a few glasses of fine Scotch can't put right—hey, James?' James nodded and winced as he tried to make his own way across to the house. Edward rushed to support him, as Elizabeth dismissed Ranjit from the scene.

'Put the horses away, and don't forget to tell the stable boy about Kowloon, he'll need checking out too.' James called back across the yard, as, one by one the riders went into the house and through to the drawing room where tea was being served. Elizabeth brushed frantically at his riding jacket with her hands to remove the dust and dirt before they went indoors.

'Bad show old chap—better rest up for a few days. We shan't expect you in the office for a while. Better pamper him Elizabeth,' Charles added, piling a plate with sandwiches and cake and taking it over to where James had settled, leg resting on a footstool.

'What happened?' Elizabeth sat next to her husband. 'Are you sure it's just the leg, shouldn't we send for Dr Hetherington?'

James reached over and patted her knee. 'No need my dear—just a shock that's all. A twisted ankle and a sore knee. I was very lucky.' He gestured towards Edward. 'Although, I have to say, if it wasn't for the major, I might have been down the ravine. We were on a very narrow and steep pathway. Kowloon stumbled twice on loose stones, lost his balance, went down on his hindquarters, I lost my balance and dragged him down the rest of the way as I fell, still gripping the reins for dear life, and started a slow slide over the edge of the cliff. It was only the quick thinking of the major here that saved me. He just happened to be right behind, jumped from his horse, bent down, grabbed my wrists like a vice, and loosened the reins from my grip as he pulled me back up. I was limp with shock at the time.'

Elizabeth looked across at Edward, 'How can I thank you? How brave! And, oh, we were never properly introduced this morning.' They shook hands and forced a *pleased to meet you*...even though they already knew each other's names.

'Oh, it was nothing, I doubt he would have slid any further, but it was awkward at one point manoeuvring the horse out of the way.' He took a long drink of tea and picked up a sandwich. 'Not sure about the horse though—might be a bit traumatised—perhaps better keep him for easier rides for a while.'

'Good idea, we'll keep him quiet for a day or two.' James looked towards Elizabeth to concur. 'But apart from the incident, it was a good ride, and I think overall we all enjoyed it, what, chaps?'

Mutterings and nods of approval rumbled around the room, most men now busily wolfing down the food.

'I need to show our overnight guests to their rooms, James, now sit comfortably and still, until I come back. When you're ready, Edward, I'll take you up, if that's alright with you. You can have a rest before dinner.' And addressing the others, 'dinner is seven-thirty for eight, by the way.'

She led Edward up the curving staircase and along the galleried corridor to the room she had allocated for him. A little embarrassed by their earlier brief exchange, she put on her best hostess voice, explaining where the bathroom was situated, showing him the wardrobe and drawers for his clothes, and explaining about times for breakfast and what to do if he wanted anything to eat or drink in the middle of the night.

'Thank you. It's a pleasure to be here, and to meet you, and, of course, James. Lucky man he was. I could see, given a few more moments, he would have slipped out of reach.'

'I know, and I am so very grateful for your rescue, er, please stay for a while—I...we would like to show you the area. I take it you haven't been to Shimla before?'

'First time here, but I'm on secondment for a while, and between you and me, I wouldn't mind moving here permanently—more my type of people, if you know what I mean.'

Elizabeth adjusted a curtain, and fleetingly looked into the mirror, checking the comb securing her gleaming auburn hair. 'Well, I'd better be getting back to my other guests, if you'll excuse me, I'll see you at dinner,' and as she headed past him towards the door, he caught hold of her arm.

'I *do* hope to be posted here permanently, Mrs Delaney.' She flushed, looked up into his face, and freeing her arm, turned before leaving the room.

'So do I. And please call me Elizabeth.' Head down, she closed the door and made her way downstairs.

Looking at Edward now, five years on, and being with him tonight, Elizabeth wondered again why she'd not had the courage to leave James. But then, she knew it was because of Jessica. They'd played their secret game of love for almost five long years because she was not prepared to have Jessica dragged into some sleazy separation and divorce. It suited both Edward and Elizabeth. Yet their love for each other had grown deeper as the years went by.

5

Shimla 1997:

They bumped along the rough hard road choosing a taxi rather than a rickshaw, but Jessica was not taking in much of the scenery. Her mind was focused on the meeting with Sebastian, and his presence in this taxi taking them across dilapidated suburbs. She thought him kind to be spending time with her when he'd come here to work. But he seemed to have dismissed the conversation they'd had over breakfast. It was highly unlikely his father would have the picture she sent to Meredith. Yet the co-incidence baffled her, and Sebastian's father definitely knew Meredith Bateman.

As the driver turned, asking if they were sure about going right to the end of Longon Road, a bus shot out of a side street. The driver was too late in responding and, slamming on the brakes violently, the taxi slewed sideways into the side of the bus. Chaos ensued—car horns blared, people screamed. A rickshaw tipped its load onto the ground. Their driver bashed his head hard against the side window, and Jessica and Sebastian instinctively reached out to hold onto anything. Passengers on the bus started to get out and sit by the roadside.

'Are you alright?' Sebastian straightened himself and looked at Jessica. She had ended up half on the floor, her head against the back of the driver's seat and the side window.

'I think so.' She sat back into the seat holding her head. 'I bumped my head and started to slide off the seat. I'll be alright—just a bit shaken, that's all.'

Sebastian looked over to their driver and asked if he and the car were intact. More people got off the bus and crowded round. A sea of Indian faces peered at them through the windows. Jessica suddenly felt claustrophobic. Their driver got out and started an arms-flailing heated conversation with the bus driver. Sebastian leaned over to the front of the car and pressed on the car horn. But the noise was lost amongst the hooting cars backed up behind them.

'I think we'll have to get out and get away from here. The road is blocked now anyway, so we'd be better trying to get another taxi back to The Mall, and sit somewhere quietly with a cup of tea.' Sebastian took immediate charge of the situation.

Jessica nodded vigorously, as he took out a handful of rupees and put them on the driver's seat. He helped Jessica out of the car, and they pushed through the crowd, getting as far away as they could.

'Are you sure you're not injured? it looks like you hurt the side of your head.' Jessica felt a bit sore, and said it was nothing but a bruise.

Crossing the road, holding firmly onto Jessica's arm, Sebastian hailed another taxi and instructed the driver to take them to The Mall.

They found a table in a café and Sebastian handed Jessica the menu. Rubbing her head, she was just happy to sit quietly while she regained her composure.

'I can't believe it, the first day out and this has to happen. Just my luck. But I'm alright, I'll survive.' She smiled at Sebastian who was looking concerned.

'Yes, bad luck. Pot of tea and some scones? You'll feel better afterwards, I'm sure.'

They sat enjoying the tea, both deep in thought. 'I hope the driver and the car are alright, I wouldn't be surprised to find there's not much in the way of insurance to fall back on here.'

'Doubt it myself, too.' Sebastian looked into his cup. 'Still, I'm glad I was with you and you weren't left to deal with it all on your own.'

'Yes, thanks—I think I'll have to take you with me everywhere now. When did you say you were going back to Delhi?'

'Well, being freelance, and unless I have a definite deadline, there's never any real minute-to-minute news to report. I mainly do in-depth writing, and it's circulated on the wires to whichever publication wants to buy it. Occasionally we get current stories to report, requests from our clients, but that news is covered by staffers and stringers who have hot lines to the world's press.'

'How exciting—you must get a lot of satisfaction from your job. Can't say that about mine.' Jessica thought about her school pupils.

'What do you do?'

'I'm a teacher, and you know what they say about teaching!' She paused. 'I got into it because it seemed the best thing to do. But it's changed through the years, teachers don't have the autonomy they used to have, and even in the private school where I work pupils don't respect us.'

Sebastian seemed surprised she had a career, she seemed to be more a lady of leisure. 'That's sad, but I know what you mean. Thankfully, at the moment there are no children in my life, but who knows? One day, perhaps.'

'Sebastian, I think I'm going to forget today, go back to the hotel, and have a rest. I'll start again tomorrow as though today never happened, apart from the visit to the town hall. Perhaps I'll go back to the municipal offices and see if they've found my parent's death certificates before I go gallivanting around the place. Get the feel of it first.'

'Come on, I'll escort you back to the hotel. No—let *me* pay the bill.'

They left the café and hailed a rickshaw. Jessica was disappointed, but realised there was plenty of time. She had over a month, if necessary, to unravel the mystery of her parents' deaths. She bade Sebastian farewell and he said he hoped to see her at dinner time, suggesting a drink in the bar at six. Jessica nodded in agreement, and disappeared upstairs.

She examined her face in the mirror for bruising, the bump was on the hairline, and if it did turn into a bruise, hopefully it wouldn't show. She lay on her bed and closed her eyes. What a stupid accident to happen. After all this time, she was looking forward to seeing the house where she was born. She decided to go as soon as possible, making sure they hand-picked the taxi next time. She breathed deeply and eventually drifted off to sleep.

'Hello—Jessica?' She was dreaming about a bumpy cart full of luggage banging over cobblestones. 'Hello!'

'Oh, yes, just a minute.' It was Sebastian drumming softly on her door. It was dark in the room and she was disoriented. 'Hang on, I must have overslept.' She opened the door, inviting him in.

'I just wanted to check you were alright. We were going to meet in the lounge for a sundowner—you've had a bump on the head today, and I was concerned. I'll go and order some drinks, shall I? About ten minutes—you *are* alright, aren't you?'

Jessica yawned. 'Of course, so sorry. I must still be tired from the journey. I'll see you in a little while. I won't be long.' She closed her door, switched on the main light and drew the curtains. She sat on the bed with her head in her hands, wondering what to wear. She hadn't brought much with her, just layers of versatile clothing. Evening wear hadn't crossed her mind.

She had hoped to buy some silk fabric somewhere in India, but so far hadn't had time to shop. She intended to go to a dressmaker in Delhi before travelling back to England, and have something made for a fraction of what she would pay in London.

Looking at her uninteresting wardrobe, she chose a safe beige dress and adorned it with the pearl necklace she'd been wearing all day. She brushed her hair and did her makeup, picked up her tan leather handbag and made her way to the lounge. It was heaving with people who looked as though they'd just arrived—a mix of westerners and Indians. She spotted Sebastian in the corner where they'd had coffee that morning, and walked over to him.

'Sorry, I didn't know how late it was—thanks for waking me up.' She looked around. 'Who are all these people?'

'Largely tourists. I think most of them came in a group, there might be some business people. It's so central to everything in town. I've been sitting here reading for most of the afternoon, and saw them come in. A bit of a bind having to give your passport to the front desk, it took them ages. Like everything, it's all very antiquated and labour-intensive.' He shook his head. 'Anyhow, what'll you have to drink?'

'Something long and cool—a large gin and tonic should do the trick. And have them charge drinks to *my* room this time. Please!'

Jessica was beginning to relax now in Sebastian's company. Feeling the bump on her head, she began to see the irony of what had happened—she had achieved just about nothing today. But she had plenty of time ahead of her. The new school year was still weeks away, and she only had to be back a few days before start of term.

Sebastian was aware of her watching him as he made his way nonchalantly towards the bar. She admired his style. He wore his well-cut casual khaki jacket over a dark blue linen open-necked shirt paired with light fawn Chinos. She observed how he nodded and smiled at other guests, allowing them to pass, or, in one case, helping an elderly grey-haired lady to her feet as she rose from her chair. He's not much older than her daughter, she mused. Still, it was reassuring to have his company, and even nicer he was English and could relate so well to her history with his own family connections in India.

A lot of the other guests were leaving the bar, presumably going in to have dinner. They looked tired and travel weary. Jessica smiled at a couple who passed by and wondered where they were from.

Sebastian came back with two large gins. 'Was it something I said?' he joked, looking round as the room cleared. Jessica laughed.

'Must have been,' she joked back, taking a long draw on the ice-cold drink as soon as it hit the table.

'Cheers, and here's to tomorrow—let's hope we get a bit further than today. Literally. Um, that is, if you still want me to help?'

'Would you? I'm grateful. You're at home here and know your way around so well. But I'm not sure now whether I'm ready to try to find The Laurels yet. Maybe Christ Church, and the cemetery.'

'Splendid idea—bottoms up!'

6

Shimla 1947:

Lola and Charles led the way—the men to the smoking veranda, the women back to the drawing room. Elizabeth headed straight for the powder room. She never liked having to sit with women and talk small talk about clothes, flowers and recipes. Much more the outdoor type, she could hold her own with most of the men at the dinner table tonight when it came to politics, horses and business.

She and Edward had talked endlessly about starting an export business. She'd never told James—he would think it a stupid idea, and anyway, she didn't think he liked Edward very much these days. At first, after the cliff-fall, he couldn't do enough for him. He helped introduce him into the social life in Shimla and nominated him for club memberships. James had pulled strings in high places and managed to have Edward based in Shimla for months at a time. He'd persuaded the Shimla Club to allocate a permanent cottage for him when he was in town.

Elizabeth's friend, Fredah, entered the sanctuary of the powder room.

'Phew! Thank God we can get away from them all. Clever you for coming here first. It shouldn't be long now before the men come in—it's cold out there tonight. I say, I think your hair looks spiffing, I wish I had hair like yours, it's the colour of polished copper, how lucky you are.'

'Well, I inherited it from my mother. It does seem to run in the family—even Jessie has it. She's turning into a very pretty little girl, she's four now, you know. And becoming very demanding. But we don't mind, we don't have plans for any more children. God, it takes it out of you. It's a lot easier now, of course, and Chandra takes on a lot of Jessie's care, she's very good with her. We're looking at schools, but we're not sure if we'll still be here when she's old enough, so it makes it difficult to plan anything.'

'Well, we're happy we managed to get Annabelle into a good school back home. We miss her terribly of course, but she does get back every year and we go to England with her afterwards. We stay with relatives when we're there, but I can tell you it's wonderful to get back to India and Shimla.' Elizabeth followed Fredah as they went to join the after-dinner party.

Elizabeth had applied more lipstick and a little more rouge to her flushed cheeks. She felt as stunning as she looked, the green silk of her dress draped provocatively over every curve of her body. She walked straight past the women. Some of the men had come indoors to join them, and she went to sit with James. Edward wasn't far away, and the chemistry between them began to work its magic.

She knew she had to see him again soon. They had to make a time and date. She was trying to remember James's movements for the next week or so. Wasn't he going to be off to Delhi for some strategy meeting or other? She should have checked his diary before coming out. Refusing the offer of a liqueur, she rose and deliberately walked past Edward, sliding close by him on her way, and greeting him as a friend. She made her way to the veranda and shut the door. It was cold—she pulled her wrap around her. She knew he was on his way, he'd be here soon, as practiced on previous occasions, via Charles's study door.

As expected, Elizabeth heard the opening and soft closing of the door behind her and turned to face Edward. He slid his hands over the smooth satin clinging to her thighs, and round her waist and breasts. She bent her head back exposing her delicate neck, waiting for him to kiss and caress her.

'This is very risky!'

'I know! But I know you like it—the risk!' He pulled her closer, teasing, before they embraced, moulding their bodies into one. 'So, when?'

'I'll have to call you, no, you call me, tomorrow at ten.' She pressed into his warmth and he looked deep into her eyes.

'I can't wait. We'll speak tomorrow. We have to go in—no you go first, you're freezing.'

Elizabeth straightened her clothes, wrapped her flimsy chiffon stole round her shoulders, flattened her hair, and left to go back into the house.

James stood up abruptly as she came into the drawing room and walked towards her. He took her by the elbow and steered her towards

Charles and Lola.

'Taking the air, I presume—must have been damn cold out there. Surprised your ardour wasn't dampened, dear!' Elizabeth could have cut his sarcasm with a knife.

'What *are* you talking about? dear James—now come on—a girl has to cool down sometimes you know. Ah! Look, I haven't spoken a word to Celia all night—do excuse me my dear, I must tell her all about Jessie. Its ages since I saw her.' She broke away from James's firm grip and made a beeline for her friend.

James watched her walk across the room, certain he'd crack soon—she was becoming so blatant, and it must be obvious to all their friends. They may, of course, have accepted the status quo over the years—after all, it had been more than four years since Edward walked into their lives. Sometimes, he mused, perhaps Edward thought James still owed him something for saving his life.

Perhaps he thought Elizabeth was fair exchange.

7

Shimla 1997:

In spite of the sore head and the trauma of the traffic incident yesterday, Jessica had slept well. Sitting at the breakfast table she turned to a new page in her notebook and began to write. Eager to make the most of her time here, and being a stickler for neatness, she also wanted to do things in order, and be precise.

But her thoughts began to wander. She thought about England, her home, and Saffron, her daughter, and even though Aunt Catherine had died over a year ago, Jessica missed them both. She had sent a letter and post cards from Delhi but was never sure if mail got through to the remote part of the Scottish Isles where Saffron lived in a hippie commune, with hippie friends and dropouts. She grew her own food and lived very frugally. In the winters they had to pool their resources to make sure they all survived should the worst happen if they were cut off from the mainland by bad weather, when neither a boat nor the small commuter aircraft could reach them. Jessica had ventured there to see Saffron only once, for a week. On the return flight home, she burst into tears.

It was not the life she would have wanted for her daughter. However, it seemed a natural progression from being born a love child in nineteen-sixty-four, Jessica herself falling pregnant in the summer of freedom and love at the tender age of twenty-one. Saffron's father never knew about his baby, and as the free spirit wanderers broke up and went their own way at the close of summer, Jessica had to go home and break the news to her aunt and uncle. They all tried to track down the father, but eventually gave up and had to accept the fact the baby would be born out of wedlock. Aunt Catherine was not at all pleased—they were a respectable family, pillars of the local community; bastions of proper society where norms were maintained to a high degree of morality, and where people frowned upon any kind of behaviour breaking the mould.

Yet they doted on this new addition to the family—a beautiful baby girl with grey-green eyes, whom Jessica named Saffron because of her mop of ginger hair. She relied upon her parent's seemingly never-ending trust fund to pay for Saffron's upbringing, and when the time was right, Jessica attended teacher training college. She subsequently managed to get a job at the prep school where she had enrolled her daughter.

What a lot has happened since, Jessica mused, as she watched the comings and goings of people in the dining room. Now I'm here in Shimla, eager to find my roots and to try to make sense of what Aunt Catherine told me just before she died.

Sebastian came into the room and she smiled at him as he joined her at the table.

'How are you feeling this morning? Rested, I hope.' He sat back in his chair and placed a wadge of travel brochures on the table.

'Much better, thanks—and hoping to start again where we left off yesterday before the pile-up.'

Sebastian picked up the menu. 'Sad to say, those incidents are commonplace in India. Vehicles aren't exactly maintained to any degree of road worthiness, and most simply get run into the ground. Literally!'

'So, it's a bit of a gamble, choosing a good taxi?' Jessica joked.

'You could say that.' He nodded back and raised his eyebrows at her.

He gave his breakfast order to the waiter. 'Oh, sorry, have you ordered yet? I assumed…'

'Don't worry, yes, I have and they're being very slow this morning! I'm happy just sitting here writing notes, but my mind wandered, and I started thinking, and wondering how my daughter is getting on. She lives in Scotland, and winter's coming.'

'How silly of me, I didn't realise you were married with children. Somehow, it never occurred to me…'

Jessica interrupted, 'No, not married. But I do have a daughter. Yes, naughty me—I had a child out of wedlock.' She grinned back at him.

'Well, that's nothing to be ashamed of, for goodness' sake.'

'It was though—you know, being brought up in a respectable family, going to all the best schools; having loads of money whenever I wanted it, travelling when I felt like it, and joining the flower people— make love not war! You don't remember the swinging sixties, but that was me.

'After sixth form college and a finishing school in Switzerland, I kind of went off the rails. A lot of what people imagine about those days did exist. Huh—the swinging sixties, and I seemed to be in the thick of it. Wearing flowers in my hair, popping purple hearts, smoking pot and running naked through summer meadows. And free love. That's how I came to have Saffron, my gorgeous daughter. She turns thirty-three this year, and I'm ashamed to say, has done nothing at all with her life in spite of the expensive schooling and good middle-class upbringing she's had. She's living the *good life* with a bunch of dropouts on an island in the Outer Hebrides, growing food, and fishing. I despair!'

Sebastian had been listening intently at her extraordinary story. 'Crikey! And here was I thinking you were a *Spinster of This Parish*, a staid schoolteacher, and a mainstay of English society,' he smiled and peered at Jessica quizzically.

She laughed back. 'That just goes to show—never judge a book by its cover.' He shook his head in disbelief. 'But I'm not *that* frumpish-looking, I hope. Perhaps I ought to let my hair down a bit. I suppose I came here *wanting* to give that impression, because of the mission I'm on—perhaps I thought people might take me more seriously if I looked the part. To be honest, at home I'm normally slopping around in jeans and baggy tee-shirts with a scarf around my hair and bare feet—once a hippie, always a hippie. I enjoy my life, my garden and my aging pony, Trixie. My cottage is isolated, and I like it that way! I've a studio where I paint, a vegetable garden and a greenhouse. Oh, and I try to grow exotic orchids in my conservatory. So, I suppose, in a way, I am a bit of a country bumpkin.' She grinned.

The waiter brought their breakfasts. 'Well, this food will bring you back to earth with a bump. It is only *just* adequate, isn't it?' Sebastian pushed aside the pile of leaflets he'd brought to the table, and began to eat.

'I guess so, but it is homely here, although the hotel on the hill—what's it called, The Grand Imperial, looks more like the sort of place I might stay at next time.'

'We can go there for dinner tonight, if you'd like that. You can have a good look around. I've never stayed there, but occasionally meet up with colleagues who prefer to live it up a bit and have bigger expense accounts than me.'

'Only thing is, I *am* on a budget! But oh, well, I don't suppose one meal out would hurt, and I do like the sound of the place. I imagine this is not going to be the last time I come to Shimla now, so checking out another hotel is a good idea. To tell the truth, I expect Aunt Catherine's probate to be sorted out soon, and I have great plans after that. I'll retire as soon as I can, but my priority will be to try to coax Saffie to leave Scotland. She *must* have learned *something* about agriculture whilst she's been away, and there are plenty of opportunities in landscaping these days. I even thought about offering to get her a place at college so that she can get into what she enjoys most, and make a living out of it, instead of wasting her life freezing to death and living a subsistence lifestyle.' She looked up at Sebastian.

'She sounds quite a character, your daughter. In a way, a free spirit like you were, it seems.'

'Yes, but I was restricted by convention, and the fact that I had *her* to bring up. We haven't always seen eye to eye. She wanted to find out who her father was but I had to tell her the honest truth, that I didn't know. She wanted me to describe him to her, which I did, but that is all she has—a recollected sketch from my memory bank.

'I never thought my life would be like it is.' Jessica paused and swallowed, feeling tears pricking the back of her eyes. She took a deep breath, 'Come on—that's enough of me! Let's finish our breakfast and go and have a coffee in the lounge, and you can tell me all about *you*. I'm intrigued by *your* lifestyle, too.'

8

Shimla 1947:

dward—just the man I'm looking for!' James had been into Charles' study and back searching for him, knowing that he had been out on the veranda with Elizabeth.

'Hello, James, I was hoping to see you, too. It's a while since we talked. I say, I'm pleased to hear that Jessica is doing so well, and that you're hoping to get her into Christ Church Prep school next year.'

'I bet you are my dear boy, I bet you are. And just what, may I ask, is *your* interest in *my* daughter?' James' derision showed clearly in his tone of voice.

'Well, I *have* known you all since she was born, you know. Yes, I *do* have an interest in my friends and their families. As you know, Elizabeth and I are very good friends, and she does tell me about your plans and hopes for the future. I thought you'd be glad to share good news.' Edward scanned the room briefly and swirled the brandy round his glass. 'Jolly good evening, don't you think? I had intended to introduce myself to that lovely lady over there—can't remember her name, isn't she related to Celia and Bert? Perhaps I'll go over later.'

James swallowed the last large mouthful of his brandy, and choking back his anger snarled at Edward. 'Top up, dear boy?'

'Not for me, thanks, James, I'm already full to bursting.' Edward replied as he started to walk away.

'Don't mind if I do? I feel like having a good time tonight...' James slewed his words as he lunged towards the bar to pour himself another large brandy.

Edward turned, went after him and whispered in his ear. 'Steady now, don't you think you've had enough, James—you've got to drive Elizabeth home up that bumpy road in the dark you know. Come on, we don't want another accident now, do we?'

'If you're referring to that bloody horse incident years ago, I'd rather you didn't.' James turned on Edward belligerently. 'All I ever heard for years was how you saved my bloody life. Huh—YOU save MY life?' He staggered back and found the sideboard to lean against. 'You...you saving my life—well, how about saving my WIFE?' James's raised voice delivered silence to the room, and all eyes turned his way. Edward took James's glass, and placing it on the sideboard steered him to an armchair, smiling apologetically at everyone now staring at them. Elizabeth made towards them, but decided to stay away, at least until people started to talk to each other again.

'Where's my drink? Get me my drink!' James mumbled at Edward who made his way over to the sideboard to get James's brandy glass. He knew he'd had far too much. Elizabeth carved a pathway through the guests, smiling, and went to sit on the arm of James's chair. Hubbub returned to the room briefly. Lola, wishing to lighten the atmosphere, clapped her hands for quiet.

She made sure she had everyone's attention. 'How about a little music and dancing to round off the evening? She went over to the gramophone where Charles was already waiting and suddenly the place came alive with a cheery swing rendition of Chattanooga Choo-Choo. Those who were in the mood got up to dance and the party became louder. James shrank further into his armchair, much to the relief of Elizabeth and Edward.

Elizabeth sheepishly sidled over to Edward. 'Shall we dance?' she joked, stifling her mirth, one eye on James.

'Well, he's got to get you home don't forget—that is if your car starts. Not sure where they pushed it to, we'd better ask him. It might even be better if I take you both home anyway, looking at the condition he's in. I can't say I've ever seen him in this state before.'

'He knew we were on the veranda.'

'Yes, I know. He was picking a fight about it. Hope you're not too embarrassed. Do you think they all know about us, anyway?'

'Well, you know how they gossip in Shimla—of course they do. But we're not the only naughty people around. I wouldn't be surprised if James hadn't sewn wild oats himself—now who would be the most likely lady, do you think? Hermione? Celia? Or how about Fredah?' Elizabeth held up her hand to her mouth disbelieving her mischievousness. 'I mean, look at them all—here to have a good time, to enjoy the freedom of being away from home. No, trust me, we're not the only ones.'

'Do you think I'd better go and broach the subject with James about getting back, whilst there's music and frivolity? I want to avoid another confrontation if I can. Perhaps we'll go and have a quiet word with Lola and Charles and tell them we're thinking of taking James home.'

'Yes, that's the best idea. He might cause another scene if we leave it too long. I hope he can stand. He's usually the only one who's sober.'

Edward looked across the room for Lola. They both went to her, explaining. She agreed it would be for the best, and they found Charles who was taking a breathless break from trying to boogie with Hermione.

'Charles, we're off. We've got to get James home. He's had a few too many, I'm afraid. Thank you both so much for such a wonderful evening. I'm sure we'll be reciprocating soon, and we look forward to seeing you before too long at The Laurels.'

Charles took Elizabeth's hand. 'And we hope so, too, dear girl. Do you want a hand with James?'

Elizabeth looked at Edward. 'We're hoping he'll come quietly, without a fuss, so we'll try that method first. If we need reinforcements, it'll be pretty obvious.' She made light of the situation, and they went to dig James out of his half-asleep state in a deep armchair.

'Get away…just, just…'

'Come on, James, we *have* to get home. Get up, Edward will drive us both back in his car and we can come back tomorrow to get ours.' They managed at last to pull him to his feet. As he stood up, he swayed, straightened his back in a gesture of composure, and marched out stiffly, flanked by the two of them.

'Watch the steps, James, you're doing fine now. We have to get over to Edward's car.'

James tore himself away from them and rounded on Edward, mumbling drunkenly about never going in his car even if it was the last car on earth. The door was opened, and he half fell into the front passenger seat. Elizabeth went around to the back seat and settled in for the ride. They waved goodbye to their hosts, and as Edward went through the tall iron gates of Hilltop House, James seemed to sober up a little in the cold night air, pulling his coat around him and smoothing his hair.

'How are you feeling, James?' Elizabeth was genuinely concerned but wanted him to stay subdued.

'Bloody brandy. Don't know why Charles always pours such bloody big ones! I'm...oh God...I think I'm going to throw up. Stop the damned car...STOP!' And as Edward skidded off to the left, perilously near to the edge of the cliff, James opened the car door and lunged violently to get out.

9

Shimla 1997:

Sebastian and Jessica discussed a plan for the day. Still wanting to go and find The Laurels. She thought Sebastian's idea the best; that they kill a few birds with one stone and go first to the Church to try to get access to baptism, marriage, and funeral records.

The air was thick with vehicle fumes, cow dung, and smoke as they stepped outside the hotel. Jessica's eyes watered and she fished out her sunglasses from her bag. She had willingly become accustomed to Sebastian calling taxis and rickshaws and helping her aboard whatever their transport was for the day. She'd found him delightfully courteous as they became easier in each other's company. He suggested they go to check out the Imperial on the way, have coffee on the terrace and book a table for dinner.

They walked together through the imposing doors, opened by a meticulously uniformed, turbaned doorman, who stood to attention and briefly saluted. They passed through the marble hallway towards the foyer of the hotel. Jessica looked left and right at the walls that were adorned with memorabilia from India's colonial days and gilt-framed oil paintings of proud looking Maharajas.

'This place must be new. Do you know how long it's been here, Sebastian?'

Sebastian said he thought it was built about four years previously to attract a certain calibre of tourist whose demands are more than just a homely old-fashioned place to stay. 'It's obviously much more modern, with international standards,' he explained. 'I think it rates five, or at least four stars. The terrace is to the right, through the bar and lounge. Let's go and find a place to sit.'

As they walked through the huge timber-framed glass doors the vista that suddenly came into view brought Jessica to a standstill. Spread before them was the most beautiful view she had ever seen. The panorama was magnificently topped by the mighty snow-capped Himalayan mountains that seemed so close she might put out her hand and touch them. The air was clear and fresh. A rich cobalt blue sky contrasted snowy peaks and sun shone down on the lush green of the valley below.

'I'm speechless. This is the most amazing view I have ever seen in my life.' Jessica couldn't take her eyes off the mountains that appeared to gift-wrap the picture, rugged, white, and majestic.

Sebastian pulled out a chair for her to sit in. 'Yes, it is incredible. No-one could ever imagine it without seeing for themselves. It kind of puts you in your place, doesn't it?'

'The sheer scale of those mountains has taken my breath away— and what a place to stay. I must definitely stay here next time, even though it might cost me an arm and a leg.'

Sebastian hailed a waiter and ordered coffee while Jessica walked over to the stone balustrade to look at the hotel's gardens. A large blue pool sparkled in the morning sun. A lone swimmer was leisurely taking exercise.

Back at the table they had to attend to the job in hand, and sketching out a rough map, Sebastian worked it all out. Getting a taxi from this hotel would be safer, as they tended to engage only the best of vehicles and drivers, and he suggested they keep the driver for the whole day.

After coffee, reluctantly tearing herself away from the view, Jessica followed Sebastian to the reception desk where he booked a table for seven o'clock that evening. At his request, the concierge hailed a taxi, and a deal was made with the driver for them to employ him for the rest of the day.

Pulling up outside Christ Church it was obvious to Jessica that it was still very much part of the life of this community. Entering the hallowed space inside, she looked for an official to ask about church records. They were approached by an Indian man who introduced himself as the verger, and Sebastian asked him if they could have access to records from around fifty years ago.

'There are many record books, so if you let me know your interest, I can look for you.' He politely led them down the aisle to an anteroom next to the vestry, where he bade them sit down in front of a table. 'Is it records of deceased persons you are after?'

Jessica explained her reason for coming to Shimla as succinctly as she could and introduced Sebastian as a good friend who was here to help her. 'I was born here, and my parents lived here in the summers, for ages. And my grandparents before them, although I think *they* stayed mostly in Delhi. I can't even remember them, but I was only four when my parents died.' She explained.

The man busily put large books of records before them and helped find the right dates.

'We're looking for my christening and my parents' burial,' Jessica explained as she carefully turned page after page. 'So, the fifteenth of April nineteen forty-two for my birth would make the date for christening around a month or two after that. My parents died about four years later.'

'I'm so sorry to hear that—so you're now back in Shimla to find your past and see where you were born. I hope we can help you, Miss.' He smiled kindly at them both, in turn.

'Thank you.' Jessica's eyes returned to the nineteen forty-seven entries. Scanning down the lists of perfectly scripted handwritten names, she turned the page. 'It's here—look, Sebastian. I've found it. *Delaney E; Delaney J. Died August 10th 1947. Burial service September 6th 1947.*'

Sebastian checked the entry. 'That seems a long time before burial. Does it say where they're buried?'

'No. Excuse me,' Jessica called over to the verger. 'Sorry, but how can I find my parents' graves? It doesn't say here where they were buried.'

'If the service was here, they would have been buried in Sanjauli cemetery. That's in Sanjauli suburb about ten miles from here. But I have to warn you that most of the monuments have lost their inscriptions, the stones have been vandalized, shrubs are growing around them and many of them are buried under moss, grass and mud.

'You might also find empty bottles and other rubbish in there, even on the graves. Some of the gravestones are broken and it is difficult to associate them to their respective plots. We have tried to keep the British India cemeteries in good order, but because there are no relatives of the dead here to help, it became more and more expensive to maintain them. But Sanjauli is a bit better kept than most.'

Closing the book, Jessica looked at Sebastian, shocked. 'We'd better go there.'

'Thank you so much for your information,' she said to the verger

43

'but before we go, can I see if I can find my Christening?'

'Of course, give me the name and date of birth again, and I can find it for you.'

They sat in a front pew whilst the verger disappeared into the vestry. Returning almost immediately with the register, he sat next to them and flipped through to the date of birth and looked for the Christening record. 'Delaney? Here we are—look. He smiled triumphantly. 'Jessica Elizabeth Delaney. The date of Christening is June the first.'

Jessica carefully took the register from him and disappeared into a world of her own. She marvelled at being here, in the town of her birth, a million miles away from what she knew, looking at her name on an old yellowing page of a book trying to picture the scene. She sat silent feeling detached from the day. Her two companions seemed to understand, and waited patiently until she'd taken it all in.'

'So sorry—I'm feeling emotional, never thought I would, but I'm so happy I've found this. Thank you very much for digging out the records for me. Although it seems surreal, I also feel quite content.'

Turning to speak to Sebastian, she said, 'Shall we go and see what we can find at the cemetery?'

They began to walk back down the aisle and Sebastian asked the verger where they could leave a donation to the church.

'Thank you, sir. You may put the donation in the box near the font, at the top of the aisle.'

Sebastian took Jessica's hand as they emerged outside the church and helped her into their car. 'Are you alright? You must be feeling a little scared?'

He told the driver where to go, and he put his arm around Jessica's shoulders in support and sympathy.

The driver stopped outside the cemetery and pointed to a pair of rusty iron gates. They pushed them open and entered. There was debris everywhere. Grass grew waist high in places. A narrow footpath drew them in, amongst fallen headstones and broken crosses. The area was vast, and Jessica at once thought the task impossible. Few people came here, it was obvious, even though it was apparently on the tourist route for relatives of those buried here to look for their ancestors. An old man was hacking away at the undergrowth near a wall, and a bent old woman in a scarlet sari emerged and passed them on the path, lowering her head, she pulled the sari across her face. Jessica stared after her thinking it strange to see such a well-turned-out Indian woman in this, a British cemetery.

Jessica looked left and right. 'Where do we start.' she sighed. Her hypothetical question was delivered with hopelessness.

'Why don't you do that side, and I'll look on the other side of the path. Check the easy bits first, and if we have no luck, we'll go on into the jungle.' Sebastian joked.

Following the path, Jessica read one name after another on stone tablets that had been partially overgrown with moss. 'No luck yet,' she called across to Sebastian who was scouring the broken stones.

She followed freshly trampled grass to look at a few more headstones and was drawn to a grave with a few bright flowers. She looked across towards the man who was clearing debris. He was staring at her.

Jessica approached the flower-strewn grave, bent down and brushed leaves away from the inscription with her hand. *Here lie the remains of Mr and Mrs James Delaney who died tragically on the day of our lord 10.8.1947. May their souls re-unite in Heaven.*

'Sebastian, Sebastian, I've found it.' she shouted as she picked up the flowers. Water still glistened on the stems. 'Oh, God! The woman—the one who passed us—she must have left them. The stems are still wet and the flowers are fresh.' Jessica stood and looked towards the gates.

Sebastian walked towards the old man who was now trying to pile leaves and rubbish into a rusty wheelbarrow. 'Hello! Hello! Excuse me—do you speak English?'

'A little,' he replied.

'Do you know who the woman was who was here just before us? Did she leave those flowers?'

Jessica wanted to head towards the gate. 'Come on, we might be able to find her and ask her if we hurry.'

'That was my wife,' said the old man. 'She comes here to bring my food and sometimes puts flowers to that grave.'

'Why that grave, why *that* one?' Jessica wanted to find her.

'She remembers,' the man lowered his voice. 'She was there.'

'Where, tell me, where was she?' Jessica was getting more and more frantic.

'At the fire, at house Laurel, when that terrible thing happened. Long time ago. She remembers and prays. It is very sad.' He carried on raking leaves.

Sebastian turned, 'Come on, she can't have gone far. She'll be easy to spot in that red sari.'

'Thank you,' Jessica said to the man. 'Your name, what's your name—oh, and what's your wife's name?'

'Madam, I am called Harish, and my wife, she is called Chandra.'

10

Elizabeth muffled a scream. Edward leapt out of the driver's seat and raced to where James knelt on the ground, writhing and retching. His knees were just inches from the cliff edge. Swaying back and forth, his head was hanging over the abyss.

'James,' Elizabeth shouted to make herself heard over the noise of the car's engine. 'Stay exactly where you are—do you hear me? Don't move.' Both she and Edward could see that with any attempt to get to his feet, he could tumble over the edge.

The only source of light was from the car's headlights. Edward managed to reach James before he moved. Grabbing him by his collar, he dragged him to safety. He told him to stand up. He looked a mess. Vomit and gravel caked his jacket, his tie hung loose, and his trousers were muddy at the knees.

'Sorry, Elizabeth, but can you sit in the passenger seat and I'll put him in the back. I don't want him going near the side of the road again.' Edward steered him towards the place Elizabeth had just vacated, closed the back door and drove off as swiftly as he could.

'Any excuse! Sitting close enough, are you...?' James leaned forward onto the front seats. His words reeked of brandy and the stench of vomit.

Elizabeth gagged at the odour, and sat as far away from him as she could. 'Shut up, James—we'll be home soon, and you'd better sober up. You've been a disgrace tonight, an absolute disgrace.'

'Huh—me? You two having it off on Charles' veranda and it's *me* who's a disgrace. You do know how to turn the bloody tables, Lizzie.' he slurred his words, slumping back into the seat as The Laurels came into view.

Elizabeth was relieved. 'Thank goodness all the lights are on, hopefully we'll be able to get in without waking Jessie and Chandra— I'd die if they saw the state of James. Although Chandra will most likely have to deal with his clothes tomorrow.' She pulled her stole tighter around her shoulders in preparation for helping James out of the car and into the house.

Edward turned the vehicle, stopping right outside the front door of the house. They all opened their doors at the same time, and James couldn't wait to get out. Fumbling with the door handle, he almost fell out of the car. He leaned for a while against the bonnet, breathing deeply, took off his jacket, folded it precisely and neatly, hung it over his arm, and step by careful staggering step, made his way through the door that had just been opened by Ranjit. Elizabeth and Edward weren't far behind.

'James, you'd better come upstairs with me, and while I go to check on Jessie and Chandra, you can change into clean clothes, or better still, pyjamas. You can go to bed or we'll meet you back in the drawing room. Good that Ranjit has kept the fire burning. Edward, help yourself to a nightcap—I'll be down in a tick.'

Elizabeth steered James into their bedroom. She went to her dressing table where she smoothed her hair and removed her earrings and necklace, locking them away safely in a jewellery box, before tiptoeing across the landing into Jessica's room. Chandra had a bed in the nursery for babysitting, and Elizabeth found them both fast asleep. She bent over Jessie, wanting to stroke her hair, but afraid to wake her. Elizabeth knelt by Jessica's bed for a while, marvelling at her beautiful gift from God and patted the eiderdown snugly around her daughter's tiny frame.

She found Edward sitting in a fireside chair with a whisky, reading the newspaper. 'All alright up there?' he asked.

'Yes, both fast asleep, and James is changing. I think he's sobering up a bit, but I'd rather he went straight to bed. Never wanting to be outdone, though, he'll most likely be here in a minute demanding another large brandy. What an evening. I think you ought to stay the night. Are you alright Edward?' She poured herself a sherry and stood by the fire. 'Gosh it's cold for the time of year, or is it just the trauma of tonight?'

Edward put his glass down and went to close the door. Elizabeth melted into his arms and sighed with relief. 'What shall we do?' he said. 'We have to resolve our affair. I can't go on like this any longer, any more than you can, I dare say.'

'We've got to make a decision. Whatever we do it will be final and dramatic. And there's Jessie—he'll want custody.' Elizabeth clung to him tightly. 'Oh God.'

'I know. Don't think I haven't thought about it, too. The consequences would be huge. His position, India—where would we go? Back to England? I couldn't bear to be parted from you, you know that, don't you? I love you so very much.' He kissed her passionately.

The door burst open and James stood in his dressing robe, eyes black as thunder. Swaying towards them his voice was low and calm.

'I have it now, you barefaced cheats. I heard every word, in fla…gran…te!' He spoke the damning word threateningly slow, staring wildly at Edward. 'I didn't need to, but proof is a powerful weapon, don't you know.' James approached his wife, grabbed her by the arms and pushed himself against her lewdly.

'Stop it, James we can sort this out.' Elizabeth fought him off. 'Please—stop it, leave me alone.' James pushed her away violently, her dress caught under the heel of her shoe, and as she stumbled Edward lunged forward to catch her. His fingers slipped on the silk of her dress as she fell backwards, smashing her head on the marble mantelpiece. As if in slow motion, he watched as she collapsed into the hearth, powerless to stop her. She called his name as her body convulsed, then limp and lifeless her last screaming breath diminishing to the bitter end.

Edward felt her pulse as blood began to gush from a cut in her head. He shook her again and again, looking for signs of life. Pulling her body away from the fire, he screamed her name in desperation as he cradled her head in his hands, staring in disbelief at her unresponsive eyes.

James stood by, unable to speak, looking on through a haze of alcohol, still not realising Elizabeth was dead until Edward turned on him. Shouting viciously, Edward instinctively picked up a fire iron and wielded it at James's head.

'My God, look—do you realise what you've just done? You've just *killed* your wife, my…my…only love. You've never loved her like I did, you…you…murderer! She was the most wonderful person in the whole world and meant everything to me. I was going to take her and Jessica away from here. Away from your uncaring hateful marriage.' Edward raised his shaky voice through tears of anger. 'You…you've been cold and calculating all your life. I know all your secrets, how you rose to this position, how you used Elizabeth and other people to get what you want. Always you—never a thought for anyone else.' Edward was in despair, as the reality of the situation hit home.

He cornered James who shouted for him to get out, to go away, pushing him, which enraged Edward. 'So now, you bloody cad, you've killed her. Its over James, all over. You're finished.' He looked back at Elizabeth's distorted face. 'Look. Look, oh my God—she's...*dead*!'

Edward reached for the poker and lifted it as high as he could and in uncontrolled and hysterical rage smashed it into the side of James' head. James yelled out and fell, casting his brandy around the room. Edward, now panic-stricken, repeatedly smashed the weapon into his bloody skull. Leaving James slumped on the floor, he went over to Elizabeth and lay with her, distraught. The fire crackled merrily in the silence, unseeing and unknowing the destruction and devastation in its presence.

Edward had to think quickly. Knowing what he'd done, he also had to tell the story of how Elizabeth died. Rushing towards the hall he thought about Jessie, Chandra and Ranjit. He'd have to go to the police. It was past midnight, there'd be no-one at the station. He sat on the bottom stair with his head in his hands, trying to decide what to do first. He couldn't leave the house without Jessie, and how could he wake Chandra and tell the servants before the morning?

He looked at the open drawing room door. The fire had sprung to life—flaming like spirits of the soul, lighting up the entire room. As he made his way back to look at the horrors of the night, he realised that sparks from the fire had ignited the fireside rug, and dense bright flames flickered and played around Elizabeth, devouring her dress and enveloping her body. He stared helplessly at the horrific scene. He saw the fire quickly take hold of the carpet and furniture, following along the trail made by the spilt brandy and towards where James' body lay.

Water, he had to get water. He shouted out for Ranjit, but as the intense blaze drove him out of the room, Chandra was right there at the bottom of the stairs. Taking stock of everything before her, she began to panic and whimper. Edward took her by the arms. 'Chandra—there's been a terrible accident, we'll have to get out of the house, the fire is going to spread.'

'Jessica. I have to get Jessica!' She ran back up the stairs, Edward striding two at a time behind her. He heard hissing and crackling as fire engulfed more and more of the house below.

He forged his way ahead of Chandra, and scooping up the child he quickly made his way back down the staircase. Flames licked their way through floorboards on the landing just as Chandra, who was trying to carry blankets and Jessica's teddy, ran across to the top of the stairs. The fanning flames caught hold of her clothing and she screamed, dropping blankets and teddy over the balustrade to the floor below, waking Jessica and alerting Edward.

'Lie down, lie down and roll.' He shouted till he was hoarse, watching as the blaze surrounded her. He ran to the car and put Jessica in the back seat. Then charged back into the house to save Chandra. The staircase had almost collapsed by the time he climbed back down it, half dragging Chandra's badly burnt body. She sat sobbing in pain next to Jessica, who, shaking with fear, was screaming hopelessly for her mother. Edward needed to go into the house again—his car keys had been left on the hall table. He spotted Jessica's teddy and blanket on the floor and quickly picked them up as he escaped through the front doors of The Laurels for what he knew would be the last time.

He had to get help. Ranjit was nowhere to be found. He'd go to Lola and Charles, perhaps they were still up and about after their party. He could use their phone to call police, ambulance and the fire brigade. Panicking, he turned the car towards Shimla. Stopping near the main gate to The Laurels, he looked back. In a stupor, he witnessed an inferno devour the house, lighting up the night sky as it burned like a funeral pyre. Shaking, but now silent, Jessica clung desperately to Chandra who had passed out on the back seat.

11

Shimla 1997:

'C handra.' Jessica turned sharply and looked at Sebastian. 'I know that name—I remember now!'

She turned back to the bent old man. 'Your wife, Chandra—you say she was at The Laurels? She must remember me. I'm Jessie, Jessie Delaney.'

He placed his rake on the wobbly wheelbarrow and stared at Jessica. 'Ah, my lord. Jessie—Chandra, she talk about you a lot. After we marry, after the court and everything, she told me all about it. She said she wanted to know what happened to you.'

'Chandra told you about what, exactly. A court case, what happened?' Jessica urged him to try to remember, as her mind flipped the words he'd uttered. She immediately thought a crime had been committed by someone for him to talk about a court case.

After precious minutes of difficult probing questions, with the old man trying his best to recall what he had been told by his wife, Sebastian suggested they go as soon as possible to find Chandra. He managed to get Harish to tell them where he and Chandra lived, and how to find their house. Jessica wrote the address in her notebook with a few directions, and they hurriedly made for the cemetery gate to get back into their waiting car.

Jessica gave the driver the address. As they set off back along the road towards town both she and Sebastian scoured the busy streets, looking down the myriad alleyways, still hoping to catch a glimpse of the woman in the red sari.

'My God, Chandra! Yes, of course, I do remember her now. She must have been young when she was my nanny at The Laurels. I remember us having fun together—she must have been like a second mother to me. One thing sticks out in my mind about a grand party my mother was entertaining, and I sat with Chandra on the balcony—or perhaps it was the landing of our house—and we watched as all the ladies in their finery arrived, escorted by uniformed officers and men in dinner jackets. I remember it because my father got cross with me. He came upstairs and ordered us to go to the nursery. Oh, Sebastian, we've got to find her. I hope she hasn't forgotten me. Fancy her putting flowers on my parents' grave after all this time. I wonder why? Do you think they were both working at The Laurels?'

Sebastian, peering out of the car window, said he thought Harish would have said so if they had worked together.

'What do you think he meant by *that terrible thing*, Sebastian? And *court case*. Something bad must have happened.'

'Don't know. He mentioned a fire too. I guess we're about to find out, if the driver knows where he's going.' Sebastian turned to look at Jessica and instinctively put his arm around her in a gesture of camaraderie.

'We'll get to the bottom of things, and I'll help you bear the burden. The more I hear of your story, the more I feel for you, and I sincerely want you to discover the truth.' He held her close and she tilted her head on his shoulder, feeling comforted and secure. Her mind was full of images as she tried hard to remember her parents, their home, and Chandra. She wanted to find out everything she could.

'Sebastian, listen, I've just decided to stay in Shimla until I know the whole story of what happened. There is so much I need to know. If I don't get to the bottom of it now, when will I ever have another chance?'

'Will you let me stay with you?' Sebastian sounded concerned.

'What about your work? Don't you have to get back to Delhi?' She thought it odd he could just take off whenever he wanted.

'Well, to tell the truth, they're not expecting much from me at the moment, and…'

'But I thought you were in Shimla to work, to do some research…?' Jessica sat up.

'Driver—slow down, I saw a flash of red. There—out in the middle of that crowd. Look, Sebastian, see, winding along the road?'

'Oh yes, driver, can you stop here?' Eyes scanned constantly moving traffic and people, this way and that. Flashes of red just became a flower stall or a shop selling fabrics. But no woman wearing a red sari.

'Never mind, we'll go to the house—no rush, driver, take your time. We don't want to get there before she does.' Sebastian said.

The driver explained that where they were going required some walking and there were footpaths to negotiate. He offered to walk with them to help find the house. The car veered to the left up a winding narrow lane flanked by pink flowering shrubs and blue hydrangeas, and came to a stop.

'The house is down there.' He pointed to a well-worn footpath leading to a row of small individual houses, each painted in bright or pastel colours, with tiny gardens behind picket fences. 'I will walk with you.'

A young woman wearing a mix of modern and traditional dress was sweeping dust from her front step. She stopped and smiled as they walked past, and watched them continue along the path. A few small boys played an impromptu game of cricket on a small patch of level ground, using a bat that was far too big, and stumps that were far too small. At another house, a toddler was playing in the dirt with a yellow toy truck, banging it with a stick, his chubby cheeks streaked with dust. All around them wafted the evocative fragrance of cooking spices, and the unmistakeable smell of wood-smoke. Jessica looked at Sebastian for support. She was beginning to feel very uneasy at the thought of meeting Chandra, not knowing what she might find.

'Are you sure this is it?' she asked the driver, who replied by showing them the address and pointing to the street name and house numbers.

The three of them started further down the path which became steeper, until they reached a neat little white-painted house with rose bushes in the garden and scrubbed stone steps to the front door.

'Here we are. This is the house.' The driver stepped back. 'Do you want me to stay?'

'No, thanks. You can go and wait in the car, but we may be some time. Here, go and get yourself some food.' Sebastian fished some money from his pocket and gave it to the driver. 'We'll see you back at the car.'

People in nearby houses looked through their windows inquisitively at the couple of strangers standing outside Chandra's door.

'Here we go.' Jessica said, taking a deep breath and holding on to Sebastian's arm. 'Shall I knock?'

But Jessica didn't have to knock. The door suddenly swung wide open.

The two women stared in disbelief at each other, until a frail voice emerged.

'Jessie! Jessie, I knew you'd come back.'

The old woman pulled the red sari across her face and stood in the doorway, beckoning them inside.

12

Shimla 1947:

Edward drove like a man crazed, over the uneven terrain with his precious cargo. He was sweating profusely. Unnerved, his mind whirling, he tried to piece together the last few minutes of the disaster he'd left behind him. From the moment that he, James, and Elizabeth arrived back at The Laurels from the party, to the surreal sight of the homestead being consumed by fire.

The beams from the car headlights bounced around on the road in front of him, making him feel dizzy, and Edward saw the horses only at the last minute. They were running wild, spooked and panicked. Fleetingly, he thought the stables behind The Laurels must also have caught fire. Jamming on the brakes, Chandra slid forward in the back seat, rousing her into consciousness. She shouted out in pain, causing Jessica to scream. He managed to drive the horses to the inside of the road to be near the rock face of the cutting, and left them far behind as he forged forward to reach Hilltop House as quickly as he could. The car had been filled with smoke, and he couldn't get the acrid smell of Chandra's burnt flesh out of his nostrils.

He accelerated as he approached Hilltop House, relieved to see lights in the windows. Stopping the car close to the steps, he leapt out and ran up to the front door, hammering with his fists. His strangled shouts filled the still night air like the echoes of trapped ghosts. He looked sideways to the veranda, where, only a few hours before, he and Elizabeth had embraced. A startled Charles opened the front door and Edward staggered forward, sobbing, urging Charles to come to the car. Lola appeared in her dressing gown, and, clasping a hand to her mouth, ran down the steps trying to make sense of Edward's garbled words.

Between the three of them they managed to get Jessica and Chandra into the house. Jessica was crying and Lola enfolded her in her arms to comfort her. She instructed the men to phone the fire brigade and ambulance. Chandra was drifting in and out of consciousness as they laid her on the soft leather sofa. Lola called the maid, and Charles went into his study and immediately rang Doctor Hetherington. He fetched an eiderdown for Chandra, whose burnt blistering skin oozed blood. Parts of her sari had fused with the skin on her face as she'd tried to protect herself against the flames.

Jessica was led into the kitchen where she was given a glass of warm milk and a biscuit. Lola wiped the child's ruddy tear-streaked face, gave her the comfort blanket and teddy rescued from the fire, and sat her on a chair in front of the stove to keep warm.

'They're coming—I called Doctor Hetherington, and he's getting the ambulance mobilised.' Charles strode into the drawing room and went straight over to look at Chandra. 'She's coming round. Chandra, Chandra! Answer me—can you hear me? We'll get you to the hospital as soon as possible.' Chandra was moaning in pain and trying to move. 'It will be alright, Chandra, try not to move too much. The ambulance will be here soon.'

Charles took Edward aside. 'What the hell happened? Where are James and Elizabeth?'

Edward chose his words carefully. 'I couldn't save them, Charles. I tried, we—Ranjit and me—tried to put the fire out. They were in the drawing room, James insisting on more brandy. I can't remember. Elizabeth had checked on Jessie and Chandra, and James had changed out of his filthy clothes—he was still inebriated.' Edward paused.

'Oh God—I might have known something awful would happen. I went out to the kitchen for a cloth because James had spilt brandy all over the carpet. When I got back, I heard them arguing. As I approached the drawing room he was ranting on at Elizabeth. I saw him push her into the fireplace. She screamed out for him to stop, tripped over her long skirt, and I ran to help. I think James picked up a poker and lashed out at me. There was a struggle and I must have taken it off him. He was threatening me with it. He picked up another fire iron and prepared to hit Elizabeth as I bent to pick her up. It's all a blur...I think, yes, she must have died the moment her head hit the stone hearth. Charles. I'm sorry, but I have to sit down...'

'Of course, tell me later, dear boy—it's all too much.'

Edward sat for a moment, trying to recall the shocking sequence of events. He heard Chandra cry out, and went to her side. He asked Charles if he could stay with her, and he went to see Jessica.

He found her in the kitchen staring into the dying embers of the stove. Lola was comforting her. As soon as she saw him she started to cry again and ran towards him. Edward reached out, needing so much to comfort her, but was afraid to get too close. The last thing he wanted was for Jessica to refuse his succour. He crouched before her and held her tiny hands. But she leaned towards him and he took her in his arms.

'Where's my mummy and daddy? I want my mummy and daddy. Please, I want to go home.' Her pleading voice struck his heart strings like a heavy hammer.

Lola looked on empathetically in response to Jessica's plaintiff question. 'Shush, now, dear, you'll be alright with us for now. When you've finished your milk, we'll take you up to sleep in the softest bed ever.'

'Where's Chandra. I want my ayah.'

'Come, now, dry your eyes, and, look—you can hug your teddy tight and take him with you.' Edward bent to pick her up. He buried his face in her shoulder, fighting back tears. 'I'll stay with you. We'll have you tucked up in bed in no time—and I think we might just find another teddy or two in your room.' Edward remembered staying at Hilltop House in Charles and Lola's guest room.

'Will mummy come here in the morning?'

'Come on, now. Up the wooden hill. We'll see, in the morning. Auntie Lola will be with you...' Edward was lost for words, and overcome with grief and anxiety, as he and Lola took Jessica upstairs and out of the way of the commotion unfolding downstairs. He sat, his heart filled with love for the little girl, now an orphan, whose young life had changed in an instant. He stroked her face and hugged her tight, his feelings spilling over into unexplored possessive longing for Elizabeth's child. Elizabeth's child whom they had thought their own creation.

Edward hugged Jessica as Lola closed the curtains and fluffed up the bed ready for Jessica to sleep in. He whispered to the child that he loved her very much, seemingly oblivious of Lola's presence. 'I know you're mine. You're my precious daughter—made in the beautiful image of your perfect mother, my only love.'

13

Shimla 1997:

Stepping over the threshold of Chandra's house, Jessica held back an urge to hug her. She sensed a feeling of calm trepidation. Sunshine filtered through windows into every corner of the living room. Incense pervaded the air, arousing an exotic and sensual fragrance. The room was simply furnished with sturdy dark wooden chairs, tables, chests of drawers, and a bureau in the corner. Richly coloured Indian rugs were scattered thickly over the floor, partly covered by large cushions. A heady aroma of cooking spices filled their senses. Chandra ushered Jessica to sit on a sofa in front of the empty fire grate.

The two women looked silently at each other, lost for words. They both spoke at once. Jessica was urged on first, and she patted the sofa for Sebastian to sit next to her.

'Chandra, this is Sebastian. He's been helping me and showing me around Shimla. Sebastian, meet Chandra—she was my ayah.' As soon as Jessica uttered those words, she burst into tears, quickly apologising to them both and explaining that she couldn't believe she was here after all this time.

Sebastian put his arm around her, as she straightened up and looked at Chandra.

'Chandra, I can't remember very much about my life here, yet I do remember your name and I remember you as a young lively woman teaching me and playing with me. Did I have a doll's pram and a doll? And I seem to remember a lacy parasol. My teddy. Oh, Chandra, my teddy was passed on to my daughter and she still looks after it.'

Chandra lifted both hands to her face, remembering those details from her past as if it were yesterday. And she remembered saving Jessica's teddy from the burning house.

'Tell me what happened, Chandra. All I remember is our house in the hills, running through gardens, swinging on a swing, playing with bats and balls...and a tricycle. I think I had a happy time there. I remember watching as people came to the house, but I can't remember my parents, even though I have a few photographs. Isn't that awful?

Everything must have happened so quickly, because all I know is that I was taken from here to England and adopted by my Aunt Catherine.' She searched Chandra's face which was still half-covered by the sari. 'You see, I never thought much about my short life here until recently, but knowing about it is now the most important thing in the world.'

Sebastian shuffled his feet, feeling superfluous. 'Sebastian, do you mind staying with us, or would you rather be somewhere else?' Jessica asked.

'Of course not, I wouldn't dream of it—not after being so involved over the past few days.'

'If you're sure, okay. Listen in, and if you think of anything I haven't asked, do say. Won't you?'

Sebastian nodded, and Jessica turned her attention back to Chandra, who was sitting uneasily on the edge of her chair.

'Dear Jessica, I do not believe this, either, but I can say how pleased I am that you are here. I always hoped you would.' Chandra's English was excellent. Jessica realised that she must have used it as her first language in her early years. 'All I remember of you is as a dear little girl, red hair under a hat, running across the lawn at The Laurels, full of fun and laughter. After that awful night I never saw you again. Ever. When I came out of hospital...'

'Hospital? Tell me Chandra, what happened? I don't understand.'

'Your mother and father had gone to Hilltop House that night for a dinner party. Your mother looked beautiful, I will never forget her, she wore an elegant green silk gown. After Ranjit had locked the house, you drank your cocoa and I took you to the nursery and we read picture books until you fell asleep.

'I always slept on a bed in the nursery when I was looking after you at night, but there was a commotion downstairs, and I woke up. I thought someone had broken into the house, and I went downstairs to call Ranjit. When I got to the bottom of the stairs, I heard your mother and father arguing, raising their voices, and their friend was there, too. I think he brought them home in his car.'

Jessica thought that Chandra might have forgotten a lot over the years.

'But Chandra, why did we have to escape?'

Chandra raised both her arms and gently took hold of the gold-etched edge of her sari. Pulling it behind her head she turned to Jessica and Sebastian. Her once jet-black hair, now white, was drawn back in soft waves framing the grotesque sight of half of her face which was twisted and scarred. Her right eyelid looked permanently closed and the dark wizened skin on her neck was wrinkled.

Jessica gasped. She was stunned by the dreadful sight. 'Chandra, did that happen that night? But...oh!' She turned her face away.

Sitting back in her chair, Chandra continued. 'The whole place burnt down. All except the west wing where your parent's room was, beyond the chimney stacks. Your poor mother and father...'

'But, do you mean to say that The Laurels *burned to the ground?* That can't be, I was told that my parents died of dysentery...why would my aunt and uncle tell me that? They *must* have known. Sebastian, don't you think they would have known the truth? And anyway, what about death certificates...and...well, their graves. *Both* of my parents didn't perish in a *fire?* Surely not.'

Chandra took a deep breath. 'It is true, Jessie. I was there. We were taken by your mother's friend to Hilltop House. You were in the bedroom and we both went to rescue you. He took you straight to his car and I tried to get some things for you from the nursery, but I had to drop them as I came down the stairs and flames caught my clothes. He rushed through the flames and he somehow got me out and into the car. I can't remember much after that. I was taken to hospital, and after I came out, it was all over. Everything. You had gone to England, and your parents had been buried. I asked about what happened, and later went to look at The Laurels. I never found out what happened to Ranjit. When I met Harish, we were told we could never have any children.'

Jessica stared in silence, wondering what to say next, for fear of bringing back bad memories for Chandra.

'Look,' Chandra rose and went to the bureau. 'This ornament—I found it in the ruins. It sat on top of your mother's dressing table.' She held out a small china horse no bigger than a teacup. 'I want you to have this. Take it, Jessica, please.' She held it out for Jessica to take from her.

'But this should be yours, in memory of my mother and me.' Jessica hesitantly accepted the gift. 'It's beautiful, Chandra. Thank you so much, I'll cherish this forever.'

'Chandra, there must be more, think hard. Who lived at Hilltop House, and who was it who drove us to safety that night? Did you ever ask anyone about it? Nothing seems to be right, somehow. Ashes, jewellery, ornaments. Dysentery?'

Jessica implored Sebastian, 'You do understand that I need to know the truth, don't you? I have to find out.' Jessica was once again in despair wondering what else she didn't know.

14

Shimla 1947:

Edward sat at the end of the divan bed where he'd lain Jessica, to try to get her back to sleep. She was cuddling her teddy as she turned over and buried her head in the pillow. He pulled up the blankets. Suddenly, headlights of what he assumed to be the ambulance flashed dancing shadows around the bedroom walls. He kissed Jessica on the forehead and stood, wearily adjusting his crumpled soiled shirt and smoothing his trousers, before tiptoeing out of the room and descending the staircase.

Downstairs, Dr Peter Hetherington greeted Edward with a fleeting glance as he bent over Chandra, administering sedative with a syringe. He checked her eyes and held her hand, feeling for a pulse. A nurse and the ambulance driver stood by, awaiting instructions.

'We need lots of bandages and sterilisation fluid, nurse,' the Doctor said. He beckoned them to one side, and subdued his voice. 'We must get her to hospital as quickly as we can. I'll try to cover as much as possible but she'll need extensive skin grafts. The poor woman has suffered third-degree burns and there's fusing of fabric to the skin on her face and arms. Looks like she's fortunate that her hair didn't catch fire. She's in a pretty bad way. Barely alive.'

The nurse sprang into action, and Lola offered her help. Peter Hetherington stood up slowly, staring at the wretched sight of Chandra lying on the sofa, now heavily sedated. Steadying himself on the arm of the sofa, he walked over to Charles and Edward.

'What the hell happened? This is as bad as it gets, she'll be lucky to survive...'

Edward spoke, his voice shaky and hardly audible. 'Terrible accident, Peter, terrible. I don't know where or how to start...

'The Laurels caught fire. The house went up in flames, and we only just managed to get out in time...'

Peter settled his lean frame back in the chair and stroked his fair hair with both hands. 'Good lord, Edward. But how? Where's the family, Elizabeth, and James? How did it happen? And the little girl, Jessica, isn't it?' Peter was dumbfounded.

Edward took the doctor's elbow and they went to sit in a huddle with Charles. Head in hands, he tried his best to piece together the events of the night. From the time they left Hilltop House, to the drinking, the arguments, and the impossible situation when he saw James push Elizabeth into the fire; to the speed the flames caught hold of the drawing room furnishings and curtains and began to spread upstairs, the intense heat forcing him back. He told how he managed to get Chandra out of the house just in time before the staircase collapsed.

'What? James and Elizabeth? And the girl?' Peter Hetherington was incredulous, as Edward poured out his story.

'I rescued Jessica from the house and put her in the car. Chandra went back to get some blankets and Jessica's teddy, and that was when her clothes caught fire.' Edward continued. 'The horses have bolted and are running wild, scared.

'The first thing I did was to rush upstairs for Jessica. She is unscathed, but obviously confused and frightened—she's tucked up in bed in Lola and Charles' guest room. We managed to keep her away from Chandra and the commotion, and get her upstairs. She's only four, and I'm not sure what we're going to tell her about her home and her mother and father. Charles and Lola were the first people I thought to come to. We'd all been here earlier at a dinner party. That's how James got so drunk. He just wouldn't stop drinking. You saw him, didn't you Charles? we had to almost carry him out of here. Even when we got home, he kept helping himself to more, before he started on Elizabeth. His car's here, broken down, so that's why I took them both back to The Laurels in mine.'

Edward was interrupted by the nurse who summoned the doctor to check Chandra before they got her onto a stretcher and loaded her into the ambulance. Peter Hetherington bade farewell to the trio of friends who were standing in silhouette, on the top step of the entrance to Hilltop House, and climbed into the back of the vehicle with his patient.

Edward, Charles and Lola stood silent as the rear lights of the ambulance eventually faded and disappeared round a bend in the driveway. Tears tumbled down Lola's face and landed onto her gown. She was overwhelmed by confusion and sadness. She took hold of both men's hands. Clouds scudded across the now moonlit sky as a cold wind blew icy blasts from the mountains. 'Come on, come on in—I'm suddenly feeling frozen.' She said.

'Yes, let's go in, we ought to try to sleep. It's late, and there's going to be an awful lot to do tomorrow,' Charles said, locking and bolting the front door behind them.

15

Shimla 1997:

Sebastian and Jessica began to talk about where to go from here, while Chandra made some tea.

'I hope this is to your liking, it's local tea, nothing fancy.' Chandra apologetically placed a tray on the table in front of her unexpected guests. 'I sometimes used to make tea for your mother, and I can see her now, sitting on the back veranda, entertaining friends. Jessie, I have to say, you look like her—you have her hair and manner. Your mother was a beautiful person, so generous, kind, and caring. I remember the awful day when your father had a bad accident on his horse and they brought him back home all bruised, and she fussed over him so much. Nothing was too much trouble for her. They had a house party that night, I remember it well and...'

'Sorry to interrupt, Chandra, but can you tell me, do you think they were happy? I seem to remember you taking me upstairs at one time and I went back on to the landing, I recall, and heard shouting.' Jessica chuckled and smiled realising that events were coming back from her childhood. 'It might be my vivid imagination. I think we usually only truly remember the good things from our past, yet I hope I'm able to put all these random memories into some kind of order, because right now, there appears to be a lot to unravel.'

'You are right about memories, but...no, no...I'm not sure, but...' Chandra hesitated.

Jessica looked intently into Chandra's face. 'What is it, Chandra, have you remembered something? Please tell me. I know it was a long time ago, but I want to know as much about my parents as possible, and you are the only person in the world who can tell me. I'm so pleased I've found you—and what a coincidence. And to think, we might never have met if I hadn't gone searching in that cemetery.'

'I think it was to be, Jessie. It can't have been a coincidence. But you know, at the time—nineteen forty-seven when the British left. At that time the whole country was restless, and there had been trouble between Muslims and Hindus as well as between Indians and the British. It was just before India took over self-rule. Some people, some of their friends, had left already by the time your parents died. The rest were just waiting and making the most of what they had here—especially here in Shimla, where living was easy in the summer away from the heat of the plains. It was a good life for them.'

Jessica hung on to Chandra's every word. Sebastian listened patiently, having taken a back seat in this conversation.

'Your mother, in spite of her being like an angel to everyone…well, I hope you don't mind me telling you this, it is, after all, such a long time ago, but, well, everyone in Shimla knew that she had a man friend—you know what I mean? It all seemed very open. Your father and he were friends, too—in fact it was your mother's friend who saved your father's life that day on the horse ride. I don't think he lived in Shimla, but he was here for a long time, they would be seen together. He would stay at The Laurels when your father was away on business. Servants notice things, you know, and talk. But I never said a word to anyone until now—your mother was too good to me. I would never ever say bad things about her…'

The revelation took Jessica by surprise. 'Oh, my God! Who was he, Chandra—can you remember his name?'

'It was that man who rescued you and me from the fire that night, yes, I think I remember…he was a real hero. He took us to Hilltop House. I must have been unconscious but he saved your life, Jessie.

'Now, let me think—I can even picture him—tall and elegant. Very correct and treated everyone with respect. He was in the British Army—a Major, I think. Oh, my memory isn't good my dear. I didn't have much to do with him. I remember the people at Hilltop House because I went there after I came out of hospital and they told me that you had been taken back to England. I was very upset to hear all about The Laurels, and about you and your mother and father. Their names were McAllister, yes, that right, Charles and Mrs McAllister.'

'Don't worry, Chandra. It has all been too much for you, I'm sure you'll remember more now that we have met again, and I intend to come and see you again—tomorrow, if…' Jessica stopped mid-sentence.

'I've got it!' Chandra, now animated, became very excited after dredging her memory. She sat forward in her chair.

'Of course—how could I forget? His name was Edward—yes, that's it, his name was Edward Shelley. Major Edward Shelley.'

16

Shimla 1947:

Edward said goodnight to Charles and Lola, as he was shown into a bedroom lavishly furnished with embroidered silk curtains, plush chairs and a thick patchwork eiderdown on the bed. He had no night clothes, so Charles had given him a pair of pyjamas to wear. After getting changed, he looked into Jessie's room. She was lying on her back, fast asleep. He pulled her bedclothes straight, picked her teddy off the floor and put it on the bed and sat on the rug next to her.

How was he expected to sleep? Still trying to understand the events of the night, and come to terms with his loss, he went over and over every detail he could remember, but his mind became blurred with too much information. It had all happened so quickly. Death and total destruction after a night of joy and happiness. Suspecting he would have to give a statement to the police tomorrow, he must try to keep a clear mind, but he felt too stressed to see things straight. He wasn't sure if he wanted to go back to the scorched remains of The Laurels, but knew he'd have to.

His officer training told him that he had to prepare to face every possible form of questioning, to deliver answers forthrightly and to the best of his knowledge. He knew he must prepare himself for the mess of the aftermath. Much of the fine detail had already been erased from his memory. All he could think of now was living his life without Elizabeth and Jessica. Edward sat on the floor for what seemed like half the night, leaning against Jessica's bed. Emotion bores down on him like a heavy black cloak.

He thought about his quarters at the Shimla Club. He'd managed to keep the cottage for years, his retreat when he came to the mountains. It had given him the bolt-hole he needed to enable him to continue his affair with Elizabeth.

He wasn't sure what tomorrow would bring, but knew that he'd be here for some time. There would be letters to write, phone calls to make to Elizabeth and James' families in England—they would have to know the dreadful news. He hoped Charles and Lola had contacts.

He couldn't recall names and places that Elizabeth had told him about. There would be records somewhere in the government offices—next of kin, and contacts for emergencies.

With the help of friends, he would have to take care of everything. He would have to piece together a list of people to phone or write to. He had no idea what might happen to Jessica, but hoped she would settle with Lola and Charles until they heard back from relatives in England.

He was cold, and decided to be sensible and try to get some sleep. First placing a hand on the tiny sleeping body, he left Jessica's room to go to his own bed. As his head touched the pillow, overcome with heartache and sorrow, he sobbed unashamedly until he fell asleep, exhausted.

Waking abruptly, Edward heard a loud commotion in the driveway outside his window. He glanced at the bedside clock through sleepy eyes. It was after nine-thirty. He heard voices. Charles was instructing a servant to sweep the front steps, and Lola was in a waiting car with the driver, calling goodbyes. Edward sat on the edge of his bed, head in hands, and paused for thought before jumping into action, washing, dressing, and making his way to the landing. He saw Jessica's bed was empty, and assumed Lola had given her breakfast and was looking after her. He was still piecing together the events of the night before, as he entered the kitchen.

'Dear boy—please, do come and sit and have some breakfast.' Charles asked the maid to make some fresh tea, and asked Edward what he'd like for breakfast.

'Lola's just left to take Jessica to town to buy her some clothes, and to go to Hermione's house—she sees their little boy at Sunday school apparently. Lola thought it best to keep the girl occupied, and try to get her mind off what she went through last night. She has been asking to go home to her mother, so Lola has gone with her to speak to the Vicar, to get some advice on how best to help her.'

'That's a good idea, Charles, and perhaps she'll stay and play with their boy. I've got to phone around and find out what's happening now. Do you think I ought to go back to The Laurels?'

'Leave it for now. Have something to eat. I think the police will be in touch with you as soon as possible. It must be a complete mess up there, and I would let them sort it out first. I'll go with you tomorrow when you'll be in a better state to face it.'

Edward sat at the table. Hot tea, toast, and marmalade was put in front of him as he wrote a list of what had to be done—and what he and Charles should do next. Charles was to tap into his contacts at the Viceroy's lodge, check records, and find family links to Elizabeth and James. Jessica was his priority and he had to take advice on what should happen to her now. Dismissing his first thoughts about wanting to care for her himself, and discussing it with Charles, they decided to consult Elizabeth's family in England. Family had to be found as soon as possible, and told of the tragedy. Elizabeth once told Edward about her sister in London who she hoped would be Jessica's guardian in between semesters after she was shipped off to boarding school in England. She had mentioned a name, but he couldn't remember.

'Charles, the authorities do have records—next of kin, names and addresses, don't they? There's so much traffic between here and England, they must know their employee's and senior staff's family background and details. Surely?'

'Don't worry about that, when I was a mere junior officer, one of my tasks was to document everything, file it, and keep all manner of records up to date. I drowned in paperwork some days. I should jolly well hope they can come up with something for us to go on, otherwise we're in a terrible situation.' Charles's offer of more tea was declined by Edward, who excused himself from the table.

'Come on, Charles, let's put our heads together. Jessica is our top priority. We have to make a plan for her future. I hope to God you can help me find where to start. We can't just abandon the girl, and we can't legally just foster her or have her adopted. Family must be traced. I doubt there's anything left at The Laurels that hasn't been burnt. Documents, legal or otherwise. Let's go into the drawing room and make some notes, we have to get the ball rolling to tell the families. It's not going to be easy, but I think best done together with our friends first we'll resort to the authorities. There'll have to be a funeral...' Edward stopped abruptly, lowered his head, and wondered what, if anything, would remain of the bodies. Charles sensed Edward's sobering thought and patted him on the shoulder.

'Edward, I'll help you through this. It'll be alright. There's a lot to do, but by Monday it should all look a lot clearer. Let's see to the business of making those plans and we'll set them in action as soon as morning breaks in England. I'll call a colleague to ask about family records and see if we can't get them to open up the office. It will be closed today, Saturday, but this is an emergency. Why don't you call as many people as you can who you think might have some information about the Delaney family.'

'Oh, Charles, can I borrow a jacket from you? I feel a damn fool in this dirty evening wear, but it's all I've got till I can get to my house and change.'

'Help yourself. My bedroom closet, left hand side.'

Edward crossed the landing and entered the room Jessica had slept in. He was going to lose her from his life soon. There was no way she could stay here in Shimla. Not now. He picked up the blanket from her bed and stared out of the window.

The sun was high in the sky, bathing the foothills in an early Autumn glow. He opened the window and breathed in fresh mountain air. Out of the stillness of the morning came the piercing cry of a lone eagle soaring high over the valley, and a flurry of fallen leaves blew across the driveway beneath him like an attempt to sweep away memories of yesterday. He thought he sensed a faint whiff of smoke hanging in the air.

He heard the phone ringing downstairs, and, placing Jessica's blanket back on the bed, he went to Charles's closet and found a Harris Tweed jacket that fit him perfectly. When he reached the drawing room, Charles was still on the phone. Edward settled into a deep armchair with notebook and pen, and began to write, trying to piece together the one-sided telephone conversation. At last, Charles replaced he receiver.

'Edward, that was the police. They have scant details of what happened last night, and want to come and interview you. I asked about Chandra, and they said she was comfortable but critical, and would have to be removed to Chandigarh today for more treatment and extensive skin grafting.

'I told the police they could come in about an hour. Is that alright? In the meantime, I'll get back on the blower and try to find someone in authority who can get phone numbers. Oh God! What a mess, and not even Chandra can help us with anything now.'

17

Shimla 1997:

Clearly shocked at Chandra's words, Sebastian launched himself out of his chair. He staggered around, head in hands, trying to take in this complicated scenario now presenting itself. He looked at Jessica who sat, open mouthed, staring at him. Chandra looked back and forth between them, innocent of what she'd just revealed.

Sebastian spoke first. 'This is unbelievable! *My* father. *Your* mother.' He looked first at Jessica, and across at Chandra. 'Edward Shelley was—is my father. I knew he lived here for a while, and he sometimes talks about it. But he's an old man now.' He smoothed his hair with both hands.

'This explains a lot. Jessica, we have to go. I have to tell you something, alone. Chandra—can we come back tomorrow morning, please?' Sebastian and Jessica rose and walked towards the door.

'Yes—I am here always at the house. But what is it I said? I just remembered that name. I am sorry, I was not meaning to…'

'No, no. Good Lord, Chandra, it's not your fault. You did well to remember, and we thank you so much, don't we, Jessica? Here, don't be upset, you remembered everything so well. I know I'm shocked—well, we are both shocked, but it's not your fault.' Chandra refused the clean handkerchief Sebastian offered. In silence she pulled her red and gold sari across her broken face, and turned to go back into the darkest corner of her room.

Sebastian held Jessica's arm as she pleaded with Chandra. 'Chandra, please don't think you've said anything wrong. Not at all. In fact, you have done exactly the right thing, you've made it possible for me to finish what I came here to do. To discover the truth.' She and Sebastian said their goodbyes and promised to come back the next day.

Sebastian ushered Jessica through the low doorway, and out into the bright sunlight. They walked in silence until they were at the corner of the road. The driver was still there, waiting. Jessica stopped, holding on to the railing. Sebastian stood with her. She didn't know what to say. This had changed everything now. It was Sebastian's father who would be able to tell her more than anyone else about what happened to her parents, the fire, the fateful night. But why hadn't he ever tried to contact her?

He must have known she went back to England, and according to Sebastian, he followed a few years later.

'Did you know, Sebastian? Were you sent here by your father? Don't pretend you didn't know all along. But how would your father have known I was coming to India? This changes things. You have to tell me everything you know. What has your father told you?' She looked up at his face. He was speechless, staring into infinity.

He placed an arm tightly round her shoulders. 'Jessica—we have to go somewhere. Let's get back to the hotel. I need to talk to you. I need to get through to my father in England. Come on.' He turned her towards the waiting car, he held her hand until they got into the back seat together.

They sat in silence as the driver took them back to the hotel. Sebastian paid him and they made their way upstairs.

He turned as they reached her room, took hold of both her arms, and pulled her towards him. Jessica slowly pushed him away, suggesting a practical plan to freshen up and go to the Imperial Hotel early, for sundowners. He had booked a table there for dinner, and they could talk all they had to. He could tell her all he knew. She needed some space to think, and said, 'I'll meet you in the lobby at five.'

She leaned against the back of her closed door, looking across the room and to the vista of houses that so entranced her on her first morning in Shimla. Her head spun with the revelations of today, and she couldn't decipher the information still whirring around her brain.

The more she thought about it, the more she suspected Sebastian of dishonesty. Had he entered a pact with his father? He *must* have been asked to come to Shimla to seek her out. He seemed genuine in his assistance, but was there an ulterior motive?

He had a lot of explaining to do to convince her why he was here. She lay on her bed and had thoughts of home, and of Saffie. She'd call her, too, and tell her what had happened. Jessica had a few more weeks left in India before she flew home, and she resolved to solve the mystery of all this conflicting information she'd been bombarded with, before she left.

Preparing herself to wait patiently until this evening, Jessica made a mental list of urgent questions she needed Sebastian to answer.

18

Shimla 1947:

E dward and Charles started unravelling the tangled pieces of catastrophic events that had occurred the night before. As they sat in the drawing room of Hilltop House flourishing pens and paper, making notes of what to do first, one of their major concerns presented itself immediately in front of the house. Rushing out to see what the noise was all about, they were confronted by five distressed horses with makeshift halters, being restrained by the same number of stable boys.

Not wishing to scare the horses further, Charles slowly descended the front steps of the house, finger to his lips in a sign of silence to the horse handlers. His own two boys were in front of the throng. The animals pulled at their constraints, kicking and whinnying. Dust clouds blew across the driveway like spectres. They contorted and disappeared through the trees like spirits seeking a home.

Charles whispered to his boys to take the horses to stable them wherever there was room, and asked his senior hand how they managed to get them here. They quickly and quietly exchanged information.

'Mr Charles, we are all hurt. It is very awful. The horses are ruined, sahib. You must go to where we say and shoot the lame ones.' He pointed to the mountain track. 'They are below the ridge. They have fallen.'

'How many others are there, Sanjay? And can we get to them by road? You must take us there when you've settled this lot.'

'Yes, Sahib, we will be soon. There are some injured.'

'Get to it at once!'

Sanjay took charge of the handlers, leading them and the horses single file towards the stables. Edward immediately realised that one of the missing horses was Kowloon, James's beautiful chestnut stallion, the one that had thrown him before Edward's life-saving rescue, all those years ago. The horse must be injured, not to have made it back with the others. Elizabeth's dappled pony, Rainbow, was also missing.

Edward looked at Charles as they went back into the house. 'The horses were on the road last night. I steered them away from the cliff edge with the car, but I had to carry on driving here. I think we have to make that the first priority. They may be badly injured and in pain. They can't be left.'

'I forgot to tell you, Edward, the alarm was raised by police on their way to The Laurels, and they called me. I sent the handlers to find the horses.'

'We'll have to wait for Sanjay to report back first. Those boys have done a damn fine job collecting the ones they found. Not sure how they'll be, though. I'll get the vet to check them out thoroughly, tomorrow.' Charles indicated for them to sit back at the table with their notes.

'What time did you say the police are coming, Charles?'

'Soon, so it would be best to see them before dealing with the horses. Not sure how long they'll want, but you'll need to give a full statement, no doubt. We need information from them, too. I assume the police and fire trucks have already been to The Laurels.' Charles said, gravely.

'Yes, and I think we ought to go there after we've found the other horses. How long do you think Lola and Jessica will be?'

'Not sure. I'll ring Hermione and ask if they can stay until tea time. That will give us more space, and when they get back, you can spend time with Jessica. Poor little girl—perhaps Lola and Hermione have come up with a plan of what's going to be best for the child. I can't see her staying here at all. I mean, who would look after her?' Charles's question was more of a statement.

'No,' Edward replied, 'it has to be family. There are definitely relatives back in England. I expect to hear more about them by tomorrow. Perhaps I ought to tell Jessica something about going away—prepare her, if I can? I'm at a loss for ideas. I'll talk to Lola tonight. I do hope that she's been playing with Hermione's little boy and that it's taken her mind off what's happened, if only for a while.'

Edward changed position, sitting awkwardly in his chair. 'You know, Charles I have to tell you, I love that child…' He dropped his head in his hands, staring at the floor.

Charles patted Edward on the knee. 'I know, dear boy. We all know. You needn't worry about what people think. All the best-kept secrets don't last long in Shimla, you ought to know that, old chap.

Now don't worry.'

'No, you're right, but maybe some people might think...'

Charles was still trying to take in Edward's confession. He tried to remain calm. 'Look, it all has to be faced one way or another, just tell the police what you told us last night, and they'll take it from there. Yes, there might be a few searching questions, but just tell them the truth, there's no more can be done. I'm not sure if there'll be an inquest, it'll all depend upon what's found in the ruins. If there is, it will most likely be a verdict of misadventure, or accidental death. And don't forget, we're here for you—and all your friends in Shimla will help you get through this.'

Edward could only hear half of Charles's advice. He was too worried about giving his version of what happened to the police. He, too, tried to remain calm.

'I suspect everyone knows about the fire by now. In the meantime, let's get on with the job in hand. Ah! Wait. That sounds like the police vehicle coming up the drive.' Edward stood and peered out of the window.

Charles and Edward put their notebooks to one side, and waited for the doorbell to ring. The maid ushered in Inspector Mullins and Police Constable Chapman. They were steered to a seat in the drawing room. Edward watched Mullins take out a notebook.

He listened carefully as Mullins delivered an up-to-date report.

'We have just come from The Laurels. We left the fire department there to salvage as much as they could. They have been instructed to place any personal possessions they find in metal boxes, which will be locked and stored in the safe at the station. The brigade is also making sure there is no chance of the fire re-kindling.'

Mullins lowered the tone of his voice. 'Not much remains of the house, I'm sorry to say—two stories on the west wing are still intact, but the collapse of the stairs brought down much of the upper floor on the other side of the house.'

He paused, clenching his hands together. 'We have managed to recover the remains of two badly burned, and, as yet, formally unidentified bodies.'

Edward reached for his handkerchief, briefly covered his face and wiped over his brow as the inspector continued.

'They were found in close proximity to each other in what I presume was the drawing room of the house. A few sticks of furniture survived, and most of the outbuildings. Someone will have a terrible job to do sifting through everything.' Mullins looked at Edward, realising it would be he who would most likely have to take on this unenviable task.

'It must be most painful for you to re-live what happened last night, so you may take as long as you like in telling us what exactly occurred. We need a full statement for to the coroner's office when the time comes.' The inspector explained.

Edward sat up straight and mustered enough energy to slowly recount what happened, and as he remembered it, up to the time he was forced to abandon the house to its fate.

Mullins and Constable Chapman took copious notes, occasionally asking Edward to stop to clarify something they didn't understand.

Edward explained how he remembered the party and James being too drunk to drive home. About James's car being broken down, necessitating Edward driving them home in his car. He told them how he heard James and Elizabeth shouting and arguing, and when he heard screaming, he tried to intervene. He formulated an explanation about how James had pushed Elizabeth into the fireplace, accidentally sloshing brandy over her and himself. He explained how he tried to drag Elizabeth away from the fireplace and was forced back by ferocious flames. And told them that he went to find Ranjit to help put the fire out with buckets of water.

'It was then I realised that...Elizabeth was dead.' Edward began to stammer, vividly reliving the truth of the night, yet summoning enough strength to tell them that when he returned from looking for Ranjit to help him, the whole room was on fire and James had fallen to the floor.

'I shouted again for the houseboy to come, but he wasn't there. I remembered Jessica and her ayah, Chandra, upstairs. I rushed up the staircase and grabbed Jessica out of bed, shouting to Chandra to get out of the house quickly. The flames were whipping into the hall and licking round the bottom of the staircase by that time. She ran back screaming, she had to get something, and when I'd put the child in the car, I went back into the burning house to find her. She was crossing the landing; her clothes were alight. She'd been back to get a blanket and Jessica's teddy. I told her to roll on the floor, and went up the crackling stairs to get her. I managed to save her from falling through the burning floorboards, carried her outside and put her in the back seat with Jessica. She was almost unconscious from smoke inhalation. She was bleeding, and blistering burns were all over her face and upper body. I left them in the car and had to go back inside to get the car keys from the hall table, but I had no other option but to leave the house to the mercy of the fire, and to take Jessica and Chandra, who were terrified, to a safe place.

'We came here. Chandra was taken to hospital. We've been told she's being moved to Chandigarh for specialist treatment. Jessica is here with Mr and Mrs McAllister. Thank God she was unharmed, except of course, she doesn't yet realise the full horror of what's happened to her parents.'

'Thank you, Major Shelley, I am so sorry you've been through such a terrifying ordeal, so sorry. But tell me, were there any other witnesses at the scene last night? Where is the houseboy—Ranjit did you say his name was? And you say Chandra slept through all of that arguing and shouting and commotion downstairs?' Inspector Mullins stared at Edward, waiting for answers.

'It's...it's all a bit of a blur, as you might imagine. I went to the kitchen door and called for Ranjit across the yard as soon as I realised that I needed his help to try to tackle the blaze. I'm not sure where he was. He may have been keeping an eye on the stables. I don't know.' Edward shifted uneasily in his chair, sat back, and stared at the ceiling for inspiration. 'As for Chandra, I recall she was upstairs on a bed in the nursery when I went to get Jessica.'

'Thank you. If you think of anything else we should know about, please come over to see me. We'll get this statement typed up and leave it for you to sign at the station at your convenience, sometime in the next few days.'

The handwritten statement was given to Edward who was asked to read it. He nodded and handed it back to Inspector Mullins. The two officers said their goodbyes and Charles showed them to the door.

Edward wiped the sweat from his face, sighed a huge sigh of relief, and slumped back into his armchair head in hands, wanting to weep. He was drained of all energy.

19

Shimla 1997:

As Jessica dressed for the evening, she came to the realisation that the information Sebastian had given her on their very first meeting must hold some truth. She thought about Meredith Bateman and the Stonehenge photo of her. She knew that Aunt Catherine had been in touch with Meredith before she died, and that they had always been friends even after he'd finished with his business and semi-retired. He was part of the family and such a delightful old man. Jessica made it her business to keep in touch. He had kept her trust fund going and invested her inheritance right from the time she went back to England, after Shimla.

Shimla. She still couldn't believe she was here. But her meeting with Sebastian was obviously not a chance encounter. The truth had been spoken by Chandra, and she vowed to go back to see her in the morning to get to the bottom of what happened to her parents. What puzzled her most was why didn't Aunt Catherine know? And, if she did, why did she not tell her, instead of her having to find out by chance?

It was true she'd told Meredith she was coming here, so perhaps he made contact with Edward and arranged for Sebastian to meet with her somehow. Yes, that must be it. Meredith knew about Sebastian being in Delhi, and he got in touch with him through Edward Shelley. She had phoned Meredith before she left, telling him about her trip. It all started to make sense to her. And there was Sebastian's rat-tat-tat on her door.

Jessica went to the door to unlock it. 'Come in, Sebastian—I'm nearly ready.' She twirled to check her appearance in the mirror. She'd had to wear the only thing that looked faintly like a cocktail dress, but she still wasn't sure about the vivid mid-blue colour of the silk crepe.

'You look nice, Jessica—and I didn't say before, but that's a stunning string of pearls you're wearing around your neck.' He touched them briefly.

'They were my mother's. I did get her jewellery, and I cherish it. Now I realise what happened, though, I'm wondering what survived the fire and what perished that night. I'll ask Chandra more about it tomorrow, but let's forget it for now. Shall we go?' She smiled at Sebastian, putting him at ease.

He'd felt left out and had expected a cold reception from her after she'd had time to think things through, and felt relieved at her relaxed attitude.

'I've ordered a taxi, it ought to be downstairs waiting for us.' He held the door open for her and they made their way down the staircase and through the lobby. Akash bade them a good night as they headed towards the cab.

Once seated, Jessica turned to Sebastian, who was just about to speak. 'No, me first. Sebastian, I have to tell you that I think I know why you're here. I've worked it all out, you see—and I don't think you're to blame for anything. I did at one time think you'd been lying to me, but now I realise that even if you had, there's a good reason. Meredith is behind your being here, isn't he? And that photo in your father's study *must* be of me, to remind him of my parents. Well, remind him of my mother, who, according to Chandra, was having an affair with him. But what's puzzling me, is why wouldn't your father at some time have been in touch with me in England?'

Sebastian put his hand on hers. 'I'll tell you all about it over a drink and dinner. Well, as much as I *can* tell you. I had to mention the photo to make sure you were you, but when we exchanged names that was all the proof I needed. I haven't exactly been father's *confidant* all my life. Until recently, and even after retirement he's been involved in making as much money as he can—it does seem to come easy to him, I have to say. We've drifted apart a bit. I go down to see him on high days, holidays and birthdays. In fact, this December, he'll be eighty, and I plan to throw a party for him.'

The taxi pulled up in front of the Imperial Hotel, and the door was opened by one of their porters. Jessica got out and Sebastian paid the driver. He thanked the doorman as they made their way down the corridor towards the bar.

'We're a bit early for our table so let's enjoy the veranda view before the sun goes down, over a cold G and T. What say you?'

'Sure—I think we deserve it after all the revelations of the past few days, not forgetting the recent confusion and misunderstanding.'

Jessica said.

They settled themselves at a table for two and ordered the drinks. Nuts and olives were placed before them and when the drinks came, Jessica and Sebastian clinked glasses before greedily downing a good deal of the ice-cold liquid. Jessica took her camera out of her handbag, much to the amusement of Sebastian.

'So that's what women keep in their handbags, is it? Apart from the obvious lipstick and powder and notebook and...'

Jessica chuckled. 'Of course! We never miss the opportunity of a brilliant shot.' And with that she quickly snapped him close-up, laughing.

'Steady on, I don't want that picture of me to become a point of discussion in your album. Remember, our family aren't very good at explaining photos.' He joked.

Jessica turned and began to take pictures of the breath-taking views and of the hotel grounds and gardens. The Himalayan mountains unfolded in a spectrum of gold and orange as the sun caught peaks and valleys. Raucous peacocks roamed the lawns below, foraging for seeds.

An elderly couple sitting two tables away watched, and smiled at them.

'Perhaps you'd like me to take a picture of you both?' The silver-haired man stood up and walked towards them.

They looked at each other and agreed, and Jessica gave the man her camera.

'Sit closer. That's it—what a lovely picture with the mountains in the background.' He gave the camera back to Jessica. 'I hope you'll treasure it forever. On honeymoon, are you?'

They both laughed. 'No, not at all, er, just good friends.' Sebastian said politely whilst Jessica sat, bemused by the bold assumption.

She said, 'I'm here to explore the place where I was born, and where my parents lived when they were here during the British Raj. Sebastian is helping me discover my roots, if you like.'

'Ah! I see. Well, good luck with it all. Isn't it a glorious place?'

Jessica glanced at the view. 'Yes, it is,' she said, 'thanks for taking the photo.'

'My pleasure,' said the man as he walked back to join his wife.

'One for the album when I get home,' said Jessica.

But her mind was concentrating on what else Sebastian might reveal about why he came here. Mistrust reared its ugly head again.

20

Shimla 1947:

An awkward silence filled Charles's drawing room for a while after the police left. Edward realised it was crucial for him to remember every word he'd told the police. He was confused, yet very aware that his version of events differed from the statement he'd given. He assumed it would be closely scrutinised at the time of the inquest into the deaths of Elizabeth and James, and he must remember what he said. He felt panic stirring inside.

'Lunch?' Charles got up from his chair and went towards the kitchen.

'Yes, please,' said Edward. 'Anything will do—a sandwich or something, and a cup of tea. We'll have to get going up the valley to find those horses immediately afterwards.'

Edward began to write notes about what he'd told the police, about how it was, and about what action to take to ensure Jessica's safety and future. He'd have to ask for extended leave to sort it all out, and move into his cottage at the club for the duration.

His departure from India must be listed already, for his dispatch and de-mob back to England, even though he hadn't officially heard anything yet. He'd wanted to start a business on the back of his residency. He'd seen opportunities for exporting goods to England. He and Elizabeth had thought about it years ago, but nothing ever came of their idea. Pipe dreams, she'd thought. But he saw it as a way of escape for them to be together, for her to break her ties with James completely and for them to marry. Was now the right time to start the ball rolling? Even though she would never be able to share it with him? He realised he'd have to eventually get back to real life, and on his own. Thinking he needed a diversion more than ever he decided to make tracks with his business plan when the time was right.

Charles came back into the drawing room, and suggested they go to the veranda to wait for lunch to arrive. The maid came along shortly with a plateful of sandwiches and a pot of tea for two.

'I'll take my Land Rover, and we'll dust off the shotguns and take the revolvers. Remind me to get plenty of ammunition from the store.'

Edward added, 'We'd better warn Sanjay he's coming with us. We've about five hours of daylight left. That should be enough to clear up what remains of the horses. I'm not looking forward to it."

'You got the stomach for it, Edward? You've been through hell already. Are you sure you can deal with it? We can manage without you, I'm sure'

'I'll be alright. Rather me do it than anyone else. Elizabeth would have wanted that.' Edward gulped down the last of his tea, wiped his mouth and stood, looking grim, ready to take on what had to be done.

Charles found coats and hats and sent for Sanjay. He went to the gun room and unlocked the gate. He took out double the number of cartridges and bullets he thought they'd need, two shotguns and two revolvers.

'Do you think we ought to get Carmichael involved? I mean, he has to deal with sick and wounded animals on a daily basis. Perhaps we'd better phone him and tell him what we're going to do. He might want to come along anyway.' Charles said.

Edward considered Charles's proposal. 'Yes, perhaps we should. When word gets out, he might feel he hasn't done his duty as a vet to let us deal with the horses ourselves. I'm sure he'd want to get involved.'

Charles headed for the phone. 'I'll call him now, he can drive here and we'll all go together.'

Edward carried the guns to the door and waited for Charles in the doorway. Looking down the driveway he noticed the maples were turning to Autumn shades of red and orange. Leaves had begun to fall and flowers die. Soon there would be movements of British officers leaving the hilltop town to its wintery mantle. The snow would creep down the mountains to eventually settle silently upon rooftops. Summer homes would be secured against the vagaries of the winter weather, and laid to rest until next year.

But next summer, Edward would be gone, along with most of the British. The sub-continent would be handed over to the Indians, and the Viceroy would rule no more. Colonials would be forced to forge new lives in Britain and abandon the land of their forebears.

At least Elizabeth had been spared that ordeal. She wouldn't have known what to do with a suburban home in Surrey or Kent, Edward mused.

Clutching the guns, he turned towards the sound of Charles's approaching footsteps.

'Is he coming?' he asked Charles, expectantly.

'Had a long chat with him, and yes, he'd like to be with us under the circumstances. Says he's had to perform the unsavoury task more often than he'd like. Let's load up the vehicle and wait for him. Sanjay will be round in a moment. You alright, Edward—you look a bit peaky?' They walked towards the Land Rover.

'I'll be okay. I've just been wondering what Shimla will be like next summer, after we've all gone. Do you think you and Lola will leave soon? I'm going to try to get out of India and back to England within the year, but I have an idea about setting up an export business, so I may stay behind for a while.' Edward loaded the guns and hats and ropes along with other supplies into the back of the vehicle and sat in the front seat with Charles to wait for Andrew Carmichael. He checked the time on his pocket watch.

'We'll have to get a move on, I hope he gets here soon. Ah! here's my trusty stable boy.'

'Get in the back, Sanj, we're waiting for the vet.'

Edward had a thought, 'Would it be better if Sanjay got in the front and I rode in the back with Carmichael—he's got to direct us to where they saw the horses.'

'Good idea! Sanj, come here, you can be the spotter.'

The vet's car came to a screeching halt next to the Land Rover, and after exchanging greetings with Edward and Charles, he emptied the boot of ropes, sacks, and other likely-looking equipment.

'Get in Andrew, glad you're here.' Charles offered his hand.

'I heard the buzz around town—terrible job, terrible. Edward, please accept my sincere condolences. I hear you did all you could. So very sorry. What a dreadful state of affairs.' Sitting in the back seat with Edward, he patted his knee in sympathy, as Charles spun the Land Rover into action.

Edward turned to Andrew and tried to speak, but words were hard to find. How could he still not be in shock?

'I...I couldn't save them, Andrew, I couldn't save anything. Jessica is safe and well, thank the Lord, but the nanny, Chandra, suffered third-degree burns and has been transferred to Chandigarh hospital. I pulled her down the burning staircase just in time…'

'Don't talk, dear boy, no need to upset yourself more.' And to Charles, 'How long before we get to those injured horses, Charles? We'll have to get a move on to beat the light.'

'How far, Sanj?'

'Sahib, round the next corner, and towards the Viceroy's house turn to The Laurels. Sir, they will not move themselves. They were down, right down there in that valley. After we caught the ones we brought back, two very very badly damaged could not get up. Sahib, they are broken, together.'

'You mean they are next to each other?' Charles quizzed him.

'Yes, Sahib—very close.'

Edward sat stunned, almost afraid to ask the obvious question. 'Sanjay, the two horses together, do you know them?'

'Sahib, I think. A tall chestnut stallion with white flash—very very heavy horse, and the pony Memsahib at The Laurels rides.'

Edward closed his eyes. James's stallion, Kowloon, and Elizabeth's pony, Rainbow. Head down, he pinched the top of his nose, hoping to staunch tears. Kowloon, the old stallion that James fell off over the cliff top the first time they rode together, when Edward saved James's life. The same day that Edward first met Elizabeth. He pictured them, horses, friends, lovers, all lying next to each other in death. Vivid images now too much for him to bear. He flung his head back, taking a deep breath.

Andrew turned and placed his hand on his knee again, in a gesture of understanding. 'C'mon, courage. I'm here to take on the emotional burden. You don't have to be involved, you know.' Andrew spoke empathetically. Edward nodded, eyes still closed, as they bumped and bounced around at Sanjay's instruction in the oft-driven direction of The Laurels.

Edward thought about when he had to stop the car, driving home from the party, to let James out to be sick by the side of the road. Just two nights ago—it all seemed so surreal. He remembered horses running wildly, scared. They'd lost their way in the dark after his car left them behind. He imagined them tumbling over the cliff. Tumbling to their death.

'There! Down there!' Sanjay pointed to a clearing on the valley floor. 'Sahib, they all fell together, down.'

Charles stopped the vehicle. 'Okay, chaps, it looks like we've got a hike. Let's go.'

The men carried everything down the steep slope to the valley floor. Sanjay whistled hoping they might hear some sound from the fallen horses. And there it was. A deep snort, not more than a few feet away. The fallen horses were hidden by scrub and long grass.

Edward hesitated, moving forward slowly, deliberately, trying not to alarm the already frightened animals. Nervously, he fingered the butt of the service revolver and just as anxiously removed his hand and stared. Two of the horses lay side by side. It was almost as if, having fallen together, they could comfort one another in their pain and grief. Grief? Do horses experience grief, wondered Edward, his mind racing, unsure of his next move. He knelt on the soft ground between the stallion and the pony, first stroking Kowloon's neck and gently brushing his mane. He cradled Rainbow's head in his arms, and felt a tiny shudder run through the pony's broken body. Rainbow looked up at him—was that a tear in her limpid eye? Do horses cry? Another quiver, her legs scrabbling at the ground in a feeble attempt to get to her feet. Edward could feel tears streaming down his cheeks. First Elizabeth, now this. How to cope...?

He looked again at Rainbow's face, no longer twisted in pain, those brown horse-eyes now closed as if in resignation of her fate. Carefully Edward removed the revolver from its holster, placed the barrel against her forehead, and gently squeezed the trigger. He turned his face to the sky. It was not a deafening bang, loud, but not deafening. Another shudder. He felt her relax and go limp, her head heavy in the green grass.

Kowloon, startled, tried to raise his body. Edward turned. The pure white flash oozed red as he put him out of his misery.

It was done.

21

Shimla 1997:

Sebastian looked at his watch as a fiery sun dipped behind the mountains, leaving its glow on wispy clouds. He looked at Jessica who was settling into the soft cushions of her wicker chair.

'Time for another?' he looked at his empty glass.

'Oh, why not, it's so lovely just sitting here. I could stay forever.' She smiled at him and drained the last drop of gin and tonic.

Sebastian summoned the waiter as Jessica pulled her cashmere wrap close against the cooling air. She glanced again at the elderly couple along the veranda. She wasn't exactly a seasoned traveller and thought the couple brave to be touring India at their advanced age. She felt the urge to engage them in conversation, but Sebastian leaned forward to speak to her.

'I suspect you didn't want to say too much tonight about our quest, but I still feel I have to tell you I was totally unaware of my father's affair with your mother. It was such a long time ago. But I now see why he asked me to seek you out. And I have to say, I'm so pleased I did—you're not at all how I imagined you to be after my father's description.'

'But your father has never met me, so how would he know what I'm like. He must still remember me as a child.' Jessica sat puzzling. 'Do you think he was the one to contact my Aunt Catherine?'

'Don't see how he could—unless…'

'Unless what?'

'Well, they must have met when you were small, perhaps your aunt and uncle came to Shimla after the fire, for the funeral, to escort you back to England. Did they ever tell you anything?'

'I suppose I should have asked. I swanned through life unquestioning, without a care in the world. I was aware they had adopted me, but I remembered nothing about being here. Growing up, I always had plenty of money, and I did what I liked. Hence my swinging sixties hippie stage. I never asked them about my parents. They told me when I was older, but obviously were mistaken about my parents' cause of death. I think I knew they were not telling me everything. I sensed there was more to discover. That would be why

Catherine urged me to come here. It's strange, but I guess in nineteen-forty-seven communications weren't easy, but she found out more later and never told me.

'They weren't here anyway, in Shimla, apart from—presumably the funeral, and to take me back to England. But perhaps I'll never know more than I do now.' The waiter came with fresh drinks and Jessica proposed a toast. 'Here's to lost family, friends, and to new beginnings.'

'To lost family and friends, and new beginnings. We'll try not to jump the gun, but tomorrow, when we move hotels, I'll phone my father and ask a few pertinent questions.'

'Yes, I'll drink to that,' she said. 'And I need to get in touch with Saffron, too. It seems a long time since we spoke.'

The elderly couple got up from their table and began to make their way inside. The man gave a perfunctory nod as he passed. 'Have a good evening,' he smiled, following his wife.

Jessica leaned forward and whispered to Sebastian. 'They seem awfully nice, but I can't help thinking they're brave to be travelling in India on their own at their age.'

'I thought the same, but somehow, they seem at home. They could be regular visitors. I doubt they live here. Yes, quite adventurous.' He looked after them pensively.

'I guess you're always looking for stories,' replied Jessica. 'I wonder what theirs is.'

'If they're here tomorrow, I might find time to talk to them. In the meantime, drink up, and let's go in for dinner—it's getting chilly.'

Dusk descended rapidly, along with the temperature. Cool Himalayan air tumbled down the mountain slopes, subduing everything in its path, carpeting valleys and forests.

This is magic, thought Jessica, watching the last remnants of mountains disappear into the night. Seductive, sensual and too irresistible for words.

Catching up with Sebastian, she slipped her hand into the crook of his arm. He squeezed her hand and she allowed him to steer her towards their table.

The hotel was well patronised. Most of the places were occupied by couples. Here and there were single men or women, dining as

Sebastian usually did—his trick was to bury his head in a book to prevent unwanted attention from other guests. But tonight, he wanted Jessica with him—he was pleased that she looked up to him for help and guidance, and their deepening attraction for each other was reciprocal.

Jessica, in return, wanted him as her escort, as well as realising that their bond was leading to something more than friendship. The task in hand would be very difficult without his local knowledge and ease of communication. Better than sitting alone in the dining-room of a hotel, she realised, glancing round at their fellow-diners.

His chosen bottle of wine was uncorked and tasted. Sebastian looked across the table, smiling.

'Well, here we are! And here's to you.' He lifted his glass. 'Looks like we're in this together, you and me.'

She answered succinctly, 'Well and truly, more than we could ever have imagined.'

'And in more ways than one,' he replied, looking over the rim of his glass straight into her eyes.

Sipping her drink, Jessica replied, 'That's more than alright with me,' she averted her eyes, feeling her cheeks flush. She was overwhelmed by the moment, and lost for words.

22

Shimla 1947:

A sombre mood blanketed Hilltop house. Edward and Charles, finding little conversation after their gruelling day, returned with heavy hearts at dusk, having discussed with Andrew Carmichael how the horses' carcases would best be disposed of. They agreed a cremation in situ. Andrew was to take care of all permissions and arrangements as soon as possible.

Clambering back to the Land Rover, Edward had hinted that he and Charles carry on up the road to The Laurels. His proposal met with a resounding *no*, Charles suggesting instead that they find time tomorrow morning. Another day would have passed, and this late in the evening, there would be nothing either of them could possibly do or see, and Charles said it would only depress Edward more after this afternoon's dreadful ordeal.

Lola returned to Hilltop House that evening with Jessica, just after they all arrived back from dealing with the horses. She and Jessica had spent the day with Hermione. Jessica had played happily with Hermione's four-year-old son, Peter. They promised to get together for Jessica's sake every day, for playtime. Hermione had suggested that the girl stay with them until plans had been sorted out for her to return to England.

Jessica went with the maid to get ready for bed. Half an hour later, she was brought into the drawing room to say goodnight to everyone. Her face was sullen.

Edward held out his arms. 'Come here Jessie, give uncle Edward a goodnight hug.'

Jessica ran towards him sat on his lap and buried her face in his shoulder. He hugged her tight and had to throw back his head as he felt tears prick the back of his eyes.

'Come on, now, up the wooden hill. Were's teddy?' He tried to make his voice light and lilting.

'I want my mummy. Where's my mummy I want to see her? Where is she?' She clambered down from his lap, looked at the floor and started to cry. 'Can I go home now to mummy? I want to go home.

Please, please!'

Lola rushed forward, not knowing what to say. They hadn't practiced what to tell Jessica, or even thought of a feasible story that might mollify her for a while. What do you say to an innocent little girl who had just lost both her parents? Tell her the truth? Not say anything until they had to? or wait until she was older? Either way, she will come to realise that her parents are no longer here, thought Lola, who didn't relish being the person to break the news to her, and try to get her child's brain to comprehend the significance of her plight.

'Hey, Jessie—tell Uncle Edward what you did today. We went to see Hermione, and Jessie went to nursery school with Peter, didn't you? We went back to Peter's mummy, and had tea and supper. Remember that yummy cake we had?' Lola sat Jessie on her knee. 'And tell him about when we went shopping...'

Jessie's eyes brightened. 'Yes—oh, Uncle Edward—we saw a naughty monkey sitting in a shop and running around.' She laughed and looked at Lola. 'It was very naughty, wasn't it? And...and it jumped onto the counter and stole something, and everybody ran after it down the street.'

'Did they catch it?'

'No. Silly Uncle Edward—it just jumped and ran and laughed. Ha haha—like that.'

'Tell Uncle Edward what we bought at the shops, Jessie.'

'Can I get it?' Jessie looked up eagerly at Lola who nodded, bearing a thin, forced smile.

'Yes—go on—then we'll get you tucked up in bed with Teddy.' Lola gently pushed Jessie towards the hall where they'd dropped their bags. Jessie went running out, excited, to show them what she'd bought.

Lola looked knowingly at Edward and Charles, shaking her head. She dropped her head into her hands as Jessie came walking back into the room, carefully carrying a bright-coloured box.

'Look, Uncle Edward,' she undid the wrapping, took the top off the box and opened the fine tissue paper. 'Look...' She offered it for him to look at, excitedly.

'I bought mummy a present...'

Edward stifled a sharp intake of breath and raised his hand to his mouth.

Inside the box was a delicate silk scarf in the same sage green that Elizabeth last wore to the dinner party, here in this room. Nestled on top of the scarf was an exquisite amethyst brooch.

Edward looked at Lola, her head still in her hands, and tried to make light of Jessie's announcement, 'Oh, darling, that is so beautiful, Jessie, you must keep it very safe. Let Auntie Lola look after it for you. Here—put the top back on the box and let me help you wrap it up again.'

Edward choked out the words, swallowing often, in an attempt to stabilise his voice. He passed the box to Jessie who gave it to Lola.

'Will you keep this for my mummy, auntie? She'll be surprised when I give it to her. I know she'll like it, it's her very favourite colour.'

'Yes, of course she will,' Lola inadvertently fell in with Jessie's plan, not realising what she was saying. The gravity of the atmosphere in the room had at least lightened. Pulling herself together, Lola urged Jessie to go to bed. 'Right, little madam—come on, say goodnight to everyone. Time for bed.' She took the girl's hand, and they chatted non-stop all the way up the stairs. Lola read her a story and she fell asleep almost at once.

Lola sat with her for a few minutes, enjoying the solitude, feeling distraught for the child who had no reason yet to feel anything for herself. She was still wiping tears from her eyes as she went downstairs to join Charles and Edward for dinner. They needed to talk urgently about what to do with Jessica.

23

Shimla 1997:

Sebastian and Jessica couldn't get out of their stuffy hotel quickly enough. Colonial it may be, but there was no scrap of charm to connect it with India's bygone era. Jessica had begun to dread the oppressive drabness of the dining room, the obsequiousness of the waiters, and was more than ready to make the change, even though the hotel was almost twice the price. Her luggage, by comparison to his, looked enough for four seasons, as, with the help of the porter, they piled the taxi high with their belongings, ready to drive to the Imperial Hotel where they'd requested an early check-in.

They'd been allocated adjacent rooms. Sebastian smiled and shrugged, looking at Jessica.

'Alright with you?' he grinned, waiting for an answer.

'Of course. All the rooms face the mountains, don't they?' She looked at the girl behind the front desk to confirm. 'Let's get settled and go out. Chandra's expecting us back today, and I can't wait to see her again.'

They arrived outside their rooms, and agreed to meet in the lobby in fifteen minutes.

Inside, Jessica was immediately drawn to the French doors leading onto a wide veranda that swept the full length of the hotel past every room. She noted wryly that it would be easy for her and her neighbour to walk outside to meet. White painted chairs with bright silk cushions, and small tables had been placed outside each room. It was just her style. Window boxes bursting with multi-coloured blooms lined the classic colonial style veranda wall.

She hastily arranged her clothes into neat piles on shelves, and hung the rest in the wardrobe. She checked her hair and face in the bathroom mirror, looked at her watch, and hurried downstairs.

Sebastian had a car waiting. He'd given Chandra's address to the driver. Jessica was happier, having come to terms with the mysterious revelations that were unravelling, but she still needed to find The Laurels. She turned to Sebastian, 'Do you think Chandra would like to come, too?'

'We can ask,' he replied. 'It might be a good idea to get her to come along, now I think about it.'

'I'll try to persuade her, but she may not have been there for the past fifty years, and who knows what we'll find, if anything.'

The steep stony path to the house was familiar now. Smoke perfumed the air along the way as they passed by tidy little painted houses. Pots of herbs stood on pathways, and flowering gardens made their walk worth every step. Chandra saw them coming and opened the door. They entered the small, neat room, sitting where they'd sat the day before.

Chandra was wearing a green sari etched in silver. She let it fall on her shoulders, no longer ashamed or frightened of them seeing her ugly scars. Jessica stood up with an immediate urge to embrace her, and took hold of her hands. She looked down into the tired old eyes.

Chandra's smile struggled to hide her uneasiness. 'I have tea. Will you take tea?' she asked, formally.

'We'd love to. Thank you.' Jessica looked at Sebastian, who agreed.

Chandra disappeared into the kitchen alcove. Jessica re-joined Sebastian on the couch. During the silence that followed, they remembered the earlier conversation here in Chandra's house, and her revelations that had stunned them both. But Jessica still wanted more information about the accident, the fire, and how Sebastian's father had rescued them from the blaze.

Placing a tray in front of her guests, Chandra went over to a cupboard on the other side of the room. She opened the top drawer, took out a box of matches and an incense stick which she lit and stood in its holder. Transfixed, they all watched as the thin line of pure white smoke ascended to the ceiling, curling to disperse the sweet and unmistakable scent of jasmine.

Jessica sank into the sofa. She leaned closer to Sebastian as Chandra sat on a wooden stool to pour the tea.

Sebastian spoke first. 'Chandra—we'd like you to come with us to the site of The Laurels.' He added, 'We'd very much appreciate it, wouldn't we?' He glanced at Jessica who nodded.

Chandra raised her hands to her face, covering her mouth, digesting what he'd said and nervously pulled her sari back over her head to cover the scars.

'Jessie. I am not sure. It is nothing now, someone told me. I went only after you had gone, after I was better. I wanted to see again.'

'What did you see, Chandra? Tell us, was the house still there?'

'Jessie, it was a long time ago, I cannot remember. I walked around and picked up that little china horse I gave you. It was always on your mother's dressing table. Always. I came back to town in the cart with Harish. He did not know anything about it.'

'Please come with us, Chandra. It would mean so much to me. Will you come? We have a car waiting to take us.' Jessica pleaded, eagerly searching Chandra's face for her response. 'Please!'

'I do not remember anything now. I will come with you, but do not hope that I can show you and tell you what happened.'

Jessica stood up, unable to contain her excitement. 'Oh, thank you, Chandra, thank you very much,' and to Sebastian: 'Shall we go as soon as we've finished tea? You do have the map and the address?'

'Jessie, I will tell you the right road.' Chandra explained that it was a long way and the road was not used anymore. 'Since for a long time when the British left, their houses were not used. No one could get to them in the hills. None of us had any car.'

'Of course, but I have seen remnants of British buildings all over town.' Jessica thought of the municipal buildings, banks and the clock tower, and of course, the church.

'They are still used well.' Chandra said as they made their way to the waiting car, Jessica holding on to Chandra's arm to help her up the stony path.

Sebastian had gone on ahead. By the time they arrived at the car he was poring over the map with the driver. Jessica helped Chandra into the car and sat beside her. Sebastian seated himself next to the driver and they began their journey into the unknown.

24

Shimla 1947:

A re we all agreed?' Lola looked across the table at Charles and Edward. 'Shall I take up Hermione's kind offer to look after Jessica? I think it would be better for her to be with a family and another child. She can go to nursery school every day. She'd have company and it may take her mind off what's happened.'

'I agree that's the best solution,' said Edward, trying to imagine how Jessica would react. 'But we'll need to tell her about her mother and father, and I've no idea how to approach that. We'll have to tell her in a way she'll understand. Perhaps we should just say they're sick in hospital.'

Charles thought this a good idea and said that once she'd accepted their absence, to tell her in simple terms that her Mum and Dad may not be coming back because they're very ill. 'But we ought to hold off telling her anything until she asks. She'll take it in better when she *has* to be told the truth.'

The truth. Edward jolted himself wide awake. What *was* the truth? He'd given his statement to the police, and it was all accepted as the truth. He'd yet to sign it, remembering that he had to go back to the station to check it before it was submitted to the coroner. Would he be questioned? In detail? Possibly not, he thought, but his conscience was troubled. Even though there was much confusion that night, he knew he'd glossed over what really happened. He said he'd threatened to strike out at James in self-defence, but the fact remains that he struck repeated blows to his head, that had brought Elizabeth's husband down and rendered him unconscious. He could have tried to help him, to get him out of the room, but by the time he came to that decision, the fire had caught hold and it was too late.

He turned towards Charles and Lola. 'I think it best if I take on the responsibility for Jessica. I'm Uncle Edward to her, and we've been through this together, don't forget. I may have to tell a few white lies at first, but the sooner the transition to a near-normal life takes place, the better. She's not a baby, so she may remember the night of the fire for a long time.'

'Yes, but funny she hasn't mentioned it at all. All she's cried for is to have her mummy and daddy back. You've done a wonderful job, Lola, taking her to Hermione's and persuading her to help. Keeping her occupied is best.' Charles finished talking and put both hands on the table in front of him in a show of finality.

'First, though, I have to go to the police station, we'll go to The Laurels. I assume our vet has been able to arrange the disposal of the horses' bodies? What a task that was.' Edward couldn't believe it was only yesterday he knelt by their broken bodies to put them out of their misery.

Charles followed Edward towards the door. 'Andrew told me the carrion and vultures would take care of them very quickly even before he could cremate the animals.'

Edward nodded grimly, and promised to be back at Hilltop House within the hour to collect Charles, to drive to the police station.

He was shown into the chief superintendent's office. The door was closed firmly behind him. Sitting on the opposite side of the polished desk, Edward eyed Chief Superintendent Henderson as he stood and walked over to a wall safe. Unlocking it, he revealed a thick pile of documents. Carefully selecting a thin green folder, he sat back at his desk and opened it without saying a word. Placing his hands on the contents, he turned them to face Edward, and pushed the folder across the desk for him to read.

'Major Shelley,' he now spoke formally to Edward, 'this is the statement you gave to my officers, Mullins and Chapman when they interrogated you at Hilltop House. Please read it, and if you have any further information to give us regarding the tragic events of that night, please feel free to let me know. We are able, at this stage, to add to the statement, but not detract from it.'

The chief superintendent rose and left Edward alone to read his statement. Running his shaking fingers down the typed document, he skimmed most of it in a haze of anxiety and wretchedness. What could he add? He only remembered that his love, Elizabeth, and her husband, James, were no longer here. Leaning on the table, his head in his hands, he tried to believe what he was reading.

His own words leapt out at him, crowding his memory, disturbing him...*arguing...screaming...ferocious...flames...no other option...I was forced to abandon the house to its fate…*

All he saw was Elizabeth's face, blood oozing from the gash in her head caused by her fall. Fall? James had pushed her, killed her, Edward knew *that* to be true…that's why he became his other self, enraged, distraught and angry to the point of losing control. That's why he threatened James. Drunken James, who had struggled to stay upright. Rage swelled up again in Edward, soon to be overtaken by more guilt and horror as he clearly remembered striking James to the ground and leaving him there to die.

Edward clumsily signed and closed the folder and pushed it away from him across the desk in a gesture of wanting it all to disappear. He sat back in his chair. He sensed Henderson re-enter the room. Sitting opposite Edward again, he took the folder, asking if there was anything further to be added. Edward shook his head, once more tormented by mixed feelings of grief and dread.

'No, inspector. That's what happened to the best of my knowledge and memory.'

Edward was escorted to the door and informed that he would be told the date of the inquest in due course. He would, of course, be summoned to attend.

'Thank you, Chief Superintendent. I am going to go to visit the scene of the fire today at The Laurels, I trust that will be in order?'

'Ah! Yes of course it is. I forgot to tell you that apart from retrieving the charred remains of Mr and Mrs Delaney, various other items were also found, mostly of a personal nature—a box containing jewellery, remnants of a photograph album, and household items such as ornaments. Do you know who will take possession of these? The daughter is very young, I hear.' He stared at Edward.

'Yes, only four years old. We are currently deciding where she's to live, and what's to happen to her, but we're getting in touch with family in England today. I believe there's an aunt and uncle who will most likely take care of her. There are no relatives here in India. I'm the one who was closest to the family.'

Inspector Henderson looked away. It was no secret, even to the police, that Elizabeth and Edward had enjoyed a long-term illicit relationship.

Edward continued. 'I think you should put aside those personal things until the family come over. When they arrive, there'll be a funeral service after which final details of what to do with Jessica and all those possessions can be discussed.'

Once outside, Edward breathed deeply. A gardener lazily sweeping the pathway stood aside, and with a bow of the head made way for him to pass. He sat in the car for a while before making his way back to Hilltop House to pick up Charles. He didn't relish the thought of making that journey to The Laurels. The bumpy driveway, so familiar, the ornate gate and high laurel hedge.

The burnt, and possibly still smouldering remains of the house, and his life...both now destroyed forever.

25

Shimla 1997:

Turning off the main road, the driver questioned Chandra again, in Hindi. He shook his head in disbelief, but she spoke insistently, raising her voice. Still shaking his head, the driver made his way to the start of the track to the hill, changing to low gear and swerving regularly to avoid fallen rocks. In the back seat, Jessica peered down the ever-increasing sheer drop by the side of the road, and looked nervously at Sebastian. They drove over bumps and lumps and through grass that became thicker the further they progressed. Chandra turned to face them.

'The road to The Laurels was very very rough, you know,' she reassured Jessica, smiling. 'Always having too many rocks falling. This *is* the way, I remember it now.'

Turning back to the driver, and addressing him in Hindi, she pointed ahead. The driver nodded and changed gear.

Grass now covered most of the road ahead, which levelled out after a hairpin bend, allowing the driver to speed up.

'Look, look ahead, up—you see the ground? Flat. You see?'

Jessica strained to see from the back seat until a small plateau came into view. Did she expect to remember anything? 'Chandra, is this where the house was?'

'Yes, this is where you lived.'

'But I can't see anything. Can the driver get up there?' Both she and Sebastian scanned the expanse of undergrowth before them.

'Let's get out now, can we?' Sebastian spoke to the driver who turned off the engine and applied the handbrake.

'Yes, yes…' He waved his hand towards the wasteland and shook his head again.

Simultaneously, the three got out of the car. Jessica and Sebastian followed Chandra, her skirts held high enough to clear the patchy vegetation. The ground was hard beneath wispy stalks of weeds, and as they approached the end of the track, Chandra exclaimed and pointed to the right.

'Look. Look—over there is a gatepost that was the entrance to

The Laurels. There—and look, there are still laurel bushes. They made a hedge all around the garden. Jessie, the garden you played.' She was now smiling and excited.

Jessica stopped walking and surveyed the scene, in the near distance was the wall of a building. Through her troubled and muddled brain, a clear picture was developing. Closing her eyes, she saw herself as a child, running through a garden, laughing. Parasol in hand, a teddy bear in a doll's pram. Her senses reeled as she sank to the ground, her head in her hands, as she remembered the sweet smell of freshly mown grass, and her mother's voice calling *Jessie, Jessie*.

'Yes,' she whispered, 'this is the place, the place where I was born. I can feel it.'

Sebastian and Chandra stepped ahead to give Jessica space to be alone. She had a strong feeling of déjà vu, of belonging. Her spirits seeped into the earth below and floated in the air above, untying constraints as though releasing her from slavery. Tears of joy and sadness mixed spontaneously as a heady sense of freedom descended upon her. Smiling, she looked up at the two figures walking ahead, and took several deep, cleansing breaths before rising to join them. They drew closer to the ruins of the house.

Catching up, she took hold of Sebastian's hand. 'I'm so happy. So, so happy to be here. I've dreamed of this for years.'

'But this can't exactly be the picture you dreamed of,' Sebastian replied.

'No, not at all, I imagined a grand old house covered in ivy, with impressive steps down to a magnificent garden with a summer house and pond. I stupidly expected it to be in mint condition with other people living here, never knowing it had been razed to the ground. What a lot I've learned, and how strange it feels to be here. It's as though part of my soul stayed behind when I left that day, and now I have it back—all together in one place. The smell of the earth, the blue of the sky and the scenery all somehow seems familiar. I feel I've found home.'

They stood gazing at the vista taking in the clean, clear mountain air. 'It's a feeling of belonging—can you understand any of that? That missing thing in my life. That gap of incompleteness—it's all now mended. It may sound daft, but I feel more whole than I've ever felt in my life. I feel I belong here. It's as though I've been forever seeking something, anything, and now I've found it. Oh, Sebastian...'

He put his arms around her and hugged her tight, feeling her need to have human contact, to share her emotions. Even though he was somewhat surprised at her reactions, he also tried to imagine what life must have been like here, fifty years ago. His own father regularly making the slow drive up the bumpy track to a clandestine rendezvous. Romance, he thought, would have come easy in these dreamy blue-remembered hills here, in Shimla.

Jessica watched Chandra wandering back and forth, seemingly surprised by the remaining bricks and timber still scattering the ground. She thought that she, too, might find it easy to bring back memories of her time here as she walked along the line of the outside walls picking up remnants of lacy iron balustrading that once enclosed the veranda. The veranda where she'd play with Jessica, showing her how to fit together a jigsaw puzzle or dress her dolls, where she'd catch glimpses of Elizabeth entertaining friends for tiffin, or sitting with James for a sundowner in the evening.

Chandra, too, looked deep into the past and found a new contentment at being there once again with Jessica in this forgotten chapter in both of their lives.

26

Edward was reluctant to get to Hilltop House too quickly, delaying the inevitable seemed like a good option to him although it went against his principles. His heart felt heavy as he stopped outside to pick up Charles. Tooting the horn to announce his arrival, he waited until Charles appeared and descended the red brick steps to meet him.

Edward felt overdressed in the formal smart clothing borrowed from Charles for his meeting with the police inspector. But he had nothing else to put on until he'd found time to go to the club and collect more of his own clothes. Charles was dressed far more appropriately for venturing up the hill to The Laurels.

'How did it go, Edward?' He was eager to hear all about Edward's meeting with the police.

'Oh, alright, I just went over the formal statement I gave them and signed it. Inspector Henderson said he'd keep in touch and let me know about the inquest. They'll want me there as a witness. He said they have retrieved things from the wreckage and they're in safekeeping at the station.'

'Well, that's all good and over now—and I've some news for you.' Charles' enthusiastic manner did little to encourage Edward to participate.

'About...?'

'Well, my man has been through the staff personal contacts at the Viceroy's offices, and found a comprehensive list of names and numbers of family members in England relating to James and Elizabeth. James was very precise, you know—he used to make sure that every I was dotted and every T was crossed.'

'I'm very relieved. Does that mean we can make those phone calls later—shall we do it from your place?' Another task to overcome, thought Edward, as he struggled to see just how he would break such news to families overseas.

'I'm all in favour of getting the calls made as soon as possible, too. One more job to tick off. I say, you know you can stay at our place as long as you like, old boy…' Charles was thinking ahead, planning.

'Thanks, Charles, but I'll go back to the club. When we've sorted out Jessica, and made permanent plans, that's where I'll be for the duration, until after the inquest and funeral. I think we should wait till Elizabeth's sister gets here before we have the funeral.'

'We'll write a list of questions for Catherine and her husband. There will be a long-time delay in proceedings if we don't do it from here, I suspect. Perhaps we can make their arrival coincide with the funeral, we should be able to get Jessica booked back on the ship with them.'

The car had just passed the area where they found the injured horses. Instinctively, both men looked down, lost in their own thoughts. Nearing the house, Edward stopped the car.

'Charles, I'm not sure if I want to see the devastation now. I think I've been too impulsive in the need to come back.'

'Come on—you need do it only this once. A sort of cathartic experience you'll regret later if you don't. Do you want me to take over the driving?'

'No, I suppose you're right. I must see The Laurels for the very last time,' Edward determined, as he started the car again.

The gates came into view, and the summer house. Enormous piles of bricks and debris were scattered as far as the eye could see. A breeze eddying around the still-standing chimney sent swirls of ash into the air, whisking them away towards the foothills.

The garden remained defiant as a sentinel, untouched by the damage to the house. Sweet-smelling roses bloomed amongst lavender. Elizabeth's favourite flowers, he remembered.

Steps still led to the burnt-out hallway, the black-and-white tiles broken and blackened by falling timbers. The upper floor had collapsed apart from two adjoining brick walls. Edward struggled to envisage the house as it was. Scorched furniture was unrecognisable, most of it charred.

Broken glass littered the whole area and as they walked around in silence, Edward stepped up on to the back veranda—the lacy ironwork was still warm from the fire. The devastation was too much for him to bear as he thought about his lost love. Not a word issued forth from either man. There was no need for words, no need for explanations.

No need for anything but shock and horror.

Edward looked over towards the stables—most of the doors had been broken down by the panicked horses in their desperation to get away. He noticed that Rainbow's door remained intact—perhaps it was left off the latch. Elizabeth's pony must have bolted and followed the others in fright. No sign of life or the servants could be seen. He mused that they, too, most likely fled...

He looked up to where Elizabeth's room had been. There was nothing, nothing but half a wall still standing. Picking his way through the ash, he saw piles of smashed crockery and ornaments. A short strong breeze picked up the dust and flattened it back into the ground. Edward noticed items that had miraculously survived. He wondered if they ought to retrieve them for Jessica. His eye caught a flash of sunlight at his feet. He bent down to look and found the silver jewellery box from Elizabeth's dressing table. Smashing down to the floor below, it had fallen open, revealing her emerald necklace. Nearby he found the gold and emerald brooch he gave her for her birthday last year. He picked them up, and smoothing the ash from the gems, held them tight in his fist looking to the sky for deliverance.

Charles came over and took his arm. 'Come on, old chap—we've seen enough. Let's just take a few things back to bequeath to Jessica when she's older, when she is able to understand.' Charles tugged Edward away and into the garden. 'I'll go and rummage to pick up what the police didn't take. Sit here for a while.' He pointed to a garden bench and Edward sat down obediently. He clutched the necklace and brooch, and, opening his hand to look again, slipped them into his pocket.

He needed that talisman for comfort and remembrance of the plans they had, the days of beauty and nights of love. Wherever his life took him, he would always hold it close and never forget.

'Elizabeth.' He spoke her name to heaven and knew she'd hear him...

27

Shimla 1997:

Lost in their own thoughts at the place where The Laurels once stood, Jessica and Chandra tried to remember their lives there half a century ago. The house where they escaped death and were rescued by Sebastian's father. The place where he and Jessica's mother conducted her love affair. Jessica took photographs and they made their way back to the car.

The driver, relieved to be back on a proper road, snaked his way back to Chandra's house.

Jessica looked at Sebastian. 'Well, that's it, I suppose! All my ideas as seen through rose-coloured glasses of what I expected to find, have brought me firmly down to earth with a bump.'

He reached for her hand. 'Quite a blow, I imagine, but at least we made it. I was sceptical on the way here thinking this can't be right. Chandra knew better. Thank you, Chandra—it's a good job you came with us—we would never have found it. Even the driver thought we were all bonkers.'

'So, disappointed? Perhaps, but I still feel we have a lot more to discover. When will you call your father? Perhaps later today?' Jessica made a plan.

'Sounds good. We'll take Chandra back, go to the hotel for lunch, and get on the blower before dinner.' He leaned towards Jessica and winked as she turned and nodded in agreement.

'Chandra—do you mind if we go back to the hotel straight away after taking you home? We'll see you soon when we've done more research and called home this evening.'

'Jessie, no. I can meet you again, and if I think of more, I will write it down for you.' She looked back to the road as they approached the entrance to her pathway. 'Please—you don't come with me. I can go from here myself.'

'Are you sure? Sebastian was just about to get out of the car to walk her home.

'No, please.' She got out and waved as they drove off again to the other side of town.

'Lunch?' Sebastian asked as they arrived back at the hotel.

'Yes please—now?'

'Why not, but before we go in, I'll check to see if we need to book an overseas call. You still can't just pick up the phone and dial from here. What time should I say, bearing in mind they're four hours behind us?'

'Afternoon for them. Perhaps seven this evening for us?'

'We should be able to dial internationally, but in my experience, it doesn't always connect first time.'

'Okay. We'll go for lunch. Do I have time to go to my room and tidy up? I feel a bit of a mess having just trekked through the Himalayan undergrowth. And my shoes definitely need a clean.' Jessica left Sebastian standing in the lobby.

He spotted the elderly couple who had taken their photograph on the veranda. They came towards him and stopped.

'Hello. How are you both today?' Sebastian smiled.

'Very well, thank you. Lady friend deserted you?' The old man joked.

Sebastian laughed. 'We've been into the country this morning and she needed to freshen up. It feels like we've been halfway up Everest.'

'Jakhoo Temple?' the old man queried.

'No, er, we found the house—well, the remains of the house— where she was born. It's been an emotional morning. She couldn't remember much, but she felt some connection, she said.' He looked up at the couple. 'Would you like to join us at our table for lunch? She'll be down in a moment.'

The wife thought it exciting and said she'd be interested to hear all about it. 'We lived here, too, in those golden days long gone.'

'Ah, well, that's a coincidence.' Sebastian stood up. 'Not sure we introduced ourselves properly.' He thrust out his hand. 'Sebastian, pleased to meet you.'

They shook hands. 'Likewise—oh and I'm Charles, and my wife, Lola. Smiling, they agreed to take a table together, just as Jessica appeared.

'We're having lunch together,' Sebastian told her. 'Shall we go in?'

Settling at a round table, Charles extended a hand to Jessica.

'Charles and Lola.'

'I'm Jessica,' she said as she sat next to Sebastian.

'Hmm…Lola, we knew a Jessica, didn't we? But it can't possibly be you, my dear—far too much of a coincidence.' Charles dismissed his comments with a wave of his hand.

'But Charles, think of the story and Jessica and Sebastian's reason for being here.' Lola looked from one to the other, eyes widening. 'We left here fifty-one years ago, Jessica. We lived in a house called Hilltop House. Don't suppose you remember?' Lola persisted.

'I don't remember much, I was only four. After my parents both died, I was whisked away to England with my aunt, who later adopted me. I've lived there ever since.' Jessica scanned the faces around the table as an eerie silence descended upon everyone's lips. 'Oh, you don't mean, do you think that…'

Lola interrupted her abruptly. 'Jessica, what's your second name?'

'Delaney-Hartford, why…what?'

'And your father was James, and your mother was Elizabeth?' As Lola spoke her parents' names, they leaned forward waiting for what was to come next. Jessica clamped a hand over her mouth in astonishment. Lola continued. 'Co-incidence or not, we knew your parents very well indeed, and were part of the horrible and nasty events that led them to perish in their own home, at the place you've just been to visit.'

'So, you would have known *my* father,' Sebastian aimed the obvious searching question, pausing to look the couple in the eye. 'My father, Edward Shelley?'

Charles and Lola gasped in unison.

28

Shimla 1947:

Edward allowed Charles to lead him to the car for the drive back to Hilltop House. He stopped to gaze at the ruins of The Laurels, eyeing the destruction with photographic sight. The air was calm. Smoke still rose silently like ghosts from the ashes of his past. He felt dead and empty.

Charles waited in the car, trying to understand what might be going through Edward's mind. He observed his tortured face as he settled into the passenger seat, and saw in his friend the embodiment of grief, sadness, and despair. Charles recognized that Edward just wanted to be left alone. Manoeuvring the car and pointing it through the gates, he left this scene of carnage and misery, keeping the speed down as they descended the driveway to join the road back to Shimla.

The house was quiet, Jessica had gone to stay with Hermione for the day, to play with her son. Charles walked through the drawing room and into the kitchen. He asked the maid to bring coffee for him and Edward, who had settled himself on the sofa, still looking miserable and depressed.

Now that reality had hit home, Edward knew it would be a long hard slog to find his equilibrium. Thoughts and images swirling round his head oscillated from when he and Elizabeth first met, to the first time they made love, to Jessica's birth, to how this gradual deterioration between James and his wife had somehow passed him by in the euphoria of love and lust. He was beginning to fear that it was all his fault—not Elizabeth's, not James's. But his. He could have just walked away from the affair, no matter how profound and deep their love had been.

Charles flopped down beside him, once again placing a reassuring hand on Edward's knee.

'I can't even start to imagine what's going through your mind, chum, but never ever think it was all your fault.'

Edward was comforted at his friend's perception, but reckoned anxiety and sadness must be written all over his face.

'Don't read too much into it. It's always taken two to tango, you know, and it's so common here—one day you'll find out about other friends of yours and realise you were not alone. I know that's no excuse, but it happens all the time. Don't get caught up in some sort of self-denial or self-denigration. Please, Edward, it will drag you down, and you can't change the past. Also, remember we have much work to do until the episode is over. Look on the bright side—at least you still have Jessica, and anyone can see that she's the apple of your eye. Try to count what few blessings you still have.

'Coffee's here, and I have a load of things for us to go through—the file is on the table.'

Charles stood up and walked over to the table as the coffee arrived, hot and steaming.

'Look here, my man has compiled this list of all known relatives of Elizabeth's family in England. He confirmed there were no relatives left in India, just as we suspected. The only person in Elizabeth's family appears to be her sister, Catherine, but there is a phone number for her and her husband, Elizabeth's brother-in-law.'

'Do you have addresses, Charles? We might need the authorities to mail documentation to them after our phone calls. Otherwise, we'll get their address when we phone. Also, anything on James's family?'

Charles slid the file over to Edward who scrutinised details. He noticed that Elizabeth's contacts were a lot more concise than James'. He knew, from her, that James' family was based in India for generations. He had no siblings listed, just his parents who apparently had gone back to Scotland after his father's retirement. Like so many expats, they'd read the writing on the wall regarding India's impending independence. All the main details of those he needed to contact were there.

'I guess that if there is any other family anywhere, they'll make contact between themselves.' Edward collected the papers together and closed the file, satisfied they had all that was needed to break the bad news.

He rose. 'I'm going to the club, Charles, what time do you want me to come over to make those phone calls? I'll sort out my things, have lunch and try to get some sleep, too. Thank you for everything—I don't know what I would have done without your support and guidance.'

'It's nothing, my dear boy. You'd do the same for me, I'm sure.'

They finished their coffees and walked out into the driveway. Edward noticed James' car still parked under trees.

'I suppose we ought to do something about selling that car. I'll put a notice up at the club.'

'Good idea. Come back for sundowners, and we'll get a line through to overseas. Fingers crossed we'll reach our target tonight.'

'Bye, Charles. I'll see you later—before Jessica goes to bed.' They both managed to raise a knowing smile at that, and Edward waved as he drove away from Hilltop House on his way to taking up residence once more in his cottage.

29

Shimla1997:

Charles stared at Sebastian across the lunch table. 'Good Lord! Of course we knew Edward Shelley. Shimla was a small place in those days, cliquish and privileged...and rather hedonistic you know. Has he not told you about his time here? You and Jessica know each other, so surely you'll know what happened to your father and Jessica's parents?' Charles looked incredulous, memories now flooding back.

Jessica looked at Lola and Charles, not believing her ears.

'We, er, are only just beginning to unravel the story. I came here to trace them, to find their graves, and piece together their lives before they died. We've been to public records offices, the church, and we found their gravestones. We also found an elderly woman called Chandra...'

'No! Chandra, your ayah? I don't believe it. Edward brought you both to our house after the fire. She was taken away to Chandigarh hospital. Badly burned, she was, it was terrible. We never knew what happened to her, I don't think we ever saw her again. So, she's still here, here in Shimla? Well, I never, she must be very old by now.'

'She is old, and she still bears the terrible scars from the fire. We saw her this morning, and took her with us to the place where The Laurels used to be.' Jessica lowered her tone. 'It was moving. Lately I've wondered and tried to imagine what my parents' lives were like here, and I thought I'd find beautiful gardens with a summer house, and a grand old colonial mansion covered in ivy, still being lived in and cared for. But there was nothing, nothing at all, except a broken gate and piles of overgrown bricks and debris. The track was almost impassable.'

Sighing audibly, Jessica continued. 'I took photos, but there was nothing to see. Though strangely, I found some peace there, some spiritual tranquillity of belonging I can't explain. After all, that *was* where I was born, and where my parents lived and perished together. And all along I had been told they died of a rare form of dysentery. I still don't know why my aunt and uncle would lie to me.'

She looked wryly at Sebastian, shrugging her shoulders. 'Last year my aunt died. Before she passed away, she told me something strange. She urged me to come here to find the truth. I assumed she was delirious because towards the end of her life she rambled on about all sorts of things. I dismissed the remark, assuming it was just another of her stories.'

Jessica paused to take a sip of water. 'I always knew that one day I would come to Shimla to pay homage at my parents' graves. I also wanted to find records of their marriage and my christening, and anything else I had no idea about. Now I understand why there wasn't much of their personal property that made it back to England.'

Sebastian put his hand on hers and suggested they all adjourn to the terrace for coffee. Following behind, their new-found friends were stunned at what they were hearing.

They settled into comfy chairs on the veranda. The mountains were partly cloaked in drifting white clouds, which threw shifting patterns across them.

'It's quite a story, Jessica, and I'm sure we can add much more to it.' But Charles felt reticent to impart too much information, and remembered the inquest, and how Edward was tied into knots by the presenting counsel.

Charles turned to Sebastian. 'But first, tell me. Your father, is he still alive, if so, where does he live? We were such good chums. When we all dispersed and went back to England, he stayed behind to start a business, I remember. We lost touch with most of our friends from India. I guess that's why we like to come here every now and again. It takes us back to what is sometimes referred to as *the good old days*.' He reached out for Lola's hand and they both smiled at the thought.

'Yes, my dad is indeed still around, although he's not been well of late. In fact, it was he who urged me to come to Shimla at the same time as Jessica. I live part-time in Delhi. I'm a freelance journalist, so unless I'm in the middle of some investigation or in-depth story, my time is my own. I also have a flat in London that I go back to frequently.' Pausing, Sebastian turned to speak to Jessica. 'Yes, it was my father's idea that I seek you out here, and, yes, he did divulge some scant information about you, and why you would be here, but it is true I never knew about the fire or about our parents. Nothing at all.'

'It's alright, Sebastian, I've already worked it out, so please don't think I consider you a spy.' Jessica laughed at her own joke, along with the others, breaking the ice between them.

Coffee arrived and Lola poured everyone a cup to their liking. As she did so, she questioned why Jessica and Sebastian had apparently only just met.

Jessica told the story about her meeting with Sebastian, '...and I have to say, that without Sebastian's advice, I wouldn't have known where to start. He's been more than helpful to me.

'We're going to phone our families later and tell them what we've found. Sebastian also has a few pertinent questions for his father. Chandra has been our link with the past, and we were so fortunate to make contact with her.' Jessica looked at Sebastian. 'It's as though it was meant to be, isn't it?'

Sebastian nodded and told Charles and Lola about the encounter. 'It was uncanny. We'd been directed to the old overgrown cemetery at Sanjauli. It was a total mess, untidy and unkempt. The verger at Christ Church told us it was in bad repair because there was no funding anymore to tend British cemeteries and it was only kept open by local volunteers. Hardly anyone ever went there nowadays. When we found it, there was an old Indian man attempting to tidy the gardens with a broken rake and rusty wheelbarrow. After we'd found Jessica's parent's gravestone, which was fairly easy to pick out from the rest because someone had placed flowers on it, we asked him about the flowers. It turned out he was Chandra's husband, and it was Chandra who regularly tended the grave. We saw her leaving the cemetery.'

Jessica took over the story as Charles and Lola sat looking on. 'The old man gave us the address and the driver took us to the exact house. We scoured the streets as we drove along, looking for the old woman in the red sari, but by the time we reached the house she was already there.'

'What an amazing story,' Lola said, sitting forward in her seat. 'So, you met Chandra? Your old ayah from The Laurels? What I remember—and correct me if I'm wrong, Charles—that dreadful night after the fire, Edward brought Jessica and Chandra back to our house. We'd had a dinner party earlier that evening, and he'd driven your parents back home to The Laurels because your father's car wouldn't start, Jessica.' Pausing, Lola continued in a barely audible voice, 'Your father had also had far too much to drink that night.' She stopped abruptly, looking at Charles.

Jessica, sensing Lola's reticence to tell more, took up the story again. 'It's alright, Chandra told us about my mother and Edward's affair. The revelation shocked us both. That's why we have to talk to Edward today to find out more, and to clarify suspicions I have concerning what exactly happened to me here before I was taken back to England by my Aunt Catherine. You didn't know that she and my uncle adopted me, eventually?'

Charles said they never heard anything more after she left that day, and it was soon afterwards that Edward was discharged from the British army and left Shimla, as they all did, after independence.

Sebastian looked at his watch. 'I say, can we see you later today, or tomorrow morning, Charles? We must phone my father and Jessica's daughter.'

'Of course. We've been rambling a bit, but in the meantime, Lola and I will put our heads together and try to remember more about what happened.' Charles shook his head. 'I still can't believe it. Tomorrow after breakfast alright for you?'

'Perfect,' said Jessica as she stood and shook hands. 'We'll see you here on the veranda. We'd better go and make those phone calls.'

30

Shimla 1947:

Edward called at the club for a bite to eat before making his way back to Hilltop House. He was overwhelmed by friends and even people he hardly knew, who came over to offer their condolences and help. All wishing him well with the task ahead.

Once refreshed and rested, he felt more able to face the monumental job of making phone calls to England. He decided not to have wine or an aperitif, needing instead to keep a clear head.

Lola met him at the door and ushered him into the drawing room. Jessica was there, playing with some toys that had been donated by the nursery school and friends. She looked up as Edward came into the room.

'Uncle Edward—look, look at all the toys I have to play with.' She beamed at him and went back to dressing a large doll. 'Look, her name is Anna, and she's a queen, and she has real hair like mine that I can brush. Isn't she beautiful?'

'Jessie she is lovely. Anna, you say? Well, I think that name suits her—Queen Anna.' He held out his arms and she came to him for a cuddle. Look, why don't you finish dressing Anna, you can take her to bed with you and Teddy. Is that a good idea?'

'Yes, Uncle Edward, and look, when I lie her down, she closes her eyes, so she can go to sleep.'

The child was excited at being given so many presents, and seemed to Edward that she was beginning to accept her stay here with Charles and Lola. He smiled at her, as much as in relief as with gladness at her own obvious joy.

'What a clever queen she is. Bring her to me when you've found the right clothes for her, and we can settle you all down for the night.' Contentedly lost in her new doll, Jessica sat on the floor.

Edward sat next to Charles as they prioritised their telephone list, thinking that the first person must be Catherine, Elizabeth's sister. She would have to be the one to break the news to the rest of the family. And also, possibly to any family of James they might know in England.

'Better wait until Jessie is in bed, Charles, she doesn't need to hear anything.'

Edward refused the offer of a drink, '...to give you courage, dear boy!'

Just at that time, Jessica came over to them, with arms full of toys she wanted to *put to bed*, she said.

'We're all going to sleep in my bed now!' she announced, and turned to go to her room, Edward followed in her wake waiting for her to drop a few on the way upstairs.

Charles and Lola shouted goodnight to her, as, determined, she took one careful step at a time, clutching the toys. 'I will ask Anna to read my story tonight, Uncle, so you can go if you like,' she announced.

'Alright, hop in, and let's settle Anna and Teddy and everyone else round you comfortably and you can close your eyes just like Anna.'

'Yes, Uncle Edward. Night-night.'

He bent over to kiss her forehead, pulled up the eiderdown, and said goodnight, relishing his new role as father. Pausing at the door, he gazed upon her tiny body, and love flooded his whole being. 'Goodnight my angel—I love you, Jessie.' He whispered.

Re-joining his friends, he took out his notes and found the telephone number. 'Here goes,' he said as Charles brought the telephone over to him at the table. 'I'm ready.'

It took a mere three minutes for the call to be connected. A female voice answered with a clear-sounding *Hello*.

'Er...' Edward cleared his throat, 'hello, is that Mrs Hartford? Catherine Hartford?' He waited anxiously for confirmation. There was a noticeable pause on the line. 'Hello...'

'Yes, hello, this is Mrs Hartford to whom am I speaking?' Her voice, brusque and business-like, unnerved Edward.

'Um...you don't know me...um...I'm calling from Shimla, and I'm a friend of your sister Elizabeth and James, your brother-in-law. My name is Edward Shelley.'

'Yes,' Came back the curt response. 'Yes...' she paused. 'Is there anything wrong?'

'I'm afraid I have some bad news for you. Some very bad news, Catherine—may I call you Catherine? You see, there has been a terrible accident, terrible...'

'What? you're not trying to tell me...'

'Sorry to have to tell you like this, Catherine, but both your sister and her husband...they...er...two days ago there was a fire. It destroyed The Laurels entirely...' He heard high-pitched moaning sounds on the other ends of the phone, and then silence. 'Hello, Catherine, are you still there?'

A shaky voice responded. 'Are they...? Oh, my lord! Oh no. And Jessica? Please don't tell me they're all gone.' She was now audibly sobbing loudly.

'Jessica is alive. But...everything...'

'The poor child, the poor child.'

Don't worry, Catherine, she's safe, and being well looked after by me and other friends, but she doesn't know yet about her mother and father. We decided to wait until the time was right—if it ever will be the right time.'

'Their um...the bodies? Were they badly burned? Were there...' she stopped again, Edward imagined her to be taking deep breaths and trying to calm herself. 'I must come over—will there, yes, of course there will be a funeral, won't there?'

'Yes, of course, and I had hoped you would be able to come, you and your husband. And...'

'What, Edward? And what?'

'Jessica has no other family now...er...' His awkwardness was interrupted immediately by Catherine.

'Can we bring her back to England? Would that be in order, do you think? Oh, the dear child. We often received letters and photographs from Elizabeth. She was so proud of Jessica. In fact, I received one only a few weeks ago, telling me she had been enrolled in Sunday school and was already going to nursery school.' She paused again. Edward heard her breathing deeply. 'You see, we could never have any children of our own, and Elizabeth wanted us to share in Jessie's upbringing. In fact, we already offered to have her after her boarding school semesters when she eventually came over for her education. But, oh dear, I can't take all this in now, and I must tell my husband. Can I call you back tomorrow?'

Edward commiserated and gave her Charles' number. Catherine said she'd try to get through about the same time the next day.

'Thank you, Catherine. Thank you...and, sorry to be the bearer of such devastating news. I will be here whenever you want to phone, any time. Oh, and one more thing before you go. Can I leave it to you to make contact with as many other family members as possible over there, and James's family, too? I think he has a cousin in Scotland, if you've ever had the details. Most of his family were here in India, and most have passed on now.'

'I'll do that, Edward, and we'll talk again tomorrow. I have to go and rest now, and take it all in. What a blow. What a shock.'

'Goodbye, Catherine.' Edward replaced the receiver and took a deep breath. 'Thank you, Lord. thank you,' he said to the empty room.

31

Shimla 1997:

S ebastian and Jessica retreated to their hotel rooms, with thoughts on how they were going to address the current situation and tell their respective families what they had discovered together. Both hoped that they would get lines through to England and Scotland easily, and have explanations over and done with quickly.

They were connected simultaneously. Jessica to Saffron, and Sebastian to Edward.

'Saffie? It's Mum.' Jessica pressed the handset close to her ear. She wished the telephone reception could be clearer.

'Mum,' came back a surprised excited-sounding voice. 'Mum, where are you? Are you still in India? There seems to be a lag on the line.'

'Yes, Saffie. I'm in Shimla—been here for a while, and I've found what I'm looking for.'

'That's wonderful news, Mum. When will you be coming home?'

'Well, not yet. You see, I've met a man.'

'What? Did you say you'd met a man? Mum...Mum—crikey. Do tell. What's he like? Never too late, Mum, I've always told you that. I've also got news, but not as exciting as yours...wow!'

Jessica chose her words carefully. 'Saffie, it's not like that, it isn't...' She heard giggles.

'Come on, Mum. What do you mean? You've fallen in love, haven't you—admit it.' Saffron giggled again.

'Saffie, no! Don't jump to conclusions. He's a journalist, and he's younger than me. But, well, it's a complicated story, and it will take ages to explain in detail, but it turns out he's the son of my mother's lover.'

'What? Did I hear that straight? Your mother, departed long ago in India, had a lover? But...you were her rightful daughter? So how come you've found all this out only now?' Saffron sounded confused.

'I know—and yes, you will be confused until I tell you the full story. I'm calling from the Imperial Hotel in Shimla, and have to make it brief, in case we get cut off. But he—er, Sebastian Shelley—made contact with me here, and we have been able to piece together what happened to your grandparents. Sebastian has been so helpful, and we have become good friends. When we both make it back to England, I'll have a fuller story for you. I've met up with my old nanny, Chandra, it's been a rollercoaster of experiences, and it's not over yet.'

'So, Mum, is all this info bona fide? Have you checked it out? And did you find records anywhere? And how could Sebastian help you with all this?'

'He works in Delhi for a news agency, and knows the place like the back of his hand, but there's a mystery I've yet to solve, regarding his father. I think his father knew I was coming here, and told Sebastian to meet me and keep an eye on me. I think there's something I'm not being told.' Jessica stopped to take a sip of water, lapsing into an area of uncertainty.

'Wow, Mum, are you safe? Don't say you're afraid of this man.'

'Oh, no, of course not, but…well…look, Saffie, I've had fleeting thoughts—he had a long-term affair with my mother.'

'Oh, surely not! But if that is that case, it means that my situation could be the same as yours—history repeating itself?'

Jessica knew this was coming once she told Saffron the story of what happened in Shimla. Saffron had given up the search, but had never forgotten that she was a love child of that era, and had come to terms with it. She knew there was no hope of finding her biological father. Jessica had borne the guilt of the situation all her life.

'No, Saffie. For that, I'm sorry every day that dawns.'

There was a difficult pause in their conversation. Saffron decided to break the ice.

'Mum, listen! I have news. I'm leaving the Hebrides. For good. I've had enough of everything, the place, the people I commune with, the hardship and this awful weather, so next week I'm coming back down south…'

Jessica took a deep breath and smiled to herself. 'What a relief! Thank God you've at last made a sensible decision in your life, Saffie. Look, I won't be back for a while, but go and stay at the cottage. You can take over looking after everything 'till I get back, and we'll decide what to do. Trix needs a good ride, and you can do all the things the neighbours are helping out with while I've been away. There will be apples on the trees no doubt, and maybe some veg and soft fruit in the garden if it isn't overgrown already. I told the neighbours to help themselves to any produce, but the tomatoes in the greenhouse should be just ripe. Oh, I'm so happy, so happy now! You've still got a key? If not, there's one under the plant pot in the usual place near the porch.'

'Thanks, Mum, it'll take me about a week more to make sure I get away from here without a fuss, but I'll let you know when I am at the cottage. I'm also a happy bunny. I don't know how I've put up with everything here for so long. Back to civilisation for me. Do you have a number I can phone you on?'

Jessica rummaged around the desk and found the hotel's main number. She read it twice to Saffron. They bid each other a long farewell, till next time.

Jessica sat back and tried to relax. She'd heard raised voices on and off from Sebastian's room, but all seemed quiet now. She walked over to the bed and kicked off her shoes, swung her legs on the bed and lay back, closing her eyes to recall the conversation she'd had with her daughter.

32

Shimla 1947:

Sitting in Charles' study, Edward felt reassured after his phone call to Catherine. She had taken it badly, but seemed to have the resilience to maintain control.

Just like Elizabeth, he thought—always able to organise things in a crisis. His inner voice reminded him that she was gone, except for in his head and heart. He had begun to see her everywhere. Sometimes it was a comfort, other times it was a sadness, a deep dark sadness that made him panic as his heart was dragged to a depth from which he feared he might never emerge. How would he ever get over this? How could he live without her? Why did this have to happen before they could do the right thing and make a clean break? These questions were irrelevant now, he told himself, shaking his head, trying to get her out of his mind.

He hadn't heard Charles enter the room, so lost was he in his own jumbled thoughts, as he stared out of the window onto the veranda where he and Elizabeth had had their last clandestine meeting. She had looked dazzling in her favourite green silk dress. The dress that caught fire as she fell, helpless, into the fireplace. With a kiss, they had promised to meet as soon as they could, and discuss their future together. But now, all that was left were memories. And Jessica.

'Edward!' His friend's voice startled him. He stood up immediately.

'Sorry, Charles. But everything is alright. Better than I had hoped. Catherine took the news well, although very shocked of course. We touched on everything I wanted to say, and it was she who volunteered the perfect solution for Jessie. They'll take her back with them to England, after the funeral.'

'Dear boy, what a relief for you. Just what you had hoped would happen. So, they will be coming over? Best thing, they need to meet Jessica on her home soil, so to speak. We'll try to prepare her for what's going to happen.'

'She might not understand fully, but I think if we make it sound exciting, that she'll be going on a big ship to England to be with her aunt and uncle…' Edward paused, realising Jessica hadn't been told, about her parents. Neither did she ask any more. He knew that hurdle was going to be the most difficult to jump. But she would have to be made to understand that her mother and father would not be coming back. 'Charles, I have to start thinking about a funeral, and also about the inquest. I'm surprised the court hasn't set a date yet. And we'll have to wait until we hear back from Catherine about their arrival date before we can arrange a funeral. Will it matter that it's delayed?'

'Well, it's not like a pyre, you know, having to take place immediately. No, the coroners will keep things on hold until you tell them.'

Edward followed Charles into the drawing room, and they made themselves comfortable. Charles asked the maid to bring them tea.

'Catherine's ringing us tomorrow, on this phone, so I'll be hanging around, I'm afraid—about the same time. After that, I'll get the ball rolling with final arrangements. And I must ask about the inquest. Between you and me, Charles, I'm a bit worried about that. I still feel I could have done more to stop the fire taking hold. There has to be a verdict of some sort, and I'm not sure of the options.'

Charles sat forward. 'Look, Edward, you must stick to the statement. Whatever they ask you, don't be deflected. They know you must have been terribly confused, but they have accepted your full statement of what happened that night, and that's that.'

Edward's thoughts flew to what could happen. Might they tie him up in knots? Would there be further evidence from the pathologists? He just wanted it to be over and done with. 'I know, but clever counsel can divert anyone from the facts and turn them into fiction.'

'Edward, it won't be like that, trust me. It's an inquest to determine the cause of death, not a trial. Just keep your cool, and it will be over in minutes. It's a cut-and-dried case, and I shouldn't think they'll even have the full complement of judge and jury. I imagine it will be conducted by a government official. They usually are.'

'I hope you're right, Charles, I damned well hope you're right.'

33

Shimla 1997:

From her room, Jessica could hear that Sebastian was still on the phone to his father. During her conversation with Saffie, she'd heard raised voices from next door. *This is turning out to be something of a nightmare* she thought, questioning her motives and her growing dependence upon Sebastian. Yet, there was no denying that all she had learned and discovered could never have been achieved on her own. For that she was grateful. The rest of their connections and co-incidences had tipped a balance between inquisitiveness and reality.

She walked across the room. Opening the French windows, she hesitated before going outside to watch the last rays of orange sunlight play on the mountains. Sebastian's doors were closed, so she moved away, along the veranda, and sat down, pulling her wrap around her shoulders against the cool air. Suddenly, she was looking forward to going home. Saffie would be in residence, and Jessica could recount the whole story of her incredible expedition to India. She relaxed into her chair and breathed deeply.

She heard Sebastian's door open and close. He pulled up a chair beside her. Jessica looked round to say hello, but he sat looking down, elbows on the chair arms, hands clasped over his mouth.

'Well?' Jessica leaned forward. 'What's wrong, Sebastian? Did I hear you having angry words with your father?'

He looked at her intently. 'I don't know where to start. I don't.' He wavered, his voice quivering.

'Come on—whatever you discussed can't be any more revealing than what we already know, surely.'

'Huh! Forget the affair with your mother, how about him being grilled by police about the fire? about suspicions being thrown at him at the inquest as to what happened that night? And how about him telling me that he has been in league with Meredith all the time your trust fund was being administered. And, listen to this…what would you say if the truth was that your funding was provided all your life by my father, ever since you got back to England as a child? Oh, and by-the-way, you were right, Meredith did send him the photo of you at

129

Stonehenge.'

He went on, angrily banging a fist on the table, 'Think about it—was it an accident? Could my father have set fire to the house deliberately, to get rid of your father? How do we know *what* happened? Yes, Chandra told us *her* version of that night, about how he rescued both of you from the house and took you to safety. But could it simply be a case of eternal triangle meets angry lover? Oh, God. I just don't know now. If it weren't so real, it would make an amazing book, or film. Or a mystery story for my agency.'

Calming now, Sebastian continued, taking hold of Jessica's hand. 'Jessica, listen. There's no easy way to tell you this…but my father told me that he thinks you're his daughter.'

Jessica stared blankly at Sebastian, not knowing what to say after his angry outburst. She wondered—was it that he'd never been told anything of this before, or was it that he suddenly realised that she might, in fact, be his half-sister. Or perhaps he was irritated at the funds coming out of what was to be his rightful inheritance?

'Hell! He said that? All that! No wonder you're so exasperated.' Jessica felt that she was a pawn being used in some extraordinary game. He thinks he's my father? No!' She sat, wondering why he would say such a thing. 'This puts a different slant on everything. Although, most of it we could have deduced, or at least suspected, ourselves.

'But if he wanted to get rid of my father, why did my mother also have to perish? And surely, he would have confessed.

'Oh, Sebastian, think of how this must have haunted him all his life. Think of what he must have gone through, the angst and uncertainty, and still, to this day, not knowing the truth.'

'I know. I shouldn't have got angry with him, but he should have confided in me before. And he should have told me the reason he sent me here to make contact with you. And your trust fund manager—accountant—whatever he is, why the lies and secrecy? I told Dad we'd met Chandra, and that we'd met this couple called Charles and Lola. There was silence, and after that it gushed out. All I can say is that I hope it was a relief for him. And painful as it must have been, I hope he feels better for sharing this with me. He's not well, you know, and in spite of the fact that his businesses have made him a very wealthy man, I doubt he's ever been happy. His marriage to my mother lasted no time at all.'

Jessica reached across and put her hand on Sebastian's. 'Look, I'm *sure* he's not my biological father. I was almost five when my parents died, and there would have been a divorce or something before that if he was. But fancy him supporting me for that length of time and putting me through school. Aunt Catherine said it was a fund set up by her and my uncle from my parents' legacy.' She had a sudden flash of clarity. 'So, just think it through, my adoptive parents must have known your father. And about you. And about everything...they must have! I never suspected anything, and they never told me. No wonder my aunt, on her deathbed, urged me to come to India to find the truth. She must have been in league with your father and Meredith Bateman all the time. Now *I* feel angry! Oh my God—why these secrets? And they must have thought that history was repeating itself when I had Saffie.'

Sebastian stood up and walked to the veranda balustrade, Jessica went to stand by his side. Together they looked out to infinity.

'Please don't be angry, Sebastian. This happened such a long time ago. People lived different lives—very straight and very narrow. Moral values were different. These things happened, and I've heard that the colonials were the worst offenders. In those days it was swept under the carpet, not flaunted like it is today. And couples *did* stay married, and carried on with mistresses and lovers. I guess people turned a blind eye to it all. Your father and my mother were no different to thousands of other adulterous ex-pats in India.

'The fire? I'm inclined to believe Chandra's story. She was there that night, nearly lost her life.'

Sebastian turned and moved towards her, searching her face. 'Jessica, would you mind if I gave you a great big hug?'

'And me, you?' She replied. Their need for comfort was mutual right now as she pressed her face into his shoulder, feeling relieved and safe with his arms wrapped around her.

Sebastian suddenly stiffened, holding her at arm's length. 'Didn't we arrange to meet Charles and Lola tonight?'

She laughed. 'No, relax, tomorrow after breakfast. We have the night to ourselves.'

'I have a bright idea. Why don't we send for room service, and have dinner together out here in this romantic spot?'

'Yes!' Jessica was excited at the thought. 'We can carry on imagining what may or may not have happened. And I will tell you *my* exciting news!'

'I'll call the waiter, but first things first, how about a stiff drink? Immediately.'

'A large G&T, please, barman…'

34

Shimla 1947:

Edward was rousing when the knock came on the front door of his cottage at the Shimla Club.

Glancing at the clock, he noted it was not yet eight. The knock came again. This time, louder.

'Alright. Alright, I'm coming,' he shouted across the expanse of his living-room as he headed for the front door, wrapping his dressing-gown around him.

He opened the door to a messenger boy nervously holding out a large official-looking envelope in both hands. Edward rubbed his eyes and took the envelope.

'Please, Sahib. You sign. Please.' The boy handed him a pen and a paper for him to sign. 'From the Court House. Sahib.'

At once, Edward knew it was the summons for him to attend the inquest. Handing the signed paper back to the messenger, he thanked the boy and, fingers trembling, began to open the envelope. Walking back into his living room, he made himself comfortable, preparing to read and digest the contents. The date set for the inquest was just two days away. Instructions enclosed were for him to give evidence as the only witness to two deaths, and the conflagration of The Laurels.

The wording was formal and to the point. Edward had to fight back a mixture of anger and sadness at the thought of telling the irrefutable facts of what, to him, was the most life-changing event he was ever likely to encounter. There was no choice for him to opt out, no proviso for him to excuse himself. He had to be there. He had to give evidence, and had to base it on the account he'd given to the police the morning after the tragedy.

He tried to remember the statement he'd signed—the true and accurate record of what happened that fateful night. He remembered Charles' words telling him it would all be over in minutes and he would merely have to agree to it all before the coroner. *Highly unlikely to have a jury for a case like this...merely a formality,* he'd said. But Edward was still convinced he'd break under questioning and become tied up in knots over the economical truth in his original statement.

Making breakfast, Edward started to recall the events of that night, and the actions taken. *How could I ever forget striking James so cruelly? So violent, so out-of-character for me.* Words rattled round his brain. What if he were boxed into a corner by questions, *self-defence, accidental?* Perhaps.

Or would he simply have to verify his statement to the court? It was, after all, as Charles had said, not a trial. Merely for the record, to determine the cause of death of Elizabeth and James. *Still, I don't have much longer to worry about it now, and at last I'll be able to get on with arranging the funeral.* He determined to do that this very day, and to go and see Charles and Lola this evening. He'd stop by at Hermione's as he did every day before Jessica went to bed, to read her a bedtime story. His sole focus in life was Jessica now, her wellbeing and safety, and he was pleased that she'd settled well into Hermione and Andrew's household. Their son, George, had proved to be a good playmate.

'Uncle Edward!' Jessica ran towards him, arms outstretched. 'Uncle Edward, come, come and look what I did today at nursery school. Come.' She tugged his hand and he obediently followed her upstairs to her room, looking back at Hermione who also urged him on with a serious look on her face.

'Look at my picture, Uncle Edward.' She rummaged through the sheets of paper on her table and proudly held out today's creative effort for him to see.

'Oh! Oh…that's…er…very good, Jessica…'

'Look. There's mummy and daddy. And there's me and...'

Edward stared at her picture. 'And…?'

'Oh, and that's a big big fire, and Teddy, and look…see, there's you and mummy again!'

Stunned and upset, Edward was doing all he could to stave off the emotion welling up inside him. He stared at the images neatly drawn by this four-year-old innocent child who didn't ask questions anymore about her missing parents. It was obvious to him that her mind was in turmoil.

This graphic insight into her inner self told him more than she could ever say in words. In this picture, she was telling everyone what she knew but never talked about. How was he going to deal with this window into her young mind? He took the picture and went downstairs, steadying his hand on the handrail, with Jessica trailing behind him. Hermione was waiting in the hall and searched Edward's face as he descended the last step.

'Jessica did well at nursery today, Uncle Edward, didn't you, Jessie? She painted lots of pictures, and she's starting to read. Aren't you, Jessie?' Jessica nodded, trying to take the picture from Edward who was still mesmerised, not knowing whether to ask her about it, or simply dismiss it.

'Yes, it's all very good, Jessie. Very good.' Attempting to pull himself together, he placed the picture on the table in the hall at the foot of the stairs. 'Now, young lady, how about a nice bedtime story?' He forced a joyful attitude and ushered her back to her bedroom. 'Come on angel, you must be very tired doing all these pictures and reading books. George is already asleep, shh. Into bed now, here's Teddy.' He picked up a story book and sat next to her, stroking her hair. He read a few pages of *Winnie the Pooh*, and tucking her in, kissed her forehead and stayed with her until she fell asleep.

'Hermione—how are you? Sorry to barge in again, but glad I did. What do you think about Jessie's picture?' He sat on the edge of the sofa, waiting for Hermione's response.

'I thought you'd be shocked, Edward. The poor little girl must have demons inside her head, but she never talks about it, you know. It's almost as though she's blanked it out. But not completely, obviously.'

'I know. But what can we do? She doesn't mention her parents, but thinks it alright to paint a picture of them. And everything else in it, dear God—do you think she needs special help?'

Hermione shook her head. 'No, Edward, leave it alone. In her own way, she'll find a way to cope, and the memories will fade. She's very young, and as soon as she goes to her new life in England, she'll have other things to occupy her mind. The poor mite, we must all give her as much love and support as we can.'

'Yes, that's all we can do.' Edward stood up and sighed, heading for the door. As he passed the hall table, he picked up Jessica's picture, folded it, and put in his pocket. 'I have to go to Hilltop House now— I've just had notification about the inquest, and I also need to make funeral arrangements and tell the family in England. Lots to do, and we still have to sell James's car.'

'Bye Edward. We'll see you tomorrow?'

'Till tomorrow, goodbye, Hermione, and thanks. Give my best to Andrew. Bye!'

35

Shimla 1997:

The flickering candle on Jessica and Sebastian's table, was the only illumination on the veranda that spanned guest rooms to the left and right. Bathed in this, and in memories, reminiscences and revelations, their evening had turned softly into night. They digested every word, along with the splendid food and wine that kept arriving. Jessica adjusted her warm wrap as chilled air tumbled down from the mountains.

Sebastian reached over and took her hand in his. 'Shall we go inside? You're looking cold.'

Jessica smiled at him. *Why was he so attentive? why was he so...so...gentlemanly and, well, kind?* As their eyes met, she had a sudden and powerful sensation she was being seduced. She thought the impossible. Could she be falling in love? *Or is it simply animal instinct and raw lust?* Whatever it was, she didn't fight it, but allowed him to lead her into his room. They sat on his bed saying nothing. Jessica began to feel embarrassed.

'Sebastian...' She looked up into his face as he drew her towards him.

'Shhh...we've talked enough.'

'But...!' She stiffened, as his lips brushed hers. 'It was never meant to be like this. We were never meant to be more than just friends. Friends shouldn't, can't, be like this.'

He placed a hand over hers, his other forefinger pressing her lips to stifle her protests.

'It *is* exactly like this is. It always was. It always will be. I love you, Jessica—I've loved you from the moment I first set eyes on you.'

Jessica reached up and cupped his face in her hands, searching his eyes. Was he leading her on, or did he mean what he was saying? She couldn't be sure. But nor could she stop herself surrendering to his will. She could feel that he wanted her, there was no doubt about that. And she wanted him, too, more than she could have ever thought possible. She allowed her body to yield, folding herself softly into him, as he half turned away from her and switched off the light...

The telephone rang and Jessica was instantly awake. Sebastian was already up and dressed. She leaned on her elbows, watching him as he rushed to answer the phone. She noticed her dressing-gown on the bed. She shrugged it on, thinking how thoughtful of him to go and fetch it for her. Standing, she smoothed her hair with her hands, stretched, and wandered across the room. He was listening intently to the caller, not replying other than the occasional *hmm* or, *yes*. Finally, he stood, and whilst still listening, put his hand over the mouthpiece and said good morning to Jessica with a wink of his eye.

'Okay, thanks, dad. Yes, I'll call later. Bye.'

Knowing that he was talking to Edward, Jessica looked quizzically at him as he walked over to embrace her.

'Dad!' He spoke over her shoulder. 'He wants me to ring him after we've met with Charles and Lola. Says they might not remember everything that happened, so not to take too much notice. He gave me the rundown of what happened at the inquest. They were there, apparently. I guess he needed all the support he could get having to deal with the fire and your parents' death, the funeral, and everything else before you left.'

'I know. I often wonder what it was like here, and how things must have been so different and difficult, compared to today. I try to imagine my parents' lives, but it's so long ago, I'll have to delve into the history books to find out more.' She looked around for her clothes, preparing to go back to her room.

Jessica stood in front of him, having first scooped up all her belongings. 'So...look at us, here, now. Finding ourselves in this maze of confusion like rogue waves crashing over each other on the shore.'

Sebastian smiled at her analogy. 'Go on—let's get ready for the final crash. We have to meet Charles and Lola in an hour.'

Jessica carefully opened his French doors and poked her head out to the veranda to check she was not being observed. Smiling, she blithely tiptoed next door to her room, still bathed in the afterglow of last night's passion. She showered and prepared to go down to breakfast.

Spotting Lola at a table in the middle of the dining room, Jessica and Sebastian headed over to join her and Charles. They passed the buffet table that was groaning with a variety of delicacies that anyone might possibly want or need. Charles stood up as they approached, hand outstretched.

'Good morning, Jessica, good morning, Sebastian. I trust you had a relaxing evening?'

Jessica shot a glance at Sebastian. 'Um, yes, very good, thanks. We had dinner on the veranda. You should do it, magnificent views of the mountains even after the sun goes down.' She smiled and looked once more at Sebastian, who had an urge to reach out for her hand as they sat down.

'But before that, I managed to have a good conversation with my father. And Jessica talked to her daughter, too.'

'Oh, do tell us.' Said Lola, leaning forward.

'Well, firstly, he hopes you'll get in touch when you get home, and if you can, travel to Devon to see him. He said he'd love to see you after all this time, and how clever we were to have met you, here in Shimla, of all places.' Sebastian fished in his inside jacket pocket, pulled out a piece of the hotel's notepaper, and handed it to Charles. 'Here, before I forget. Here's his address and phone number. I also talked to him this morning. He rang me before we came to breakfast—heck, I've just realised how late it must have been for him—and he said he'd try to fill in the fifty or so years since you saw each other. You must have been very good friends.'

'Very good friends, Sebastian, and I can tell you, after the horrible times we went through together, the shocking way he was treated at the inquest, and how so-called friends talked about him after he left…well, I won't say too much. But some things you never forget.' Charles, animated now, wanted to continue just as a waiter approached them to take their orders.

Jessica wanted to know more and asked Charles if he could remember specific incidents. She asked him who looked after her before her aunt and uncle arrived for the funeral, but Lola interrupted before he could open his mouth.

'Oh, my dear, it was very sad for you. As far as I can remember, you went to stay with a friend—oh, Charles, what were they called, the couple with the little boy? Fredah—yes that's it, and her husband…?'

'Lola, I just can't remember, you know, but all I can say, Jessica, is that you were very well looked after, and Edward did all he could for you. You were heartbroken and kept asking for your mummy and daddy. It was all very sad indeed.

'Now, here comes breakfast. Delicious food here. Don't you think, Sebastian?' Charles shook the napkin out on his lap and looked expectantly at the waiter adjusting the cutlery lined up before him.

Jessica and Sebastian exchanged glances, both sensing his apparent sudden lack of interest in them now. Jessica held her hand to her mouth, to cover her amused expression, whilst Sebastian shot her a knowing wink, and smiled sardonically. They both thought their companions just might be able to dredge up some more information, even though they now realised they were likely to be very unreliable memories.

36

Shimla 1947:

Images and invented scenarios had been jostling around Edward's brain for most of the night.

He stood in front of his mirror realising how little he knew about what might happen today. He had no knowledge of what procedures would take place, or even who the officiating judge might be, or whether there would be a jury.

He'd kept his remembered statement at the forefront of his mind, silently rehearsing salient points. Knowing the likelihood of him being questioned and cross-questioned, he suddenly felt alone and in the dark. Edward adjusted his uniform, pinned his ribbon bar on the left chest and tucked his officer's hat under his right arm. He sat, staring at his highly polished shoes for what seemed like hours, waiting for Charles to collect him and take him to the courthouse.

They arrived early, announced themselves to a guard, and were ushered into the courtroom. A few people were already sitting in the public benches, and a policeman stood on the raised dais next to a door to the rear of the building. The sign *Jailer's Entrance* over the door did nothing to quell Edward's rising anxiety. The dais was fully enclosed with carved mahogany railings, a lectern and judicial chair behind. The punkah wallah took his place, cross-legged on the floor, and began his job of activating the slow movement of fans above the officiating area. Dark timber panelling covered the walls to a height of about four feet, finished off with an ornate dado rail.

Edward was shown to a side table at right angles to the dais, set with writing paper and pen and ink. He put his hat on the table in front of him and looked around. Opposite him was another table for official use. Charles took his place on the front row of benches. The room gradually filled with friends, curious spectators, students, and locals. A large clock hung on the wall above a portrait of King George VI. Edward stared at it absent-mindedly. Turning, he glanced up at the stranger's gallery and down to the benches. Familiar faces smiled at him, which helped to release some of the tension he was feeling. Opposite him a clerk sat down, flanked by the police constables he recognised from the day after the fire. They nodded acknowledgement across the void separating the two tables. A stack of papers was laid in front of them, and Edward thought he caught a glimpse of a glossy photograph.

Sitting back in his chair, he observed the jury stalls and his heart sank as one by one, twelve men filed in and settled into them. Three minutes to go. He assumed proceedings would commence on time.

'Please rise for the Judicial Magistrate.' A heavy gavel loudly hit a small table on the dais. Everyone in the courtroom stood as the First-Class Judicial Magistrate entered through the jailer's door, looked around the room, and made himself comfortable behind the lectern.

He addressed the crowd. 'Please be seated. I have been appointed by the government to make inquiries in this courthouse today. I represent the coroner and will officiate in hearing evidence to the circumstances of the tragic and sudden death of Mr James and Mrs Elizabeth Delaney, who perished in a fire at their Shimla home, The Laurels, on the night of July the fifteenth, in the year of our Lord, nineteen-forty-seven. The remains of the bodies have been examined to ascertain their identity. These are kept in the mortuary, pending the outcome of this hearing, and subsequent interment.' He continued with the known facts from a prepared script, assisted by the police constable from time to time, as to location and timing of the occurrence.

'This court is not a court of trial, it is a court of inquiry into the cause of death, and as such, I first call on Major Edward Shelley, who appears to be the only witness to the scene of the incident. Major Shelley supplied the police with a full statement immediately after the event, and subsequently signed the papers as being a true and accurate account of circumstances of this incident. I will now call on Major Shelley to recount those circumstances, after which I will be able to make an informed assessment, and declare my verdict. Major Shelley, would you please take the witness stand.'

Edward, trying to conceal his uneasiness, walked over to the stand, and turned to face the throng before him in the courthouse. He grasped the rail nervously, feeling blood rush to his face, and ran a finger along his collar. Placing his right hand on the Holy Bible, the oath was read to him. He agreed to tell the truth, the whole truth and nothing but the truth.

He turned back to face the magistrate.

'Major Shelley, you were at the scene of the fire on the night Mr and Mrs Delaney died?'

'Yes, your honour. I had taken them both home from a friend's house.'

'And can you tell me why you took them home?'

'Mr Delaney's car failed to start, so I offered. I had a long-standing friendship with the Delaneys.' Edward shifted his stance as he heard mumblings in the crowd.

'So, Major, tell me what you remember about what happened after you all arrived at The Laurels. I have a copy of your statement to hand.' The magistrate held up a file, waving it at the police officers and jury.

'We arrived at the house and decided to have a nightcap in the drawing room. Ranjit, their houseboy had stoked up the fire in that room for Mr and Mrs Delaney's return. I entered the room first, and poured drinks for myself and Mrs Delaney. She had gone upstairs to help her husband, who had seemingly drunk too much at the party we had been attending, and Mrs Delaney thought he might go straight to bed.' Edward heard whispers from the public benches.

'But Mr Delaney must not have gone to bed, because his body was found next to his wife's in what was left of the drawing room, after the fire.' The magistrate grimaced, raising his eyebrows.

'Yes, Your Honour, that's correct. Elizabeth—Mrs Delaney—came downstairs and we were recalling the evening over the nightcap, when Mr Delaney staggered into the room in his robe and pyjamas. He demanded a large brandy which I poured for him.'

'So, from that convivial, albeit somewhat drunken state, how could this tragedy have happened, Major Shelley?'

Lowering his head, Edward took a deep breath, wishing he had the statement in front of him. 'Mr Delaney became abusive towards his wife, your honour. He was accusing her of adultery.' He looked up as a sharp intake of breath was heard in the room.

The magistrate looked up, too, quickly returning to his questions. 'So what happened, Major?'

'Suddenly, and out of character, Mr Delaney struck out at his wife, causing her to trip and fall backwards. I tried to stop him but he pushed her so hard that she hit her head on the marble mantelpiece before collapsing into the hearth. In his fumbling, he had accidentally spilled his brandy from his glass onto her dress, which caught fire almost immediately. I tried to pull Mrs Delaney from the flames, and prevent the fire taking hold. She appeared to me to be unconscious. At the same time, I found myself warding off Mr Delaney's attempt to push me into the fireplace, too. He staggered into the drinks table, smashing his hands on a glass before crumpling to the floor.'

'Major Shelley. Bear with me. I am just trying to establish whether you could have rescued Mr and Mrs Delaney at that time. Can you tell me what happened after that?'

'Your Honour, I suppose I panicked, ran out and shouted for Ranjit to help with water to extinguish the fire, but he was nowhere to be found. I thought about ringing the fire brigade, but it was after midnight, and I knew it would be futile. By the time they got there, the damage would have been done.' Edward saw Charles in the sea of faces and wished he could take over for him. 'When I re-entered the drawing room, the fire had spread rapidly, and trying to forge a way through to the bodies, I realised that I was endangering both myself and the other occupants of the house. Upstairs there was a child and her ayah in the nursery. I could not believe how quickly the fire took hold, and I was unable to locate a source of water sufficient to tackle the flames.'

'How long would you say between the first onset of the fire to the house becoming unsafe, Major?'

'Oh, huh, I lost all track of time. I knew I had to rescue their daughter, Jessica, and her nanny, and by the time I decided to abandon the flaming room, I retreated to the hallway, and found the nanny standing there, transfixed. I think I rushed up the stairs through the smoke and took Jessica from her bed, went downstairs and outside to put her in the car. I yelled at Chandra to get out quickly, but she insisted on going back into the house and climbing the flaming staircase to fetch Jessica's Teddy and some blankets. I also realised I had left the keys to my car on the hall table, and fought my way through the flames and smoke to find them. Chandra was shouting for help on the landing. The fire had caught hold of her clothes. I managed to clamber up the burning staircase and carry her down just before the landing collapsed.' Edward wiped his brow, not wanting to answer any more questions.

'I appreciate this event was extremely traumatic for you, Major, but just one more thing, if you don't mind?' The magistrate turned and asked the clerk to pass some papers to him. 'I have here, Major, the pathologist's report after his brief inspection of the remains of the dead. I just wondered, can you throw any light on his finding that Mr Delaney appeared to have suffered a blow to the head so severe that it broke his skull? You see, to all intents and purposes, the deaths were caused by asphyxiation, but there are other observations that need to be explained before I can close this inquest and decide upon a verdict.'

'Your honour, Mr Delaney fell alongside his wife's lifeless body and may have suffered the same injuries as his wife. I was not able to see exactly how Mr Delaney died.'

The magistrate paused, silently reading Edward's statement. 'Major Shelley, according to your statement, you were forced to abandon the flaming room. The police report of the aftermath states that the remains of Mr Delaney's body were found three feet away from his wife's. So, forgive me, but why would you not have tried to lead Mr Delaney from the room? Could the nanny not have helped? Did she witness the scene before the fire became critical?'

Edward looked to the ceiling pretending to recall clouded memories. 'Your honour, everything that night happened so quickly. I think Mr Delaney fell onto the flames. I cannot know if he hit his head as he fell. I was in and out of the room, trying to find water, to get help, and planning to save the other occupants of the house. I'm sorry, but I cannot explain what might have happened. Chandra may have seen events, but I'm not sure. She's still in a critical condition in Chandigarh hospital.'

An eerie silence fell on the courtroom. Edward glanced across the faces as he was ushered back to his chair. He stiffened and looked at the magistrate. The clerk and the jury were still scribbling in notepads, and the police officers sat expressionless, squaring up their papers on the desk for something to do. The magistrate spoke to the clerk and to the jury, and closed his file. People in the room shuffled their feet and waited. He sat behind his table as the Jury retired to consider their verdict.

One young man, dressed in smart mufti, whom Edward didn't recognise, stood, acknowledged the magistrate, and left the courtroom.

The magistrate cleared his throat as the jury filed back into their benches. The gavel hit the table once more and silence descended.

'Major Shelley, honourable ladies and gentlemen, we are now decided upon a verdict and propose to bring these proceedings swiftly to a satisfactory close.' He turned to the jury and nodded.

Beads of sweat gathered on Edward's brow.

37

Shimla 1997:

While Charles and Lola tucked into their breakfast, Sebastian and Jessica walked over to the buffet table to choose their own. They followed each other around the table, collecting healthy-looking food, and taking the opportunity to exchange a few private thoughts with each other at the same time.

'Sebastian, I think your father might be right, you know, about them not remembering much. I'm not sure I believe what they've said.'

'I was thinking the same thing, perhaps we should take it all with a pinch of salt—but if you think about it, they haven't had the need to bring back those memories for what must be a good fifty years.'

Plates brimming, they stood chatting before going back to join Charles and Lola. Jessica suggested they simply go with the flow and not ask too many more questions. 'Let's just humour them, Sebastian, and we'll take them, as planned, to see Chandra. Perhaps we could leave soon after breakfast.'

'Good idea, come on, let's go and eat, I'm starving!' They took their seats at the table, and Sebastian waited for the opportunity to remind them about going to Chandra's.

Charles stiffened. 'Oh dear! Ah!' He looked at Lola. 'Um, I don't think we'll have time, we suddenly realised this morning, that we have to leave this afternoon. We were thinking we had a few more days, but when we checked our tickets, it came as a complete shock—good thing we did, hey, Lola?'

'We have to go and pack, and make arrangements to get to the station,' Lola explained. 'I'm so very sorry—I think we've just lost track of time. I guess it's easy to do, staying here at this beautiful place. I'm sorry, Jessica, but now that we have Edward's contact details, I just know we'll all see each other back home.'

Jessica fished her notepad out of her bag. 'Here, I'll give you my phone number and you can call me as well, and perhaps…write yours here, and your address. We'll see each other again you can guarantee that. In fact, I should be back in England in a week or so. We're going to book my return ticket today.' She looked at Sebastian.

'Yes,' said Sebastian, 'and I have to return to Delhi soon. But I intend to travel back to England for a while to see my father. We have lots to talk about now, and he'll have to answer a few of my questions...'

'So, all back to Blighty. Just like the old days—because regardless of whether we were born in India or not, we always called England home.' Charles cocked his head and smiled perceptively, remembering how it was.

'I can't believe the co-incidence,' Jessica said. 'I just think our meeting was meant to be. I've been here long enough now to get to the bottom of what happened to my parents. I've seen what I want to see, and felt the energy of the places we've been taken to, including the ruins of The Laurels. I've cried, been shocked, and I've learned a great deal. Yes, it did come as a massive surprise to me. It all seemed so simple before I left home—go to Shimla, find my parents' graves, find the registry for dates and events in the family, and have a bit of a holiday in the meantime. My mind has been set on doing this for such a long time. I just needed to turn those last pages and close the book.'

Sebastian added to the story, 'I came onto the scene, not exactly by chance, I'll have you know. My father wanted me to make contact with Jessica and steer her through what he knew would be a minefield.'

'Yes, and it has been, but I don't know how I would have been able to find my way without Sebastian. And, well...we're close friends now.' Jessica lowered her eyes, wiped her mouth with her napkin, and glanced at Sebastian, trying hard not to give anything away. She looked across at their table companions, wide-eyed and innocent.

Sebastian took up the conversation. 'How will you travel back? I guess you're off on the train to Chandigarh, Delhi, and fly back to London? Pretty much what we'll do, although I'll spend some time at my office before flying back.' He looked at Jessica, taking her hand. 'I'll take this lady as far as Delhi and put her safely on a flight first.'

'But today, after we've been to see Chandra, I'm going to do some shopping, and later we're both going to climb the steep hill to the Monkey Temple. Sebastian says it's a must.'

Lola became animated. 'Oh yes! You simply have to do that. That view...'

She was cut off by Charles. 'Now, Lola—don't tell her too much, it has to be a real surprise.'

'Well, I can't wait, even though I've been told it can be an arduous walk. But I'll have this man to hang on to…' She put her hand on Sebastian's arm. 'Won't I?'

'Of course!' replied Sebastian, smiling, and, turning his attention to Charles, 'Won't you let us help you later with your luggage, and go with you to the station this evening?'

'Dear boy, that's a very generous offer, but we have it all in hand. The hotel knows us well, and they take care of everything, but if we need anything at the last minute, I'll call you. We leave at about four o'clock.'

'I hope you have a good journey back. It's a long one to take, but you're used to it, I guess.' Jessica smiled at Charles and Lola.

'This will be the last time, Jessica. We're definitely getting past all this travelling now. Yes, we'll be saying a fond farewell to Shimla today, as the train pulls out of the station.' Lola said, mournfully, getting up from the table and helping Charles to his feet. 'You see what I mean?'

'Well, goodbye, and bon voyage. We can all look forward to meeting again back in England.' Sebastian and Jessica shook hands with them, and they watched as the couple left the room.

'Shall we go? I think we'd better get our tickets sorted out first before we go to see Chandra.'

'It's going to be another big day, but let's get it done. And tonight…tonight I'm going to take you out to dinner to a very special place…no, I'm not telling where, but you'll love it.'

Jessica leaned closer to him hooking her arm into his with a new self-confidence and intimacy. 'You lead, I'll follow,' she whispered in his ear, already looking forward to the evening.

38

Shimla 1947:

L adies and gentlemen. The evidence presented here today at this inquest into the deaths of Mr Mrs James Delaney has been considered by the jury. The verdict had more than a few options to be determined before conclusion. The cause of death in this case could range from asphyxiation to fatal blows on the head caused by falling debris or other heavy objects. Or by incineration.

'By the time the remains of the bodies were discovered, the surrounding building had been razed to the ground. The only plausible evidence we heard was from Major Shelley who was the only witness at the scene. In light of this uncertainty, the jury has therefore reached an Open Verdict.' The magistrate paused as a flurry of whispers echoed through the courthouse.

'Should further substantial evidence come to light at any time in the future, the court has the right to re-open the case and present that evidence. However, re-opening a coroner's inquiry is extremely rare. The court records will therefore be archived for fifty years from today's date.

'I expect this to be the end of this case, and the hearing is now officially closed.'

An air of relief settled around court officials, jury and the police. All stood as the magistrate left the chamber. Papers were cleared from desks, the crowd began to talk animatedly, and Edward, still tense and worried, took a clean white handkerchief from his pocket and wiped the sweat from his brow.

Charles was making his way over to where Edward remained seated, elbows on knees, trying to relax and take it all in. He was grinning from ear to ear, and congratulated Edward on his sterling performance.

The courthouse began to empty. Edward looked at the number of people there. Friends and acquaintances departed without a backward glance.

'Come on, Charles, I need a stiff drink. Let's go to the club.' Edward left the room, followed by his friend. He placed his hat firmly on his head as they walked towards Charles' car.

They drove in silence for a while. Edward was still digesting the proceedings of the morning. He was clearly worried by the verdict.

'Charles, what if someone comes forward? What if word has got around? People read between the lines you know, and maybe...'

'Look, only I know the truth of the matter. I don't think even Lola knows, and anyway, even if she did, there's no way she'd upset the apple cart on a vague notion that all was not exactly as presented. We can't bring back Elizabeth and James.'

Edward thought about it. 'You're right, Charles, of course you're right. I need to dismiss those thoughts and get on with what lies ahead. Later, before I go to see Jessica, I'll get a date set for the funeral, phone Catherine, and set the wheels in motion. And I have to sell James' car.'

'I'm sure you'll sell it easily, old man. In fact, why don't you put an advertisement on the notice board at the club right now.'

Edward was more positive as they turned up the hill towards the Shimla Club, and began to relax. 'I'll do that. What do you think I should ask? I'd like to think the proceeds will pay for Jessica's passage. If there's a surplus, I'll open a bank account for her at Barclays. If not, I'll put in some funds of my own.'

The Club was busier than usual for the time of day. Edward noticed immediately that many people from the courthouse had decided to go there as well. He felt intimidated, not knowing their reactions, not knowing what they had privately discussed. He straightened his shoulders, took a deep breath, smiled bravely and walked towards the bar. Charles ordered drinks, as some members stood up. One person began to applaud. Others joined in. Edward turned to look and the applause became louder. Faces smiled at him from the throng as the ovation died down.

'For your bravery, Edward, for doing all you could in those difficult circumstances.' Fredah spoke for them all as a chorus of *hear, hear,* rang out and glasses were raised in a toast.

Embarrassed, Edward bowed his head. 'Thank you, my dear friends, thank you—your sentiments are much appreciated.' He turned and picked up his glass from the bar and raised it to them, in gratitude.

Immediately his anxiety melted away, and his guilt-ridden thoughts turned towards his courage and daring on the night of the fire. He and

Charles sat at the bar and Charles slapped him on the back. 'Here's to you, old chum!' They both downed their whisky and Charles ordered more. 'No need to worry, Edward, it's all over now. Let's get on with the necessary tasks, and make plans for the next few weeks.'

'Yes, we must,' replied Edward, 'I can feel another list coming on…' his tension was released.

'How about coming over for dinner tonight? I'll tell Lola to cater for you, and you can do your phone calls from our house.'

'Thanks, Charles. My first priority is to set a date for the funeral, and I'll be able to tell Catherine when she has to book her passage. I'll have to allow enough time for her to get here. Would you think, say, three weeks hence would be enough? I've also to book a berth for Jessica, back on the same ship. Or perhaps we can do that when they get here from England for the funeral…'

Already, Edward could see more clearly, and was keen to get on with everything. There were lots of things to do, and he made mental notes to prioritise. Immediately, his future planning took centre stage. He felt a pat on the back, and Philip joined them at the bar.

'What now, Edward? I guess it's fallen to you to tidy up the mess left behind. If there's anything Fredah and I can do to help, please let us know.'

'Very kind, Philip. Thanks. In fact, you don't happen to know anyone who might like to buy James' car, do you? I have to raise money for Jessica and her passage to England. Also, there's the funeral to organise once we have a date for Elizabeth's sister and husband steaming over for it. They're going to take Jessica back to England to live with them. She's staying at Hermione's. Their three-year-old boy, George, and Jessica play well together, and it serves to keep her occupied. The poor little girl.' Edward's expression changed to one of sadness.

'Yes, but you've set her on the right track, so let's hope she'll be alright. Have you told her yet about the plans for her to go to England?'

'Philip, no. In fact, she's stopped asking about her parents, and we don't know how to broach the subject. I mean, she must remember the night of the fire, but all she's done is draw pictures. It's as though she knows but doesn't want to hear it. We decided to wait until she was ready so we've told her nothing. As far as her meeting her aunt and uncle from England and travelling back with them, well, she might not be able to grasp it all anyway. We'll explain when the time comes.'

'Good luck with it all, Edward. And please, remember, we're here to help—and, I imagine, so is everyone else. I'll put out some feelers for the sale of the car and let you know.'

Edward collected a piece of paper from the office and wrote a quick advertisement for James' car to put on the notice board. He and Charles left the club house. They set a time for Edward to go over for dinner, and shook hands before parting.

As Charles drove home to Hilltop House, Edward retreated to his cottage, relieved and buoyed by the reception he'd received. He took off his uniform and donned civvies, eager to get things moving along, to plan ahead and to close a few chapters of the book of events that had now changed his life.

39

Shimla 1997:

Jessica returned to her room while Sebastian waited in the hotel lobby. She gathered up what she needed for the day out, and for shopping. She wanted to buy Chandra something, as well as silk fabric and clothing to take home for Saffron. She wondered if she needed to take a memento back for Meredith Bateman, and thought if she found something appropriate, she'd buy it for him. Believing that today might be her last day with Sebastian, she felt a pang of sadness, but realised she'd been in Shimla long enough.

Sebastian had ordered a driver for the day, and the car was waiting outside.

'All set?' He smiled at Jessica and guided her into the car. 'So, where to first, madam?'

'I think our priority is to see the travel agent and get my…our tickets booked, don't you?'

'We'll go to see Rafiq at Sunpex Travel, he's been arranging my train tickets and flights for years.'

Sebastian gave instructions to the driver and settled into the back seat with Jessica.

and instructed the driver to pull in and wait, as they arrived at the travel agent's premises.

It took them a good hour to get everything organised, with Rafiq spending an inordinate amount of time on the phone making copious notes. Finally, checking the itinerary he'd prepared for them, they were asked to return in the afternoon to collect the wads of paper tickets for their travel.

Sebastian asked their driver to proceed to the morning markets. Time went by quickly as they meandered between fruit and vegetable stalls set out beautifully to attract the crowds of shoppers. They picked their way through pools of muddy water past sad sights of birds and puppies in cages, and stopped briefly to watch a man try to charm a snake from its basket. Powerful smells of spices drifted through the air, together with a whiff of rotting vegetation. Jostling crowds pushed and bumped into them, and traders tried to attract their attention, waving bright scarves and ornaments. But they were on a mission, with little time to spare.

Jessica shuddered at the animals in cages, and walked briskly towards the fabric stalls, steered by Sebastian. Women crowded around, lifting beautiful filmy swathes of sheer, raw, and embroidered silks, holding colours to their faces and checking in the mirrors. Sounds of excitement surrounded her as she stroked bolts of silk, admiring the shine, or colour or fineness. Ready-made saris were selling fast as she pushed her way to the front of the stall to get attention. Sebastian said he'd be back in fifteen minutes, explaining that he wanted to find something for his mother.

Jessica chose a bright turquoise sari edged in gold for Saffron. It shimmered opalescent like a dragonfly's gossamer wings. Calculating how much yardage she'd need to make a long evening dress, she also chose emerald green silk-satin, and a deep blue translucent shot-silk to take home. No sooner had she fished out the money from her purse than she felt a hand on her shoulder and turned to see Sebastian standing right behind her.

They forced their way through the throng and Jessica asked where she might buy something for Chandra.

'Hm…you know, I think she would be thrilled with a small sari clasp.'

'Or perhaps a pair of earrings? I noticed she likes her earrings.' Jessica said.

'Right, come this way.' And Sebastian once again steered her away from the fabric stalls to a quieter area where men and women alike fingered and admired gold chains, pearls and amethyst jewellery.

'Here, Sebastian, look—lots of gold earrings.' Together, they chose the earrings, large discs of gold surrounded by a delicate tracery of filigree silver, dropping from a pearl stud. She put the packet into her bag and grabbed his arm.

'Let's get out of here, Sebastian. I'm starting to feel claustrophobic!'

They got the driver to drop them at the winding pathway to Chandra's house. The cricket-playing boys must have been at school today, but clanging pots and sweeping brooms were busy, and mouth-watering cooking smells enveloped them on their steep climb.

The door was open, and sweet smells of incense wafted through it as they stood back waiting for a response to their knock. Jessica tapped the dust from her shoes and smoothed her skirt. She held the roughly-wrapped present behind her back.

Chandra appeared at the door, tightly holding on to the sari half-covering her face. She beckoned them in.

'Dear Chandra, we're leaving Shimla the day after tomorrow, so we wanted to say goodbye before we go. Oh, and...' Jessica stood up and offered the gift. 'I want you to have this to remember me by. I hope you like it.'

Dropping her sari, Chandra held both hands to her face. 'Oh...dear Jessie. Thank you.' She took the small package and placed it down on the table, and took Jessica's hands in hers. Her dreadful scars were now plainly noticeable.

Jessica lifted a hand and raised it to touch Chandra's face. Tears welled in her eyes and she paused, unable to speak. Swallowing, she picked up the present, forcing it into Chandra's hands. 'Here—please open it...we do hope you like it.' Jessica's eyes dropped as she forced a smile.

Chandra appeared overwhelmed by the generosity of her guests. She held up the earrings to her ears. 'Thank you very much. When I wear these, I always remember you, my Jessie.' Looking from one to the other, she invited them to stay for tea.

Sebastian spoke for both, 'Chandra, it is so kind of you to offer, but we have little time today, and we want to go to the temple before getting back to the hotel.'

'Yes,' said Jessica. But we couldn't leave without coming to see you. And I do feel I will be back soon. I feel that part of my heart will be in Shimla forever, now.' They embraced briefly and said goodbye.

Chandra watched as Jessica and Sebastian stepped outside into the bright sunlight and made their way up the footpath. They held hands as they went.

She turned back into her house, as tears rolled down her cheeks.

40

Shimla 1947:

E dward awoke at five-thirty in the afternoon. The strain of the past days had taken its toll, and he'd fallen asleep after the courtroom ordeal and the release of tension at the Shimla Club. He dressed quickly, preparing to go and see Jessica before she went to bed.

He liked to take her a present every day if he could, but today he hadn't had time to buy one. He thought he'd see what he could find for her at the club house. Perhaps a few biscuits if they'd put them in a bag.

He rushed up the steps to the club and came face-to-face with the smart-looking Indian man he recognised from earlier in the day, who'd left the courtroom before the session was officially closed.

'Ah, Mr Delaney?' asked the stranger.

'Yes—didn't I see you in the courthouse this morning?'

'Let me introduce myself. Sonny Singh, junior reporter, *The Shimla Recorder*. I was there to cover the inquiry for the paper. There is a lot of interest by the local press in this inquest. Terrible story, terrible!' He stepped back, sensing Edward's displeasure.

'But you left before the verdict was announced. How can you write an informed report of what occurred at the inquest if you weren't there throughout?' Edward was agitated.

'Ah, Mr Delaney—the rest was just an either-or situation. It was either going to be one thing or the other. I had a deadline to meet for tomorrow's paper.' Singh smiled sweetly.

'Why are you here, now?' Edward was on the defensive.

'Ah, Mr Delaney, you see, I wanted to get other people's opinion to add to the story. But it seems I'm too late. The club is almost empty, you see.'

'Well, I'm sure you can get a transcript from the court to get your facts right, can't you?' Edward waited for an answer.

When it came, it infuriated him. 'There are rumours, Mr Delaney, you know. Rumours. You see, we are aware of goings-on, oh yes, we are aware. There are those in Shimla who think that all is not what it seems…'

'Get out, get out of here. Right now. Don't you ever come back, and if I find any scurrilous reporting published in tomorrow's paper, I'll sue the lot of you.' Edward scowled at the reporter and turned sharply on his heel before walking into the club bar, leaving the man speechless.

'Edward, what can I get you? The usual?'

'Oh, no, no thanks. I came to ask if you had anything I could take to Jessica, it's been such a long day I didn't have time to buy her a present today.'

'How about…err…I know, I bet she'd like a little bag of chocolate buttons? We sometimes serve them with morning coffee.'

'Perfect, Joe. Yes, please, she'd love them.' Edward waited while Joe reappeared holding a small white paper bag. 'Thanks a lot, I'd better be off, I'm late.'

Edward drove to Hermione's, arriving just in time to catch Jessica before she went to bed.

'Uncle Edward!' She ran to him. 'Uncle Edward, you came!' Aunty 'Mione said you might not come today.' She hugged him, all the time looking behind his back, feeling in his pockets and hoping he had brought her a present.

'Yes, Jessie, I have!' Jessica squealed with delight as Edward produced the small paper bag from his inside pocket.

'Thank you, thank you, uncle.' She turned to peck him on the cheek before rushing off to discover the contents of the bag.

Hermione led him into the drawing room. 'How are you, Edward? I heard the inquest was a bit gruelling. Are you okay?'

'I'm fine, just fine. How's Jessie been today?'

They talked about Jessica, and Edward told her about the inquest, explaining that he was now able to arrange a funeral and Jessica's passage back to England.

'I don't want to appear rude,' said Edward, 'but I'll have to get to Charles and Lola's to phone Jessie's Aunt Catherine before she goes out for the day. She has to be told when to book their passage. Tomorrow I'll fix a date so I can think about Jessie's ticket home. Funny, but Shimla's her home, yet we always refer to England as home, don't we?'

He kissed Hermione and gave Jessica a big hug, failing to avoid her sticky chocolate-covered face, and wished her goodbye and sweet dreams.

Apart from the interlude with the reporter, the day had gone well for Edward. He felt light in step and free from anxiety as he drew up outside Hilltop House. He noticed that James' car had been covered with a tarpaulin. He'd have it cleaned before it was sold.

Lola and Charles were waiting for him, and as soon as they'd welcomed him, a glass of whisky was put in his hand. They sat and recalled the morning in court. Lola hadn't been there, so she questioned Edward intensely, raising her glass to his good health and to the future. They decided to call England after supper.

'It'll be a good time, Charles, to get Jessica's aunt and uncle organised and inform them about what to expect when they get to India and Shimla. I'll pin them down to dates, too.'

'Sounds like it's all in the planning now, Edward. You need to get Jessie's passage booked, and the funeral organised.'

'Tomorrow I'll see to all that. Where do you think they ought to stay? I'll book a room for them.' Edward was thinking in detail about their visit, and he wanted to make them feel welcome and comfortable.

'Try the Grand. Paying in Sterling, they'll find it cheap, even though it's the best place in town,' Charles suggested.

'I've just had a thought—I'll pay all the funeral costs, and, if they ask, I'll be clear that I want it that way. It's the least I can do.'

Edward recalled Elizabeth's smiling face. He felt distraught, alone and unloved. If only things had been different, if only James hadn't attacked her, if only she'd left him earlier, if only...

Charles broke his reverie by announcing that dinner was ready, and Edward made up the trio who were served roast beef followed by apple pie. The lovely meal gave Edward a feeling of homeliness, a feeling he desperately needed.

'Oh. Charles!' Edward said. 'You didn't see in court this morning because you were sitting at the front, but a smart Indian fella just got up during the proceedings and left the courthouse. I bumped into him just now leaving the club. I asked him why he left before the verdict was announced, and he told me who he was. A reporter from *The Shimla*

Recorder. I asked him why he left early and he said he had a deadline, and intimated that he knew what the verdict would be. He added, cheekily, that there had been rumours around town.'

'What?' Charles was incensed.

'Quite. I told him to get out in no uncertain terms, and that if anything slanderous is published in tomorrow's paper, I'd damned well sue them.'

'Good for you, dear boy, they're all out now for anything to disgrace us, now that we're leaving India. Sometimes cocky and sometimes dangerous, you know. I believe there have been more attacks on the British in Delhi, as well as on those poor Muslims trekking out to their new areas. They're leaving early, in their droves, while they can, before complete anarchy sets in. At least we're somewhat protected here in this backwater. I hope.' Charles looked concerned.

Edward looked at his watch and decided to get a line through to England, excusing himself from the dining table.

'Hello. Hello? Can you hear me? Is that Edward?'

'Yes Catherine, Edward here. I'm afraid the line isn't very good at all. How are you? I'm calling to say that you ought to book your passage as soon as possible. We're over the inquest, it was an open verdict, and tomorrow I'll arrange the funeral. If you can get here in three weeks, I'll set the date for the funeral early in September.'

'I've been doing some research and I'm booked on the Stratheden. She arrives in Bombay on August 30th. Do you think I'll get to Shimla in time?' Catherine sounded doubtful.

'Easy. Go to your agent, and see if he can get a through ticket. Ship, train, train. Train to Chandigarh, train to Shimla—oh, and try to get a daytime one—you'll get to see the scenery as you approach Shimla. Just be sure and ask the agent, there are many trains being used to transport people to Pakistan. You don't want to be anywhere near them. Please ask for first-class luxury. I'm sorry, but I have to tell you that you may be witness to thousands of people on the move. And there has been violence, too. People have been killed in hate and anger. But you'll be alright, so don't worry. We look forward to your arrival, and tomorrow, I'm going to book your stay here. Just let me know what time you'll be in Shimla and I'll be there to greet you.'

'Thank you, Edward. Yes, we've heard here in the news that the partition and the Muslim problem is turning out to be awful. I've been advised to employ an armed guard in Bombay to travel all the way with me, oh, and I hope you don't mind, but I will have to come over on my own. Harold has some urgent ongoing business to attend to. I'll let you know my final plans in a day or two. Goodbye, Edward, and thank you.'

'Bye, Catherine—speak soon.' The line had started to crackle badly and Edward was unsure if she'd heard him clearly. But he was glad to see progress and now wanted to organise funeral details, and Jessica's tickets.

Edward's day had been a real roller-coaster, but the next phase had arrived, and Jessica's last days in India loomed closer.

41

Shimla 1997:

It was lunchtime. Sebastian and Jessica found the café in The Mall where they'd taken refuge after the taxi crashed into a bus on their very first day.

Sebastian said, 'It seems ages since we were here on that disastrous outing.'

Jessica looked around her, remembering little of that day. She looked at him across the table and smiled. 'And look at all that's happened in such a short time. It seems like an impossible dream. Me finding my roots at last, and discovering the truth about my parents' death.' She hesitated. 'And now, there's you and me.' She stopped abruptly, with a feeling of disbelief, recalling her impulsive actions of becoming attached to a younger man with an unlikely familial connection. Jessica tried to convince herself that their relationship was, and only ever could be, a misguided, mad passionate fling. Today was their last day in Shimla. All of a sudden, and even without computing the big confusing picture, she felt ashamed of herself.

Sebastian reached across the table, and she put her hand in his. It was as if he could read her mind. 'Don't be glum, Jessica. Please don't be sad or ever regret anything that's happened. I believe that everything happens for a good reason. I also believe in fate…'

'Sebastian…what happened between us in Shimla, has to stay in Shimla. I know we'll see each other back in England, and I want you to know that I'll never regret anything, and I want today to be our best day ever. I leave tomorrow, and we'll meet up again in Delhi, but let this episode in our lives just be a happy memory to recall when we are both older,' she added, 'and wiser, too.'

'If that's what you want, so be it. I do love you. I do…'

'It's impossible, Sebastian. There's your father, and, God forbid he *could* be *my* biological father. And there's my daughter, Saffron. I'm just trying to get her out of the mire she ended up in and I'm practically doing the same thing myself. No, what happened between us will be a happy memory for me, never to be forgotten.'

Sebastian squeezed her hand, paid the bill, and hailed their driver to take them to the foot of the climb to the Jakhoo Temple. An eager group of tourists assembled behind them.

'Come on, let's go climbing.' Sebastian took Jessica's arm, and together they began the long steep walk to the temple.

Jessica fished a scarf from her bag and tied it around her head. They developed a rhythm to their step, keeping pace with each other, unable to talk, and catching every breath they could muster. She stopped and leaned on a low wall to get her breath back.

'It is steep. I'm gasping.'

'Just stop when you want to. We're more than halfway there. Just about another half kilometre to go. And trust me, it's worth it.' Sebastian took her hand, helping her along the way as the climb became steeper, until eventually the trees opened up, sun poured down on them, and the temple came slowly into view. Monkeys scurried around looking for food, but soon left disappointed. They lined the steps to the temple, sat on top of the roof, and hung from surrounding trees, looking as though they were about to pounce. Jessica felt uncomfortable, and Sebastian used a stick to scare them off.

She gazed around, spellbound, her hands covering her face. The majestic mountains rose like sharp shards of white icing.

Sebastian watched her reaction and smiled. He had a sudden urge to take her in his arms, lift her up, and kiss her. Dignity amongst strangers prevailed as the tourist group arrived behind them, puffing and panting, also awestruck by their surroundings.

'Come into the temple, Jessica. Here, take my hand,' said Sebastian, entering the hallowed space, she reached out and took his hand as they climbed the worn steps trying to ignore the ever-present annoying monkeys.

'Thank you for being with me,' whispered Jessica as Sebastian put his arm round her shoulders.

They stared at colourful painted ceilings and walls, and intricate images surrounding them, and wondered at the magic of this tiny place. Candles burned everywhere, flickering around the inner temple, casting eerie shadows. Gold frescos glinted in the glow that brought to life the painted icons hanging on walls everywhere. She wanted to light another candle and felt like saying a prayer as she breathed in the heavy scent of incense. They walked out into the bright sunlight, and put money in a silver collection bowl near the door. Sebastian had to tear her away from the dramatic view to begin their descent. Hand in hand, calf muscles burning, they laboriously made their way to the bottom of the long, steep path.

Their driver got out of the car and opened the doors for them before driving them back to the hotel.

'Don't know about you, Jessica, but I think I need a rest after the day we've had.'

'Yes, and I need to put the finishing touches to my packing before we go out tonight.' They headed towards their own rooms with a brief *see you later.*

'Come in, Sebastian,' Jessica called out knowingly at the soft knocking on her veranda door.

'How are you doing? Wow! You look stunning!' Sebastian looked at her admiringly.

Jessica looked down and smoothed the bottle green silk dress. 'Thank you, kind Sir!' She curtsied and laughed. 'You don't look so bad yourself, I must say.'

Mutual admiration continued as Sebastian led the way onto the veranda. He pulled out a chair for her at their table on which stood an ice bucket containing a bottle of French champagne and a platter of extravagant-looking canapés.

'Best view in the hotel, just for you, madam.'

'You must have been planning this for ages, Sebastian. It's lovely.' He bent down and kissed her cheek before taking a seat and summoning the waiting attendant to uncork the bottle.

They raised their glasses. The intense colour of the setting sun turned the bubbles orange.

Jessica raised her glass. 'Here's to Shimla, here's to you, here's to me.'

'And here's to us!' added Sebastian.

Jessica felt the familiar prick of tears behind her eyes. Blinking, she buried her nose in the glass of Champagne and taking a sip, allowed the cool bubbles to dance around her mouth.

The sunset. This was the last time she'd see the colour on the mountains, the mist sliding down to the valley as the evening drew to a close. The last time she could feel a sense of belonging here, and the last time she'd feel comfortable with her churning emotions for Sebastian. In a few weeks she'd be back at school, looking strait-laced and teacher-efficient.

Sebastian sensed her mood. 'A penny for them.'

'Oh, just thinking how this experience has changed my life. Just thinking about you, and me, and what will happen when we get back home.'

'Well, we have one last night together.' He looked at his watch, 'In forty minutes, your golden coach will be here to take us away for a lovely evening.'

'Apart from my last night in Delhi. I've decided to take up your offer of a bed for the night.'

'Great…here, let me top you up, we have the rest of the evening before us.'

Dinner was a sumptuous delight. The restaurant didn't disappoint. Jessica had never seen such opulence—not even at the Imperial. She'd never been one for entertaining or going out. All her life she'd been unconcerned with indulgence.

Fed and amply watered, they arrived at the hotel weary and ready for sleep.

'Early breakfast?' Sebastian asked Jessica as they arrived at her door.

'Not too early though. We don't leave 'till the afternoon train, you know.' Turning the key to enter her room, she looked round at Sebastian. 'Night cap?' she suggested.

Before closing the door behind him, he hung the *Don't Disturb* to the outside, as she stood arranging wine glasses at the mini-bar fridge.

'The only night cap I want is you, Jessica.'

She turned, 'No, Sebastian. We can't go on like this, we both know that. We've got to find out more about your father and my mother. In fact…'

But he embraced her, reassuring her that he also wanted to get to the truth. 'I think we just need to be close to each other tonight, Jessica.' She relaxed, sleepily as they collapsed onto her bed.

165

42

Shimla 1947:

Edward's next few weeks flew by rapidly. He'd managed to sell James' car for a good price, and with the proceeds he opened a bank account on behalf of Jessica. He' tell Catherine about it when she arrives, along with anything else relating to Jessica. He had obtained a copy of her birth certificate to be taken back to England, and compiled a file of useful information about Jessica and her nursery and Sunday school education. It contained all the personal details he could think of. He also wrote an account of what happened at The Laurels on the night of the fire, for her to take back and keep safe.

He had received details of Catherine's return passage, and booked Jessica a berth in her cabin. He and Hermione began to pack a trunk containing clothes and the few belongings Jessica had.

While driving to see her that afternoon Edward had composed his lines. She had to be told, and needed to understand what was to happen. He'd also wanted to broach the subject of her parents again. She had never asked. It was as though she'd forgotten them. It would have helped if he'd had a photograph of her Aunt Catherine. But at least he'd managed to obtain a picture of the ship she was to travel on, and he made a story for her out of that which had seemed to make her very excited.

It was just three days before the funeral, and he was collecting Jessica to drive to the station to meet her aunt, and to take her to the Grand hotel. He imagined she would be exhausted after her long journey.

'Jessica, come on, we're going to the station. Isn't it exciting? Remember the big ship I showed you the pictures of? Well, your Aunt Catherine has come here on that ship, and on the train, and you'll meet her soon. Your uncle will be waiting for you when you arrive in England.'

Jessica looked puzzled. 'You're my uncle, and Uncle Charles. I don't have an aunt.'

'Yes, Jessica, you do. But they live a long way away.' Edward took a long breath. 'Your Aunt Catherine is your mother's sister, and she lives in England with her husband, who is your uncle. You will be going on the ship to England with your Aunt Catherine.'

'And mummy? Where is my mummy? She's not here, I know she's not here, and I know where she's gone, they told me at nursery. Why did she go...' She shouted at Edward. 'I don't want my aunt, I want my mummy back from heaven. Please, Uncle Edward...why can't she come back? Please make her come back...'

Jessica's sobbing rendered Edward speechless and his own tears welled up. He stopped the car and took hold of her, wiping her eyes, trying to distract her.

'Dearest Jessica. You know I love you very much, but your mummy is looking at you from heaven, and is with you right now. She will always be with you wherever you go, and we'll take care of you for her. When you meet your Aunt Catherine, you'll have a big exciting journey to England in a huge ship, and even when you get there, your mother will still be with you, always.' He held her close until her crying abated.

'Come, now, wipe your eyes, and hug teddy, and think about your mummy up there in heaven—she wouldn't want you to be unhappy, now, would she?'

'No, uncle, and I want her to be happy, too,' Jessica lifted her eyes to the deep blue afternoon sky, 'look, I can nearly see her up there in heaven. Will you hold my hand?' Edward reached out his hand and they drove the last bit of the way to the station. 'I love you, uncle,' she said, looking at Edward.

They went onto the platform to wait for the train. It was bustling with porters and passengers, cleaning wallahs and uniformed officials. Edward noticed three military policemen standing by. He took Jessica into the waiting room—an open-fronted structure with newly varnished timber benches. A man and woman were sitting on one, talking animatedly, looking up the track every few seconds to see if the train was approaching. Edward tipped his hat and he and Jessica sat down. He pushed aside a lock of her golden hair, and straightened her floral dress. 'There, you do look pretty. The train will be here soon. Look, look down the track and wait for it to appear.' He pointed in the direction that the train would be approaching. No sooner had he said it, than there it was, chuffing and puffing out smoke after its long climb.

Jessica stood up, clutching her teddy. 'Look, Uncle, the train's coming. Will it make a noise?'

'No, it will rest here at the station before moving on again. Hold my hand, and we'll wait until it stops. We'll look for your Aunt Catherine getting off.'

Edward was nervous—for Jessica, as well as for himself. He scanned the coaches and waited for the doors to be opened. Young men seemed to be the only passengers, some in uniform, some in mufti. They walked along to the First-Class coach and two doors were opened by porters. A man in a dark blue suit climbed down onto the platform and turned to help a woman down the steps from the carriage. The blue-suited man made his way through the crowds, holding a small placard on which was written *Shelley*. Holding tightly onto Jessica, Edward made himself known to the man, and followed him to the woman on the platform. He knew immediately she was Elizabeth's sister. Looking at her, his heart skipped a beat. They could have been twins. Her auburn hair, the way she moved, her blue eyes that sparkled as they shook hands. She was wearing a pale green dress and a jaunty hat embellished with pink felt flowers and a half-face net veil. And she carried a large crocodile-skin handbag.

'Mr Shelley—Edward. Oh! and I do believe this is my dear niece, Jessica.' Catherine bent down and tried to take Jessica's hand, but the timid little girl clung to Edward's leg and ducked behind him.

Edward turned and lifted Jessica in his arms. In doing so, she dropped her teddy on the platform, but immediately, Catherine picked it up.

'Here, my dear, what's his name?' She smiled at Jessica as she handed teddy back to her.

Prompted by Edward, Jessica replied softly, 'He's just called Teddy.'

'Well, I can't think of a better name, he's very handsome, isn't he?'

'Yes, and he lives with me and Aunty 'Mione and George in their house.'

Edward put Jessica down on the platform, and she looked up at Catherine. 'I haven't got a house, because my mummy is in heaven, so I live with 'Mione and George and my other uncle.'

Catherine turned, both enchanted and distressed by what Jessica had just said. She took out her handkerchief and dabbed her eyes, as the porter approached her with luggage neatly stacked on a trolley.

'Well, do you know, I have a big house that you will live in, in England. And I have a big garden for you to play in and there are lots of toys for you to play with, and so many picture story books, you can't even count them all.'

'Is there a swing in the garden? Is it on a big ship?' Jessica seemed confused, so Catherine and Edward thought it time to gather up her belongings and make their way to the hotel. Catherine walked over to the blue-suited man who was waiting patiently a few steps away, and fished some money from her handbag. He gave her a bow, and she joined Edward and Jessica walking towards the station exit.

Catherine explained, 'That was Rashid. He's been with me all the way from Bombay. I couldn't have made the journey without him. He's very well educated, and told me about the sights we passed by on the journey.'

Catherine sat with Jessica in the back seat of Edward's car, and they made their way to the hotel. He'd booked the best room for her, and soon she was checked in. She looked at Edward and Jessica.

'Jessica, I will have to rest now, but I will see you both tomorrow, and Jessica, I might have a present for you in one of those suitcases— what do you think it might be?'

Jessica looked puzzled. 'Erm, is it a book? Or sweeties? Or…'

Catherine took hold of both her hands. 'My dear, you will just have to wait and see. Tomorrow, Mr Shelley will bring you here and we'll have a long chat and I'll show you some photographs. Goodbye, Edward, goodbye Jessica.'

Edward left the hotel and took Jessica into town for an ice-cream before returning her to Hermione's house. He drove back to his cottage at the club feeling light-hearted and relieved that their meeting had gone so well, and that Jessica had come out of her shell so quickly. Yet only two days away and he had to endure Elizabeth and James' funeral. Once more, he felt a sinking feeling in his stomach.

43

Shimla 1997:

Jessica woke to a commotion coming from the veranda outside her room. She glanced at the clock.

'Oh, my God! Sebastian. Wake up, we've overslept.' She jumped out of bed, smoothing the clothes she'd slept in. 'Sebastian!'

She rushed into the bathroom, splashed cold water over her face and peeked through her curtains.

'What's going on? Hell, wow, what happened? It's eleven thirty!' He sat up in bed casually rubbing his eyes, as reality set in.

'We've not had breakfast, not packed, not checked out, not…'

'I know—and the manager is outside my door, wondering what to do.'

Jessica composed herself, and in her most perfect English manner, opened the veranda door to the startled handful of onlookers outside.

'Oh, hello, I do hope you don't mind, but I needed to sleep this morning ahead of my journey.' She turned to the manager who seemed embarrassed and backed away. 'I'll be checking out in approximately one hour.'

'Of course, Miss Delaney-Hartford, of course…we were just a little concerned that everything was alright. Um, do let us know when we can help you today.'

'Thank you, I will.' Jessica closed the door and drew the curtains. She looked at Sebastian who was gaping at her incredulously and they both began to laugh.

'Didn't think you had it in you—saw them off sharpish, I'll say. But, hey, we have to move fast. When do we have to be at the station? Come on, let's get organised I'm starving. Last night's dinner is all but a luscious memory. I'll order room service now and we can eat as we pack.'

'Good idea, I'll have an omelette and toast, and lots of coffee,' called Jessica as she took her suitcase out of the cupboard. 'And you'd better get back to your own room, I'm kicking you out!' She reached out to him. 'By-the-way, did I say what a great way to end our last day in Shimla? No? Well, I feel on-top-of-the-world happy. And I want to tell you...I do love you, Sebastian. As difficult as all this is going to be when we get home, we'll have to face the music.'

'Maybe, who knows? But for now, let's get prepared for the journey.'

They took their room-service brunch outside on the veranda. Jessica had sorted out her luggage, but not yet packed.

'When do you think we should ask the hotel to take us to the station, Sebastian?'

'In my experience, we need to be there a good half hour before the train is due to depart. Same old bureaucracy, checking and re-checking of tickets, stamping and re-stamping of documents, luggage porters, etc. It's not like London where you can just run for it and jump on.'

'I guess I'll miss some of that though, when I'm home. I've got used to the pace here, and I think it suits my disposition. Back home everything seems to have to be done yesterday, but I'll be back in my little cottage in the middle of the green meadows of Hampshire, with my pony Trixie and my daughter. Life will be good. I start back at school in two weeks, so I should have time to re-adjust and get settled.'

'I'll be home at my Barbican flat a few days after you, and I'll be travelling down to Devon to see my father as soon as I can. I'll need to see you again as soon as possible, you know. Before you leave Delhi, I want to exchange dates with you.' He looked at her, eyebrows raised.

'Dates, yes, me too. I'll have only one spare room now that Saffron's in residence, so perhaps a stopover en route to Devon? We'll work it out. There'll most likely be lots of things I have to see to before I start work again, and I'm expecting probate to be finalised on Aunt Catherine's estate. Not sure what I'll do with the inheritance, but I think I'll definitely retire from teaching and throw myself into something more beneficial to the community. The Pony Club is always wanting me to try helping with riding for the disabled. We'll see. I'd better go and secure my luggage now. We'll call for the hotel porter to collect everything at the same time.'

Jessica fingered her mother's tiny china horse that Chandra had given her. One memento and a connection to her past. She wrapped it into her clothes and packed it in the middle of her case, smoothing the sari over it. She had bought the beautiful sari for Saffron, and a pair of silver filigree earrings she thought she'd like. Not much to show for the time she'd spent in India, but shopping wasn't on her main agenda. She'd lots of photographs to develop, and she looked forward to compiling an album of memories.

Looking at herself in the mirror, Jessica saw a totally different person to the one who had first arrived in Shimla, slightly lost and scared. Sebastian had steered and helped, propped her up and given her strength when it was necessary. When she heard the porter at his door, she opened hers to allow her bags to be taken, too. Sebastian came over to her and they both walked onto the veranda to take one more look at the view.

'I feel I'll be back, you know,' Jessica said solemnly.

'Together?'

'I'd like that, Sebastian, I would.' She turned and pecked him on the cheek. They quickly caught up with their luggage in the lobby, paid their bills, and piled into the hotel minibus.

Strapping her handbag across her body, Jessica jostled behind Sebastian through the crowds at the station, as the porter waited patiently for paperwork to be scrutinised. Their luggage was taken to the correct part of the platform for embarkation.

As they held hands, neither of them noticed the figure of a bent old Indian woman in the shadows, with a red sari pulled across her face. Chandra was smiling behind it through her tears, as she bestowed a silent blessing on them from her gods.

44

Shimla 1947:

Catherine stood motionless outside Christ Church. She wore a dark grey tailored suit with jet black accessories. A downdraft of icy air scuttled dry leaves down the pathway towards the lychgate and into the street below. Edward stood beside her as they waited nervously for the hearse to arrive. Only when bearers began to carry the two caskets towards them did Catherine's tears spill down her grim face hidden behind her black net veil.

Her sister, her brother-in-law. She dared not imagine the contents of those coffins. Floral tributes overflowed the dark wooden boxes. The procession shuffled into the narthex and halted to allow the chief mourners to line up behind them.

Catherine and Edward walked side-by-side. He staring straight ahead, she looking down at the floor. The coffins were placed in front of the altar, and the vicar entered the pulpit. Catherine and Edward led, followed by Charles and Lola, and close friends filled the front pews first. Around forty other mourners filed into the church. Organ pipes fell silent and all focus was on the reverend.

All except Catherine, who felt as though she was in another world, at another time, living in a bad dream. She kept her eyes firmly on Elizabeth and James' coffins laden with pure white lilies. She wanted to hold her sister, talk to her, and to remind her of their lives together before she'd married and left India to go to live in England. But Elizabeth was gone, and Catherine would never see her again.

The Reverend John King began to offer tributes to Mr and Mrs Delaney, saying words Catherine could not bear to hear, images she could not imagine, about places she did not know. Instead, she saw Elizabeth playing hide and seek with her, skipping in and out of the shadows in their garden in Bombay. Pushing the swing for each other, laughing, playing tag, dressing up in fairy costumes and eating cake at the children's garden table and chairs they used, for pretend tea parties and picnics.

Catherine felt Edward's hand on hers, and she knew he'd sensed her grief. She felt comforted by his touch and realised that he, too, was feeling devastated. Hymns were sung, but were drowned out by the playing of the organ. She didn't hear many of the words spoken by the vicar, but she knelt to pray for her sister's soul.

Too soon, the procession was moving back up the aisle and out of the church, where the funeral vehicles were waiting to take them to the cemetery for interment.

Reverend John King sat with Catherine, Edward, Lola and Charles for the journey, which seemed to Catherine to go on forever. The Mall was lined with people, some bowed their heads and removed their hats in respect. The cleric made futile attempts to break the silence in the car, pointing out various landmarks to Catherine. She looked at Edward and he frowned back. The vicar's monologue seemed to have annoyed him, too.

He was glad it had all gone smoothly. He'd dreaded this day – and hoped against hope that he wouldn't break down with sheer and uncontrolled grief. Having Catherine there somehow gave him courage to withstand the deep emotion of the day.

Few other mourners came to the interment. The grave had been beautifully prepared. The short ceremony was finalised as Edward and Catherine each threw a handful of soil on to the coffins now deep in the ground. Both were staunching tears as they performed this final act of farewell. Leaving the leafy shade along the pathway, they walked back between well-tended graves.

Back at Hilltop House, Charles and Lola had a buffet lunch prepared, and Catherine was relieved to be there. Exchanging hugs of support, Lola showed Catherine to a bedroom to freshen up. They all gathered in the drawing room where Charles was already pouring glasses of whisky. Catherine nodded approval, sat back, sighed, and began to relax.

They discussed a headstone and Edward said he'd see to it. Lunch, followed by afternoon naps, was the order of the day. Catherine surprised herself by sleeping soundly for about an hour. Before dozing off, she remembered the meeting with Jessica two days earlier.

'Jessica, darling—please, come in. Hello Edward.' Catherine had closed the hotel room door behind them. Jessica held back when Edward and Catherine shook hands, so Catherine, smiling, walked over to her.

'Jessica, remember I said I'd brought something for you from England? And you were trying to guess what it was?'

'Yes.' Jessica spoke softly, shyly.

'Well, come and look here. Look in the big bag over here.' Catherine coaxed her across the room.

'What is it? Er…'

'Jessica, I want you to call me Catherine. Will you do that?' Catherine almost pleaded with her.

'Yes…Cafrin.' Jessica looked into the bag, and with Catherine's help, took out a large box.

'Go on—open it, it's for you, dear. I hope you like it. Shall I help you?'

'Yes please,' said Jessica, pulling at shiny blue satin ribbons that secured the lid on a large box, and lifting the lid to expose white and pink tissue paper. 'Oh, I know what it is.' Jessica was excited. 'Look, Uncle Edward. Look!'

She lifted the beautiful doll from the box and held it tight in both arms. 'Thank you, thank you, Cafrin. What's her name? Look at her lovely white dress and blue bonnet with flowers round it. And she has eyelashes. Uncle Edward, she has proper eyes. And her arms and legs move, and she's got shoes on…and petticoats.' Jessica's face lit up with joy and excitement.

Catherine knelt next to her. 'Well, she hasn't got a name yet, so what shall we call her? I know, do you think she looks like a Belinda…or a Jennifer.'

'Um…yes! Jennifer, she's called Jennifer! Uncle, she's called Jennifer.'

'And have you noticed, Jessica?' Catherine gently helped her lie Jennifer on her back. 'Look, when she's put to bed, she closes her eyes!' Jessica was enthralled. She held out her arms to Catherine saying thank you over and over again, before giving her a hug.

Edward couldn't help but notice the tears of joy in Catherine's eyes. It had been achieved—a bond had been forged, albeit tenuous and delicate. He sat down and watched as Jessica and Catherine played with Jennifer. He took a deep breath, smiled quietly and rested his eyes, mentally preparing himself for the funeral in two days' time.

45

Delhi 1997:

Jessica stepped into Sebastian's apartment, followed by the janitor carrying her luggage. Sebastian gave him a tip and walked over to join her at the window. This part of Delhi bore no resemblance to the Ashok Hotel area, where she stayed before. Neat tree-lined streets and green spaces stretched out ahead, and from this bird's-eye-platform on the fifth floor, she could just make out the mellow golden sandstone of government buildings. Immediately below, flash cars and limousines were parked outside pretty colonial-style bungalows and well-kept houses with lush tropical gardens and exotic flowering shrubs she couldn't put a name to. The area was free from the usual litter and clutter she had come to expect in India.

Sebastian circled her waist from behind. 'Some view, hey?' he said.

'This is so different to anything else I've seen in India. What a lovely area, and away from the madding crowds.'

'If you look down below—see the yellow-painted bungalow with a gardener doing some watering? That used to belong to my father. After he left Shimla, he came here to start up his business, and bought himself the bungalow as a pied-à-terre for his frequent visits from England. He'd come over to do deals with manufacturers and silk merchants to export his purchases over to England. It must have been around nineteen seventy when he eventually sold it, and invested in this apartment. I suppose he still felt the need to keep a foothold here.'

Jessica was intrigued. 'So, you now occupy it—very handy.'

'Yes, and believe me, in this area property prices have gone sky-high.' Sebastian suddenly looked melancholy. 'Dad will never be back here now though. And I'm not sure what to do if the place is left to me. I could move back to London permanently, and work for the London office of the agency, but I'd miss Delhi, I think.'

'Well, it's nice that you'll have that choice.' Jessica turned back into the room and he guided her to her bedroom.

'Yes, two bedrooms, each with single beds…' He apologised, not stating the obvious.

Jessica smiled at him. 'Perhaps we'd better prepare for later today and not think any more about...'

'Oh, and why?'

'Because. Because in Shimla things were different. We're now going back home and our behaviour has to be adjusted accordingly.'

Sebastian felt as though she'd just smacked him in the face. 'Well, you're definitely in charge now,' he said, looking surprised, 'so, tell me what you want to do for the rest of the day, before getting up early tomorrow morning to fly away.'

'Shopping! That's what I want to do. To go on a shopping spree. I never found the time before, but I would like to buy some silk fabric and perhaps a ready-made kaftan. Any idea where I should go?'

'I'll get my driver to take you to the best shops in town. Don't worry, he'll wait and stay and you can ask him to go anywhere. He also knows where to find a dressmaker's shop to have a garment made, if you want to,' Sebastian said, looking at his watch, 'you have three hours before you need to be back here so that we can go out for an early dinner. In the meantime, I have this mountain of correspondence to deal with, not to mention getting in touch with the office. I have a story I want to run past the editor.'

Jessica turned her attention to her luggage, clothes for travelling in tomorrow, and making space for anything she might buy. She sat on her bed and looked around. Sebastian kept a neat and tidy home. Books and bookshelves were everywhere, lining walls from floor to ceiling. She walked over to take a closer look at photographs standing on the windowsill. Mostly photos of Sebastian, either alone or with a young Indian woman. In one, he and she were laughing and had their arms around each other with a backdrop that looked like the Gateway to India in Bombay. Neat piles of magazines were stacked for a guest to read, and she couldn't help notice the hand-woven rugs everywhere, some well-worn, obviously made somewhere in Asia.

She also noticed some exquisite Indian furniture when she went to join him in the lounge and assumed he inherited most of it from his father's house. An intricately carved armoire, small barley-twist legged polished tables and a beautiful burgundy leather-topped desk in a bay window, where Sebastian sat sifting through his mail.

As she approached him, he picked up the phone and began to dial. 'I'll get the driver here straight away. Are you ready to go on this mammoth shopping spree?'

'I think so, I'll have to stop at a bank to cash some traveller's cheques first. Will he know where to go?' she asked.

'Oh yes, and you can trust him implicitly. His father worked for my father years ago, and now he works for me and my neighbour. We share his services. He runs errands, cleans the apartment, goes grocery shopping, everything. He's almost part of the family. His name is Jayesh, but we call him Jay. 'I'll take you down to meet him, and the rest is up to you.'

Three hours was all she had, but Jessica wanted to do it in two. First, they stopped at the silk emporium, and Jay told her that if she were to choose some fabric and a pattern, they could make up a blouse or a dress by the time they came back this way. Tempting as it sounded, Jessica declined, but bought metres of different coloured silks. One colour, she decided she'd call coffee, in a lightweight slub, she'd make up herself when she got home, into an evening dress ready for the winter season. She was usually invited to various Christmas and New Year parties.

'Memsahib, you like sari?' Jay asked Jessica. 'Oh, I bought one in Shimla, and I had one given to me, but...'

'Memsahib, I know best place. My brother he have shop.' Jay made it sound irresistible. 'Also, jewellery! Indian silver...Memsahib...'

'Oh, no thanks, Jay, I won't have room in my suitcase for it all. But perhaps we could go by the sari shop. Yes, okay.'

Jay carried her shopping bags to the car and locked them in the boot as she got in the back seat.

It seemed to take forever through back streets and busy roads dodging traffic. Jessica looked at her watch.

'Jay, I'd like to be back at Mr Shelley's in less than an hour, do we have to go far?' She was feeling nervous not knowing where she was or where she was going, and wished she'd not agreed to go further than the silk emporium.

However, eventually they did arrive, and were welcomed royally. Sari after sari was fluffed and shaken to show off its beauty.

'The red one, that red one there. Please can I see it?' Not looking at the fabric, Jessica held it in her hands and stroked the shiny golden border. This was it. This was like Chandra's sari. 'Yes, I'll take this one.'

And, to protestations, 'No, no other, no better or worse, please let me buy this one.'

The airport was chaotic. Jessica had checked in and watched as her suitcases with their precious cargo disappeared. She and Sebastian strolled towards the departures gates. He took hold of her hand and they turned to face each other. She wanted to be with him, but she put on a brave face, as did he.

'This is it. It's goodbye.' She looked up at him, her stomach churning. If only she could stay, if only they could go back to Shimla together and not have any other cares or commitments. If only...

'Let's just say au revoir, Jessica. Until the next time. I'll call you when I'm back in London.'

They reluctantly let go of each other, Jessica turned and started to make her way to immigration, passport ready. She felt a tug on her arm and willingly turned around. Sebastian held out his hand. The tiny parcel was wrapped in tissue paper.

'Here, take it, this is for you, Jessica. Safe travels, wherever you go.' She took the present and put it in the pocket of her jacket and kissed him on the cheek. And she was being called to show her passport. Looking back, she waved as she made her way down the long corridor towards departures. She looked again and he was still watching. They exchanged waves.

At the very end of the corridor just as she was about to turn, she looked back again, searching.

But Sebastian had gone.

46

Shimla 1947:

Edward had to drive into town. He was going to buy Jessica a present before collecting Catherine from the hotel. He'd asked Hermione what to buy, and she suggested a straw sun hat for onboard the ship.

'Where are we going, Uncle Edward?' Jessica asked, looking bewildered, hugging Teddy close. 'Are we going to go to Cafrin's hotel and the station.'

'We are, but I just thought that I might like to buy you something first.'

'What will you buy me, Uncle Edward?'

'Well, here we are. Come on, come with me into the shop, and I'll show you.' Edward helped Jessica out of the car and into Mr Gupta's Fine Millinery shop. 'See that lovely straw hat with the blue ribbon around it? See, try it on, it will look splendid on you to wear on the big ship when you go out on deck.'

'What's deck, uncle?' He'd noticed that Jessica had become a lot more curious about things around her—he assumed she was at the learning stage of her life, every sentence was inquisitive.

He put the hat on her head and stood back. 'There you are. That's just the job.'

'Your daughter she look good, and with her red hair...' The shopkeeper joined in the admiration.

Edward felt a flush of pride and smiled sheepishly, not correcting the man. 'Yes, she does, doesn't she?' he replied, as he adjusted Jessica's hat.

Catherine was waiting in the lobby of the hotel, surrounded by trunks and suitcases. Edward had already given her travel documents for Jessica, together with any other official information she might need to show at the port before embarking on the journey back to London. She wore the hat she'd arrived in just over a week ago. She bent as Jessica ran towards her.

'Well, Jessica—what a lovely hat! It suits you perfectly.'

'Uncle Edward bought it for me. Do you like the ribbons? They're like the ribbons on Jennifer's hat.' Jessica twirled around slowly to show Catherine the back.

'Perfect, dear, just perfect.' And, to Edward. 'I'm ready to go.'

The car was loaded with luggage, Jessica's and Catherine's. One trunk had to go on the back seat, squashing Jessica to one side. They piled out of the car at the station surrounded by porters vying for tips. Catherine spotted Rashid. 'Oh, thank goodness, I thought he'd forget to come!' She stood tall and called to him.

'Rashid! Rashid! Over here.' Rashid made his way towards them and Edward told him to follow the porters with the luggage.

A conductor came over and checked their tickets, before sending them off to the first-class platform area. Edward paid the porters to look after it all, and they disappeared with Rashid.

Edward and Catherine walked along the platform with Jessica in the middle, holding hands with both of them whilst Edward carried Teddy. They settled themselves onto a bench to wait for the train.

'It has all been very quick Edward, I've hardly had time to get to know you, or Elizabeth's friends. But it was nice to meet James' family at the funeral. They were devastated. I think they were more upset than I was.' She took hold of Jessica's hand.

'Well, I expect to be back in England soon. But first I have to return to Delhi. I want to set up an export business. In fact...' he hesitated, 'I had talked to James and Elizabeth about it, as an idea for what we might do after the British leave India. I believe there's a market in Britain for Indian cotton clothing and cotton bales, and silks.'

'What a good idea, I can see it being snapped up in England now the war is over and the New Look is in vogue. Oh, listen, Jessica—is that the train?'

Jessica stood up and looked along the platform. Everyone surged forward at once and she was almost lost. Edward ran to her side and grasped her arm. 'Stay with us, Jessie, stay with Aunty Catherine, and you'll be alright.'

The train pulled up with a sigh as porters went to open doors to carriages, and people began to pour out.

'Memsahib!' their porter shouted above a cacophony of voices and the hissing of the engine. 'Memsahib—this is your carriage.' Rashid came over to lead them.

'Jessica, I will say goodbye now. I hope you have a good time on the big ship…'

'Uncle Edward, come with us, please.' Jessica pulled him towards the carriage door.

'I can't right now, Jessie, but I promise, when you're in England and playing in Aunty Catherine's big garden with all those toys, I will see you there as soon as I can.' He picked her up, hugged her, and placed her in her seat on the train, near the window.

'Goodbye Catherine, please write to me and I promise I'll keep in touch with you, too.' After they embraced, Catherine joined Jessica in their compartment, slammed the door shut and opened the window to look out.

'Jessica, come and wave goodbye to Uncle Edward.' She made way for the confused little girl and held her close. Edward waved back over the heads of surging passengers, all eager to stay clear of the train when it moved away. Porters struggled under the weight of travelling trunks and suitcases. Third-class passengers jostled towards the station exit, women struggled with long, brightly-coloured saris. Men in different-coloured turbans manoeuvred cages crammed with chickens, and heaving with livestock tied to ropes. Waves of heat and dust wafted exotic odours along the platform in the affray.

The engine built up steam, and let out an ear-splitting screech as steam hissed and smoke puthered from the funnel. The guard blew his whistle, and the train began to pull slowly and noisily out of the station.

Edward stood helpless and forlorn on the platform. He suddenly realised he was still clutching Teddy. 'Jessica!' He sprinted, panicking, dodging everyone on the platform as the train picked up speed. 'Jessica,' he came level with their compartment, and saw Jessica crying. 'Jessie, Jessie, here.' He stretched out his arm as he ran beside the moving train. 'Here's Teddy—you nearly forgot him. Hold him tight and don't let go.' He forced Teddy into her eager outstretched arms. Smoke billowed around them as he shouted into the haze. 'Dry your eyes, Jessie. Please don't cry.' By the time the smoke had cleared, the train had gone, taking Jessica with it, and out of his life forever.

Jessica had been distraught and had cried loudly, unnerving Catherine, when she realised Teddy was missing. But was now tightly hugging her precious furry friend.

Edward found the nearest bench, collapsed on to it and wept.

Part Two

England 1997

47

London September 1997:

With a soft thud, and a screech of brakes, the aircraft landed at Gatwick Airport. Early morning mist hung over river valleys in the familiar countryside Jessica loved so dearly. After India, the fields of green were blinding. She'd been in another world, in another life, and discovered a lot more than she'd bargained for. Now, she had to focus her thoughts on the immediate future. Going back to school, and settling back home. She also had to confront what she'd learned in Shimla and seek further answers from Meredith Bateman. A big chunk of her family jigsaw puzzle was still missing.

Through the welcoming hordes, she immediately spotted Saffron, her shock of short red hair a curly halo around her smiling face. Saffron saw her mother and moved quickly through the crowds to greet her.

'Saffie, oh, Saffie—I can't tell you how good it is to see you.'

'Me too, Mum, I was beginning to think you might find an excuse to stay on in India.' They hugged each other tightly.

Holding her daughter at arm's length, Jessica looked her up and down. She was wearing a blue jersey dress with black stockings and black leather boots. Multi-coloured beads hung around her neck, and long matching earrings bobbed against her cheeks. Jessica noticed she'd slicked on shiny lipstick and applied eye shadow and a little blusher to her porcelain features, and thought how pretty her daughter looked. They walked out into the chill morning towards the parked car, rolling Jessica's luggage behind them.

'Well, I must say, Saffie, you look a damned sight better than you did in the frozen north when I came to visit you. And happier. I do hope you never ever think about going back there again. I never told you, but when I flew back from seeing you on Barra, I cried my eyes out, having seen how you lived. It was never what I'd envisaged your life to be. I wanted you to go to Uni, be someone in the community, have a good education and a career. But, do you know, you were doing what I did at your age—dropping out, and looking at the world from a different perspective.'

'Oh, Mum, I'm sorry, but perhaps I had to do it. Perhaps it all helped shape my life, and enabled me to move on.' Saffron shot a sympathetic smile towards her mother as she manoeuvred the Land Rover out of the car park.

'I'm so glad you're back, Saffie. I need you now more than ever.' Jessica's words fell on Saffron's ears like a cry from the heart.

'And I'm glad you're back, Mum. I'm dying to hear all about it, and all about this mystery chap you've been hanging out with. What's his name again...?'

'Sebastian, Saffie, his name is Sebastian Shelley. He was a great help, and he thinks there's a connection between my family and his, when they were in India.' Jessica was flagging. 'I'm so tired, I think I'm going to crash out when we get home. How's the cottage? And Trixie? And the garden?'

'Mum, you're exhausted, put your head back, it'll be a while before we get home. By the way, you'll love the early autumn colours. All the fields have been harvested, and the farmers are already out sowing their winter crops while the sun shines.'

'I suppose there's a lot of mail?' said Jessica. She had asked Saffron to sift through it and throw out any junk.

'Not too much. But you remember you asked me to open anything that looked important, and I did open a largish envelope that turned out to be from your accountant. Or was it your solicitor? Bateman, I think his company is called. But I didn't think it worth calling you, so I stuffed it all back in the envelope for when you returned. I hope you don't mind. It looked like legal stuff.'

Jessica sat up, wide awake again. 'Ah! That will be to do with Mum's will and probate, I hope. He said he'd get it all wrapped up by about now, when I last spoke to him a few months ago. I wanted you to be there at the funeral, you know. I miss her even now—she was my mother's sister and I couldn't have been adopted by a more loving person.'

'I know. Mum. I'm so sorry. I should have come down from Scotland to say farewell to Gran.'

Jessica sat deep in thought. 'Well, if the probate has been finalised, it means I'll be able to re-organise my life. I'll have money to make a lot of changes. I would like to retire, and spend money on the cottage to modernise it. I might even think about buying a bigger house away from Coombe Lacey. You can help me make decisions. I hope you're staying now, and not planning on galivanting round the world.'

'No, Mum, I'll be here as long as you can stand having me around.'

'Good—now, let me have a nap, the jet-lag's beginning to take hold.'

Sensing the car slowing down, Jessica woke. They were going through the village. They were almost home.

'Here we are, Mum, nearly there.'

Red yellow and brown autumn leaves were blowing in the wind, swirling around houses and piling up in gutters. Jessica hadn't been away long, but so much had happened to take her mind away from home. It seemed like years. She didn't want to think about Sebastian and their discoveries, preferring to just settle quietly back into her home and get her head straight first. She felt Saffron needed to know about her past, her heritage and her ancestors. Jessica would tell her what she'd discovered, and go over her time in Shimla. She resolved to tell her later over a glass of wine.

Wandering around her home she looked bewildered and felt a little lost. Saffron took the luggage up to her bedroom and suggested she rest right now.

'Here, Mum—I've made the bed fresh for you. Have a good long nap, and I'll wake you in time for tea.' Jessica obeyed willingly, kissed Saffron and walked over to close the curtains.

'Be a darling Saffie, could you hang my jacket in the wardrobe. I don't want it to crease. Saffron picked up her jacket off the chair and found a coat hanger.

'Mum, there's something in the pocket.' Saffron held up the gift that Sebastian had given Jessica at Delhi airport.

Jessica had forgotten about Sebastian's gift after opening it and replacing it back in her jacket pocket on the plane. She'd promised herself that she'd ignore it.

'Oh! Saffie, I-er-I…'

'Come on Mum—it looks like a present to me.' She began to undo the string, and before Jessica could explain, she'd opened the package containing the exquisite sapphire ring. 'Mum, who gave you this, it's gorgeous? I know,' she chuckled, 'I bet it was Sebastian.'

189

Jessica took the box out of Saffron's hand. 'Yes, it was. At the airport as I was leaving. I tried to resist it, but he slipped it into my pocket just before I disappeared to find my gate. I was so shocked when I opened it on the plane, and I didn't know what it meant. But I decided I couldn't accept it.'

Saffron sat on the edge of the bed. 'So, your friendship *was* more than that. I'd say he wants to be serious.'

Jessica raised her voice. 'Saffie, look, it was nothing. I guessed he just wanted to help me. But yes, I suppose we did become close....'

'Mum! Don't tell porkies. I bet...'

'Saffron, leave it—there's a lot more I have to tell you before you understand what happened in Shimla, but, my dear girl, not now.'

'Sorry, Mum. In any case, it's none of my business. Sorry.' She kissed her mother on the cheek and left the bedroom.

'Saffie!' Jessica had just noticed the welcome on her bed.

'Mum?'

'You brought Teddy back. What a lovely gesture, Saffie. He'd also had enough of the Outer Hebrides, too, I guess. But he belongs to you now, you know! First worn out by me, and he's yours until...well, until perhaps I have a grandchild.'

Mother and daughter smiled, both glad to be together again. Jessica looked at Teddy, shaking her finger at him. 'You've travelled far, Teddy, now you have to stay home where you belong.' Her mock admonishment made them both laugh.

48

Hampshire September 1997:

Try as she may, Jessica couldn't sleep. She spent the best part of two hours lying on her bed, mulling over the reunion with Saffron. She loved her home, her solitude, and her seclusion, but she felt it had somehow been invaded. Saffron had made herself at home in the last two weeks, and now had an air of being in charge. Jessica resented taking her repeated instructions to go and sleep off the jet lag, and her offers of tea, caring though they were. She was also angry with herself for leaving Sebastian's present in her jacket pocket, and even angrier with Saffron for discovering it, with the accompanying inuendoes.

Jessica had to come to terms with the fact that Saffron was here to stay. She couldn't see any other way. She had hoped to be able to welcome her into the fold again with open arms, but feared they had drifted apart. Neither knew about each other's lives, not for the past few years, anyway. But here she was, her daughter, doing what Jessica had wanted her to do for a long time, yet now in a quandary as to what was to happen next.

She picked up Teddy from the bed. *I'm being unkind*, she thought, *I'm sure Saffron means well, doesn't she, Teddy?* She made him nod his head, making her smile, and she set about unpacking her case. She had presents for Saffron. She shook out the red silk sari she'd bought for herself, and the turquoise one she'd bought for her daughter. Everything seemed dreamlike to her now—the journey, the meeting, the discoveries and the childhood memories that had been shaken violently from her subconscious. Everything that had happened in Shimla was already becoming a surreal experience.

Then there was Sebastian. How was she to approach this with Saffron? Deep down, Jessica felt attached to him and didn't know how she might get over their brief encounter. Trying not to second-guess herself, she started sorting clothes. She stacked Saffron's presents of silk, the sari and silver earrings.

Preparing to go downstairs, she first went into the guest room—now Saffron's room, usually so tidy, to find things scattered about and her own nick-knacks taken away in order for Saffron's to be displayed. Jessica felt uncomfortable.

Placing the packages on a chair in the hall downstairs, she spotted Saffron through the open doorway, down the garden. Jessica's garden was her pride and joy. It had taken her years to develop it into a beautiful and serene place to sit in on a warm summer's day. She'd had the large pond dug with a stream leading into it and a little bubbling waterfall that emptied into the main pond. She'd stocked it with carp and orfe, and made areas of rocky interest for the fish to dart in between. In the summer, purple and white waterlilies floated wax-like on the water, and the pebbled edges led to a circle of natural wildflower meadow. An arbour-covered bench, alive with climbing pink clematis completed a feeling of sanctuary and calm. Jessica walked along the garden path under the apple trees towards the vegetable garden she'd made near the greenhouse. Her aim was to get to the paddock and say hello to Trixie. She paused to talk to Saffron.

'There you are, Mum. I guess you didn't sleep much.'

'You're right. But I have unpacked all my luggage. And I thought I'd go and say hello to Trixie. Did you ride her at all, Saffie?' Jessica perched herself on an upturned log and watched Saffron as she cleared dead vegetation from the greenhouse.

'No, Mum, but look what I've done in the garden. This is a doddle compared with the cottage garden I tried to tame on Barra. I thought I'd put in some brassica and sow a few winter veg. Also, it will soon be the time to put in spring bulbs, so you'll have to tell me what's there already, and where you'd like more planted.'

Once again, Jessica felt she was being usurped by her daughter, who seemed to think she could just walk in and claim the house and garden as her own. She resented Saffron's attitude of taking it all for granted. *Don't be mean, give her some leeway. She may tire of it anyway, so there's no point in getting angry or upset. Just accept her as she is and see how it resolves.*

'Yes—I'll give it some thought.' Jessica walked away towards the fence between the garden and the paddock. Her face lit up when she saw Trixie, head down, pulling grass. As soon as she clicked and called, the horse pricked up her ears, shook her mane, and appeared to dance towards her, tossing her head and whinnying.

'So, you do remember me, Trix?' Jessica smiled, stroking her forehead and neck, and whispering to her gently. 'I've been away, but I'm here now, to stay.' The animal snorted and whinnied again, turned and cantered along the fence and back. 'I'll come and take you for a ride in a few days. You're looking sleek and healthy.'

Making her way back to Saffron, Jessica relaxed, happy to be home.

'Shall I go and make us a cuppa?' she asked Saffron. 'You're so busy here. Why don't I bring it out and we can sit by the pond and you can take a break?'

'No, Mum, I'll…'

'Saffie—now, no more of this! I'm quite capable of making a cup of tea. And I don't want you to feel you have to look after me, or pay your way by working in the house and garden, you know.'

Saffron looked at her mother quizzically, feeling as though she'd just been told off by her teacher. 'Alright—I surrender. Go!'

Sitting at first in silence sipping their tea by the pond, Jessica began to recount her days in Shimla. From the sad discovery that The Laurels had been destroyed by fire, to her close relationship with Sebastian. Saffron had lots of questions, and was interested in the story surrounding the fate of her biological grandparents. Jessica told her about the chance meeting with Chandra, and how she'd begun to remember events from her childhood. About what she'd been told by Chandra of that fatal night, and how she'd clung on to Sebastian's father, Edward.

She continued to tell Saffron what Sebastian had said about his father, and about the chance meeting with an elderly couple at the hotel who'd lived in Shimla at the same time. That they'd known Edward, and Jessica's parents, and they remembered what happened that terrible night. She told her about Chandra's revelation that her mother and Sebastian's father had a long-term affair, and about how she and Sebastian thought they could be half-siblings. Jessica expected Saffron to be shocked, ashamed, disapproving, but she took it all matter-of-factly.

'Well, Mum, I look forward to meeting Sebastian.'

'Saffie, I had a wonderful time. Sad, scary and sometimes worrying, and I'll never forget any of it. And, yes, Sebastian's duplicity is still on my mind at times, but I took him at face value. He said he'll call me when he gets back from Delhi. His father lives in Devon, so he thought he might stop off to see me en route from London. He has a flat in the Barbican.'

'Look, Mum, you deserve to spread your wings a bit. I'm the one that ought to be getting more serious, after the life I've been living, shacking up with whom I please, whenever I felt like it, without a care or responsibility in the world. But you're in danger of becoming an old maid, a spinster of this parish, and spending the rest of your life knitting socks.'

'Perish the thought, Saffie. All I've done in my life so far is to take on a safe job, make enough money for us both, yes, you too, have benefitted from this staidness of mine. Look at this place—it doesn't come cheap. But I have other news. I'm going to hand in my notice at school and retire at half-term. October this year. I want to make the most of things before I'm too old, and get as much out of life before it's too late. That, at least, is what my Indian journey has taught me. I'm determined to turn over a fresh page and mould a new life out of the remnants of the old!'

49

Hampshire September 1997:

Jessica sat at her green-leather-topped desk. The largest white envelope was at the bottom of the pile of mail. Pushing the rest, she delved straight into the bulky package from Meredith Bateman. She had been expecting it, and had hoped that her mother's probate would be completed before she left for Shimla. Sliding the contents onto the desk, the first sheet of paper was an account for work done by Bateman's, listing numbered receipts in tracing and collating assorted legal and formal documents. Placing it to one side, she looked at the death certificate of her adoptive mother, Catherine. She eagerly opened up the will. Catherine had appointed Meredith Bateman as her sole executor.

Along with the will were bundles of papers carefully sorted and collated. Her own original birth certificate was there, along with her parent's marriage and death certificates. Scrutinising the documents, she saw nothing unusual, and the cause of death given on her parents' death certificates read simply 'asphyxiation'. The sheet of yellowed paper tucked underneath the certificates was headed 'Shimla Court Coroner's Office'. It was the court's findings at the inquest following their death, and referred to a jury determining an open verdict. *Open verdict on what? So why did Catherine tell me they died of dysentery, and not hint at anything else until she urged me to go to Shimla? And why was there an inquest?*

Scanning through the mass of papers, Jessica knew she had discovered all about Elizabeth and James Delaney. Yet there was still a mystery to be solved which may affect not only her, but Saffron, too.

She spotted a separate envelope, also from Meredith's office. Reaching for her letter-opener, she opened it and sat back. Its contents were what she had hoped for. It was a personal letter. Meredith had summarised her mother's will, and Jessica's legacy, in an easy-to-read document.

She sat back when she'd finished reading the letter, and rehearsed her lines. She heard Saffron in the kitchen, preparing supper, and suddenly felt the need for a stiff drink. Brushing aside other mail, she folded the letter and stuffed it into the pocket of her jeans.

'Hi Mum. I hope you don't mind me cooking dinner tonight? I put a casserole in the oven a while ago.'

'All smells good to me. I think I'll have a gin and tonic—how about you?'

'Brilliant, we can go and sit in the conservatory until dinner's ready. It should be about another hour.'

'Perfect.' Jessica began assembling ingredients for their drinks. 'I've just been trying to get through all that mail, and I've managed to sort out the all-important correspondence from Bateman's. She nodded to Saffron to lead the way into the conservatory as she carried out their drinks. 'I've got something to tell you.'

After they sat down, Jessica produced the letter from her pocket. 'Cheers, Saffie!' she lifted her glass.

'Cheers,' Saffron took a mouthful of the cool liquid and waited anxiously for her mother to speak.

'Well, Saffie, cheers it is. I—we have something to celebrate.' Jessica smiled at her over her glass before placing it on the table and opening up the letter.

'Come on, Mum!' Saffie was excited, urging her to read it.

'Well. It appears that I've been left a large amount of money, along with jewellery, personal and heirloom items.' Jessica paused and looked at Saffron.

The cash value of my mother's legacy to me is four million two hundred thousand pounds, and sixty-five pence.'

Saffron put her hand to her mouth and gasped. 'Four million two hundred thousand pounds,' she said incredulously. She started laughing. 'And sixty-five pence.'

'Oh, Mum, oh dear! Sorry, it's too much to take in, but I can't help laughing at the sixty-five pence.' She stood up, put her arms around her mother and held her tightly. They both burst out laughing.

'Sit down, Saffie. I've been thinking. Look, you've had time to make a decision about where you're going from here, and so have I. This now simply enables both of us to follow our dreams and change our lives for good...'

'But, Mum—it's *your* inheritance, yet...'

'That is so, but you are her granddaughter, and she always said that she wanted me to share my inheritance with you. I don't think she understood what you were doing with your life, why, or where, and she trusted me to look after you when the right time came. Well, that time is now, and I would like you to think hard about my proposal to you.' Jessica lifted her glass. 'And can I have a refill, please! The last time I had a G&T as good as this was with Sebastian, sitting on the terrace of our hotel in Shimla—what memories it conjures up.'

Settling back into their chairs, Jessica roughed out what she thought might happen and what they might do with the legacy. She put it to Saffron that perhaps she'd like to live in the cottage for a peppercorn rent. Jessica said that after retirement, she'd like to move west, either Devon or Cornwall and buy a house somewhere on the coast.

'That sounds like a possibility, Mum. And it all depends, of course, how you think you'll share the inheritance.' Saffron said, shrugging her shoulders in an attempt to cover up her enthusiasm.

'Well, it's something I've been thinking about for a while, and now that you're here, and I hope, to stay, it would make sense for you to live here. You love the garden, and riding, and this country life. The villagers are very supportive and all on the same wavelength—country people who wouldn't be seen dead in a town or city. And me? The chance for a new life? Who knows?'

'Wow! Mum. You've thought this through, haven't you?'

'Sort of, but I have to go to see Meredith as soon as possible. There remains a lot of unanswered questions. I'll ring him tomorrow, and make a plan to drive to Cornwall. Have you been using my mobile? It needs to be well charged, and I'll have to take the Land Rover, so we can either hire you a car or—hey—we can go and buy another one. Right now, if we choose!' Jessica suddenly realised that her life would no longer be dictated to her by how, or whether, she could afford things.

'Of course—all of a sudden, money's not so much of a stumbling block.' Saffron raised her eyebrows as she, too, began to hope that she would never again want for anything. 'I think you'll enjoy the freedom you'll have, Mum. And I think I'll fit in here. What a turn of events, and now I know I made the right decision to leave Barra.' She looked towards the kitchen. 'I think that casserole must be done by now.'

'Saffie, I hope this doesn't spoil either of us. There'll be no rearrangements until I'm sure, and until I've talked to Meredith Bateman and sought his advice. I don't intend to rush into anything.'

'Except, perhaps another car? I will need one.' Saffron suggested audaciously.

'Not so fast. I'll think about it. Now, let's eat, shall we? I'm starving.'

50

Hampshire September 1997:

A gravelly voice, clearly that of an elderly man answered the call. 'Hello, Meredith? This is Jess.' Jessica adjusted the phone so that he might hear her better. It's Jessica Delaney-Hartford. I'm back from India, Meredith.'

'My dear, welcome back—where are you now?'

'I'm at home. At Willow Cottage. How are you?'

'Oh, chugging along, you know. Did you get the mail I sent you?'

'That's what I'm calling about. Yes, thank you. My legacy came as a surprise, and I need to get some advice from you regarding certain aspects of Mum's will, too.'

'Well, I'm always here when you want me, at the other end of the phone, you know. Tell me…'

'No, Meredith, I need to sit down with you and talk to you face-to-face, so I thought I'd drive down to Cornwall either tomorrow or at the weekend—will you be there?'

'Of course, my dear. I don't go far these days, and even though I still have a share in Bateman's I'm just a sleeping partner.' Meredith chuckled at his little joke and cleared his throat. 'Any time that's good for you. I used to find it better driving down here before the weekend. I'd love to hear your stories, and all about your travels in India.'

Jessica took a deep breath. 'But before I come down, perhaps you can just clarify a few things for me?'

'Of course.'

'Meredith—er—do you know Sebastian Shelley?' Meredith paused. Jessica waited.

'Hello? Meredith?'

'Jess, yes, I do. He's the son of a great friend of mine, Edward Shelley.'

'And did you know he was going to meet me in India, in Shimla…'

'Jess, can we discuss this when I see you? Yes, I had been told. Look, there's a lot you need to know. When you get here, I'll be able to explain better. Now that Catherine has passed away, there's no more need for subterfuge. I've wanted to be honest with you for a long time, but my hands were tied. I'm sorry, but I can explain everything.'

It was Jessica's turn to be silent. What was he trying to say? And what more secrets could he reveal that she didn't already know? Was Catherine the reason she was never told about how her parents died? And if so, why not? And if it were true, what Sebastian had told her that first day they met, Meredith was connected to him and his father.

'Jess? Are you there?' Meredith sounded anxious.

'Yes, I'm here. I was trying to make sense of what you've just told me—sorry.'

'Jess, why don't you come to Cornwall tomorrow? We can go for a pub lunch or tea somewhere, and I'll tell you the full story, and I'll explain why it's only now you're finding out the truth.' He paused. 'Can you get here?'

'Yes, I can and will, but I think I'll travel down this afternoon, and stay at Fowey Hall where I usually stay, and come over to Bodmin Moor in the morning so that we can have a lot of time together. Will that be okay with you?'

'You have my number—call me when you get to Fowey, and we'll set a time at my office—or perhaps even better at my house.'

'Yes, I'll do that. I know there's mystery concerning my parents' demise, and I think I've found out why. I'll wait to hear the rest from you.'

'Look forward to hearing from you, Jess, and seeing you. It's been a long time.'

'Till tomorrow, Meredith. Bye.'

'Goodbye dear girl.'

Jessica heard the faintest click just before she put the phone back in its cradle. Through the gap in the study door, she caught a glimpse of Saffron descending the stairs. Getting up from her desk, she surprised her daughter in the hallway.

'Oh, Mum—I didn't know you were up yet. I...I came down to make the coffee. Is everything okay? I mean...'

'Saffie, have you just been in my room?'

'No! Why should I, Mum?' Saffron was indignant. 'I didn't even know you were up.'

'I've been on a call to Meredith Bateman and I thought I heard the bedroom phone click.' Jessica walked ahead of Saffron into the kitchen.

'I must have been mistaken. Now—do you have yours black or white?'

Jessica felt uncomfortable, but decided to leave the subject alone, as she joined Saffron at the kitchen table.

'I'll be driving to Cornwall later today.'

'Oh?' Saffron feigned surprised.

'Yes, I have an urgent meeting with Meredith tomorrow, and I must get a few things clarified. I'll have to take the Land Rover. Don't let me forget my mobile. I suggest if you need to go shopping, this morning would be the best time, as long as you're back by lunchtime— I'll have to get on the road. It will take me about four hours. I'll make a reservation at the Fowey Hall Hotel.'

'Of course, Mum—can I do anything for you before you go?'

Jessica considered Saffron's offer. 'Oh, yes, you can do me some breakfast if you like.'

'Ah, I was just about to go and have a shower, but…'

'No problem, I can just as easily put a slice of bread in the toaster and boil an egg.' Jessica took a deep breath and huffed. 'Go on. I'll see you later.'

It was becoming apparent to Jessica that the relationship with Saffron she had hoped for on their reunion didn't seem to be working yet. She didn't want to perpetuate hostility in the house, but Saffron's behaviour wasn't very endearing. But as was her way, Jessica decided to give it more time and see how things unfolded, but she was sure that Saffron had been listening in to her phone call on the bedroom extension. They didn't need to always be on the same page but, to avoid any confrontation, she decided to bite her lip for now.

Jessica scooped up all the documents pertaining to her inheritance, and the will. She packed them to take to Cornwall, also to keep them away from Saffron's prying eyes. She called the hotel and made a reservation for two nights. And she drafted a letter of resignation to the headteacher at Coombe Court School, which she would email before she left.

There were ten more days before she needed to go back to her job, and she hoped to be free by half-term. By that time, she hoped to be well on the way to relocating to a new home, and a new life. That space would give her plenty of time to decide where she wanted to live, and give her and Saffron time to sort out both their futures to mutual satisfaction. She no more wanted to be at odds with her daughter than she wanted to be secretive, but she sensed an awkwardness between them.

She hadn't realised her daughter could be so self-centred. Perhaps she'd had a bad time in the Hebrides. She decided she'd find out more about that period of her daughter's life before passing harsh judgement. But the edginess in the household had to stop before it got out of hand, so that they could live together harmoniously, at least for the time being.

51

Hampshire September 1997:

As she drove away from the village Jessica felt a sense of relief. She still wasn't sure whether it had been a good idea to welcome her daughter back, but where else could Saffron have gone? She seemed to be a bit of a loner, lost, not knowing what to do with her life. Jessica wanted to do the right thing by her, but the way things were going it might not be that easy.

Pulling up at a roundabout to let a milk tanker through, Jessica decided she'd stop at her favourite watering hole, Stourhead, for tea. She had been a member of the National Trust for a long time, and always tried to seek out their stately homes and gardens on a long drive. She loved these calm and pleasant havens where she could recharge her batteries. Choosing scones and a pot of tea, she sat and observed the other patrons. Social stereotypes, she thought cynically, in their zip-off Rohan shorts and hiking boots, walking staffs, casual sweaters slung round shoulders, and heads covered with sensible sun hats. But what's wrong with that, she reasoned, they all helped to keep these historic places maintained for everyone to enjoy.

A tall man walked towards her with his tea tray, scanning the sea of heads, looking for a spare table. Jessica lowered her gaze and busily got on with pouring her tea and dolloping cream on her scone. The scene at the hotel in Shimla came rushing back—Sebastian asking if she minded if he sat with her. She put a hand up to her face in a body-language gesture that said, *please don't sit here*. The tall man walked away and she relaxed. She was keen to get on the road again and stopped just briefly at the gift shop to buy a jar of homemade lemon curd to give to Meredith.

Determined to get to the hotel in time for dinner, Jessica pressed the accelerator hard and switched on the radio for company. As the miles melted away, her thoughts turned to how good it was to be home again, and knowing she'd be regaling Meredith with her travel stories and discoveries tomorrow, in Cornwall.

It was with drooping eyelids that she finished her after-dinner coffee at the hotel, as the sun set over the sea. Her lunchtime meeting with Meredith tomorrow had been a good plan. She would not rise early.

Jessica heard the shrill ring of her mobile next to the bed, and sat bolt upright. The sun was shining through a slit in the heavy brocade curtains, casting a beam of light across the floor of her room. She checked the time—it was already five past nine.

'Hello?' She rubbed the sleep out of her eyes. 'Hello—Jessica here.'

'Good morning, Jess.' It was Meredith, as she suspected. 'I'm so looking forward to seeing you today.'

'Me, too, Meredith.' Jessica stifled a yawn. 'I'm having a late morning. It was tiring driving down yesterday.'

'Good idea—there's no rush. I just wanted to make arrangements for our rendezvous, and I've been thinking, why don't you come to my office first? We can have a lunch later at my local. Can you get here by mid-day?' He didn't wait for an answer. 'We can go through things before we go out to lunch. See you about twelve?'

Jessica panicked, 'Yes—about twelve.'

She ordered room service and opened the curtains to a crystal-clear Cornish sky. Her room overlooked the mouth of the river and out to sea, and she watched briefly as small boats sailed to and fro. Holidaymakers were making the most of the last few days of the summer break.

Showering, she wondered if she should phone Saffron, but dismissed the idea, and concentrated instead on how she thought the meeting might go. She was intent on recalling everything that had happened in Shimla so it would be fresh in her mind when she spoke to Meredith. She had just finished dressing when her breakfast arrived. *Good timing,* she thought, and hoped the rest of the day would go as smoothly.

The one-time farm buildings emerged in the near distance on Bodmin Moor, as Jessica rounded the last corner of the narrow lane, between banks of green willow that led to Trevasey. Bateman's sign pointed down the long driveway to the extensive converted barn complex. Jessica mused that nothing much had changed since she first came here with her mother.

Bateman's offices were in a separate barn adjacent to a stable block. A riding school rented the stables, and as Jessica pulled up, three ponies trotted out in front of her to join a hacking track in the field opposite. The Land Rover crunched to a standstill on the pebble forecourt, and Jessica slid out to be welcomed at the door by a beaming Meredith, neatly dressed, but somewhat portlier than the last time they met.

'Jess!' They pecked cheeks in a friendly greeting. Now semi-retired, Meredith was still quite young-looking, and Jessica noted his smart co-ordinated clothing and his well-kept wavy silver hair he wore, just to the collar. She's always thought him to be the artistic type. 'Come in, my assistant took the day off today so we have the office to ourselves.' He took her elbow and walked her into his lavishly furnished office at the far end of the beamed and rustic main room, neatly laid out with desks, printers and computers, and many healthy-looking indoor plants. She remembered his passion was caring for and propagating orchids in an orchid house he'd had built onto his home. She was so taken with the exquisite blooms that she'd followed suit. She'd sat in there the last time she saw him, when she and a friend were visiting whilst on holiday.

'Oh, Meredith, this is so nice. It's good to be here in Cornwall again, and I'm so wanting to tell my story.'

He'd parked himself behind his imposing oak partners' desk in front of a pile of prepared documents. Jessica sat opposite, pulling files out of her briefcase. He got down to business straight away.

'Ladies first. So, tell me all about Shimla—or would you like a coffee first?'

'No to the coffee, and, well, where to start. I've been on an emotional roller-coaster, Meredith. Right from the time I arrived, to my last day in Delhi. I did tell you that I met Sebastian Shelley, didn't I?'

Meredith shuffled in his seat and nodded confirmation. 'Go on, dear.'

'I don't know what I would have done without him, to be honest, but it was weird at first, him knowing you. I was highly suspicious of his motives and, to be honest, I still am, a little.' She paused.

'Jess, carry on. I'll hear your version first, but I have a story to tell you.'

Jessica continued. 'There was some confusion about a photo in his father's study that he told me unconvincingly was of your niece. I said I didn't think you had a niece, and the issue seemed to pass by. But he took me to all the places I needed to go, you know, registry office for copies of my parents' death certificates, and council offices to try to locate The Laurels where I was born. I honestly don't think I would have been able to do all that on my own.

'We went to the church where I was baptised—it's still in use— and met the current vicar, and found out from him that my parents' graves were located not in the churchyard as I'd expected, but in a British cemetery out of town. Sebastian and I went there and we found their graves.' Jessica looked across the desk. Meredith was listening, intrigued by her story.

'That's amazing.' he said.

Jessica fished in her handbag for a tissue as she remembered that turning point in her trip. 'Meredith, we met the woman who used to be my nanny, and later she told us all about what happened in Shimla when my parents died.' She paused, noticing that Meredith's face looked blank.

'Which was?'

Jessica looked the old man in the eye. 'I think you know, don't you? And I think you, Sebastian and his father knew all along that my parents perished in a fire that consumed their home and I was rescued by Edward Shelley. It wasn't a rare form of dysentery at all, was it, Meredith? It has…'

Meredith was keen to interrupt. 'Jess, of course, you should have been told the truth, but the secrecy wasn't ours at all. I wanted to come clean with you when you were old enough to understand, but Catherine wouldn't let us.'

'You mean that Mum kept this from me deliberately. But why? As she was dying, she urged me to go to Shimla to find the truth. But I never thought there was any sort of a conspiracy going on.'

'More than that, Jess. Much more than that. You see, it wasn't a trust fund from your parents that sent you to the best schools, provided anything and everything you wanted in later life when you were growing up and facing adulthood. And it didn't come from your adoptive parents either.'

'But...that is what Sebastian told me, but I didn't take it all in.' Jessica held her head in her shaking hands, 'so...who was it...'

'It was Edward. Edward Shelley, Jess. And at last, I can tell you why...'

52

Cornwall September 1997:

M eredith helped Jessica into the passenger seat of his car. She didn't know whether to laugh or cry or be angry at the stunning statement Meredith had just delivered.

'Sorry to drop this bombshell, Jess, but it had to be done this way. Catherine swore me to secrecy until after she died, and until you and I could meet. She urged you to go to Shimla first, hoping that you might somehow uncover the truth there for yourself. I think she was ashamed of herself for not telling you at the outset. You see, Catherine never knew much about your mother's life in Shimla. I think that was why she wanted you to go there.'

'It doesn't seem fair, all these secrets being kept from me—the very person who ought to know it all. I mean, what would have happened if I hadn't gone to Shimla? Would I still be in the dark? Meredith, I feel like I've been side-lined bigtime. It's embarrassing, almost like everyone's been treating me like a child.

'But I think I found out more about my parents and their lives in Shimla than anyone else could have known.' She hesitated, deep in thought. 'Except, of course, Edward Shelley. Funny, Sebastian said he'd take me to his home to meet him.' She paused. 'So, how much of this does Sebastian know?'

Meredith swung the car into the forecourt of the Crown Inn. 'Not a lot. Come on, let's get settled and I'll tell you all I know. And you tell me what you found in Shimla.'

'I'll tell you everything *we* discovered as well as what other people told us. And in spite of opening such a can of worms, I'm so pleased I went.'

They settled into a secluded corner table and ordered lunch and a bottle of wine. Meredith went to the bar and ordered them an aperitif.

When he returned with the drinks, Jessica began to recall her story. 'After Sebastian said he would be able to help me find my way around, he pretty much came everywhere with me. It was a huge help, for which I am grateful. It wasn't long after meeting Chandra, my old nanny, that we saw the big picture, and we were both shocked to hear that my mother, Elizabeth, had an affair with Sebastian's father.

'Quite by chance, we also bumped into an old couple who lived in Shimla at around the same time as my parents. They were close friends of them and Edward Shelley, but I think they'd forgotten a lot, so we didn't push them to remember. To be honest, we'd already uncovered the whole story by that time.'

Meredith took a sip of his gin and tonic. 'Jess, I'm sorry this was all kept from you, but there was a reason, and who was to know that you'd discover the truth of the matter.'

'So, you knew they perished in a fire at their home? I always wondered what happened in Shimla. And I have to tell you, but you might laugh, but I've had an occasional nightmare for most of my life, about choking to death in thick smoke. So, how did you know, and why didn't you tell me, Meredith?'

'It was Edward. He also swore me to secrecy because he wanted to do the right thing by you.'

'Edward? Why?'

'Edward thinks he might be your father, Jess. He wanted to support you in the only way he could, with money.'

'He still thinks that?' Memories of the conversation she had with Chandra and Sebastian in Shimla came flooding back.

'Jess, your parents died intestate. You were so young, and it seemed they hadn't made a will. Catherine was the only qualifying next of kin, and she was bequeathed what small amount of equity your mother left behind.'

Their lunch arrived and Jessica didn't think she could face food with these new disclosures spinning round her brain. Meredith placed a hand on her arm.

'I want you to do something soon, Jess. I want you to meet Edward.'

Jessica put her hands to her face in trepidation. 'Yes, and I think I'd also like that,' she said, 'as soon as possible. I think he saved my life in that fire—mine and Chandra's.'

They finished their lunch in silence, Jessica thinking about her newly-discovered benefactor. Could he be her father? There would only be one way to find out, she thought, he'd have to agree to a test of some sort. She wasn't au fait with the procedure, but had heard

DNA was used by scientists and pathologists to verify family connections. What if it proved she wasn't his daughter? Her mind raced on...

Meredith piped up. 'A penny for them, Jess?'

'Oh, nothing, but I was just wondering...'

'What?'

'Well, you know Edward, and I don't, but do you think he'd be agreeable to a DNA test? I think that would be the only way to know for sure, don't you?'

'Jess, he's an old man, and he's, well, he's terminally ill. Didn't Sebastian tell you? He's dying of incurable cancer. And, sorry to say, he's not been given much longer to live...'

'No, I'm so sorry, Sebastian did mention that he was ill.'

'I think he knows how seriously ill his father is. He'll stand to inherit quite a fortune when his father dies.'

'Meredith, he and I got on well in Shimla. When we left, I stayed the night in his apartment in Delhi and he took me to the airport the next day. But before we found out from Chandra about his father's relationship with my mother, we had formed a close bond. I know he's younger than me, and I guess I was vulnerable, but I thought he felt something for me. You see, what I discovered in Shimla has changed my whole life. I was on an emotional journey from the moment I met Sebastian.'

Meredith listened attentively. 'It seems everything is coming together in your life all at once, Jess. I don't suppose you've had any ideas yet about what to do with your legacy?'

'As a matter of fact, I have. I plan to retire from teaching as soon as they can let me go, and I thought about coming west and buying a house by the sea. Somewhere I can live quietly—or in the countryside.'

'Jess, how long will you be down here? because I was thinking about calling Edward and taking you to his home to meet him. He lives just over the border in Devon. It's only a forty-minute drive.'

'Let me think about it, Meredith. I have a week before I have to be back at school, and I have to sort out what to do about Saffie.'

'Of course, but shall I give him a ring anyway, to test the water. Your meeting will be so emotional for both of you. The only way he has been able to keep in touch with your life has been through me, and

Catherine when she was alive. I've sent him the odd photo of you…'

'One of the first things Sebastian told me, by way of an introduction was that I looked like the woman in a photo that his father has on his desk in his study.'

'I gave him the one you sent me taken at Stonehenge when you came to Cornwall two years ago.'

'That's what Sebastian said—Stonehenge, and he said that when he asked his father about it, he was told it was a picture of your niece.'

'Poor Edward. I've known him for almost as long as your life, and I don't think he's ever been happy. He's a very successful businessman, but Sebastian's mother and he were totally incompatible, and over the years he confided in me that he'd never love another woman like he loved your mother. It will be so good for him to meet you.'

Jessica felt tears pricking the back of her eyes. She never knew any of this, and now a whole new world was opening up to her.

'Meredith, I've decided, I'll stay on here until I've met Edward. I simply have to, now. When do you think we'll be able to see him?'

'I'll think about it when I get back to the office. He never goes far these days. He has a married couple who live in the gatehouse at the entrance to his estate, who look after him and the house and grounds. They organise other people from time to time to come over to work on the estate. I manage his financial affairs for him, so he's able to live his days out without worrying about anything.'

'How about tomorrow?'

'Leave it to me. He's going to be so overwhelmed. I'll call him in the morning so that he won't spend a sleepless night in anticipation and anxiety. I must say, Jess, I'm also feeling emotional now it's all coming to a conclusion.'

'Me too, Meredith. Just imagine, I'm fifty-five years old, and only now am I about to find out who I am.'

53

Cornwall September 1997:

Jessica bid farewell to Meredith, who waved from the doorway of his office. It was raining again, and as she made her way through the maze of country lanes, her car became covered in mud splashes and leaves.

Coming out into the vast open space of Bodmin Moor, she found a suitable spot to pull over. She sat motionless, staring through the windscreen. The wipers were working hard, swishing away the rain water in buckets-full. She mused that it must be like the monsoonal rain in India.

She was drained, and the tears falling down her cheeks bore a quiet stillness, mimicking the sparkling raindrops. She'd never felt so alone in the world as she was now, locked in the dilemma of insecurity, uncertainty and emptiness. She slumped her head onto the steering-wheel and pressed a handful of tissues over her face.

Come on, girl. You have to face this head-on. You have to summon up the strength somehow and come to terms with it all. Pull yourself together—it's not the end of the world it's just very strange and unexpected.

She took a long, slow breath and tilted the rear-view mirror to look at her reddened eyes and tear-stained face. She fished in her handbag looking for something to remedy the damage. Neither a car nor tractor had driven past her from either direction, but, she thought, who in their right mind would go out on an afternoon like this.

Arriving back at her hotel, she was overcome by exhaustion. Jet-lag meets a day of incredibly draining feelings, she thought, and succumbed to a deep sleep. Waking to the shrill sound of her mobile, she realised she'd slipped back into Indian time. She recognised the number staring at her from the small screen as her home number. She let it go into voicemail while she pulled herself together enough to face a long, possibly awkward conversation with Saffie. She raided her mini-bar and sat in an armchair with a large gin and tonic before ringing back.

'Mum, thank goodness—I have been trying to get hold of you forever.' Saffron sounded out of breath. 'I have news about…'

'Well, as you may or may not know, Saffie, mobile signals sometimes drop out in Cornwall, and I've been out almost all of today. I had a pub lunch with Meredith Bateman. I've got such a lot to tell you when I get home, and by-the-way, I'm staying on for a couple more days. Tomorrow, hopefully, I'm going to meet Edward Shelley...'

'Who?'

'Edward Shelley—Sebastian's father.'

'Mum, listen, I had a call from Sebastian last night. He's back in London, and wants to come down to see you tomorrow. After calling in here, he said he'd head west and go to see his father. He sounds like a nice guy, Mum.'

'Yes, Saffie—he'll be charming.' Jessica hoped that her reluctance to talk about Sebastian further hadn't been too obviously laced with acerbity.

'So, Mum, when do you think you'll be home? I'd better get some groceries in if we're to be entertaining Sebastian.'

'You don't have to be excited about it, Saffie. He'll fit in very well, I think. I just hope he doesn't over-stay his welcome. But he'll want to get down here as soon as possible.' Jessica was dredging her memory, realising she had to tell Saffie all about her grandmother and Edward.

'There's so much to tell, Saffie, and tomorrow I guess there'll be more...Saffie? Saffron—are you there? Hello.' Jessica realised she'd been talking to no-one for a while.

'So sorry, Mum. I've, er, I've not been feeling too well since you left. A touch of the collywobbles, I think. I'll be alright.'

'I do hope so. Have you just been sick?' Jessica didn't wait for an answer. 'When did Sebastian say he'd be there? I may not be back home before he arrives. I gave him my home and mobile number before I left Delhi. He may have been trying to phone me, too.'

'He said it could be tomorrow late afternoon. How long will you be at his father's house, do you think?'

'Don't know, but apparently, he's not a well man, so perhaps we won't be able to meet for too long. I'm not sure what to expect. I won't go into details on the phone, but I'll tell you as soon as possible...'

'Mum? What? Is it what you were told by your nanny in Shimla?' Saffron was curious.

'Look, I hope to be able to drive home after I've met Edward, but

213

I don't like driving after dark. The best thing I can do is to call you when I'm on the road, and in the meantime, when you hear from Sebastian, tell him my rough plan. Put him in the blue room—can you make up the bed and give the room a freshen-up?'

'Course, Mum. Gosh, what an exciting and full life you lead. See you tomorrow, I hope.'

'Bye Saffie, I'll explain everything when I see you, and its lucky that Sebastian's going to be there, because he needs to be party to it. Hopefully it'll fill in the missing pieces of the jigsaw in the story we pieced together in Shimla. Look, I have to get ready to go down to dinner now, we'll speak tomorrow.'

'Yes, bye Mum. Take care. Till tomorrow. I'll go and get Sebastian's room ready now.'

54

Cornwall September 1997:

Meredith phoned early. 'Morning, Jess, I'll have to go over to Cleave Manor in my own car, introduce you to Edward, and come back to my office. I have to attend to something urgently.'

'Sorry you have to do that, Meredith, I thought I might take you and Edward out for lunch somewhere nice.' Jessica was disappointed.

'Sorry, Jess, but you'll notice that Edward is in no position to be going out too much, and anyway, he'll have had his housekeeper prepare lunch for us, I'm sure. I must call him and tell him I won't be staying long.'

'Alright, I'll meet you there—how long should I allow for the journey? And any landmarks other than the directions you gave me yesterday? I've seen the AA Trip Finder directions from Fowey. It all seems fairly straightforward.'

'No landmarks, but it's easy to find and you'll see the gates and gatehouse from the road as you approach. He'll be expecting you, so the main gate to the property will be open. Just drive in and over the hill till you see the house. Park on the pebbled front courtyard. You may find the door open as well. I'll be there before you, so you'll see my car.' He hesitated. 'He's going to be so excited, I can tell you...'

'Well, so am I—and nervous, too.'

'He'll make you feel relaxed and at home in no time. You'll see.'

'See you there, Meredith. Bye for now.'

Jessica took one last look in the mirror, and adjusted her mother's pearl necklace. She picked up her handbag, descended the old oak staircase at Fowey Hall, said a confident hello to the doorman and got into her car. Placing the AA touring map within easy reach, she set off on yet another journey into the unknown.

Boarding the Bodinnick car ferry to cross the river she stared whimsically at Daphne du Maurier's residence, Ferryside, on the banks of the river. She wondered what that great novelist would have made of her complex story.

Jessica stopped to get her bearings, also to check her appearance in the mirror. Two miles later and there it was, the gate house, the open gate and, proudly crafted in wrought iron above it, *Cleave Manor*. Another sign on the right-hand stone wall read *Private residence. Please check in at the gate house.*

Meredith had told her to just drive in, so she turned the Land Rover through the gate and onto the gravel driveway. Slowly driving over a hill, she spotted the house through a break in the trees lining the drive. It sat beautifully in its sand-coloured stone overcoat surrounded by laurel bushes and hydrangeas whose pom-pom blue blooms were turning golden.

Past the imposing front door, Jessica parked the car meters away from Meredith's. She felt like crying again. *No, dear God, no…why is this happening? Please, not now.*

She crunched her way towards the entrance. Meredith was there to greet her. He helped her up the steps and into the impressive entrance hall. Large works of art hung on walls above and alongside the huge fireplace. A log fire burned in the hearth.

The frail old man with white hair rose tall and slender from the fireside sofa and turned slowly on his walking-stick. He clumsily pulled the royal-blue jumper further around his shoulders as he stopped in his tracks to look at Jessica. His old lined face broke into a beaming smile. He dropped his stick and held out both arms.

'I know it's you.' He smiled. 'Dear Jessica. You're the spitting image of your mother.'

As Jessica moved towards him, they both held back their tears. She gently and quickly hugged him but he was losing his balance and began to stagger backwards. She and Meredith helped him back on to the sofa.

'My dear Jess—please, I'm sorry—what a day it's going to be. Come and sit here for a moment. Let me look at you properly.' He never took his gaze away from her and, as he regained his composure, he pulled a handkerchief from his pocket and dabbed his nose and eyes.

He looked at Meredith, 'See, I told you. They *are* her mother's eyes. And her mother's hair, and, oh, Jess, please tell me. Those pearls…'

'Edward. Yes, they're Mum's. They survived everything. They were in a box of jewellery that Catherine saved for me for my twenty-first birthday.' She fingered their coldness, holding them away from her throat so that Edward could see them properly.

'I'm overwhelmed. Meredith, let's go through to the drawing room. Come on, my dear, let me show you *my* Laurels. It's a fair-sized house, you know, but it has been my home for longer than I can remember…' Shakily, he rose from the sofa, and instinctively, Jessica stood beside him and held his free arm to help him to his feet. They looked at each other, Jessica smiling half in disbelief and half at meeting Sebastian's father who was not at all how she had imagined him to be.

Meredith led the way through to the drawing-room. He told Edward he'd have to go back to the office, as he parted from them, saying he'd leave them together to talk, Edward insisted he stay for lunch at least. 'I know that Annie's preparing a veritable feast for us. Oh well, I'm sure we'll manage it together, won't we dear?' he said, looking at Jessica.

'It's a very tempting offer, Edward, but I have to attend to some urgent business matters. Sorry.'

'That's alright. But do come over again soon, there are a few personal matters I want to discuss with you as a matter of resolve, very soon.' At that Meredith strode across to the door.

Edward pointed his walking stick towards a door leading off the drawing room. 'Jessica, I want to show you something—over there in my study. Walk with me. Look, my beautiful home is all too much for me now. But I wanted you to be here to see it as it is now. You and Sebastian may have to deal with things eventually.'

'Oh, Edward, I …' Jessica was taken aback by his assumption. She realised he had been waiting patiently for her. *If only someone had told me before, would it have made that much difference? Why only now when he's so old? We could have spent more time together, and the situation with Sebastian would never have happened.*

'Don't you worry, I have a rough plan.' He gestured over to a highly-polished grand piano, and beyond that, his study. 'Look, see those photographs there—on the piano and on the side table over there?' They walked towards them. Edward picked up an exquisite silver frame. 'See the woman sitting between the two men. That's your mother, Jess. I used to worship the ground she walked on. She was the only real love of my life.' He reached for the piano stool. Perching on it, he bowed his head.

Jessica stared at the photograph. It had been touched-up with colour. Just as Edward had remarked, they had the same face and same hair. Her mother was smiling, posing, flanked by two young men. She looked relaxed in a wicker chair on what looked like a veranda.

'My mother—Edward, this is amazing. I've never seen such a good picture of her. Where was it taken, and who are the two young handsome-looking gentlemen?'

'The young men? Ah! That's easy Jess. This is me—and that, Jessica, is your father. Your father, Mr James Delaney. We had some splendid times in Shimla. The place? the back veranda of their house, The Laurels. Come, let's sit over there.' He pointed to two beautiful deep-cushioned blue brocade armchairs. A shaft of sunlight streamed through the window, depositing its timely glow over the room.

Jessica was still clutching the picture. 'Edward, do you remember a housemaid in Shimla called Chandra?' Edward's expression froze into an anxious frown.

'Chandra? Of course, Chandra—now I'm not sure how much you know, or what you and Sebastian discovered in Shimla. But go on.'

'We met her.' She watched his face slowly turn to a recognition of her incredible statement. 'We met her in Shimla, and she told us so much about my parents, about The Laurels, and about me when I was a little girl. She also told us about the fire, the trauma, and, Edward, she told us about you and my mother…'

Edward held his head in his hands, as if in shame. 'It's alright, Edward. I do understand. And after what Meredith told me yesterday, I've pieced together most of the puzzle. How can I thank you enough for all those years of paying my school fees, putting money into my bank account, and enabling me to have such a free and happy life? Without you, I wouldn't be who I am today—this happy and confident lady just about to retire from her career and engineer a sea-change in her life.'

Edward sank backwards into his chair and took one long, deep breath. He opened his eyes. 'This is just like a dream—a dream come true. And I hope you will forgive me for asking Sebastian to go to Shimla and find you. Funny, I wanted him to steer you away from any information you may glean about me and your mother, Jess, but I guess it had to come out eventually. I loved you very much, too, in Shimla.

After taking you to the station with Catherine, and chasing after you as the train left because you'd left your teddy behind...'

'Teddy? You don't mean Teddy? Oh no, what a priceless story. But even more priceless is that I still have Teddy. I handed him down to my daughter, Saffron, and she's just brought him back to me.'

They looked at each other and couldn't help but burst out laughing. Edward got out of his chair. 'Come on, let me show you more pictures and mementoes, and more of the house, and after lunch, I have a real surprise in store for you.'

55

Devon, September 1997:

Edward and Jessica walked side by side through the house. She made sure she was near to him should he need assistance. He escorted her through room after room until she lost count.

'Come with me to the kitchen and meet Annie. She's been with me for many years. She and her husband, Bob. He looks after the grounds and keeps the gardens beautiful. Annie cooks and keeps a close eye on me. She organises outside staff to keep on top of housework and cleaning. It all seems too much for just them and me, doesn't it?' He smiled wryly at Jessica.

'But I can imagine why you don't want to leave here, Edward, and of course, you have Sebastian to think about. I agree it is a great family home, and I'm sure it will be again.' Jessica kept to herself her thoughts on what the future may hold.

'I suppose so, and now that Sebastian's leaving Delhi at last, there's always the possibility that he may find a woman and need a home like this. I would like that very much.'

'Here we are.' Jessica helped him open the heavy door to the kitchen. 'Mmm—smells divine.' He turned and whispered to Jessica, 'Annie's a very good cook.'

'Annie!' He called to a large round lady draped in aprons, washing her hands in the sink. 'Annie, this is Jessica. Remember I told you about her?'

Annie smiled. 'Of course. Jessica. Welcome to Cleave Manor, I hope you're enjoying the house tour, and I hope you like a good hearty steak and kidney pie.'

'It smells delicious, Annie. I'm looking forward to it already...'

Edward butted in. 'What time for lunch, Annie, oh and there'll only be the two of us, Meredith had to go back to his office. Hope that's okay.'

'How about one o'clock? And I'll lay the table in the conservatory.' And to Jessica. 'You'll love the view from back there, right over the gardens, with Dartmoor as a backdrop.'

'Thanks, Annie.' Edward led Jessica out of the kitchen.

'Where to now, Edward? The place seems so vast after my humble cottage. Oh, and I forgot to tell you, Sebastian's going down there today. He arrived back in London yesterday. Saffie's going to look after him till I arrive home. He and I were going to come here together, but Meredith wanted me to come to meet you today. I'm staying at Fowey Hall, and I'll go home tomorrow.'

Edward looked surprised. 'Oh dear, I was hoping you'd stay longer. You can come and stay here, you know. I'd love to have your company and love to reminisce about Shimla and my—our—lives there.'

'That's very kind, but…' She hesitated, 'but well, why don't I? I have so much to find out, and so much more to tell you about my visit to Shimla. Are you sure?' She looked at Edward who pointed to a sofa in the drawing room they'd just entered.

'Sure, my dear, sure? I'm certain. I'll dredge my memory and tell you as much about your parents as I can remember. My memory isn't all that bad, even though I have this…awful disease.' His voice trailed off.

'And I'll tell you as much about what we discovered in Shimla as I can fit in.' Jessica's heart jumped at the thought of getting to know her late mother's lover. She'd have to tell him everything she and Sebastian found in India, and about the couple at the Hotel.

'How do you like this room, Jess? Isn't it so calm and cool? When Sebastian was at Cambridge he'd come down for long weekends and semesters with a variety of friends. They'd liven the place up, I can tell you, but they were all fairly well behaved, in spite of the copious quantities of booze they seemed to consume. Let's sit here for a while, on the sofa.

'His mother and I bought this place, and she lived here until he went up to Cambridge. It was a sad but inevitable break-up. She had a number of extra-marital affairs over the years. I quantified it as poetic justice after my liaison with your mother all those years ago. She eventually left to live with one of her men, took Sebastian with her, and married again. Sebastian sees her more than me. I guess sons do? But he's much closer to me now, now that I'm nearing the end of my life.'

'Don't say that, Edward. You're still going strong. I'd say you had many more years ahead of you.'

'Not so, Jess. You see, I have cancer, I won't go into the nitty-gritty. The doctors say I have only a few more months more to live.' He looked at Jessica, a painful frown on his face.

'No, that can't be. It can't. Oh, how I wished I'd known you sooner, about what Chandra told us about you and my mother, and about how you risked your life to save us both from the burning house. I realised there was a lot more I should know. I suppose you know what I mean?' She fixed her eyes on his face. 'You do know, don't you?'

Edward looked away. He appeared to be deep in thought. He turned to Jessica. 'Yes, I know. We both wonder whether I'm your father, Jess.' Tears glinted in his rheumy eyes. She held his hand.

'Is that why you've secretly carried me through life financially, and is that why Meredith kept you informed of my progress? He was the one who sent you that photo of me at Stonehenge, and I guess Catherine knew everything and kept it to herself all these years. That would be why she wanted me to find out for myself. On her deathbed she urged me to go to Shimla to seek the truth. Did she also know about Sebastian?'

'I'm sorry, Jess.'

'For what, Edward? you've been a guardian angel to me, and Meredith told me why I was only now allowed to know the truth and get to meet you. Catherine didn't want me to. She must have thought she would besmirch the memory of her sister Elizabeth, in my eyes. I don't think I would have minded.'

They sat, staring through a distant window. Jessica was digesting the news about Edward's health. She realised that she had to find out soon if he was her father, but didn't know how to broach the subject of DNA testing. In fact, she wasn't sure if they would be able to do that. Perhaps a blood test would suffice. She'd find out as soon as she could, and hope he agrees. Sebastian. Let Sebastian ask him. After all, they'd been lovers albeit only for a few passionate days in Shimla, and that was something she wasn't proud of.

Planting his walking stick firmly in front of him, Edward eased himself off the sofa. 'Let's go upstairs!' he announced.

Jessica had noticed the wide sweeping staircase leading off the hall. 'I assume you are alright getting up the stairs, Edward? I'll help you.'

'I have a secret method. Come, and let me show you my elevator.'

He led the way out to the hall and across to the library. Tucked in an alcove between the shelves of books, ornaments and walls of pictures, they approached an oak panel. 'Press the knob on the right, Jess, stand back.'

The oak panel swung out, revealing a mirrored interior. 'In you go, Jess—isn't this good? I had it put in about five years ago when it was a case of sell the house or find a safe way of getting to and from my bedroom.'

'Oh, Edward, you've thought of everything.'

'I didn't want to sell Cleave until after you had been here, which I knew was bound to happen, so that's why I still rattle around these walls alone.'

Captivated by a panoramic view as they stepped out of the lift, Edward added, 'And, can you imagine ever finding another beautiful spot like this?'

Jessica was entranced. She turned to him. 'No, Edward. This is simply paradise.'

He looked at his watch. 'Ten minutes, and we'll go down for lunch. But before we do, follow me, I want to show you some paintings of Shimla, and I'd like you to tell me if you recognise anything. I want to know if the place has changed. What I hear from old friends it's much the same as it was way back in nineteen-forty-seven. The year I left there for good and went to Delhi to start afresh. It's all flooding back to me now, Jess. Even the bad times. I just want to go to my room, but carry on down the gallery.'

Jessica recognised some of the scenes in the paintings hanging on the walls. Christ Church, The Mall, and panoramas across the valley. And the unmistakeable Monkey temple that she and Sebastian visited on their last day in Shimla. He came over and joined her, explaining how he'd acquired the artworks, and pointed to a picture of a fine-looking house with a phalanx of brick steps to the front door, a profusion of blue and pink hydrangeas in the foreground.

'That's such a lovely place, Edward, it's not...?'

'No, it's not The Laurels. That's Hilltop House. It belonged to friends of mine who were very close and kind to me. And to you, too. I took you there to stay after the fire. I would like to think I kept in touch with them, but it's all so long ago, and we have little to talk about these days.' He sighed and led the way back to the lift.

She noticed him holding something in his pocket, and thought he'd been to his room to get some medication. He showed her the paintings in the galleried landing, until their descent to the ground floor, and the conservatory, for lunch.

'This calls for a celebration,' he said, filling her glass with champagne. 'Bottoms up—as we used to say in India.'

'Here's to you, Edward.' They clinked glasses across the table.

56

Devon September 1997:

That day, when I met Elizabeth, it all seemed as though it was ordained. There was instant chemistry between us. I'll never forget it, Jessica...' Edward had become very animated during the meal. He was like an excited schoolboy with an important story to tell. He hardly stopped talking, interrupted only by Jessica answering the occasional question. She heard about his first encounter with her mother, and how there was an immediate attraction. And about how, that same day, he saved James's life, as his horse lost its footing and almost disappeared into a ravine.

He explained, sometimes apologetically, about how he and her mother would have clandestine meetings, about how they fell in love and had started making rough plans to broach the subject with James. He admitted that their affair was the talk of the town, but that everyone in those days accepted such things. He regretted how he'd behaved towards James and said he still thought about what happened the night her parents perished in the fire—he said he still lived with the thought that he could perhaps have prevented the fire taking hold. He appeared pensive, worried, and struggling to remember.

They talked about Chandra and the inquest, and how he was questioned, and suspected. At that point, Edward put down his knife and fork, and stared out of the window.

Jessica reached across the table. 'What is it, Edward? Have I said something wrong?'

He shook his head and looked down at his plate. 'No—it's just that the more I think about that night, the more seems to come back to me. It was the most traumatic thing that's ever happened in my life. The scene keeps changing and, as I get older, I imagine more and more that it was me who caused it all. If only your mother and me...'

'Edward, what happened can't be changed, nor can you make it right again. It was a lifetime ago. How can you remember anyway? Even I have a problem remembering things from just a few years ago. You have enough to worry about. Don't rake up the past. Try to leave it all behind—way back there, in Shimla. It wasn't your fault. How could it have been? You loved my mother, you would never have let her die.'

'That is true, but that night…changed my life forever.'

Jessica was puzzled but said nothing. She didn't want this day to be sad, and she wanted to be able to come back and stay for a while without a black cloud hanging over them.

'Perhaps another day. Not today, we ought to be happy today, both of us, and I know that you've been anticipating our meeting for a very long time.'

'All my life, practically, just to see you again before I die and, better still, to get to know you as an adult. I've thought about it ever since I left India. I kept in touch with your life through Meredith, but we had to meet, didn't we?'

Annie came to take away the plates and asked whether they wanted dessert and bustled away.

'Jess, I've something I want to give you.' Edward reached into his pocket and pulled out a black velvet bag with drawstrings attached. He placed it on the table between them. 'I went back to The Laurels two days after the fire, after we'd settled in at Hilltop House. My friend came along with me, he thought it might be too much for me to take in. It was.

'The devastation was final, save for a couple of walls and a few remnants of the contents of the house. I remember wandering to the spot where the back veranda used to be, imagining Elizabeth and me sitting there watching the sun go down over the mountains. It was barely recognisable, as was everything except the garden which seemed to be flourishing, as if to mock me.' He paused. Jessica listened.

'Heaps of rubble and charred furniture had already been sifted through by the police. They took valuable items that they found and kept them until Catherine came over for the funeral. After that she brought you and your mother's belongings back here. Other precious personal things she had shipped over later.'

'I know, she gave me the jewellery box for my twenty-first birthday.' Jessica fingered her necklace. 'Hence the pearls.'

'You see, Catherine and I did keep in touch, but she never knew anything about my affair with your mother. Well, I assumed she didn't. Here, Jess, I have been saving this all these years until this day came as I've always hoped it would. I found this in the cinders at The Laurels, the day I went there after the fire. It was glinting through the ashes.' He gave Jessica the black velvet bag. She opened it to reveal a beautiful diamond and emerald brooch. 'I gave this to your mother for her birthday the year before she died. I want you to treasure it like I have treasured it all these years. Here—pin it to your dress.'

'Dear Edward. I don't know what to say. This brooch has a powerful message from my mother. It's so beautiful. And I'll make sure it is passed down to my daughter and kept as an extraordinary and unforgettable heirloom.' She reached over and took his hand in hers and saw the happiness in his face.

'Ah—here comes Annie's dessert concoction. When we've had lunch, I'll just show you a bit more of the estate, and I always go for an afternoon siesta. It's going to be a long day.'

Annie placed a bowl of meringue, cream and fruit in front of them, and just at that moment, three people riding horses went along the pebbled pathway in the garden, towards the field beyond.

'What beautiful horses. Are they...do they...?'

'Use my stables? Yes. I used to ride out on my own, oh, some years ago now...but now I rent the stables to a lovely lady who runs a riding school. It helps to keep the place alive with activity. Mostly on a Saturday, though, with schoolchildren being put through their paces.'

'What fun—they put my pony, Trixie, to shame. She's a bit long in the tooth now, so I don't ride her much. But perhaps I'll borrow a horse for Saffron when I get home, and we can go out together.'

'Are you a good rider, Jess? You had a small Shetland when you were a little girl—in the stables at The Laurels. He escaped with the others during the fire. It was horrible. We found them all, they'd panicked and fled and fell down the mountainside. Your mother's horse, Rainbow—your mother was an expert rider—was found with two broken legs. I cried at the carnage. We had to put each and every one of them out of their misery.'

'Oh my God, how awful for you—you did all that *and* looked after me and Chandra.'

'Chandra was taken off to hospital in Chandigarh straight away, and I never saw her or heard about her again. She was very badly burned, and we feared the worst.'

'I have her address, Edward, she would be very pleased to hear

227

from you. Between us, we pieced together most of what happened in Shimla.'

'Unbelievable, Jess. What an incredible story. I'll write to her soon. But for now, let me take you out to the gardens for a bit of fresh air. Doctor says I have to take deep, fresh air breaths every day!' He chuckled. 'And I try to do as I'm told.'

Jessica smiled at him and helped him down stone steps to the lawn at the back of the house where they'd just watched the riders go by. He indicated a wooden bench. And there they sat, side by side, like father and daughter, each lost in their own thoughts.

57

Devon September 1997:

E dward announced that he was going upstairs to take an afternoon nap. Jessica said that she would go back to her hotel. 'I'll come back in the morning after breakfast, if that's alright, Edward. I'll only be able to stay for two nights because I have to get back home by the weekend.'

'That'll be fine, and we'll be able to make a few plans for your future visits,' he said.

'I have a pre-term teachers' meeting at the school where I work, but I've already handed in my notice. I'm hoping to be retired come the half-term break. I'm so looking forward to starting afresh, getting out of my rut, and beginning to live again. If I can come back to Cleave Manor, mid-October after I leave my job, I'll be on the hunt for a home of my own.'

Edward picked up his walking stick and rose from the garden bench. She followed him into the house. 'Wouldn't it be nice for us to spend Christmas here, do you think? With Sebastian, and with your daughter, too. It's a long time since this place came alive.'

'Edward, that would be lovely, we'll try to arrange it.'

Sebastian. How was she going to handle the problem of Sebastian? She needed to talk to him privately and make it clear that there was to be no more of what happened in Shimla. She thought she'd done that, but he had seemed persistent.

'Sebastian's driving down to my cottage today, and I'd like to see him before he leaves to come here to see you.'

They reached Edward's elevator, said a brief goodbye, and Jessica popped her head into the kitchen, saying goodbye to Annie, and told her she'll be back tomorrow. Annie said she'd get a room aired and ready.

'Thanks so much for the lovely lunch. We've still got a lot to talk about. Has Edward told you to expect Sebastian in a day or two?'

Annie looked up, surprised. 'No, I didn't even know he was back in England. No matter, I'll ask Mr Shelley tomorrow. It will be nice to have the house used again.'

'Bye, Annie—I should be back by late morning tomorrow.'

Before she reached her car, Jessica was fishing in her handbag for her phone.

'Hello? Saffie?'

Yes, Mum. I've been trying to call you.'

'Has Sebastian arrived yet?' Jessica tried to sound matter-of-fact.

'Yes, Mum, that's why I tried to call you. He's here now, and is staying till you get back.'

'Well, that's just the thing, Saffie. I've been invited to stay at Cleave Manor for a couple of days. I…er, I wondered when Sebastian was going to come down. I'll have to get back home by the weekend, though.'

'That's wonderful, Mum. So, you and Edward are getting on together?'

'Yes, and we've had tons to talk about. I've more-or-less found out what happened to your grandparents, back in Shimla. But I wanted to talk to Sebastian.'

'Why, Mum? I mean, he and I are getting on well, too…'

'Oh, I thought he might want to know how his father is before he comes down to Devon.' That was all Jessica could think of immediately that sounded feasible. 'Is he there now?'

'No, well, yes. He's upstairs sleeping off some of the lingering jet-lag…'

'Right. Well, can you ask him to call me sometime today. I'm on my way back to Fowey now, and will be at the hotel till mid-morning tomorrow.'

'Sure, Mum, I'll tell him.'

'Bye, Saffie.'

'Bye, Mum. I'll tell Seb…' But Jessica had already switched off her phone.

She started the car and sped off angrily. Once again, she had been manipulated by her daughter. She thought she should practice her story for when Sebastian called her, and make sure Saffron wasn't within earshot. But she had to re-iterate what she told Sebastian in Delhi, on her last night in India. And she wanted to give back the present he gave her, regardless of what it meant. A ring is a ring. She snorted *what a cheek* admonishing herself for letting their brief affair happen in the first place. 'What a fool, what a crazy fool I was,' she shouted out loud to the roar of the engine. As anger began to take hold, she slammed her foot down on the accelerator, driving well above the limit, narrowly missing vehicle after vehicle until she reached the queue for the car ferry.

She pulled on the hand brake violently, turned off the engine and sat, numbly wondering what had got hold of her. *Oh God, I have to remain sane, I have to go back to Cleave Manor tomorrow and act normal with Edward who already sees me as part of his family.*

Back at Fowey Hall, Jessica made a beeline for the lounge. She ordered tea and sat trying to calm down, looking out at the tranquillity of the gardens, with rose bushes still in bloom, and faint autumn tints touching the trees that framed the estuary. Boats bobbed about, sails flashing in the afternoon sun's rays.

She fingered her phone in her handbag. Better wait until she was in her room, she thought. A young couple sat down at the table next to her. Jessica nodded and smiled briefly. The tea and scones were placed before her, instantly bringing her back to reality and calm. She picked up a magazine from the shelf under the table. *Cornish Life.* Sipping her tea, she turned to the property section, scanning the beautiful homes and gardens of the few chosen to advertise in its pages. The prices confirmed that the area was, indeed, as the adverts proclaimed, much sought after.

She made a mental calculation, and realised she could well-afford most of these up-market country homes. One in particular caught her eye. Close to Fowey, individually set in a small cove, with lush green lawns rolling down to the water's edge. Jessica dreamed. *Could it be? Would I want such isolation? What would I do there?* But she was intrigued enough to take the magazine to her room for later scrutiny.

Now calmed by the diversion and comforting afternoon tea, she took off her clothes and ran a fragrant bath. She stroked her body in front of the mirror, looking for something to admire about it with the imminent arrival of middle age. Still determined to call Sebastian afterwards, she remembered his face, his smiles, his easy charm and demeanour, Jessica sank into the soothing depths of the water, closed her eyes and relived their love-making in the shadow of the Himalayas. The only possibility she'd ever had in her life since her days of hippiedom and free love, to create a meaningful relationship now in jeopardy. Her misguided realisation of the impossible had placed an unbreakable barrier between them, and she'd have to navigate her way around it as best she could. She knew that it would likely break Edward's heart if he ever knew, and change what he appeared to think about her, as a squeaky-clean upstanding member of decent society.

58

Devon September 1997:

Jessica reached for her mobile just as it rang.

'Jessica?' His confident voice was unmistakeable.

'Sebastian. I…I was just about to ring you. You must be psychic.' She laughed nervously, not knowing what to say first. 'How are you? Is Saffron looking after you? I assume you'll be making it to Devon as soon as you can? Your father is amazing. He's not well, but he's been so welcoming to me. In fact, he insists I go over to Cleave Manor tomorrow to stay there for a couple of days. But I have to get back home soon, back to school.'

'Jess, calm down, stay there. I'm coming down to Devon first thing in the morning. Of course, I have to see the old man as soon as I can, but I also want to see you, too. I hope we can find some time to spend together, if only briefly. Can we, please?'

Jessica walked over to the dressing-mirror in her room. She felt a flush of pride—of self-worth, and a distinct feeling of need again. The need to be with Sebastian, the need to spread her wings at last and to be herself. More importantly, she felt joy so strong, her eyes shone as she smiled back at herself in the mirror.

'Jess? Are you still there?' He sounded concerned.

'Yes, Sebastian, of course I'm here. Sorry, I was remembering us and how we were in Shimla. Yes, please come down as soon as you can. I'll stay a bit longer, I was only rushing back…well, to see you while you were there. It will be much better here. I've seen Meredith and cleared up so many questions. I can see things better now I've met your father, and he's explained how and why things happened when they did.'

'I'm planning on being there before lunch.'

'You need to ring your father.'

'I will. Take care. See you tomorrow.'

'Yes, I should be there about lunch time, too.'

'Jess?'

'What?'

'I do love you, you know. I've had time to think things through…'

233

Jessica was hesitant, but easily seduced once more. 'Sebastian, so have I. See you tomorrow.'

'Bye.'

She clutched her phone with both hands, laughing, as she threw herself onto her bed. Hugging a pillow, she rolled around ecstatically. *Is this what I've been waiting for all my life? Is one's destiny a foregone conclusion that only unravels when the time is right? Or have I suddenly been overcome by some middle-aged revelation of life being too precious in any form to allow events to slip away?*

She heard a commotion outside her room, followed by a knock on the door. She quickly donned a robe and opened the door to find a porter holding the largest bouquet of red roses she'd ever seen.

'Madam these are for you.' The young man pushed them towards her but she asked him to bring them into the room and put them down. She was overwhelmed and didn't need to look at the attached card which read. *English roses for an English rose. Love, Sebastian xxxx*

Jessica backed away, staring at the bouquet in admiration. The scent was intoxicating. She clicked his number on her mobile. It hardly rang before he answered it.

'Sebastian, they've just arrived. What can I say? A mere thank you doesn't seem enough. They're lovely. The gesture is very generous, and I want you to know it's one of the nicest things that has ever happened in my life. Sebastian? Look, I want to tell you...'

'Wait, wait until I get there. I'll see you tomorrow.'

Jessica felt light-headed. She made a point of taking time with her hair and makeup, applying more than usual. The one extravagance in her life was the French perfume she'd worn forever, which she splashed on lavishly. She pinned her mother's brooch to the only dress she'd brought for dining out and made a plan to go shopping in Fowey the next morning before she left for Devon. She'd noticed some very nice shops she thought might stock some new and vibrant clothes for her wardrobe. *A new me. Yes, why not? About time. I already feel like a new person, ready to begin my life again, this time for my own pleasure, not to prove myself in a career, or to fit in with village society, to be the 'good egg', or to worry about the things I can't change, like my daughter.*

She made her way to the dining room with a smile on her face and a glint in her eye. Heads turned as she made her way to the table. She smiled at the waiter who brought the menu, and said good evening to the couple on the next table. *It's still me, a new me, a happy and a slightly risqué me.*

In her reckless state she ordered the most expensive Champagne on the wine list, and didn't mind if she became tipsy. She'd come to the conclusion she'd arrived at the beginning of the rest of her life.

Jessica packed early the next morning, checked out of Fowey Hall, found parking on the waterfront, and made a beeline for the shops. Helped by a friendly shop assistant, she chose linens, silks, dresses, tops and trousers, a pair of designer denims, an expensive handbag, and a pair of trendy shoes. She opted to wear at once a beautiful silk scarf which updated her appearance straight away. She was hoping to get to Edward's before Sebastian, so that she could change before he arrived. At the florist's she chose a rose bush to give to Edward. The name of the rose was *Remembrance*.

Pulling into the forecourt of Cleave Manor, Jessica saw that Sebastian hadn't arrived. She was met at the door by a young girl she hadn't seen before, who introduced herself as Beth. She took the bouquet of roses to be arranged, and showed Jessica up to her room. She was told that Edward was in the garden, so she took the opportunity to hang up her new clothes, and change.

She looked over the garden from her bedroom window, and spotted the dogs. *Edward shouldn't be far away.* She made her way outside and found him sitting on the same bench as before. The dogs woofed as she walked towards him and he tried to stand up.

'Don't stand up, Edward. I've already made myself at home.'

'Well done, Jess. I just had a call from Sebastian. He should be here in time for lunch, so we can all eat together. I can't remember when I last saw him—just before he went back to Delhi, I suppose, before he went up to Shimla to find you. And now here you both are. Indeed, here we all are.'

'I'm also looking forward to seeing him again, Edward. I have to admit, I owe him an apology.' She looked down at her feet. 'I was dismissive of him when we said goodbye at the airport. Instead, I should have thanked him and shown my appreciation. He looked after me...' She hesitated. 'We became good friends you know, and got to enjoy each other's company.'

'My dear Jessica—can you ever forgive me? I wasn't thinking when he phoned me from Shimla…'

'It's alright Edward, it's for the best that I know the whole truth.'

'Yes, but I have to…' He stopped abruptly as the dogs ran, barking, towards the open French doors. '…this must be Sebastian.'

Jessica stood to face the house as Sebastian, petting the dogs, came into the garden. She walked towards him and he took her hands in his for a moment as they looked at each other.

'Come and sit with us—we've just set the world to rights.' They strolled towards the garden bench. Edward, who had already turned to greet his son, leaned on his walking stick and observed the couple with interest as they drew closer.

59

Devon September 1997:

Jessica stood looking on as Sebastian greeted his father. It had been a few months since they'd seen one another and they were locked in deep conversation.

'You're looking well, Father—better than I expected, to be honest. It must be all this lovely fresh country air and sunshine. I hear you've had a great summer over here, now an Indian summer, which seems very appropriate for all three of us, doesn't it?'

Edward held on to Sebastian's arm as they went back to the garden bench.

'Let's sit and chat with Dad, Jessica, we can go in for lunch later.' He offered her a seat.

'I could go and ask Annie to bring out some refreshments?' she suggested.

Sebastian chipped in, 'No, I'll go and get some. What about a celebratory bottle of bubbly?'

'Not for me, dear boy,' Edward replied. 'Doctor's orders you know. But…oh, I suppose this is a very auspicious occasion. Perhaps a sip or two won't do any harm, as an aperitif.'

'That's the spirit, Dad, let's celebrate. Later we'll go in for lunch and we can tell you about our discoveries in Shimla, and…'

'Sebastian?' Jessica cut him off before he said too much, 'why don't I come in with you to help? We won't be long, Edward.'

Jessica also wanted to bring her gift of a yellow-flowering rose bush out to Edward so that he could decide where to plant it in the rose garden.

She and Sebastian walked side-by-side through the French doors of the drawing room. He stopped abruptly, pulling her towards him.

'I've missed you. I couldn't get down here fast enough.'

'And me, you,' she said as they embraced. 'Sebastian, we'll have to tell your father soon.'

'I know, and as soon as I got back to London, I phoned a chum who is friends with a pathologist in the Metropolitan Police Force, and I've found out how to go about getting our DNA tested.'

'It's been concerning me, but not too much, because the more I think about it, the more the dates don't seem to add up. Your father and my mother had an affair, for sure, but it must have been in the early days when your father spent less time in Shimla than he did later after he was posted there permanently each summer. But the most important point is that I am beyond bearing any more children, isn't it?'

Sebastian steered her towards the cellar door. 'That depends on whether we want to cement our relationship.' He drew her to him and kissed her lips. 'If it is discovered that there is a familial link, we would not be allowed by law to marry—that is, if you and I eventually decide to. So, the test has to be done, hasn't it? For now, though, let's enjoy our re-union. How about you go and fetch the glasses and a tray, and pick up some nibbles from the kitchen while I go and choose a bottle?'

Jessica turned and strode into the kitchen, emerging a few minutes later with Sebastian's requested items on a plate which she put down briefly to pick up the plant pot containing the rose bush, wrapped in pretty paper. Struggling, she placed the rose in front of Edward and the plate on the table beside the garden bench.

'Edward, I bought this for you.' She picked up the rose bush again and held it out for him to admire.

'Dear girl! What a lovely surprise. It will look lovely in the rose garden, and whenever I look at it, I will remember you. Thank you.'

'Edward, well, appropriately, it's called *Remembrance*.'

Sebastian popped the cork, allowing the champagne to cascade over the top of the bottle. He carefully poured it into three flutes, and proposed a toast.

'Here's to this reunion, here's to Dad's upcoming big birthday, and to sweet memories. And here's to Jessica. Bottoms up!'

Jessica offered Edward a handful of nibbles and suggested he not drink too much. She'd already seen the mountain of prescription drugs he took every day.

'I did tell you, Father, that I am re-basing back to the UK, didn't I?'

'Yes, on the phone from Shimla, I think. Or was it Jessie who told me? Whatever, I'm more than pleased I'll be seeing more of you. Will you stay in London?'

'I'll keep the flat on, but I think I'll look for a place in the country where I can write in peace and quiet.' Sebastian's thoughts were on his future with Jessica. He dare not divulge his real motive to his father yet.

'Well, Jessie's definitely going to come to live down here. She's told me all about her plans to retire. Have you seen any property you might like to buy, Jessica?'

She looked from Edward to Sebastian and back to Edward. 'Well, yes, I have. There was an advert in Cornish Life for a wonderful-looking house right on the beach in a secluded cove near Fowey. Polkerris House. It looked like an artist's idyll. I think I'll make an appointment to go and view it.'

'If you like, I can come with you.' Sebastian piped up. 'That is, if you'd like me to.' His subtle suggestion made her smile.

'But don't you want to spend more time with your father?' she replied.

'Look, you two, my afternoons are usually wiped out with a good long sleep, so if you can organise it, why don't you go today, after lunch? It's not that far to get there and back in time for dinner…'

'Yes!' Sebastian could hardly hold in his enthusiasm. He turned to Jessica. 'Why don't you ring the agents before lunch and see if it's possible.'

'I will, as soon as we go in. At least I'll be able to see what a million pounds can buy me down here.'

They raised their glasses again, before Sebastian put them on the tray ready to take inside.

'Come on, Father, let's go in for lunch.'

They'd taken Sebastian's red Mazda MX5, and as they approached the house in the cove, the car was clearly struggling to cope with the rutted road. Jessica had made arrangements to meet the agent, a man with the name of Ashton Greaves.

'Should've come in the Land Rover. I think.' he said, struggling with the steering wheel. If this is anything to go by, hmm…may need some work.'

Jessica agreed. 'We'll see, but it is only my first viewing, after all.'

The drive gave way to tarmac just as an amazing vista came into view.

'Oh, look! Sebastian, the sea. And the bay. How beautiful.'

Sebastian slowed down. 'It is a special place. And here's the house coming into view.'

Jessica stared straight ahead as before them the honey-coloured stone façade stood proud behind a sweeping forecourt flanked by late-flowering roses. Woodland formed a backdrop, shielding the house. The agent was standing beside his car next to the front entrance.

'Here we go,' Jessica said as they stepped out of the car. 'First impressions?'

'Isolated, lovely…'

'Mr Greaves?' Jessica offered her hand. 'This is Sebastian Shelley.'

'Pleased to meet you. Shall we go into the house first, or I can show you the extent of the grounds? As you may have gathered, this is a very special property, one of a kind. It has been in the same family for three generations, but the time has now come…'

He led the way through a massive hall and into the drawing-room with windows that beckoned with the view of the whole bay. In the forefront, calm water lapped quietly under a wooden jetty and on to a narrow pebble shore leading to manicured lawns that swept right up to the house.

Jessica and Sebastian exchanged glances as they tore themselves away from the view to follow the agent through to dining room, kitchen, upstairs bedrooms and back into the gardens via outbuildings and three garages.

'Mrs Shelley, are you looking specifically for this type of property?'

'Oh, Mr Greaves, no, I'm Jessica Delaney-Hartford, and this is my friend Sebastian Shelley.'

'Beg our pardon, sorry…I assumed…er, of course, I remember our telephone conversation.'

'That's alright, Mr Greaves—or should we call you Ashton?' Sebastian's irony wasn't wasted on Jessica, who covered her mouth momentarily to disguise her smirk.

'Yes, I'm about to retire, and feel the need to leave my old life behind and start afresh while I can. In fact, this is exactly the type of property I had in mind. I know Cornwall and love it. I have friends here—and in Devon.' She smiled at Sebastian.

They were both given a brochure for the house which had pictures of the interior and a potted history of the place.

'The current owner is willing to negotiate on price, by-the-way, should you need to proceed further. But for now, is there anything else I can tell or show you?'

'I don't think so, Ashton, but can we stay for a while and explore the cove before we leave?'

'Of course, there's no-one living here at the moment, so please do, and please call me—or I'll give you a call, perhaps, Mrs…er soon, when you've had time to think things over.'

The agent bade farewell and disappeared through the five-barred gate and up the driveway. Sebastian and Jessica turned to each other at last being able to burst into laughter as they embraced.

'See that mound of grass next to the water's edge? I'm going to drag you there kicking and screaming.'

'No, you're not!' replied Jessica. 'I'll get there first…'

60

Cornwall 1997:

They lay on the grass looking up at a deep blue summer sky. The gentle lapping of waves on the beach began to calm Jessica and she closed her eyes. She felt Sebastian playing with her hair and smiled contentedly.

'It was the first thing that attracted me to you, you know.'

Jessica turned to face him. 'What was?'

'Your crazy, wonderful hair. Not red but a deep golden auburn, wild and curly. I love it as much as the woman it belongs to.'

Jessica leaned on her elbow, the sun's rays picking out the golden strands. 'Oh, Sebastian, don't be absurd, I've always hated my hair. I could never see anything in the least attractive about it, and I've tried to flatten it all my life.'

He put this hand behind her neck and pulled her face to his. 'Well, from now on, you can start liking it, okay?'

She relaxed across his body as they kissed each other passionately, he holding her tightly until she pulled away.

'Perhaps better wait, this is not exactly the right place, is it?' she playfully scolded. And at that moment, they heard the putt-putt of a boat's engine getting louder. Straightening their clothes, they looked out to sea and saw a little motor boat that appeared to be heading towards the jetty. They stood up and walked along the edge of the water. Jessica shielded her eyes from the sun as the boat came right up to them. The driver shouted out a greeting and slammed the hull into the pebbles before shutting off the engine. He threw out a long rope to Sebastian before jumping out of the boat.

'Tie 'er off to that tree, will ya? Thanks...'

Jessica stood by, amused, watching Sebastian obey the orders of this man in a boat who'd just arrived out of nowhere.

'I'm Jake.'

'Er...hello, I'm Sebastian and...er...this is Jessica.'

'Not trespassing are yer?' Jake said with a knowing smile on his face.

'Of course not! No, we've just been to look round the house with a view to purchasing it, and the estate agent said we could stay as long as we liked.' Sebastian explained, wondering why he felt the need to go into any detail at all to this chap who might just be trespassing himself.

'Ah! Been on the market for some time, mind…'

'So, what's your interest, if you don't mind me asking?' said Sebastian.

'Me? I do t'garden. Come every week for three hours or more, depending on't time of year.'

'Oh, so you'll know a bit about the place. Tell me, who are the current owners?' Jessica's curiosity was awakened.

Jake sat on the gunwale of his boat looking at the house. 'There's only one of them left now. And it's not a very well-kept secret in t' village that it hasn't all been plain sailing, if you know what I mean. The old lady tried to stay here but her children decided she needed to be looked after somewhere else.'

Sebastian asked, 'So what's the family name?'

'Spicer-Jurgen. One of them double-barrelled jobs. Yer see, he were German, she English, and rumour has it that they combined their names. Rumour has it he were hidin' here after the war—yer know. Some did.'

'Gosh, what a history, and that would explain some of the paintings hanging on the walls. So what happened to him—Jurgen?' Sebastian probed further.

'Again—nobody knows to this day, but the story goes that he were swept out to sea and drowned. They had a boat. A big boat they used to cross t' Channel in.'

Jessica and Sebastian looked at each other. She reached out for his hand.

'It's alright though. His body were found and he's up in t' cemetery in t' village.'

'Well, I'm glad we sorted that out.' Sebastian cleared his throat and took a deep breath. He looked quizzically at Jessica, who also appeared to be astonished by the story they'd just heard.

Jake tipped his cap and excused himself saying he had to get on with the garden before the dew began to rise. 'So, d'yer think yer might buy the house? If yer do, perhaps you'll keep me on, like?'

'If we decide to go ahead.' Jessica smiled at Jake, and he walked briskly towards the outbuildings.

'What a story.' Sebastian. said. 'Could have been embellished over the years, but it's also feasible. But the house and gardens are lovely, and you could get a boat, too.'

'Perhaps not after that story, Sebastian. Come on, we'd better be getting back to Edward. We've got the whole night ahead to work out our plans for the next few weeks.'

As they got into the car, Sebastian suggested she go back to London with him and they get the DNA test done. 'Whatever the outcome, I want to be with you.'

'And me with you, Sebastian. I can't remember when I was so happy. I feel free at last – free to choose whatever I want in my life.' She paused.

'You know something that puzzles me?'

'What?'

'Does anyone ever call you Seb?'

He was struggling again with the steering wheel on the rutted driveway. 'I can't tell a lie, Jessica. I once had an Indian girlfriend in Delhi. She couldn't get her head around such a convoluted name, and I let her call me Seb.' He looked at her fleetingly to see her reaction.

'Well, you don't think I didn't imagine you'd never had other women in your life. In fact, I'd be suspicious if a handsome hunk of a man like you had not had more than a few flings,' quickly adding, 'I prefer to call you Sebastian, anyway.'

'Good, so, what about coming to my London pad? Let's get this test done.'

'I can do that, but can we stop off at my cottage? I need to give Saffie the car, and get a few things.'

'I've a lot on the horizon, too. I'd like to get a position with a newspaper as a feature writer. And there's India—I've been living in Dad's house in Delhi, and I'm going to suggest I sell it for him as soon as possible.'

'There are changes ahead for both of us. I feel I've turned the last page in the first book of my life, and I'm looking forward to being myself now, not being controlled by anything or anyone. I want to kick-start an exciting new beginning for myself that includes you, Sebastian…' she hesitated. 'I love you. Very much.'

He reached for her hand as he drove. 'And to think, neither of us had any idea that it would come to this. I came out to spy on you in Shimla, and ended up falling in love with you. But complications presented themselves, the more we found out, the more we became entwined in each other's families and lives.'

'I know, and I was just thinking, Edward may never have met me again if Meredith's orchestrated meeting hadn't taken place.'

'You're very philosophical, Jessica. It's a good way to be. The Hindus have a similar logical attitude to life.' He swung the car through the gates of Cleave Manor and slowed down.

'One other thing, Sebastian, I have a confession to make…'

'I know. The ring?'

'How did you guess?' she looked down at her finger where it ought to be. 'I'm sorry, but I haven't even tried it on yet. I opened the packet and was more than a little surprised, and I put it away again. I will now wear it all the time.'

Sebastian pulled the car to a gentle stop in the driveway of his father's house and turned to face Jessica. 'So, does that mean, that if everything works out in our favour, you'll marry me?'

'Yes, Sebastian. I will…'

61

Devon September 1997:

The inviting smell of baking met Jessica and Sebastian, as they walked through the house looking for Edward.

'Jessica, we'll get to London mid-afternoon tomorrow, if we're lucky. I've a few things to do at the flat. I've been away for a while, so perhaps we can stay three or four days?'

'Will we be able to get the DNA test done? How long will it take to get results?'

'I'll call my mate at the Met in the morning before we leave and make a plan. God, I hope it all works out. Do you think we ought to tell Dad? We'll have to get a sample from him.'

Jessica lowered her voice. 'Sebastian, I've been thinking about that, can't we just take something with his fingerprints on it? I know nothing about it, but if we can do that, we don't have to tell him we're going to get the test done. And when you think about it, it just involves me and you.'

'But Jessica, I'm sure he wants to set the record straight. He wants to know if he's your father.'

'When you ring your friend, ask him the best way for us to present our DNA for testing?'

'Good idea. The smell coming from the kitchen is making me feel hungry again, I'll go and arrange something to eat.' Sebastian walked towards the kitchen just as Edward descended in the lift. 'Hi Dad— I'm going to organise tea. Shall we count you in?'

Edward met Sebastian as he stepped from the lift. He was carrying a parcel. 'Yes, please, Sebastian. I'll see you in the drawing room. Is Jessica there?'

'Yes, I'll join you in a minute.'

Edward, his walking stick tap-tapping, greeted Jessica and sat opposite her, placing a small box and an envelope on the table.

'How did your trip to Cornwall go? Did you like the house you went to see?'

'Edward, it was just what I had imagined it to be. Secluded, romantic, on the sea-shore, in a small private cove. I fell in love with it.

246

It seems there's a history attached to it—and a mystery. But it will need some renovating. It hasn't been lived in for a while. Sebastian loved it, too...'

'I sure did, Dad...erm...' Sebastian arrived carrying a plate of small cakes. He looked at Jessica, not knowing whether to tell his father their other news.

'Dad, we're going to drive up to London tomorrow. Jessica's coming with me after we stop off at her place briefly, and we're...um...we're going to have a test. You know—a DNA test. I know the story, we all know, and we have to find out if Jessica is one of our family, don't we?'

'Sebastian, that is what I need to know for sure,' Edward looked at Jessica and tried to smile through his uncertainty. 'Even though I think I'm pretty sure already.'

'I know, Dad.'

'Sebastian. how does it work? Will you need to take something of mine?'

'Dad, first thing in the morning, I'm going to talk to a friend who's been advising me, and I'll let you know before we go.' He put his hand over his father's on the arm of the chair. 'It'll be alright you know. Just leave everything to me.'

Edward took out his handkerchief. His hands were shaking. Composing himself, he looked across at Jessica as he reached for the box and the envelope he'd put on the table. 'Jessica, I want to show you something, to give you something I've been keeping in the hope that one day we'd meet. Now that you've been to Shimla and found the truth of your parents' passing, I want you to have this.'

With trembling hands, he held out the packages as she leaned over to take them.

'Go on, open them up. But first, open this.' He nodded at her.

Carefully, she broke the seal on the large yellowing envelope and looked inside. A single sheet of paper slid out. She unfolded it and looked quizzically at a child's painting.

'Edward?' She held it up for them to see. 'What is it?'

'My dear, those scribbles and childish images were painted by you just after your parents died. It was the only indication we ever had that you knew what happened to them. You brought it home from nursery school one day, and I don't mind telling you, it broke my heart.'

Sebastian looked at the childish picture. 'You've kept it all this time. There are flames and a man and a woman—your Mum and Dad, Jessica. Somewhere in your head it was all there.'

Edward took over. 'But you never ever talked about it, nor did we ever explain why your mother and father weren't there. You came over here, and your Aunt Catherine leaked out a made-up story to satisfy your curiosity as you got older.'

'This is amazing, Edward. How can I thank you for this? for keeping it as part of my early life.'

'But that's not all. Open the box.' Edward pointed towards the string-tied box.

The wrapping paper fell to the floor as she took off the lid. Inside she found a jade-green silk scarf, and nestled into it, a sparkling amethyst brooch. She pulled them out of the box, and held them out for Sebastian to see. 'But...'

'Jessica, I've also been saving this for you. I thought we'd meet one day. Just after you did the painting, you went shopping with the lady who looked after you, and brought this present back. When you told me it was for your mother's birthday, I choked trying to hold back my grief. You were so happy that you were going to give it to your mother, saying they were her favourite colours.'

'Dear Edward—what traumas you must have had, but do you know, this is exactly *my* favourite colour, too.'

'It's the hair. You have the same colouring as your mother. Please keep these as a reminder of times you don't remember. Your early years in Shimla.'

62

Devon September 1997:

Jessica went to bed early, excusing herself after dinner. She needed to have a good night's sleep in preparation for the journey the next day. She also thought Sebastian and his father needed some time together.

They'd planned to set off after breakfast. She packed her case before getting into bed, leaving out what she needed in the morning, and sank into a warm bath before luxuriating between the cool cotton sheets on her bed.

She felt good in heart soul and spirit as she put on her nightdress. How lucky she was, how unexpected was this new life unfolding before her, like a runaway train unable to be stopped. She just had to let it go as it wished, and take her into the unknown territory of love and happiness. She didn't want to rationalise any more but simply let things develop in their own way, and whatever she was faced with she was prepared to take in her stride.

She heard footsteps outside her door, and a single sharp tap as the door opened and closed quickly. In the glow of her bedside light, she watched Sebastian walk over to her bed.

Jessica sat bolt upright. 'Sebastian! No, you can't be here. Not here, not now…'

He sat on her bed and placed his finger over her lips.

'Shhh…I just wanted to say goodnight, that's all, and to say how lovely you looked tonight.' Kissing her briefly, he stood. 'So, goodnight, Jessica. Tomorrow is another day for us. Nervous?'

'Yes, Sebastian, very nervous. Now, go!' He closed the door quietly and she snuggled back between the sheets.

Jessica joined Edward and Sebastian at the breakfast table dressed ready for the long journey back to Willow Cottage, and eventually to London. She noticed Sebastian's bag near the front door.

'Good morning, Jess.' Edward tried to stand as she sat at the table.

'Good morning, Edward, Sebastian. Looks like a good day for driving. I hope. We have to take both cars as far as Hampshire and leave the Land Rover for Saffron.'

'We can go in convoy. Or shall I race you?' Sebastian joked.

'Better not. I'd rather not get a speeding fine, thank you very much. Anyway, I doubt the Land Rover can go as fast as your fancy sports car.'

'You're right. I just have to call my chap at the Met now whilst you're having breakfast, and we'll be on our way.' Sebastian left the table and fished out his phone as he headed towards the drawing room.

'You'll drive carefully, won't you, Jess? I want you to return here as soon as you can, remember.'

'Of course, Edward. I'll sort out my work and retirement, get Saffie settled, and speak to the Estate Agent again about Polkerris House.'

'It would be so nice if you were to settle here. Just think, we could get together on a regular basis, Sebastian could come here. I'm not sure when he'll see his mother. She lives in Surrey. I suppose he'll have to go to see her soon, and tell her about his plans to leave India.'

'He didn't tell me anything about his mother,' replied Jessica, 'I don't suppose you've seen her very much since you began to live apart.' Jessica was interested to know.

'No, nothing at all. Not even heard anything from Sebastian. It's a long time ago now. And she never gives a thought for me. Neither me her, for that matter. There are times I'd wished I'd never married her, but then I wouldn't have Sebastian. He's has been my life, even though we don't see very much of each other.'

'Well, I think we need to remedy that, don't you, Edward?' They looked up as Sebastian came back into the room, smiling. He sat in his chair at the table.

'Okay. I have instructions. We need to each take a plastic Ziplock bag, tear out some of our hair, so to speak, making sure there are some hair roots on them, and carefully place them in the bags, seal them properly, and write clearly which sample belongs to whom.'

'Is that all?' Jessica thought they'd have to take a used cup or glass or fresh fingerprints.

'That's all. I'll take them to the lab as soon as I can. My chum has just given me the address. There will be a charge because it's a private request, but it shouldn't be much and I'll take care of that. It will take a day or two. They'll ring me with the result as well as give me a written report.'

Edward looked surprised. 'It seems so easy.' He looked at Jessica.

'I'll get the bags from Annie, and we can each take our own hair sample.' Sebastian said, sounding business-like. He went to the kitchen and emerged a few seconds later, handing them all a bag.

'Do you want me to help you, Dad?'

'No. I'll be alright. I just have to go upstairs to my room. I'll see you both in the hall in ten minutes.'

Sebastian collected their samples and sealed them all safely into another large envelope, with a signed note from each agreeing to the procedure. It occurred to him to question the need for his own DNA to be taken, and he pondered on it as he as he wrote the name and address of the laboratory he'd been given. He attached a note explaining who he was, together with his phone number and address. He explained it was for clarification of genetics within his family. He put the envelope on top of his bag and went upstairs to carry Jessica's bags down to the car.

'I guess this is goodbye for a while, Dad. We'll let you know how things go.' Sebastian embraced his father and took the luggage to the cars.

Jessica kissed Edward on the cheek and gave him a hug. 'Same here, Edward. I'll call you to let you know what happens. You know, about Polkerris House, my job, and when I might be back.'

'Goodbye, Jess. Please come back soon.' And with that, Edward turned and walked back into the house flanked by his two loyal dogs. He turned as the two drove out of the forecourt and watched as they disappeared out of sight, up the long drive to the gatehouse.

Silence descended around him once more, enabling him to become introspective about the surreal unfolding scenario.

63

London September 1997:

Stopping briefly to stretch their legs, Sebastion and Jessica managed to make it to Willow Cottage in good time. Saffron was waiting for them, and had prepared a chicken salad for their lunch which they ate together in the conservatory. They discussed the London visit and plans for the next day, and put Saffron in the picture regarding developments.

'Mum, I forgot—there's some mail for you. I'll get it. Quite a bit of junk, hang on, I put it on your desk...' She returned with a small pile of envelopes and Jessica sifted through them.

'Nothing very important I don't think,' she muttered as she discarded one after the other. 'Looks like this is from the school.' She ripped open the white envelope.

Saffron and Sebastian watched Jessica scan the letter, waiting with anticipation for the contents to be revealed.

'Ah! Listen to this. *...saddened to receive news of your resignation...understand your reasons for taking early retirement...we have been lucky to find an immediate replacement to step into your position, and can offer you the option of handing over your post before the beginning of term...wish you Godspeed for the future whatever path you decide to take and thank you for all your dedication and hard work...*' Jessica looked up at Sebastian. 'I can leave now. Now! This makes everything so much easier. Gosh, this changes everything, frees me up to do whatever I want. I'll write back to the Head and accept the offer first thing in the morning. What an unexpected surprise. Saffie, there are going to be a few changes.'

Sebastian looked at his watch. 'That's fantastic news. Everything seems to working out so well, but in the meantime, we ought to be making tracks. Just a couple more hours and we should get to the city before the rush-hour.'

'Yes, I'll just go to my room and get some clean clothes, and we'll be off. I still can't believe how things seem to be sliding into place so easily. I'll arrange to go into school as soon as I can, to hand over to my successor.' Jessica left Saffron and Sebastian sitting at the table and disappeared upstairs.

'Well, Mum seems to have everything going for her. I'm dying to hear her other news and find out what happened in Cornwall. Do you think she'll sell Willow Cottage?' Saffron leaned forward on her elbows and stared at Sebastian.

'I definitely think she will. And I know she won't mind me telling you, but I went with her to view a beautiful property on the coast near Fowey. We both fell in love with it. I think she'll put in an offer. Needs some work, though, but she says she always dreamed of living by the sea. I do hope she does.'

'So, are you going back to India? I got the impression you also wanted to re-base back here?'

'I've thought hard about it, and I think I will come home. My father is very ill and frail and I don't think he'll be around for too much longer, and as I'm his only offspring...'

'That would mean big changes for you, too.' Saffron looked quizzically at Sebastian, her mind racing. 'So, if you stay here and inherit your father's place, and Mum buys the Cornish house...what will happen to Willow Cottage. And me?'

'Look, Saffie, I'm sure your mum will discuss any plans with you first. I...I can't say what the future may hold, but I'm sure you're in there somewhere.' They heard Jessica walking through the hall.

'Mum. All set?'

'Yes, let's get on our way, Sebastian.'

Mother and daughter embraced briefly. 'Safe onward journey, as they say, and please let me know what's happening, won't you?'

'I will. I've left the Land Rover keys on the hall table. We're off in the MX now. Not much room for luggage, but it's much more fun. Bye Saffie, thanks for lunch.' Jessica pecked her daughter briefly on the cheek and turned to go. As she did, Saffron noticed she was wearing the ring that Sebastian had given her.

Sebastian had also noticed, and as they walked to the car together, he put his arm round her shoulder. 'Thank you. It suits you, and appears to fit perfectly.'

'Perfect, yes, it's lovely,' she said, as she lowered herself into the passenger seat. 'Let's go, let's try to beat the rush hour traffic.'

Two hours later they were pulling into Sebastian's parking place at the Barbican and unpacking the car. Jessica was surprised at the abundance of shrubs and trees decorating the corridors and walkways, and how pleasantly it was laid out with so much space and airiness. His flat was one-bedroom with a sliding partition in the living area where a sofa bed could be used. Jessica settled into an armchair, relieved to be there after the long journey from Devon.

'Tea?' He hardly needed to ask. But Jessica instead suggested a glass of wine or a gin and tonic.

'G&T it is. Make yourself comfortable. We can sort out our things later. We've got all night. Tell you what…let me take you to Covent Garden for dinner. I'll book a table at The Ivy. We might even get to see a few celebs and arty types.'

'That sounds exciting, Sebastian. I don't know London at all, so anywhere you take me will be a real treat. I like your place. Very cosy.'

'And it's very handy for the city. The complex was state of the art, a dramatic departure from the usual flats, when they built them,' added Sebastian. He walked over with their drinks and sat next to her. 'Cheers, and here's to us, Jessica. What new lives we're carving out for our future.'

'Cheers, Sebastian. Indeed, but there's a lot to do and a lot to think about.'

'I'll drink to that.' They clinked glasses as they had that last evening in Shimla, and sat looking out over the city's darkening skyline.

64

London September 1997:

After eating a rushed breakfast, Sebastian went to meet his friend at the Met. He'd carefully placed the samples in his briefcase, and hoped they would be all that was needed for the extraction of DNA. It was a long way back to Devon if his father's sample proved to be unsuitable.

Jessica took her time dressing. She wasn't sure what they'd do today, but knew Sebastian had some of his own business to sort out. Perhaps she'd take off on her own and explore parts of London she didn't know. The Summer Exhibition was still on at the Royal Academy, and she could also go to the National Gallery. She'd been before, but the thought of strolling those hallowed walls filled with old masters was too irresistible. She tidied her things, made the bed, and looked around the small space to see if there was anything else she could do.

Sebastian's desk was piled with documents and letters. His laptop sat squarely in the middle. She peered at all his books lining the walls, and went to look at his rogue's gallery of photos in frames on a shelf. Front centre was a photo of an elegant middle-aged woman, posing as if in a studio. She saw a remarkable likeness to Sebastian, and assumed it must be his mother. The smile was kindly. She looked happy. Jessica's eyes scanned the pictures, mostly family portraits, she assumed. She noticed with interest photos of his schooldays, standing in his cricket whites proudly holding a shield. Next to it a photo of a house and his mother and father and a small boy she thought must be Sebastian standing in front of the doorway.

She heard the key in the lock and turned to greet him.

'All done,' he said, 'I've been told the results should be available within the week. They'll phone me.'

'Will you have to go to collect them?'

'Yes, but there will be no need to collect the samples. I was told they'll destroy them, so we can head west again as soon as you want.'

'So? What now?' He sighed and slumped into an armchair.

'I thought I'd go to the Summer Exhibition at the Royal Academy, and possibly the National Gallery as well. Don't you have some arrangements to make of your own?'

'Yes, I do. Why don't we go downstairs, and make plans over a coffee? I'll put you in a cab and come back and start to get my head together.'

'Perfect—the day is still young enough for me to walk my legs off, and for you to get to grips with your personal business. And we have our own plans to make. I have a few ideas, but we can talk about that later, over dinner. I'll grab a bite to eat for lunch whilst I'm out, and leave you in peace for the day.'

'Come on, action stations.' She picked up her bag and pecked him on the cheek before heading down for a coffee.

Half an hour later, she was climbing into a cab. She called back, 'I'll see you later.'

They blew kisses to each other and the cab sped off for Piccadilly.

With tired and aching feet, Jessica made her way back to the apartment. She'd called Sebastian earlier to tell him she was on her way and to put the kettle on. She'd had a wonderful day gorging on works of art. She seemed to be drawn towards romantic paintings of lovers, and families. She sat for a while looking at a Vermeer of a young woman standing in front of a small ornate virginals as though about to play some music, and wondered what that life would have been like for her. Had she been sheltered in one way or another all her life, like she imagined the young woman had been? She wanted to step right into the painting, wear the same sumptuous clothes and learn to play a harpsichord. She'd always imagined her life might be like that, cossetted, out-of-this world, but she could only dream about the measure of comfort, love and mystery the woman appeared to be enjoying.

Jessica knew deep down that she was clutching at straws at this time of her life, and hoping against hope that she and Sebastian would make good and successful partners. Yet was she as blinkered as the woman in Vermeer's picture. On the surface all was calm and organised but, within, her life had no meaning or purpose except to please others.

She promised herself many visits to the gallery, and wanted to be able to come up to London regularly after they were settled. Indeed, if they ever were settled. She didn't want to burst the romantic bubble, but that might have to happen in the next few days.

She threw herself down on Sebastain's sofa and kicked off her shoes.

'Like that, is it?' He went to make tea.

'Wonderful, Sebastian. I can't remember the last time I went to the National Gallery. The Summer Exhibition was so interesting, too, and so different. Sometimes it takes too much imagination to understand those huge abstracts.'

'Well, now we can come up to London and stay here as often as we like.'

'Oh? What about...'

'I've told the agency I'm on sabbatical for the foreseeable future.' He put the tea tray down in front of her and grinned. 'I'm free, Jess, I'm free to do what I like for as long as it takes us to get our lives sorted out and decide where we want to live. How good is that? We're both able to start afresh together. And the sooner the better for me.'

'That's wonderful, Sebastian—now we can make tentative plans, and when the DNA results come back...'

'Yes, I've made headway while you've been out.' He poured two cups of tea. 'I rang the Marylebone Registry Office. We can go there as early as tomorrow, and set a date.'

'What! But...?'

'No time like the present, Jess, and what did we say just two days ago? No regrets, no turning back. So full speed ahead into the rest of our lives together now. Agreed? I'll ask a couple of chums to come over as witnesses, and you can start to meet my friends.'

Jessica was too tired to argue, and just wanted to have tea and discuss this tomorrow.

He leaned across. 'Cake?'

'Thank you, I'm feeling more human now.' She rose to go to the bathroom, passing the bookshelves she'd scanned that morning, including the collection of photos. Hesitating, she turned.

'Sebastian, is that a photo of your mother? I was looking at them this morning and thought there was a distinct resemblance.'

He came over to join her. 'How did you guess? That's my mother, and I should phone her today, she doesn't know I'm back. And this was me and dad at...'

'Yes, I saw them this morning. I like it that you have family photos displayed. Where did you say your mother lives? I guess I ought to meet her soon.'

'She lives just outside Reigate, on Reigate Heath, in a lovely country house near the golf course. She's on her own now, her husband, my stepfather, died last year, and she's thinking about selling up and moving. I think she should stay put, she's settled there and has good neighbours, and it is all very convenient. We'll pay her a visit as soon as we can.'

Jessica smiled at the thought. 'Yes, I'd like that very much. She'll want to know my story, I guess.'

'Don't know how I'm going to broach the subject about you and me. She wouldn't have a clue about our connections, least of all about you—I'm sure Dad didn't share anything with her about you. But I'll have to tell her, and the sooner the better.'

'One more hurdle to jump on our race to set records straight, I suppose. And now, we just play the waiting game until we hear about the DNA test results.'

'Yep—in the meantime, let's go out. I reserved a table. If we're lucky, the singers from the Covent Garden Opera House will come along later and serenade us.'

'Sounds great fun. I'll get ready to go.'

65

London September 1997:

Jessica took full advantage of being in London. For the next two days, she went to the V&A and the Tate Modern, as well as hitting Harvey Nichols and Harrods to do some shopping.

Sebastian came with her to the Tate, and she was surprised at his knowledge and appreciation of modern art.

During that time, she received various phone calls from the estate agent in Cornwall, and from Saffron. She managed to stall any decision about her return. Waiting for the DNA result was more important than anything else.

Day three, and she'd wondered if Sebastian should ring his friend to find out about the tests. She spoke to Saffron and told her what she was doing. She'd rather speak to her on a phone call that she could cut short if necessary, than be faced with a barrage of awkward questions.

'Sebastian, have you spoken to your mother yet?'

'I'll call her right now. But I'd have to start a very long story about you and us and Edward, by way of an explanation, to put her in the picture. She'll have a lot to take in.'

They fell silent for a moment, but Jessica suggested, 'Perhaps don't tell her anything about how you helped me in Shimla, and how we found out about my parents' demise. That way, we can explain more when we're face to face. What do you think?'

'Hmm...yes, she doesn't need to know anything yet.'

'Later, we can tell her the whole story, after we've got the results.' She paused. 'Is there any way you can ask your friend to chase it up?'

'Hmm...don't like putting him under pressure because it's not his department, but I'll phone and ask.' Sebastian checked the time and walked over to his desk. Jessica made herself useful by pouring glasses of wine and getting some olives out of a jar and into a dish. She took them over to the balcony and placed them on the small table, trying to hang on to his conversation.

He came over to join her. He was smiling. 'He thinks he can have them available by tomorrow morning. How's that for efficiency? I asked him to email me, and I'd arrange payment through the bank.'

'Fantastic. Phew—cheers! Here's to tomorrow.' They clinked glasses and both felt relaxed knowing they could move forward one way or another.'

'Sebastian. Here's to us, and our future. Now—do ring your mother.'

'Yes sir!' Sebastian obeyed her command and went directly back to the phone. She watched him dial and wait. He spoke first into the mouthpiece and called across the room to Jessica.

'It's on message bank, so she may have gone out for the evening. In which case, she'll not respond until the morning. At least I've made the effort. Let's drink up and go to dinner.'

'Good idea. I'm starving. Where are you taking me tonight?'

'Well, we won't know until we get there. But you'll like it, I promise. We'll get a cab there and back. I thought we'd go to the South Bank. It's a bit of a walk to find a restaurant, but along the river there's some great pubs and eateries. It's fairly early so the business crowd may not have left their offices yet.'

'It's a lovely evening to sit outside if we can find a place.' Jessica said as they crossed over Southwark Bridge.

They found a restaurant with al fresco tables and ordered drinks and the menu.

'Sebastian, I've been thinking. I might go back to Hampshire tomorrow. You wouldn't mind, would you? I mean, I can meet your mother later, and I feel I have so much to do and organise, and I have to go to my school to say goodbye to everyone.' Jessica looked intently at Sebastian who seemed surprised.

'But I thought we could use this time for ourselves at last, now that I'm unencumbered and you don't have to be back for any particular reason.'

'If I'm to buy the house in Cornwall, I have to discuss plans with Saffie. I thought I'd buy the house before winter sets in and definitely before Christmas. Everything seems so up in the air right now.'

Sebastian pondered and took a long swig of his beer. 'I've been pushing you. A lot has happened since we both came back from Shimla, and we need to slow down a bit and take stock.'

'There have also been a few changes in my life since I came back— not least of all us, and our relationship and…' Jessica held out her hand

'…an engagement.'

He took her hand and kissed it in the old-fashioned way.

'How gallant, Sebastian. A true gentleman. I'll head out of London tomorrow on the train, and you can stay on to get your new life organised. Don't make any further plans at the registry office—I'll be back just as soon as I can. Does that sound okay to you?'

'Quite reasonable, but I'll miss not having you around. I'll let you know as soon as I get the result of our tests, so keep your phone nearby at all times, won't you?'

'Of course. But the first thing I have to do is discuss things in detail with Saffie, and phone the estate agent to make an offer on what might just be The Laurels number two. Do you think I should go ahead and buy that house? I know there's a lot of work to do, but I'll be able to afford it, and just think, we might very well live there together and make it our forever home.'

Sebastian smiled at her romantic notions, but deep-down thought it a great idea.

'We'd get a boat, and explore the coastline. Go fishing…'

'Keep chickens and have our horses.' She leaned against him. 'Let's do it, shall we?'

'Let's do it.'

66

Hampshire September 1997:

There wasn't much Jessica needed to do in London, and back home she had a myriad of things on her list, not least to bring Saffron up to date with developments in her relationship with Sebastian.

Once on the train, she phoned Saffron. 'Hi Saffie. I'm on my way back. Could you pick me up at the station please? The train gets in at eleven thirty-five. There's so much we have to do and I don't need to stay in London at the moment.'

'Hi Mum. I know, we do have to organise a lot, and in only a day there's mail piling up for you. Will you go to the school?'

'Yes, that's the first thing I need to do, and we'll go out and buy another car. With me travelling back and forth to Devon and Cornwall now, I'll bequeath the Land Rover to you and go and get myself something similar.' Jessica stared out of the window as the London suburbs began to thin out and give way to green fields and leafy lanes. 'Now that you're back home, we need to make decisions about how and where you'll live, too.'

'Mum, I'll be...' The line crackled through Saffron's voice and Jessica only heard every other word.

'Saffie, Saffie, you're fading...' They lost contact.

Jessica desperately wanted to know Saffron's plans for the future. She wanted to help Saffron stand on her own two feet and needed to know what she intended to do with her life.

The phone interrupted her thoughts. 'Saffie! You're back. The signals aren't very good yet, are they?'

'No, Mum, and I just want to say before we get cut off again, that I'll see you at the station. I've just refuelled the Land Rover, and after lunch perhaps we can go and look at cars.'

'Yes, but I'll see if I can get in touch with the Headmistress first, and get my school visit out of the way. It will be very sad, after all these years, but I must admit it's the right thing to do. I'll see you at the station. Don't be late!'

But there was no Saffron waiting at the station for Jessica. She checked her phone, but no missed phone calls either. She called her. There was no answer. Seething inside, Jessica couldn't believe her daughter had forgotten, or didn't care enough to be waiting on the platform for her. She sat on a bench outside the waiting room and thought about taking a taxi. *I'm not sitting here forever. Damn it!*

'Taxi!'

The car moved up and the driver got out and opened the door for Jessica. 'Willow Cottage, Coombe Lacey, please.' She instructed the driver.

The taxi snaked its way down the narrow approach road to the station, and out into the mainstream traffic. At that moment, Jessica spotted her Land Rover, Saffron at the wheel, rounding the bend to the station. The vehicle narrowly missed the taxi but carried on at top speed.

'Bloody motorists! Don't care these days, driving them bloody Chelsea Tractors. They think they're kings of the road—just down from the smoke, drivin' everybody else off the road as though they own it.'

Jessica cleared her throat. 'Er—, Driver, I hate to say it, but that was my daughter, fifteen minutes late for picking me up. I'm sorry to inconvenience you, but would you mind turning round and taking me back to the station? So sorry.'

'Ah, well, miss, alright. I can, but I'll have to charge ya, I will.' He sounded aggravated and Jessica decided to keep quiet until they were back at the station. She gave the driver a hefty five-pound tip, but he continued to grumble.

Saffron was walking back to the Land Rover from the platform, phone in hand, looking puzzled.

'You got here at last?' Jessica said, sarcastically. 'Thought you'd forgotten...'

'Look, Mum...I'm so sorry, but I haven't been too well this morning, and thought it would be alright for me to drive here, but...'

Jessica got into the passenger seat, not wanting to listen. 'I was sitting there like a lemon, couldn't get you on the phone, so I grabbed a taxi. Thanks a lot! He had to turn around, and was angry and scathing about *Chelsea Tractors*. I gave him a large tip but he still went away muttering.' She paused and looked at the oncoming traffic. 'So, are you alright? What's wrong, are you ill?'

Saffron turned into the lane leading to the village, and slowed down. 'Mum, I need to tell you something. Erm…Mum…I think I'm pregnant.'

Jessica's intake of breath was audible. 'What? You—you're going to have a baby? But…'

'Yes, Mum. I'm pretty sure. In fact, I AM sure.'

'And did you know this when you left the Hebrides? Who's the father? Why didn't you tell me before? Oh God, Saffie. I don't know whether to laugh or cry or be sympathetic or angry with you.' She looked at her daughter in the driving seat. 'Saffie! Be careful, slow down and mind the bumps.'

They exchanged uncertain glances. 'Mum, I'll be alright, and I'm going to see the doctor tomorrow to confirm everything. Are you mad at me?' She pulled up outside Willow Cottage and turned off the engine.

'Get out Saffie, let's go inside. No! I'll carry my own bag.'

'But Mum…'

'No ifs and buts, Saffie.' She led the way into the hall, dropped her bags and turned to give her daughter a big hug. 'Well, I thought I had a lot to do, but this changes things. Let's go and sit in the kitchen and you can tell me all about it. And no, I'm not cross—after all, its history repeating itself, isn't it? Our family is about to get bigger. Gosh, just think, I'm going to be a grandmother. I can't believe it.' Jessica filled the kettle, smiling secretly at the prospect of a baby in the house.

'Cup of tea? What a story, what a surprise, just wait till I tell Sebastian.'

67

Hampshire September 1997:

Mother and daughter sat in the kitchen at Willow Cottage for what seemed like hours. The one shocked by the news, the other needing reassurance.

Jessica finally rose and made lunch, suggesting that Saffron take a rest in the afternoon.

'Mum, I'm so relieved you're not angry with me.'

'I just remember when I was at your stage of pregnancy, how sick I was, and how tired I used to get. The sickness goes away, but as the baby grows, you'll feel more and more tired. You mustn't worry about a thing. I'm sure it will all go well. After we've checked with the doctor tomorrow, we'll have a better idea of timing, and you should be put on a regular monitoring regime and encourage you to go to relaxation classes. I wonder what the birth date will be?'

'Mum, I swear I didn't know about it when I left Barra. You see, Adam, my partner, and I had a row. It wasn't the first one. We hadn't been getting on for months. It just wasn't working any more, and apart from that, I was beginning to hate the lifestyle, the constant pressure by others in the commune to eat this and not eat that, and to grow what they recommended. I have to admit, it was a period of my life I'm pleased I had, but I know I wasn't cut out for it. It all sounded very futuristic, green and organic, but, I'm not like that deep down. I like my home comforts too much.'

'I know, and now you're in a totally different place in your life. Take advice from your mum, please tell Adam. For the child's sake, if not for you and him. Remember when we tried in vain to find your own father, it was a nightmare for me to go through, because I knew we'd never find him. For you, it's easy, and whatever his reaction, you'll have to go along with it. Trust me, it is the best way. Otherwise, there'll be so many problems when the baby grows up.'

Saffron tidied the kitchen and said she'd go for a lie-down, but Jessica wanted to tell her about developments with Sebastian.

'Sit down for a minute, Saffie. I need to tell you what's happening with me and Sebastian. I have a problem of my own to deal with.' She looked her daughter in the eye and carried on. 'We took a sample from Edward to be DNA tested, and provided samples for each of us to go to the testing lab. Sebastian delivered them two days ago. It will take a few more days to get the results, and that's why I decided to come home and do something useful in the meantime.

'Depending on the outcome, and providing our genetic makeup isn't linked in any way, Sebastian and I are going to get married.' Jessica cut straight through the surprise gestures and fake raised-voice excitement from Saffron, and carried on. 'We're fairly sure we're not related—we checked dates of birth against the opportunities, and yes, my mother and his father did appear to have a long-term affair in Shimla, but there are so many differences between us that, well...'

'My God, Mum! Who'd have thought it? And what about Edward, where does he come into it? I suppose you'll know if, and when, you and he have familial links.'

'Yes, and that's why we wanted to get his DNA, too.

'So, Mum, there's still a chance that...'

Jessica cut in. 'Yes, Saffie, there is, and that's why I've been very circumspect about making too much of it, and setting dates like Sebastian wants to. I was even reticent to wear this ring until we've got the results of the test.'

'So, what do you do now?'

'Wait, and yes, hope. Sebastian said he'd call me as soon as he's heard. In the meantime, I'll go to see the head at the school, and say my goodbyes.'

The first day back at school after the long summer holidays was nigh. Most of the teachers, including the headmistress were busy preparing their rooms. As Jessica neared her classroom, she felt regret and heartache, knowing this would be the last time she'd open that door, stand in front of the blackboard, and set the children's homework. She knew she'd miss feelings of elation seeing the development and progress of each child during the year she had them in her charge. She'd miss the satisfaction of knowing that she had been their mentor and guiding light, pointing them in the best way she could towards further education and ultimate success. She stood in front of the empty desks and felt tears pricking.

She would remember the brightest, and those not-so-bright ones, who struggled but managed to make the grade. She would also miss not knowing where and how they ended up. The empty room echoed her past life, her enthusiasm and drive. It was waiting for eager new faces including that of the teacher who would take her place and try her hardest to fit in with the school where Jessica had been a part of the furniture. She felt sad and lonely as she left, clutching personal items from her locker. She'd keep them as a reminder of her days there. She was determined not to cry or give the place a backward look.

She arrived home just as her phone rang. It was Sebastian. He told her he was to see his mother tomorrow.

'Are you sure we're ready to tell your mother? Perhaps you can tell her about me first? When the results come through, we'll be able to tell everyone we're engaged. I'd feel a lot happier if you didn't mention it to her yet.'

'Well, if you insist, but we are pretty sure, aren't we?'

Jessica didn't answer his hypothetical question. Instead, 'I've just come from the school. It was sad, but there it is, a phase of my life over and a new one about to start. Oh, Sebastian, I feel so lucky. And, guess what? Well, you'd never guess—I'm going to be a grandmother. Saffie's expecting a baby.'

There was a distinct pause on the line. 'Sebastian—are you still there?'

'Yes, wow! That's a surprise, isn't it? But, and the obvious question, who's the father?'

'It turns out it's the chap she's been living with on Barra. She's in the very early stages, and we're going to the doc tomorrow. It was a great shock to me, but I've told her to tell the father. It just wasn't working any more between them. That's why she left. It will change things a bit, but it shouldn't affect our plans. At least I hope it won't.'

'No news yet about the DNA results. I'm going to ring my mate later and try to hurry things along a bit. I hate this waiting, and I hate not being with you. I'll ring Dad, too and bring him up to date. I think we'll head off back to Devon as soon as we hear, and wait awhile to make plans for our wedding. I think Dad would like to be part of them, don't you?'

Jessica felt relieved. Things had been going too fast and she felt they needed some more time and space. 'Of course, but you can come here and stay for a while, too. In fact, you can do that after you've been to see your mother, if you like.'

'Mm…yes, I think I might do that. I'll let you know how that meeting goes, and most likely come straight down to Hampshire afterwards.'

'Missing you tons. Get here soon, Sebastian. I love you.'

'Love you too, Jessica.'

68

September 1997:

The next few days at Willow Cottage accelerated into a whirlwind of activity. Jessica realised that she'd be away from home for a while, travelling to Devon and London, and in between going back to Cornwall for a second viewing on Polkerris house. She started by having a good clear-out of clothes, items she no longer wore, and kitchen equipment bought on a whim that was hardly ever put to use. Saffron helped her, but it was a selection process she needed to do on her own.

Saffron took her newly-acquired Land Rover to town frequently, seeking out baby equipment and clothing. The doctor had announced her fit and well, and gave her details about ante-natal classes and who to contact when labour began. A private nursing home was booked for the following June, flexible dates accepted. Jessica had commented that at least there was plenty of time for them all to get settled into new lives and lifestyles. Saffron had tried to get hold of Adam on the phone, and ended up sending him a letter.

Every day Sebastian rang to say still no news about the tests, which was making Jessica a little nervous. Final plans about her future were incomplete until those results came through.

Jessica was in the middle of packing yet another bag to take to the charity shop when the call came. Sebastian was abrupt. 'I've got the results.'

Jessica sighed a sigh of relief. 'And?'

'I'm coming down to Hampshire right now.'

'But…what? Come on, you've got to tell me. Sebastian, just tell me.'

'Can't tell you over the phone, it's too complex. I'm on my way. I'll be there in under two hours. Look, I need to be with you. Don't worry, all will be revealed as soon as I get there…'

'Sebastian, what do you mean, complex? …Sebastian? What the…'

But he'd rung off. She tried to ring him back, but couldn't get through. Putting her phone on the table, she covered her face with her hands, and sat motionless, deep in thought. This could only mean one thing. They were half-siblings. Jessica bent over the table and buried her face in her folded arms, her mind racing. There could be no wedding, and no love except perhaps platonic. Feeling anger welling up, she walked out into the garden and tried to calm herself.

She'd always thought her meeting the man of her dreams at last was too good to be true. Lack of self-worth reared its head and the bashing-down of her confidence took hold. She noticed Trixie hanging her head over the hedge form the paddock and went over to talk to her.

Her ears pricked as Jessica stroked the horse's forehead and neck, 'What shall I do, Trix? What now? All my dreams are about to be shattered to bits. I guess in the end it was always meant to be—just you and me, and now Saffie and her baby when it arrives. My own future stays motionless.' Trixie shook her mane, as if understanding every word. 'Shall we go for a ride? Come on, I'll walk you round to the stable.'

She opened the gate and went into the paddock heading for the tack room. Trixie followed obediently.

Jessica needed to get away from her feeling of doom. Trotting down the narrow lane alongside the paddock, she rationalised that she'd been hasty in jumping to conclusions, and tried to shake off her sadness. She didn't know, after all, and wouldn't know until Sebastian arrived.

She turned onto the bridle path that led to the stream. The ground was firm and oak trees were shedding their leaves on the path. As she slowed Trixie down, they rustled under her hooves. Reaching the crest of the field, she pulled her up, and sat still listening to the silence of the countryside—the countryside she loved whatever the season of the year, in its constant metamorphosis. Trixie reached down to pull fresh grass from the side of the track.

The slope to the stream beckoned and, urging the horse on, Jessica rode to the big tree where she always tethered Trixie while she wandered through the thicket and alongside the bubbling fast-flowing water. She sat on a log and felt thankful for small mercies, for being there and for her good health and now her wealth. But what was money, without a life lived with the one you love, she wondered? Purely the ability to pick and choose, to enjoy selfishly. Jessica bent over the running stream and dipped in a stick, watching as water eddied around it, wanting it to float downstream to join the river.

She must do the same, she reasoned, tossing the stick into the gushing rivulet, she made her way back to Trixie and began a slow walk back home.

'There you are.' Saffron came rushing to meet her mother in the garden. 'I looked everywhere. What's the matter?'

'I've just been for a ride down to the stream to try to clear my head.'

'What do you mean, clear your head? Are you feeling unwell?'

Jessica smiled. 'I may be—but not physically. I had a call from Sebastian.'

'And?'

Jessica paused, not wanting Saffron to see her overly upset at a notion she'd manufactured, based on a few words from Sebastian. 'He's on his way here. I can't get through to his mobile, but...'

'Come on, Mum, but what?'

They sat on the bench near the greenhouse. 'Well, he's had the DNA test results back from the lab. He didn't tell me the result. He said it was complex, and said it could wait till he gets here.'

'That sounds a bit scary—why so cagey, I wonder. When will he be here?'

Jessica looked at her watch. 'About now, I think. It's not a long journey in that fast car of his.'

'Shall I prepare some lunch for us? Oh, and come and look what I've bought for baby.' She tried to distract Jessica, realising the seriousness of her expression.

Saffron's light hearted response to the news lifted some of the gloom from Jessica's shoulders. *Maybe he just wants to break the good news to me face to face, give me hugs and smiles and make me happy. Maybe. Or perhaps the news is not good, and he wants to console me with platitudes and regret.*

They prepared a salad to eat at the kitchen table, and as Jessica filled the kettle and put it on the AGA to simmer, Sebastian's car screeched to a halt in the driveway.

Jessica wiped her hands on her apron, removed it, and rushed out to greet him. By the time she arrived, he'd taken his overnight bag from the boot, and put up the roof of his car to park it for the duration.

'Oh, my God…thank goodness you're here.' They embraced and Sebastian gave her a big kiss. 'Come on in, we've just finished preparing lunch.'

Smiling now, hand in hand, she led him through the cottage door and into the kitchen where he greeted Saffron. Not wanting to appear too eager, small talk ensued as he was steered towards a chair. They sat on opposite sides of the table, Saffron at the end.

Offering him the platter and salads, she said, trying to appear matter-of-fact. 'The news! Sebastian, come on.'

He looked up nervously, struggling to find his words. 'Well, er, look…'

'Come on, tell us the results of the test.' They watched as his face broke into a grimace.

'Well, there's good news, and not-so-good news…' He looked down at his plate again.

'What? What do you mean? I thought there'd be a straightforward we are or we're not related.'

'Oh, there is.' He changed his expression and raised his eyebrows. 'You see, the relationship between you and me is negative.'

'So, I'm not related to you?' Jessica felt the lifting of a huge weight. 'And Edward?'

'Ah, that's the problem.' Jessica and Saffron hung on tenterhooks. 'You see, my father is NOT your father.' Jessica placed her hands together as if in prayer, immediately thinking what Edward's reaction to this news might be, as Sebastian continued in a grave voice. 'BUT…neither is he mine.'

69

Hampshire September 1997:

All eyes were on Sebastian, waiting for him to say something after the stunned silence that followed after his shock announcement. Jessica didn't know what to say to him. He didn't look particularly upset, nor did he look annoyed. She thought about his mother, as he must have thought about her and the connotations attached to his statement. They began to pick at their food, trying to take in what he'd just said.

Sebastian broke the awkwardness. 'The reason the tests took so long is that they did them twice, just to make sure they'd got it right. Apparently, there's no denying—the results speak for themselves. He looked across the table. 'I've been thinking it over and over, but I don't know what to do. I mean, do I tell Dad, do I tell Mum? I know my mother had affairs, that's no secret, but this? This came as a complete bombshell. Thing is, if I tell Mum I know I'm not Dad's son, I'll need to know who my real father is. She's led Dad on all his life to think I'm his. If I tell dad the shock revelation will most likely kill him in his frail state. If I tell neither of them, I'd be living a lie for the rest of my life.'

Jessica suggested, 'You don't think your mother knows? What if she denies it, and says the tests are wrong? It's possible that she doesn't know.'

'Oh God. What a mess this all is. Can I live the rest of my life— can you live the rest of your lives keeping my secret? I'd rely on you two saying nothing, expunging this information from your memory. But in any case, where would I stand. Do I want to know who my real father is? Or perhaps I could pretend I didn't believe it, and try to carry on with my life as though I wasn't aware, in denial.'

Jessica put her hand on his arm. 'We have to tell the truth, Sebastian. Although I do think we shouldn't tell Edward about you. We can soften the blow about me not being his daughter by telling him about our plans to marry. Sort of bad news, good news. As for your mother, you'll have to work something out and prepare to challenge her. She's clearly not been honest with you. I'm so sorry.'

Saffron piped up. 'Hope you don't mind me interjecting, but from where I am, on the outside looking in, perhaps the only person right now who needs to know is Edward, and he only needs to know that mum isn't his daughter. You can be economical with the truth about you, Sebastian, and leave your mother until there's a better time. You have documentary evidence about the DNA, so it doesn't matter when you tell her, does it?'

'I suppose not. What a dilemma, and all I know is we need to get to my father as soon as possible.'

'I agree,' said Jessica, 'let's go this week. All I have to do is to finish clearing out as much as possible, tidy up my correspondence and call the estate agent in Cornwall. I have decided, depending upon another inspection, I'm going to buy that house.'

'Bravo, Mum. I'll be alright here, well, for a while, but maybe I'll move to the west country as well. Especially after the baby's born. Even along with all the upset and uncertainty, we can still start making plans to move forward.'

'Sebastian, the wedding can take place now as soon as we like…' Jessica squeezed his hand in anticipation.

Urged on by the certainty of them being free to stay together, get married and love each other without thoughts nagging at them about any familial link, it didn't take long for Jessica and Sebastian to move forward. They took two cars down to Devon with as many personal things as could be loaded into Jessica's new Range Rover. They thought they'd marry at the register office in Exeter, thinking it would be better to keep it low key for the sake of Edward's failing health. Sebastian called him to say they'd be at Cleave Manor in a day or two. Fortunately, he didn't ask about the DNA tests, but said he looked forward to seeing them both.

Saffron accepted her mother's relationship and forthcoming marriage with enthusiasm, and began to make her own plans for when the baby arrived. The birth date she'd been given by the doctor was earlier than she thought. She talked about what she might do at the time, and Jessica had promised to be with her, suggesting Saffron go to stay with them in Devon until after the baby was born. What to do about Willow Cottage didn't figure in any plans, they all assumed that Saffron would live there and maintain it as her own. Jessica would be happy with that arrangement.

Sebastian accepted that his Damocles sword would hover over him until he saw his mother face to face. He'd got Jessica now, and she was his future. He had reached the stage where he wanted to put everything behind him, even giving up his job and planning to sell his father's house in Delhi. He and Jessica had talked about going to India on honeymoon.

With mixed emotions, they drove in convoy to Cleave Manor, stopping only once to stretch their legs. It was accepted that Jessica stay at the manor house, and Annie had prepared bedrooms for her and Sebastian, as well as sending out to replenish stocks of food. She met them at the door.

'Welcome back! Come on in, Edward's in the drawing room waiting. But I have to tell you, he's been under the weather this past week. He's lost his appetite and he's feeling a bit down. The doctor came to visit yesterday, and took blood and urine tests. He told me to ask you to ring him. I think Edward might have taken a turn for the worst.'

'Oh dear, he must be feeling bad. He's usually so stalwart about his illness, and likes to carry on regardless. We'll go right now.'

'There's a roaring fire, and I put a rug over his knees earlier and took him some coffee and biscuits.' Annie helped carry some luggage. 'He'll be so pleased to see you both, so pleased. I hope it bucks him up a bit.'

Dropping their hand luggage, Sebastian and Jessica headed for the drawing room. Edward was slumped in a chair, asleep. He roused when he heard their footsteps. Donna and Glen came to them, slowly wagging their tails, then flopped beside the fire. Looking at Edward's wizened face, Sebastian was immediately overcome by sadness.

'Dad! Hello, Annie tells me you've not been very good these past few days.'

'Me? Oh, I'll be alright, just feeling lazy, and how good is it to see you both. I've been looking forward to it. I hope you can stay longer this time.' He sat up and adjusted the tartan blanket over his legs.

'Hello, Edward. We came back just as soon as we could. We've got some news, but it can wait until you're feeling a bit better. No hurry. I believe the doctor came to see you?'

'Dear Jessica—what a breath of fresh air. Yes, the new pills doc's

275

given me seem to be knocking me out. I refuse to be taken into hospital, so he's offered to come over every other day to see how I am.'

'Dad, we'll help with anything you want, but you must try to eat. Annie tells me you've not been eating much. I think I smelled something delicious for lunch. Me and Jessica will just go and settle into our rooms, and we'll see you in about half an hour, for lunch. Okay?'

'I'll get up, but I may need a hand getting there.'

'We'll come and help you. See you soon.'

The pair left Edward in his chair, and hurried out of the room. When they arrived upstairs in Jessica's room, they both sat on her bed, looking melancholy.

'He doesn't look good, does he? I'll ring his doctor before lunch and find out what the prognosis is. It all seems so sudden. He wasn't this ill when we left. What shall we do? We can't give him any bad news, not now.'

'Agreed. Ring Meredith, he'll know how to deal with the situation. In fact, I can do that while you're on to the doctor. I'll have to tell Meredith our news, anyway. He knew we were getting the DNA tests. Sebastian, don't despair. Nothing is ever as bad as it seems.' She tried to cheer him up.

'You're right. It just came as a shock to see him like this. I'll call the doc right now…'

'And I'll talk to Meredith. There'll be a simple solution to everything. Trust me.'

Jessica snuggled into Sebastian's shoulder and he held her tight. She didn't want him to see that she was near to despair over the possibilities unfolding before them.

70

September 1997:

Meredith Bateman was both shocked and happy when Jessica told him her news. She wasn't sure how much he knew about her relationship with Sebastian, so she told him the full story. She asked his advice about what and when to tell Edward, and the other problems facing them. Surprisingly, Meredith suggested they not tell him anything about the DNA results so soon. He admitted he hadn't known that Edward was so ill. Jessica took it upon herself to invite him over the following day so that they could all sit and discuss the future.

She was relieved that Meredith would be with them—after all, she had known him longer than either Sebastian or his father.

'But when Edward knows I'm not his daughter, how will he react, do you think?'

'He'll be devastated. Perhaps you don't need to tell him at all.'

Meredith asked if they'd spoken to the doctor yet, to give them all an idea of Edward's deteriorating health.

'Sebastian's ringing him now. When you get here tomorrow, we'll have a rough idea of his ongoing treatment. He looks so much worse than when I first met him. It's almost as though he was waiting for me and Sebastian, and now that we're back from Shimla, he can set his mind at rest. That's why I'm worried about telling him what could be devastating news.' Jessica paused, 'But if we can't tell him about me and Sebastian, that would be a shame.'

'When I see you tomorrow, we'll play it by ear. By that time, we'll have a good idea about his health and how to broach these tricky questions. Let's all sleep on it till then.'

Jessica knew he was right, and she discussed it with Sebastian. He phoned Edward's doctor while she unpacked and mulled over what to do next. By the time Sebastian was off the phone, she'd helped Edward out of bed and into his newly acquired wheelchair. He was a dead weight in her arms, and she found it quite hard to get him into the seat. They went down in the lift to the dining room. Annie was rushing about with food and drinks, and Edward became quite animated, talking about the house and garden.

'Jessica, I want you and Sebastian to take over the running of the manor for me. I can't do it any more, you see. I am too tired, just too tired, Jessica. I'll tell Sebastian he's to come and live here, and do everything I can't do now.'

'What a good idea, Edward. I'm sure he'd want to do that anyway.'

'And you, Jess? What about you?'

She was agitated by his question, knowing the answer but not at liberty to tell him. 'Shall we wait until Sebastian comes down and we'll talk to him?'

She wanted to change the subject, to tell him about her plans to buy the Cornish house by the sea, and the news about Saffron and the baby, then, realising that was too much information, she bit her lip and tried to steer the conversation away from family. Fortunately, Sebastian walked into the room, sparing her further questions from Edward.

'My dear boy, sit down, tell me what you've been doing.' Edward tried to move his wheelchair closer to Sebastian, but his arms were too weak.

'Dad, I've been talking to your doctor. He's coming to see you tomorrow morning.' Sebastian looked across the table at Jessica, wanting to tell her that he'd just been given the heart-breaking news that Edward had but a few weeks to live. He'd been told that the best option at this end-of-life stage would be that Edward receive twenty-four-hour palliative care, and the doctor had given him the number to contact the McMillan Trust, the cancer care organisation which would be able to deal with him in his dying days. He had suggested that Sebastian stay with his father, and prepare everything that needs to be done.

'He's a good doctor, but he needn't keep coming to see me, I'll be alright in a few weeks, you'll see.'

Jessica could see that Sebastian was perturbed and that he'd had some bad news. Annie came in with soup, and they helped Edward with his napkin and spoon. He took a few spoonsful of the hearty chicken soup, trying his best to eat what had been put in front of him. It was only then they realised just how ill he was. It was painful for them to watch him desperately trying to butter his bread. Sebastian had to look away as Jessica went round to help.

Edward put down his spoon. He'd been able to eat very little. 'Oh dear. I feel so tired now. These damned pills. I'll tell the doc tomorrow. Can you take me up to my room now, Sebastian, please?'

'Let's go, Dad.' Sebastian wheeled his father's chair towards the lift as Jessica stared after them. She carried on with her lunch while she waited for Sebastian to return so they'd be able to discuss the conversations they'd had with Meredith and Edward's doctor.

'He's bad, Jess. The doctor has only given him a few more weeks to live.' Sebastian sat, head in hands, opposite Jessica. 'I have a lot to do. I'll need your help.'

'I'm here to do whatever's necessary. Yes, we both need to prepare ourselves and him, for this. But he seems to be oblivious of his condition.'

'The doc will talk us through things, and possibly discuss with Dad. I don't think he's oblivious or in denial, I think he doesn't want us to know, and that's why he's trying to put on a brave face. He must know the end is near. He's asked for our help, and we'll be here for him for as long as it takes. Agreed?'

'Absolutely.' Jessica sighed. 'It makes our problems look very unimportant now, doesn't it?'

After they'd eaten, they retired to the drawing room and swapped their findings regarding telephone conversations. She told him she'd invited Meredith over tomorrow, and that he'd advised them to say nothing to Edward about the DNA results unless he remembers and mentions it first.

Sebastian told Jessica they were to contact the McMillan Trust and have them find a live-in palliative care nurse. They stood up and clung to each other, both distraught, Jessica near to tears, Sebastian straining to hold his back.

'Thank God we've got each other, Jessica.'

'Yes, but we should be better prepared than we are now. Suddenly our priorities have changed. The axis of our own plans has shifted dramatically, and we need to know what to do and when. It's all come so soon, and everything falls on you and me to do all we can to make Edward comfortable and cared for. I'll do everything I can to help you through this. I really will. Then we'll be able to get on with our own lives and plans. But for now, Edward is suffering and we must look after him.

'I love you so much, Sebastian. I'm sorry for everything, so sorry for you, your father—and he is your father, no matter what the DNA result said. And I'm so sorry about the results. I wish we'd never done that. I wish we'd never known.'

'But if we hadn't, you might not be here now, we might not be planning a wedding, and we couldn't share anything with Edward. I will always regard him as my father. I've known no other. He's been my inspiration and support all my life. Now it's my turn to support him. I need to make sure he's as happy as he can be, until his very last breath.'

***

Edward Shelley drew that last breath on the night of the Autumn Equinox. The sky was clear and as navy blue as a deep ocean. Stars flickered bright in the clean crisp air. His end was quick to come. Moments before, he gripped Sebastian's hand whilst stroking the heads of his two faithful companions, dog bright eyes staring. The quiet of the night shared only by his doctor, nurse, Jessica, Sebastian and Meredith. His face in death belied his troubled mind in life.

They'd talked. Edward had told them the truth about the night of Jessica's parent's death. How he had accidentally murdered her father trying to protect her mother. In disbelief they'd listened. They never revealed to him his relationship with them. He died believing them brother and half-sister. His children. He found happiness in that belief.

Surprisingly, his funeral attracted crowds of friends and his ex-wife. He was interred, as he had wished, in the corner of the coppice with the regal oak tree he'd planted forty years previously keeping watch. A simple headstone carved out of local grey granite bore the words: *Edward Shelley, 1918 to 1997. Lived tormented, died Fulfilled.* A photograph of Elizabeth was placed inside the casket with him.

He had bequeathed Cleave Manor jointly to Sebastian and Jessica. Other valuables he left for them to decide how to disperse. Annie and Bob were left a hundred thousand pounds. Meredith inherited a sizeable lump sum that enabled him to fully retire in comfort. The stables and his horses he left in joint custody to Jessica, Sebastian, and the owner of the riding school. Fifty thousand pounds went to the McMillan Trust.

The following year brought with it a frenzy of activity. Sebastian and Jessica wasted no time in arranging a simple wedding on a golden-glowing autumn afternoon at Cleave Manor, within sight of Edward's last resting place. Jessica wore her mother's brooch saved for her by Edward and made a dress from the silk purchased at the market in Shimla. Autumn leaves were falling from the oak tree, scudding across Edward's grave.

Willow Cottage was sold, and Saffron relocated to Cornwall three months before Emerald was born. Saffron's beautiful baby girl inherited the family's red hair. Trixie found a new home in the stables at Cleave Manor. Sebastian confronted his mother about his birth father. As expected, she denied all knowledge of ever having had any other lover, even though they had the evidence of the DNA test results. Sebastian was determined to investigate, all in good time.

Work was carried out on Cleave Manor and Polkerris House. Adam, Emerald's father came to visit and eventually moved down from Barra to live with Saffron and their daughter.

They started a hospitality business and grew organic food for local farmers' markets, and supplied nearby restaurants and pubs. Saffron planned to redesign the gardens and open them to the public for three months every summer. They'd serve afternoon tea with home-made scones and Cornish clotted cream, on the lawns beside the water's edge. Then came the time for Sebastian and Jessica to travel, first to Delhi where Edward's house was legally handed over to Jay. It was more than two years before their emotional return to Shimla. They were sad to discover that Chandra had died a few months before they arrived, shortly after her husband.

They never returned up the bumpy road to the ruins of The Laurels high in the foothills of the great Himalaya. Jessica was content to rest her soul in Devon surrounded by the mementoes and memories of a life she'd hardly known.

THE END